Sheila O'Flanagan's books, including *How Will I Know?*, *Anyone but Him* and *Dreaming of a Stranger*, have been huge bestsellers in the UK and Ireland; they are all available from Headline Review. Prior to taking the decision to write full time, Sheila pursued a very successful career in banking, becoming Ireland's first woman Chief Dealer. She writes a regular column for the *Irish Times* and in her spare time plays competitive badminton.

# Bad Behaviour

## Sheila O'Flanagan

headline
review

First published in 2007
by HEADLINE REVIEW
An imprint of HEADLINE PUBLISHING GROUP

First published in paperback in 2008
by HEADLINE REVIEW

1

ISBN 978 0 7553 4130 6 (A format)
ISBN 978 0 7553 3218 2 (B format)

Typeset in Galliard by Palimpsest Book Production Limited,
Grangemouth, Stirlingshire

Printed and bound in Great Britain by
Clays Ltd, St Ives plc

Headline's policy is to use papers that are natural, renewable and
recyclable products and made from wood grown in
sustainable forests. The logging and manufacturing processes
are expected to conform to the environmental
regulations of the country of origin.

HEADLINE PUBLISHING GROUP
An Hachette Livre UK Company
338 Euston Road
London NW1 3BH

www.headline.co.uk

For their continuing support all through my writing career, thanks to:

Carole Blake, who looks after my interests in so many places around the world
Marion Donaldson, for those pages of editorial notes that make the difference
Everyone at Headline and especially those of you who've been so wonderful to me on the glamorous (and the not-so-glamorous) author tours
My fantastic family still rooting for me after all these years
My friends and neighbours, who are so great to me in so many ways
Colm, who makes me go on holidays

Special thanks to the staff at the Ulster Hospital for all their kindness and support too.

And, of course, to all of you who buy my books – with special thanks to everyone who has come along to author events or said hello at bookshops and those of you who've contacted me through my website www.sheilaoflanagan.net. You don't know how lovely it is to hear from you all, especially from so many different countries. I'm truly honoured that you've taken the time to get in touch and it means so much to know that you've enjoyed my books. A million thanks!

Maths is like love; a simple idea, but it can get complicated

R. Drabek

# Chapter 1

Darcey McGonigle didn't do birthdays. These days, she didn't see the point.

It had been different, of course, when she was a little girl and birthdays were all about noisy parties with forbidden food like sucky sweets and brightly coloured fizzy drinks. Those birthdays had come with satisfyingly exciting boxes wrapped in special paper tied with coloured ribbon, and possibly even a trip to the cinema where more junk food was allowed 'just for today'. Those birthdays had been fun and magical.

But now all a birthday did was remind her that she was another year older and that somehow her life hadn't turned out like she'd expected back when she'd strutted around the place feeling like a fairy princess for the day. (Her princess phase had lasted for less than a year, during which she'd worn pink dresses and allowed her mother to use pretty clips, ribbons and slides in her wavy blonde hair. After that, she'd decided that fairy princesses were passé, had cut her hair herself with nail scissors – much to her mother's horror – and had refused to wear dresses ever again. She'd eventually given in on the dresses, of course, but she didn't do pink any more.)

Obviously, she thought, as she stepped under the shower, gasped, and rapidly turned the dial to hot from the sub-zero temperature she'd somehow left it at the day before, nobody's life turned out exactly the way they expected. She wasn't stupid enough to imagine that the things she'd wished for on various other birthdays – being a famous singer (tenth); growing bigger boobs (fourteenth); finding Mr Right (various ever since her fifteenth, but not one she'd had in the last couple of years) – she wasn't stupid enough to imagine that any of these things would all just happen. She was also realistic enough to know that what she'd wanted when she was ten or twenty or even thirty wouldn't necessarily be the same as she wanted now. But on the morning of her thirty-fourth birthday (which somehow she couldn't help thinking sounded scarily older than thirty-three) she had the nagging feeling that time had somehow speeded up on her and that she still hadn't changed into a grown-up who knew what she really wanted from life. Nothing, absolutely nothing, had panned out the way she'd originally planned. Which didn't have to be a bad thing, she supposed, as she drizzled honey and almond shower wash over her shoulders, but it would be so much better if, just once, she could make a plan and see it all work out. It was all very well to accept that she couldn't sing and that her boobs had remained a neat but uninspiring 34B and even that she probably hadn't found Mr Right, but it would be nice to achieve something from her childhood wish list.

Bloody birthdays, she muttered, after she'd got out of the shower, dressed and spent ages taming the kinks that still plagued her hair (wrestling with her dryer, her GHD and copious quantities of anti-frizz serum to achieve her objective) they were just an excuse for multinational companies to rip people off by selling overpriced cards with crap rhymes.

And so she didn't bother to check the mailbox in the hall of her apartment building for birthday cards on her way to work but breezed past it without even glancing in its direction. She already knew that she'd receive four cards to mark the occasion: one from her mother; usually a 'For my Daughter' special with flowers, ribbons and a badly scanning sentimental verse – unlike Darcey, Minette loved celebrating birthdays; one from the twins (an old-fashioned sepia-type card if Tish had bought it; a cartoon feature if it had been Amelie's turn to choose – the twins, older than her by a year, always sent their cards as a pair); a generic 'Happy Birthday' card from her father with the date inscribed on the inside – as if she didn't know what the date was; and finally a 'To My Goddaughter' card from Nerys, her mother's best friend, who would include a lottery scratch card with it and a message that if it came up trumps Darcey was to spend the money entirely on something frivolous for herself. Darcey always felt touched by the card and the gift implying that she needed the money. No matter how often she told Nerys that she was financially independent (although that independence came with her very own breathtaking mortgage and much-utilised credit card), Nerys would adopt her most sympathetic tone and tell her that every woman could do with money of her own, especially when she didn't have anyone to look after her any more. Darcey always gritted her teeth at that but said nothing. So far the total haul from all of Nerys's scratch cards had only amounted to a fiver –

which Darcey had naturally enough spent on more scratch cards, although not one of them had delivered anything in return. That didn't really surprise her. She wasn't a person who won draws or raffles or matched lottery numbers and so she didn't really expect her numbers to come up. That was why she didn't bother with wish lists of things she'd do if she won the lottery. She'd grown out of lottery-win wish lists in the same way as she'd grown out of birthdays.

She walked briskly out of her glass and steel apartment building close to Dublin's Grand Canal Dock and crossed the road in order to bask in the morning sunshine. She'd bought the apartment in one of the city's currently fashionable locations two years earlier, and she loved it despite the scary mortgage, and even though her mother thought it was far too cold and impersonal; while the twins chided her that she was shutting herself away by living on the fifth floor of the tall, thin block. (And all three of them suggested that she'd be better off back home in Galway these days than living in the stress-inducing cauldron that Dublin city had become.) It had been the purchase of the apartment that had led to the astronomical credit-card bills too. She hadn't realised just how much money she'd end up spending on (mainly unused) gadgets for the tiny kitchen or the perfect light for the living room or the scatter cushions and plumped-up pillows for her king-sized bed. But she knew that one day she'd come out from under the blanket of debt (she did, after all, and much to her own surprise, have a well-paid job!) and she loved living in Dublin, a mere five-minute walk from the Dart station and a short hop by train from her office in the Financial Services Centre.

Normally Darcey arrived at the undistinguished office building before seven thirty each day but on the morning of her birthday she was late. This was because almost as soon as the commuters at Grand Canal Dock got on to the train the driver announced – rather too cheerfully, Darcey thought – that due to a mechanical fault they wouldn't be going anywhere for a while. Darcey didn't hang around for the trains to start running again and the inevitable scrum that would ensue as everyone tried to pile on, but instead walked to Grand Canal Street and looked for a cab even though she knew that, theoretically at least, it would have been nearly as quick to walk. But she was wearing her pencil-thin black skirt and her killer-heel L.K. Bennett suede boots, and walking more than a few hundred metres at a time was simply not an option.

There weren't any cabs. She paced along the road as gingerly as the killer heels would allow, wondering why it was that there were always cabs when you didn't want them and never ones when you did. If I get a blister, she thought grumpily, I will sue Iarnrod Eireann and their damn mechanical faults! As she allowed herself the mental image of her day in court against the train company she suddenly spotted a yellow cab sign and waved frantically, managing to nab the taxi ahead of a disgruntled fellow passenger, who glared at her as she smiled sweetly at him and closed the door, glad that now she wouldn't be *too* late for work.

Late, of course, was relative. She didn't actually have to be in at seven thirty. But everyone who did well at Global Finance was in the office early and, even though she wasn't a morning person, she felt it was important to be there too. Darcey was the business development manager of the financial services company which managed its international business out of the centre. Tish and Amelie teasingly called her their high-flyer sister. That was complete nonsense, of course. She wasn't really a high-flyer. Her job was interesting, but, she told them, it sounded far more important than it was. Really it was all about being nice to people. And anyone could do that.

Despite getting the cab, the snarling morning traffic – made worse by a burst water pipe on Pearse Street – meant that it was nearly forty minutes after leaving her apartment instead of the usual twenty before she jabbed at the lift call button in the marble lobby of the Global Finance building. She sipped on her takeaway coffee, waiting for the kick from the caffeine coursing through her veins to lift her non-morning persona into someone who could be nice to people despite the hour. Even though she really wasn't ready for niceness and actually found it hard to talk sensibly until she'd downed her first coffee of the morning, she smiled in greeting at more of Global's employees as they joined her in front of the lifts, all of them with waxed coffee cups in their hands. (Global had coffee vending machines on every floor but the general consensus, which Darcey agreed with utterly, was that the coffee was sludge and it was much better to get a takeaway from the Italian barrista on the corner.)

They smiled back at her. Darcey was well liked by her colleagues, even though many of them were in awe of her ridiculously high IQ and everyone knew that Peter Henson, the managing director, was a bit scared of her himself. But she never made an issue of her IQ (she'd once commented ruefully that intelligence was entirely different to common sense), she was easy to work for, and she never bawled anyone out for a mistake even if they deserved it. (Although many people thought that her patient acceptance of the fact that they were less than perfect was bad enough.)

Darcey worked on the sixth floor. As the lift moved gently upwards, she listened to Margaret Rooney and Mylene Scott chatting in disbelief about the latest celebrity break-up and agreed with them that it was all his fault – even though she hadn't really followed the romance of the hot singer and the hotter Hollywood actress, being generally cynical about celebrity marriages. Margaret and Mylene were still talking about it as they and the other employees got out at the third floor, where most of the administration took place, leaving Darcey alone for a few moments. She glanced at herself in the mirrored walls of the lift before stepping out; her usual quick check to see that she looked OK and didn't have a coffee-froth moustache or previously unnoticed spots breaking out on her forehead. High-flyers were supposed to look efficient and well groomed, and Darcey, even though she laughed at the twins when they used the expression, secretly liked to picture herself as a tall ballbreaker of a woman as she strode through the office in a power suit. Unfortunately, though, her mental picture was often ruined by the image of her Donna Karan skirt accidentally caught in her knickers or a ferocious ladder snaking up the back of her Wolford stockings as she walked. Or her worst nightmare, tripping over her own feet and ending up flat on the floor. She'd always been clumsy as a child, even during her princess period. She worked hard not to be now.

Her reflection appeared OK, despite an errant lock of caramel and honey hair (missed by the GHD and the blow-dry styling lotion) curling over her left ear. She smoothed it down, although she knew she was probably wasting her time. Her hair had a mind of its own. Her make-up was fine, though – a tinted moisturiser applied to her evenly toned creamy skin (thankfully no spotty eruptions in the last hour), neutral eye shadow on her eyelids and a slick of dark mascara on her already long, sweeping lashes. On her lips she wore a rose-tinted lip salve. Darcey's lips were her least favourite feature; she wished they were full and bee-stung like so many actresses and models these days, but they were just normal, which obviously meant that they looked too thin. (One of the girls in corporate finance had hers regularly pumped with collagen and had offered to fix her up with an appointment but Darcey usually fainted whenever she saw a needle, and besides, she'd never seen anyone who didn't look worse when they'd had it done, no matter what people said.) So she stuck with her too-thin lips and consoled herself with the fact that she'd once been told that she was a good kisser. Besides, bee-stung lips weren't really power-woman. They implied a certain vulnerability that Darcey was determined never to show.

Darcey knew, as she contemplated her image in the smoked-glass mirror, that she had strong features, which meant that she was very definitely not beautiful. Even when she'd been younger, and before she'd hacked off her golden curls, she hadn't really been beautiful, just an average little girl with bright blue eyes and a nose that was slightly too big for the rest of her face. She hadn't changed that much really. Average was about right for her. She hadn't had anything done to her nose and her hair was still difficult to deal with. These days she wore it in a straight cut which reached just above her shoulders in a slightly severe way. She knew that trying to wear her hair straight when it really wanted to be curly was why she had to buy every new hair product that came on to the market and why her GHD was the most important piece of equipment in her life, but she liked the severe appearance. It meant that people didn't mess with her. Her black suit, with its figure-hugging skirt and tailored jacket over a charcoal-grey top, made her look almost frighteningly efficient. She liked looking efficient. It was better than looking beautiful.

She'd once talked to her mother about the advantages of being beautiful, resigned to the fact that beautiful girls got the nicest blokes and the best job opportunities and that they were simply noticed more, whereas average girls had to work so much harder on all fronts. It wasn't fair, she'd said, and Minette McGonigle hadn't tried to placate her by saying that she was talking nonsense, and instead had agreed that no, it wasn't. Minette didn't try to sugar-coat things for her children.

That particular memory always came back on birthdays. But it wasn't important any more. Darcey pushed the memories to the very back of her mind as she walked across the floor to her desk and sat down, logging on to her computer even as she slid her jacket on to the back of her chair, and noticing that, thanks to arriving later than usual, she already had a number of messages on her voicemail.

And even more messages in her email folder, she realised. Most were newsletters she subscribed to, some were from customers and one was from the director of human resources at Global Finance. She opened it and clicked on the web-page link inside. Immediately the sound of 'Congratulations' blared across the sixth floor, while a trio of cartoon bears danced across the screen holding up a banner which said 'Happy Birthday'. The nearby office staff grinned at her and waved. She made a face at them, then stabbed at the keyboard to shut down the message before picking up her phone and dialling an extension number.

'Very appropriate,' she told Anna Sweeney, the director of human resources. 'It's always good to start the day by assaulting your colleagues with dreadful music.'

'It's cheerful,' protested Anna blithely. 'And fun.'

'Yeah, yeah,' said Darcey.

'And I can do these things because in my exalted position I know everyone's birthday,' continued Anna.

'Indeed you do,' agreed Darcey. 'But I thought we agreed last year *and* the year before that that I don't do the cute message from Human Resources reminding me that I'm another year older and deeper in debt.'

Anna laughed. 'I know. I know. But it's my job.'

'You're supposed to be supportive of the staff.' Darcey's voice held a hint of amusement. 'Not bash them over the head with the notion that they're getting even closer to grey hair.'

'You're lucky, Blondie. Nobody'll notice yours.'

Darcey laughed. 'If only.'

'Anyway, happy birthday,' said Anna.

'Thank you.' Darcey grimaced as more and more messages appeared in her email folder. 'I'd better go. The whole world is sending me emails. Talk to you later.'

'What d'you think about the meeting today?' asked Anna.

'Huh?' Darcey stopped scrolling through her inbox. 'What meeting?'

'There's an email from Peter,' said Anna. 'I thought you would've read it by now. Slacking, are you? Looks like the takeover is going to happen. And looks like InvestorCorp have beaten Assam Financial to the deal.'

Darcey stopped scrolling and opened the email Anna was referring to.

> To: *All Staff*
> From: *Peter Henson, MD*
> Re: *InvestorCorp*
> *There will be a meeting in the staff dining area at 12 noon to discuss InvestorCorp and its intentions towards this company. All staff are requested to attend.*

'Um,' said Darcey.
'Um indeed,' said the director of human resources.

Everyone in Global Finance had known for some time that their company was probably going to be taken over by a bigger one. It was almost inevitable that it would happen sooner or later, since Global Finance was a profitable minnow in the sea of finance companies and therefore a prime takeover target. The rumours had been swirling around the office for months now and had popped up on the financial pages of the newspapers a couple of weeks earlier, causing Minette to ring Darcey and ask her what was happening and to remind her that there were plenty of jobs in Galway if the worst came to the worst.

'You know as much as me,' Darcey had replied. 'And I'm sure I'll be fine no matter what.'

But she couldn't really be sure. And despite what she'd said to Minette, she was worried that everything wouldn't actually be fine. It might not matter that it was Investor-Corp, of course. Things changed, people moved on. But she would have preferred the takeover to be by any other company in the world.

She twirled at her errant lock of hair as she stared at the email. Maybe she shouldn't stay around for the whole InvestorCorp deal. Maybe she should just look for some-thing else now before anything happened. It wasn't like it had been when she'd first joined the company, still wet behind the ears really and inexperienced no matter what she thought. People in the industry knew her now, and respected her. But still . . . She wiped her suddenly perspiring palms on the sides of her skirt. InvestorCorp was different. And not just because even the receptionists in their US offices had Harvard degrees.

I shouldn't have given in, thought Darcey. I shouldn't have let myself get sucked into this whole high-flying career thing. I was never cut out to be a ballbreaking career chick, no matter what other people think. And I should have had more sense than to think that being a business development manager was something I really wanted to be.

Global Finance's one hundred employees gathered in the cafeteria at the appointed time. Darcey sat on the edge of one of the wooden tables and didn't talk to anyone while they waited. Peter Henson was five minutes late, which caused one of the admin staff to mutter that he'd been the first to go and provoked a ripple of amused laughter among the rest of them. But then he strode in to the dining area, tall and confident, followed by the other members of the board, all looking pleased with themselves.

When the meeting got under way, Peter announced that the takeover was going ahead and that eventually and inevitably there would have to be some changes, but that they were nothing that anyone needed to worry about, and that no jobs would go.

'And if you believe that, you'll believe anything,' muttered Mylene Scott, who was sitting beside Darcey.

'Of course jobs will go,' Darcey agreed. 'You know what'll happen. The new set of suits will come in and they'll talk about rationalisation and downsizing. Only they won't rationalise and downsize themselves.'

Mylene looked at her, startled at such a cynical comment from the woman from the sixth floor who, despite her relatively easy-going nature, she actually regarded as a suit too.

'Well, you don't have to worry,' she said eventually. 'You're set up with that great job of yours.'

Darcey shivered. They all thought she had a great job and was brilliant, but in the end it had been a sheer fluke that had started her off on this career path. She honestly expected that one day someone would ask her a question she simply couldn't answer, and then they'd realise that she was nothing more than a jumped-up accounts temp and not a hotshot high-flyer at all.

The truth was that she'd been happy as a temp. Temping gave her a freedom that she'd never found in a permanent job. Temping meant that she didn't get involved with people and they didn't get involved with her. As well as which, Darcey knew that her boredom threshold was very low and she normally got fed up anywhere she worked after a few months, which meant that temping suited her down to the ground. When she'd come to Dublin a few years earlier, after the life she thought she was going to have had disintegrated into nothing and she'd made such a fool of herself, she'd eventually landed a job filling in as maternity cover for someone in an international bank, operating out of the financial services centre. Her job had been to check the daily trading reports for errors and exceptions – times when, perhaps, a trader had broken a dealing limit with one of the bank's trading partners or had incorrectly booked dollars as euros or something equally silly.

The woman at the temping agency had told her that it was a pressurised environment but that Amabank paid extremely well and it would be a worthwhile three-month stint. Darcey didn't care. It didn't matter to her whether she was looking for million-dollar mistakes or filing invoices. All she wanted was to be too busy to think and to get paid every week. So three days later she was sitting in the audit department of the bank where Jayne and Sinead, her two new colleagues, wanted to know all about her.

Darcey had never been the kind of person who confided in complete strangers. Besides, she was only going to be in the bank for a few months and she didn't expect to become best friends with either of them. She told Jayne and Sinead that she was from Galway and that she'd been abroad for a while and was now looking to work in Dublin.

'Are you married or single?' asked Jayne.

Darcey was startled by the question.

'Jayne's getting married next month,' Sinead told her. 'So it's the uppermost thing in her mind right now.'

'I'm not into marriage,' Darcey said, which effectively ended the conversation. Jayne looked at her huffily for not being interested and called up the website of the hotel where she was holding her reception to check once more how the room looked.

The department was busy but was hardly the pressurised environment Darcey had been hoping for. She found that she was easily able to cope with the work and never objected when she was given anything extra. She made herself extremely unpopular by actually doing work she hadn't even been asked to do, but she preferred to keep busy than to spend time staring into space while thinking about things she didn't want to think about any more; or even worse, being quizzed by Jayne and Sinead about the men in her life. Now, when she looked back on herself at that time, she knew she must have been unbearably standoffish. But she hadn't been able to help it, and she certainly didn't blame Jayne and Sinead for apparently being pleased when she was lent to other departments to help out.

Bernard Hickey, who was head of financial administration, had asked her whether she'd ever considered a job in accounting, after she'd managed in fifteen minutes to find an error in a spreadsheet that had eluded him for more than a day.

'Not at all,' she'd said firmly.

'But you found that mistake. And I checked over and over.'

'Because you were checking the computer,' she told him.

'And the mistake was in the original numbers, not the figures that were input into the computer.'

'I should have seen that,' he said in disgust. 'Did you do maths at college?'

She laughed. 'That wasn't maths,' she told him. 'It was mental arithmetic! Pure and simple.'

He grinned at her. 'Yeah, well, between computers and calculators, there aren't too many people who are good at mental arithmetic any more.'

'My father was a maths teacher,' Darcey told him. 'He made us practise.'

'Ah.' Bernard nodded. 'Well, any time you're thinking of a permanent job, let me know.'

'I don't think so,' said Darcey. 'But thanks anyway.'

It was two weeks later, the day she'd been lent out to Trader Support, that everything changed completely. And it had nothing to do with maths.

She was sitting at her desk at lunchtime trying vainly to complete the fiendish-level Sudoku puzzle in the paper when Mike Pierce, who traded in euro corporate bonds and who'd been having a telephone conversation which was getting louder and more exasperated by the minute, suddenly stood up and shouted, 'Does anyone in this damn building speak any goddam German?'

Darcey's eyes flickered upwards. Mike had torn his headset from his head and was looking around in frustration. She cleared her throat.

'I do,' she admitted hesitantly.

'Great.' Mike thrust the headset at her. 'Well in that case can you figure out what the hell this guy is saying? English

18

is meant to be the language of business, and you'd think he'd have some clue . . .'

Darcey got up from her desk and took the call.

'*Guten Tag, mein Herr,*' she said, then continued in rapid German. 'First of all, I apologise for my colleague's rudeness. Can I help you?'

The German, who introduced himself as Dieter Schmidt, told her that there was a problem regarding the interest payment for a bond in Mike's portfolio and that he was ringing with instructions about procedures that Amabank should take. His own English-speaking colleague was off sick that day, but according to their records the Amabank staff spoke German.

'Not all of us, it seems,' said Darcey as she checked his instructions again and wrote them down on her notepad. 'Anyway, it's fine now. *Danke und auf Wiedersehen.*'

She handed her notes to Mike, who was looking at her in amazement.

'You're fluent,' he exclaimed.

She shook her head. 'Not really. It might sound good to you but my accent is like nothing on earth to a native German.'

'What a treasure you are all the same.' He grinned. 'Good at maths *and* German.'

She looked at him in surprise.

'Come on!' he said. 'Bernard's been talking about you and that damn missing 50 k for the last two weeks. He thinks you're a genius.'

'He's being silly in that case,' said Darcey. 'Anyone could've spotted it. They were all just thinking the wrong way.'

'Perhaps.' Mike looked at her thoughtfully. 'Any other talents we don't know about?'

Darcey shrugged. 'I doubt it.'

'Can you speak any other languages?' he asked.

'Some,' she replied uncomfortably.

'Like?'

'French, I'm good at that,' she told him eventually. 'Italian, not bad. Spanish, OK-ish.'

'Bloody hell. You've sure been hiding your light under a bushel,' he said. 'Did you study languages?'

'My mother is Swiss,' she replied. 'She speaks German, Italian and French, although the accent – well, it's different. She moved to Ireland when she married my dad and I guess she thought it would be good for us to learn them too. I au-paired in Spain for a few months and that's where I picked that up.' She stopped, uncomfortably aware that she'd given more personal details about herself in the space of a few seconds than she'd done since she'd first joined the company.

'Ever do any other work abroad?' asked Mike.

'Like what?' she asked.

'Office work? Admin? Dealing with clients?'

She shook her head again. 'Not interested.'

'Hmm.' Mike continued to look at her thoughtfully until she found herself blushing.

'For heaven's sake,' she said sharply, 'maybe you should just get on with doing whatever it was that Dieter suggested so that you'll eventually get your interest payment.'

'Maths, languages and spirit,' he said. 'I like that in a girl.'

\*   \*   \*

It was the day after that episode when Darcey was called into the MD's office.

'I won't beat around the bush,' Cormac Ryan told her. 'I like the idea of you doing more work for us, Darcey. Specifically using your particular talents. I don't understand why we didn't know about your language skills before now.' He sounded vaguely irritated, as though she'd held some vitally important information from him.

'Hardly necessary,' she said. 'After all, I'm a temporary audit clerk.'

'But you know that our business is worldwide.'

'Of course. All the same, it doesn't much matter to me. I'm only here for another four weeks.'

'We want to offer you a six-month trial period as a permanent employee,' said Cormac. 'Everyone is impressed with your knowledge of our financial products. And your maths skills. We're also equally impressed by the language factor. We think it could be very useful in our European market.'

'Really?' She regarded him thoughtfully.

'We think you could work well with our European customers. It means a lot to someone to be able to talk in his own language.'

'Or hers,' said Darcey.

Cormac's gaze, until now firm and unrelenting, flickered. 'Or hers. The point is that sometimes we send people overseas and they make a good presentation, but the potential clients then sit around and chatter away in German or French or whatever. And it would be good to know what they're saying.'

'You want me to spy!' Darcey was shocked.

'God, no,' said Cormac. 'I don't mean for you to pretend that you can't speak to them. I want you to go in forcefully and greet them in their own language and let them know that we understand them completely. And that we've gone to the trouble of understanding them.'

'But we don't go to the trouble,' Darcey pointed out. 'Otherwise lots of people in Amabank would speak lots of languages.'

This time Cormac's look was one of irritation. 'Do you want this job or not?' he demanded.

'Not especially,' said Darcey. 'I'm happy the way I am.'

He looked at her incredulously. 'Happy using a third of your brain? Happy earning a third of what you're capable of?'

It had been like a blast from the past. Only then she'd been told that she only used an eighth of her brain. She was fed up with people thinking that she didn't use her potential and that she had no ambition. Ambition didn't make you a good person, after all.

'You're smart and you're talented and you're totally wasted where you are,' said Cormac flatly. 'But if that's the way you want it, it's fine by me. I just think it's a shame, that's all.'

'A third of what I should be earning?' She said it slowly.

'Well, depending on how things went . . .' Cormac told her hastily. 'After training, after some time. But you would be paid more as a permanent member of staff doing a specific job.'

Darcey closed her eyes for a moment. Maybe it was time for her to turn her life around. To stop drifting from job to job. To take control of things for herself. She'd changed in the last few months. Maybe it was time to prove it to herself.

'Tell me more about it,' she said eventually. 'Like – what *would* you pay me?'

She accepted the job. The way she looked at it was that she deserved the extra money. And if her personal life was a shambles, then it was up to her to make her professional life the best it could possibly be instead. The only problem was that she never really felt like a professional person. She had no real idea of how a professional person should feel.

She'd stayed with Amabank for two years, and then she was headhunted by Global Finance. Being headhunted was a strange experience. She'd never expected anyone to ring her up out of the blue and offer her another job, and despite the fact that she'd become more confident about what she was doing (even if she still wasn't very comfortable with it), she didn't consider herself to be a real expert. After all, she hadn't studied finance at college, although the concepts were easy for her to understand. It was just that she didn't really see the point to a lot of it.

But Peter Henson, the Global Finance MD, whom she'd met at a financial conference, was very persuasive.

'Come and talk to me at the very least,' he'd told her. 'I feel confident that we have the right job for your skills.'

Her task would be to find new clients in Europe and sell them the Global Finance products and services. The salary was excellent. The business development job was high-profile. It freaked her out how everyone else wanted her to be a successful high-flyer. Despite nowadays thinking that she should make her professional life as good as it could be, Darcey wasn't commercially minded at all. She liked reading for pleasure, not because she could understand financial reports in four languages. She liked doing maths puzzles for the fun of it, not to come up with some new way of making money for the company. Making money had never been important to her.

Yet, she'd thought, as she listened to Peter Henson talk about yet another increase in her salary, maybe making money was what she'd be best at in the end. Not making friends. Not making love. Just making money. Perhaps she wasn't so different from everyone else as she'd always thought. And, she admitted, she didn't know what her mother told the neighbours about her these days, but it would be ultimately satisfying if the news got around that Darcey McGonigle had turned into a kick-ass hotshot after all.

So she took the job, and because of the extra money she'd finally felt confident about dipping her toe into the property market. Minette and the twins had been getting at her to buy a place of her own for ages. Dead money, they called the rental she paid every month, and she knew they were right. A place of her own was making a statement too. That she was in control of her life again. That she could make it by herself. That she didn't need anyone else to . . . well, that she didn't need anyone else at all, actually.

'You won't regret it,' Peter Henson had said when she finally accepted the job.

Now she was beginning to think that actually she might.

# Chapter 2

After Peter Henson's announcement, Darcey spent some time mulling over the future of Global Finance with a couple of colleagues before going back to her desk and making a number of calls to various clients, most of whom had heard the news already. The financial market bush telegraph worked unbelievably quickly, she thought as she hung up from yet another client who had remarked that they must all have been expecting it.

She glanced at her watch. She knew she needed to sort out arrangements for a visit to Barcelona which she hoped to make in the next week or two, but she wasn't really able to concentrate properly on it right now. All she could think about was what might happen when the honchos from InvestorCorp walked into the offices. She swallowed hard. Nothing would happen. There had been so many takeovers in the industry over the past few years that its entire staff was probably different. So nothing would happen at all. She was getting her knickers in a twist for no reason.

It's a business thing, she told herself firmly. It's two companies merging, that's all. And I don't even know if there's any need for me to be worried about that anyway. I've got to get a grip. But her teeth worried at her lower lip even as she slid the mouse across its pad to wake her computer from sleep.

She sat in front of her screen, her hands poised uncertainly above the keyboard. And then she gave in to the thought that had been plaguing her ever since she'd read Peter Henson's email. She opened her internet browser and typed in the name Neil Lomond. She looked at the hits. Nobody who mattered. Then she typed 'InvestorCorp Neil Lomond'. There was nothing there either. She contemplated the screen for another moment and then typed 'ProSure Neil Lomond'. Her search still came up blank. Very slowly she released the breath she'd been holding as she'd waited for the page to load. Maybe he was still with them. Maybe he wasn't. Maybe it didn't really matter to her one way or the other.

She typed in her own name and smiled slightly to find it appeared in a number of different hits. She hadn't really needed to do this to know where it would appear, since Minette had Googled her at home once and had pointed them out to her with glee. One was on the Global Finance website, simply stating that she was the business development manager and giving her email address. Another was as a link in a TV interview (although that simply mentioned she'd been on the panel. Thankfully it didn't say that she'd been almost silent throughout, frozen by nerves). And the third was an account of a debate in which she'd participated at UCD about women in business. Her team had won the debate on the motion that women were still under-represented at board level in public companies. She'd argued the point well.

Three hits for her. None for Neil. Hah! She was comforted by the thought.

She probably would have stayed late at her desk, but Anna Sweeney came looking for her at six o'clock and insisted that she come for a drink.

'There's no need to hang around,' she told Darcey firmly. 'And you might not have any time for the whole birthday thing, but people will think you're a sad sap if you stay here till all hours today. Besides,' she added, 'nobody is staying late. They're all off to talk about the InvestorCorp takeover.'

Darcey logged off her computer. She knew that Anna was right but she hadn't planned to do anything special that evening and she was extremely busy, so it had seemed sensible to stay at work. Miss Sensible, she'd told herself as she'd looked through the budget reports. Miss Grown-Up after all!

Unusually, she was one of the only people left on the sixth floor. Normally, even at six o'clock, there were plenty of people scurrying around either actually busy or trying to give the impression that they were. But today nobody was bothering.

'You're right,' she said, deciding that you could take being sensible a bit too far. 'Though let's not talk about Investor-Corp. I know the whole subject will be done to death over the next few weeks and I hate idle speculation.'

Anna looked at her in surprise. She'd thought that Darcey would've liked nothing better than a bit of idle speculation about the imminent takeover. But Darcey's tone was un-expectedly firm and Anna was quite happy to talk about other things instead.

'There's a gang of us going to the Nineties Nostalgia concert on Saturday night,' she said as they settled into seats beside one of the big plate-glass windows of the Excise Bar and ordered two glasses of wine. 'There's a really good Duran Duran tribute band playing. I've got a few spare tickets. Want to come?'

'I'd love to, but I honestly don't think I can,' said Darcey after a moment's hesitation. 'I half promised my mother I'd go to Galway for the weekend, but if I don't do that I still have a few things to do before my Barcelona trip.'

'You can do the Barcelona stuff in the office,' objected Anna as she leaned back in her tub seat. 'It's going to be a good night and it'll be fun. You should come. You hardly ever come to any of the corporate dos.'

'That's because I don't need to do the whole inter-company thing like you.' Darcey grinned at her. 'All my clients are abroad. That's where I get my kicks.'

Anna smiled. 'Perhaps. But there's no harm in having a bit of a social life here too. It's not all about work. It's about getting to know people and having fun.'

'I don't need to get to know people in Global Finance, thanks,' objected Darcey. 'I know them well enough already.'

'You're missing the point,' said Anna.

'What point? I went on that terrible team bonding thing last year. Kerry McLaughlin snores! Norman Quentin doesn't wear enough deodorant. What more do I need to know about my colleagues, for God's sake?' She looked triumphantly at Anna.

'I think you could . . . well, you know . . . have more fun with them.'

'I don't need fun,' Darcey told her. 'I'm fine the way I am.'

Anna looked at her with concern.

'What?' demanded Darcey, an edge to her voice.

'I worry about you sometimes.'

'There's no need,' said Darcey impatiently. 'What in God's name is all this about?'

'It's just – well, you work really hard,' Anna told her. 'I know we're friends, but I'm also the HR director. And I care about the welfare of my staff.'

'You're priceless,' Darcey cackled. 'My staff! Get over yourself, Sweeney. You're my friend, not my HR manager.'

'You know what I mean,' said Anna defensively. 'There's burnout in this industry and I don't want you cracking up and blaming Global Finance.'

'I won't crack up,' Darcey promised her. 'I like my job.' As she spoke, she mentally crossed her fingers. She did, more or less, like her job.

'And you're good at it,' agreed Anna. 'You get on well with everyone. You're just not . . . not . . .'

'Not what?' demanded Darcey.

'You're not close to anyone.'

'What on earth are you talking about?' Darcey looked at her in astonishment. 'I'm close to you, for heaven's sake.'

'I know, I know.' Anna wished she was handling this better. 'It's just that sometimes you seem a bit distant, Darcey, that's all.'

'You'd be distant too if you spent half your life tramping around Europe drumming up business for Global Finance!'

cried Darcey. 'I really don't know why you're fussing over me all of a sudden.'

'I guess . . . it's your birthday and you were slaving away in the office and . . . you know.'

'Call me a sad old sap if you like.' Darcey grinned at her. 'But I honestly don't mind. I'll be in Barcelona in a few days. That's good enough for anyone.'

'I suppose you're right,' conceded Anna, still feeling as though she hadn't managed to achieve what she'd set out to do. Which was to somehow explain to Darcey that nobody would mind if she cut loose and did something stupid on the night of her birthday instead of making sure that she had everything for her trip prepared as faultlessly as possible.

'I'm not as much of a wonderwoman as you,' added Darcey. 'I don't have your multitasking abilities – job, kid, party animal who goes to every social event . . .'

'People don't really think of me as a party animal, do they?' Anna suddenly sounded anxious. 'I'm not. I wouldn't want them to—'

'Hey, relax!' cried Darcey. 'I just meant that you juggle everything really well.'

Anna grimaced.

'You do,' protested Darcey. 'Hell, I can hardly deal with the job and the apartment some days, but you cope with everything.'

'It's not that I'm especially good at it,' said Anna drily. 'It's just that I don't really have a choice.'

'How's Meryl?' asked Darcey after a moment's silence.

'She's great,' said Anna. 'Growing up really quickly, which

is kind of frightening. You should see the list of demands she makes these days!' She shrugged helplessly. 'To be honest with you, it's because of Meryl I'm worried about the takeover. You know InvestorCorp's reputation. What if they get rid of me?'

'Why should they do that?' asked Darcey. 'You're a great HR person.'

'Sure, but they might have someone else,' said Anna. 'Or maybe they won't give me the flexibility I have now. I mean, it's all very well that Mam is there to look after her after school and everything, but you know what kids are like. I've had to rush off two afternoons this last month because she fell in the playground or decided to get sick in class. Investor-Corp mightn't like that. And then where am I?' Her voice rose anxiously. 'I need this job. I—'

'Anna, there's no way that they'll let you go. And even if they did, there are plenty of other jobs out there.' Darcey realised that she was saying the same things to Anna as she'd told herself earlier.

'Look, I know better than anyone that prospective employers aren't meant to discriminate against anyone,' said Anna. 'But how many of them really and truly want to take on a single mother?'

'D'you know, I don't see what's so bloody different between a single mother and a married one when it comes to work,' said Darcey slowly. 'Either way, it's usually the woman who has to rush home in an emergency.'

Anna laughed wryly. 'I guess.'

'So, come on. You'll be fine.'

'I hope so.'

'I know so.' Darcey glanced at her watch. 'Do you want another drink?'

Anna nodded. 'I shouldn't really,' she said. 'I don't like leaving my mother in charge the whole time. I know she says she doesn't mind, but I'm sure she does.'

Darcey waved at one of the staff and ordered two more glasses of white wine.

'At least she's there for you and supportive,' she told Anna when the drinks were placed on the table.

'Y'see, I know that.' Anna took an appreciative sip of the cold wine. 'But let's look at things for a minute. I'm a thirty-six-year-old woman with a ten-year-old daughter. I still live at home with my mother because I need someone to help out with minding my child. But I don't want to live at home. I want to find someone and have a man in my life and a place of my own. It's so damn difficult.'

'It's always hard,' said Darcey mildly. 'Finding the right someone is far more difficult than finding the right career!'

Anna laughed. 'You're right. But it's sad to think I've made a better job of my career than my love life.'

'At least you have Meryl,' said Darcey. 'And she's great.'

'I know. I know.' Anna took a gulp of wine. 'I love her to bits and she's the best kid in the world, but I wouldn't choose to be a single mother. And yet it was my own stupid fault . . .' Her voice trailed off. 'One night,' she said fiercely. 'I mean, you don't really believe that you'll fuck it all up in one stupid night, but you do.'

'You haven't fucked it all up,' said Darcey gently.

'Oh yes I have,' said Anna. 'I can't be a glittering career woman like you. I can't be a wonderful home-baking, clothes-making yummy mummy like loads of them who live near me. And I can't be a single woman on the rip either. I have to think of Meryl all the time, and it's not that I don't want to, it's just that sometimes . . .' She shook her head. 'I'm being stupid,' she said. 'I love her and my life is fine really. It's just the uncertainty of the takeover.'

'I know,' said Darcey. 'It's unsettling for everybody.'

'You'll be grand,' Anna assured her. 'Everyone knows you're super-efficient and the best bus dev manager ever.'

'Don't be ridiculous.' Darcey squirmed uncomfortably.

'And don't you be modest,' said Anna. 'You've been Global Finance Person of the Year for two years in a row.'

'Oh, look, you know that doesn't mean very much. Besides, the competition wasn't exactly hot.' Darcey made a face. 'Mark Johnson was unfortunate to lose those clients back in September, otherwise he'd have got it.'

'Stop it!' commanded Anna. 'Stop doing that "I'm a woman and I won't accept that I totally deserve the credit" sort of stuff. Mark Johnson isn't half as good as you and you know it.'

Darcey chuckled. 'OK. OK. I'm a genius in every respect.'

Anna laughed too, then narrowed her eyes. 'Speaking of the weaker sex – any new men on the horizon?'

'Nope.'

'Well, not that I'm one to offer you advice, obviously.' Anna's voice was slightly slurred, the second glass of wine having gone to her head as she'd skipped lunch that day. 'But the only department in your life where you don't seem to have been as successful as you might is in the love department.' She held up her hand as Darcey went

33

to interrupt her. 'I know, I know, you're too busy and you haven't met the right person! But you never will if you set the bar too high. You need to let yourself go a bit, Darcey. Have a sloppy, messy love affair.'

Darcey laughed. 'I don't do sloppy, messy love affairs. They're far too much trouble.'

'I guess you're right,' Anna said. 'But then the one-night stand can be a heap of trouble too.'

'Ah, look, when it comes to men, they're nothing but trouble.' Darcey downed the rest of her wine. 'I'm going to head off,' she told Anna. 'I have plans for a long soak in the bath and a night in watching some mindless bubblegum movie.'

'Probably a better way to spend your birthday than getting involved in a messy relationship,' agreed Anna as she scooped up her mobile phone and shoved it into her bag. 'Although you shouldn't rule it out if the opportunity comes along.'

The wind was howling around the tall buildings of the Financial Services Centre when they stepped outside the bar, and both of them shivered as they turned towards the train station.

'I'm putting bets on it being another crap summer,' said Anna as she did up the top two buttons of her coat. 'What really pisses me off about global warming is that it doesn't seem to be getting any warmer!'

'I know.' Darcey, who always felt the cold, shoved her hands into the pockets of her own jacket. 'One day I'm going to emigrate to a hot climate, I swear I am.'

'What about Switzerland?' asked Anna. 'After all, you've got family there.'

'It's bloody cold in the winter,' said Darcey.

'Not damp, though,' observed Anna. 'Not grey and gloomy like here. And there's always the skiing.'

'It can be grey and gloomy,' Darcey told her. 'Besides, I'm hopeless at skiing. No, I don't see myself in Switzerland. Italy maybe. I used to dream of a nice little Tuscan farmhouse with my own olive grove where I could sell olive oil and offer painting holidays to the tourists.'

'Is there anyone in Tuscany not offering painting holidays to the tourists?' asked Anna in amusement as they reached the station.

Darcey chuckled. 'Probably not. And I can't paint, so it's a non-starter really.'

'Well, see you tomorrow.' Anna, who lived in Drogheda, outside the city, turned towards the mainline platforms, while Darcey headed towards the commuter area.

'Sure. Take care. Love to Meryl.'

'Enjoy the pampering,' said Anna.

'I will.'

'And – happy birthday.'

'Yeah, right.' But Darcey was smiling as she walked along the platform.

It was nearly eight by the time Darcey got back to her apartment, and the temperature of the spring evening had plummeted still further. She shivered slightly in her wool jacket as she pressed the keypad to open the door to her building and stepped inside and out of the fresh easterly breeze with relief.

She opened her mailbox and took out her letters. There

were seven. The four cards she'd expected were all there – she recognised her mother's slanting, continental script, the carefully printed letters of her godmother's hand, and Amelie's small, neat writing. Her father's envelope was written in block capitals. The other three letters consisted of her credit-card bill (how the hell did that always come around so quickly?), a letter from the management company of the apartment block, and a creamy-white envelope with a printed address label and a blurred American postmark. The letter had been addressed to her at her mother's home address in Galway, and Minette had forwarded it on.

An American stamp. Her body tensed and she felt her teeth clench. Minette hadn't attached a note to the envelope. Had she wondered about it too?

Darcey locked her mailbox and took the lift to her apartment. She closed the curtains (the apartment wasn't overlooked and she could have left them open, but it was beginning to rain and closing them made the place cosier), took a deep breath and began to open her mail, starting with the birthday cards. She put the scratch card from Nerys to one side without revealing the numbers to prolong the possibility that perhaps it might actually be a winner this time, and arranged the cards themselves in a neat row on her bookshelf. Then she turned to the other letters. Her credit-card balance wasn't as bad as she'd expected, which was a relief, and the letter from the management company was just a reminder about keeping pets in the block (absolutely forbidden, even though Darcey knew that at least three people had cats). The final envelope, she realised as she turned it over in her hand, also contained a card. She didn't know anyone in America who would send a card to her. She was probably adding two and two together and getting a ridiculous answer. She knew that she should just open it and be proved wrong, discover that it was some kind of junk mail. And yet something told her that it wasn't junk mail and that when she added two and two together the answer would always be four.

She didn't need to open the envelope. She didn't want to. She turned it over one more time and then tossed it into the waste-paper bin. Then she went for her promised soak in the bath, where she closed her eyes and emptied her mind of everything but the soothing music from her speaker system so that she didn't think about envelopes from America or corporate takeovers but simply allowed herself to drift with the easy melodies. Afterwards she ordered a Chinese meal for delivery and, wrapped up in her thick terry-towelling robe, ate it in front of the TV watching the latest offering from Sky Movies. After that she rang her father to thank him for his card (though she ended up leaving a message on his answering machine), did the *Irish Times* crossword, even though words weren't her forte, and then went to bed with the blockbuster novel she'd bought earlier in the week. After a couple of chapters she slid under the duvet and pulled her pillow into a more comfortable position before turning out the light. Then she closed her eyes and deliberately pushed all thoughts of the day out of her mind.

An hour later she sat up again. She'd tossed and turned but simply hadn't been able to sleep. She hadn't even come close. She pushed the duvet to one side and got out of bed.

She hesitated for a moment before going into the kitchen and retrieving the cream envelope with its printed label from the bin. It smelled vaguely of chow mein and she wrinkled her nose.

She slid her finger beneath the flap and took out the birthday card inside.

'Sorry I forgot your birthday,' it said.

She looked at it in surprise, and then opened out the card. Another, smaller white envelope fell out. She picked it up and looked at the writing inside the birthday card.

'Well I didn't, of course,' she read. 'But I've missed a lot of them over the last few years. It's such a shame we haven't kept in touch. I do hope this reaches you! By now there's a lot of water under the bridge. And we would *love* to see you at our wedding. If you are coming, you're also invited to the rehearsal dinner. Details attached. Very American, but you know how it is! And of course you can bring whoever might be in your life at the moment too.'

Darcey stared at the card in disbelief. Then she opened the second envelope. It was an invitation.

'After all this time we're finally taking the plunge', it said. 'And giving you plenty of notice to Come to our Wedding.'

The two names were printed in a silver-coloured slanting script. Darcey felt her heart hammer in her chest as she read them, and realised that the card was shaking in her hand.

She'd been holding her breath while she opened the envelope. Now she released it very slowly as she read the words again. They were getting married. Well, she'd always expected them to. But she'd thought they'd done it years ago. Hadn't that been the whole point? In the grip of a total passion for each other and wanting to be with each other for ever, surely marriage had been the only option? And now this invitation! She couldn't believe that the bitch had had the nerve to send it to her. Although God knows why she was surprised. She'd always had a nerve.

But if she thought for one second that Darcey was coming to her damn wedding, or even her damn rehearsal dinner, she sure had another think coming.

# Chapter 3

The early-morning sun was slanting through the slatted blinds of the house in Palo Alto as Nieve filled the kettle and clicked it on. Most of her friends drank coffee in the mornings (decaff now being the most popular, though some of them succumbed to skinny latte moccachinos), but she liked tea first thing. Ordinary tea too, not green or herbal or some kind of fruit infusion. Ordinary tea, strong, with milk and occasionally a spoonful of sugar too. It freaked out her friends and colleagues, but she didn't care. She never really felt as though she'd started the day properly until she'd had her cuppa.

She opened the blinds fully while she waited for the kettle to boil. The blue of the sky was already beginning to brighten and the bougainvillea outside the window swayed slightly in the gentle breeze. Across the road, Sienna Mendez reversed her brand-new Lexus out of the driveway and drove carefully along the street. Everyone drove slowly through the community roads, which had signs every few yards telling them to Look Out for Children, even though there weren't actually that many children in Pueblo Bravo to look out for.

Most of its residents were far too busy with their jobs in Silicon Valley to be thinking about children and families, but they certainly didn't want to be the ones making the headlines on the evening news for running over someone else's little darling.

Nieve looked at her fire-red Acura NSX. Not a child-friendly car. But then she didn't need a child-friendly car because she was one of those very people who were far too busy with their jobs to have children.

She hit the remote control and switched on the TV. It was automatically tuned in to Bloomberg Business News and she listened to the European and Asian market reports as she poured hot water into the small teapot to warm it. She swirled the water around in the pot and measured two spoonfuls of loose leaves into it, noting at the same time that the markets had closed higher and that the Chinese had signed another US trade agreement. She poured the now boiling water over the leaves. She didn't like tea bags and her morning tea was a ritual.

As she waited for it to brew, she watched three more cars drive out of Pueblo Bravo. Her rebellion (not that she actually needed to rebel, but she liked to think that she'd brought her own sense of self to America) was that she didn't rush out of the house in the morning and she didn't clatter into the office with a waxed cup of coffee in her hand. She normally left the house early, but not too early, and when she walked through the glass doors of Ennco, the brokerage firm where she worked, she did it briskly and efficiently and remained brisk and efficient all through the day.

She needed to be. As head of compliance she checked the

trades of men who still called themselves by nicknames like The Bear and The Stuffer and who hadn't embraced the newer, leaner, more academic trading ethos that had infiltrated so many other firms. The Bear and The Stuffer were old-style traders. Loud and brash, full of self-belief and – in Nieve's view – chauvinistic bastards. But she liked them. And though they had tried to bait her at first, they realised that it didn't bother her in the slightest, so in the end they gave her respect.

Respect, she thought, as she finally began sipping her tea. So important to her. So important to everybody. Another two cars drove past the house. Both of them the latest-model Merc. Everyone in Pueblo Bravo had the latest model of something.

She finished her tea and put the cup in the dishwasher. Then she let herself out of the house and got into her car, heading towards the glass office tower where she worked. The compliance section at the firm, which made sure that the traders stayed within their limits and didn't pull any fast stunts with the billions of dollars under their control, wasn't the glamour end of the business – that was reserved for the traders themselves – but Nieve's position was a senior one and she'd pulled in some good bonuses over the last couple of years. Bonuses they'd needed, because the Palo Alto house hadn't come cheap, and nor did the Palo Alto lifestyle. Of course both of them contributed to the lifestyle, but she was the one who was earning the eye-popping salary. She'd always been the greater earner, except for that brief time when technology people were the stars and they were the ones pulling in the big bucks. But that had gone horribly wrong for so many of them and Nieve had quickly realised that the safer money was to be made in financial services, where the banks and the finance houses and the brokerage firms might have had a downturn but were still creaming off the fees from their clients.

Which was why the job in Ennco was so great. Last month it had paid off big time. Ennco had floated on the stock market and Nieve had seen the value of the shares she held triple overnight. Right now, she was sitting on a paper profit that would set them up for the rest of their lives.

She'd always known that she'd make it big some day. Keeping her eye out for the main chance had been important to her ever since the day her father had come home and told her mother that they were going to have to move into a smaller house because he'd lost his job at the confectionery factory. She'd never forgotten how that felt, listening to her mother sobbing in the living room while her father insisted that it didn't really matter, that he'd soon get another job.

She shivered. In 1980s Ireland there hadn't been any other jobs. At least none that were suitable for a middle-aged man with no special qualifications, and certainly none that paid the same money as he'd been getting in the factory. And as she'd listened to them talk about the manager, George Lawson, and how he was still in charge despite the fact that things had gone wrong, she swore that she'd never be in that position herself.

It had all come back to her, of course, when the technology jobs had gone, but somehow that hadn't been half as frightening as 1980. Back then, jobs were supposed to be for life. In Silicon Valley they'd always been disposable.

None of it mattered any more now. Looking at the Bloomberg screen that morning, she'd seen that the share price of Ennco had gone up again. The terms of the deal meant that the employees couldn't sell their shareholding for a minimum sixteen-week period, but none of them wanted to. Word on the street was that the price had a lot further to go – at least double its current value. That was when she planned to sell. No point in being too greedy.

The only extravagant thing she'd done since the buyout was organising the wedding. She smiled to herself at the thought. She would be coming back to Ireland as the conquering heroine she deserved to be, and the wedding, in one of the most exclusive castle hotels in the country, would be an utterly lavish, no-expense-spared affair. The kind that would proclaim to everyone who came that Nieve Stapleton had hit the big time.

She didn't want to be like some of the other Irish people who came home from their jobs abroad and discovered that they were strangers in their own country and that nobody was impressed by their stories of working in the US or Australia or wherever the hell they'd gone. Because that was what had happened over the past few years, with the whole Celtic Tiger thing and Ireland seeing itself as a rich country instead of a Third World island on the edge of Europe. Nieve knew a lot of people who'd been lured back by the promise of exciting new jobs at home and had suddenly discovered that the salaries weren't actually enough for them to live on because house prices were so high and because everyone who was anyone had a sports car and an SUV, and a home cinema in the back room. She'd never bothered going back herself. There hadn't been any need. And there hadn't been anything to draw her home either.

Her US friends who visited Ireland from time to time would return with stories of pubs she'd never heard of or places she'd never been, and she'd be gobsmacked, wondering whether she'd made a mistake after all. But the Ennco deal meant that she knew she hadn't. And the wedding would prove it.

She supposed some people might be surprised that she hadn't got married before now. She'd told him she'd marry him when she'd realised her dream, when she had a healthy seven-figure sum in her bank account and when she could have a completely over-the-top, in-your-face wedding. He'd laughed at her and told her there was more to life than money and more to being married than extravagant weddings, and she'd agreed. But she'd also reminded him that it sure as hell made life a lot easier. And that as far as the wedding was concerned, she wanted it to be her very own fairy tale.

She turned off the freeway into the office park where Ennco's building was located. The car park was already full. At seven thirty she was one of the latest to arrive. She often wondered whether some of her colleagues ever went home.

The trading floor was already buzzing when she walked in. The Bear and The Stuffer were shouting at each other (a regular occurrence), and Jasmine Becker, one of the support staff, was doling out coffees and doughnuts to the traders.

Nieve shuddered as The Bear took a bite from his

doughnut, a slurp from his coffee, yelled at The Stuffer and answered a call at the same time. The pair of them were anachronisms in a modern trading environment, she thought as she walked into her glass-walled office. These days traders weren't supposed to be weirdo individuals flying by the seat of their pants. Nieve, and people like her, monitored their every move so that they couldn't make crazy trades and leave the company open to impossible positions. She'd be glad when they retired and she only had to worry about the new wave. These new traders were different. They wore sharp suits and looked in complete control of themselves. Like Jaden Andersen, who had declined the proffered doughnut and coffee and was instead drinking herbal tea. Jaden had brought in more money in the last year than The Bear and The Stuffer combined, and his bonus had reflected that.

She'd been consumed with jealousy when she'd seen the breathtaking amount of money he was taking home. She'd wondered whether she'd even come into work the next morning if she was pulling in that sort of money, but Jaden Andersen had been at his desk as usual the following day, his tailored jacket draped on his chair, his designer shirt-sleeves held up by old-fashioned sleeve-holders.

As she watched, she saw him disconnect a call, remove his headset temporarily, roll his neck a couple of times to relieve the stress, then replace his headset again. She could have been a trader, but that wasn't what had interested her. And, being honest about it, traders – whether old-style or new-style – were a different breed of person to her. She liked to have everything exactly right. Traders, even controlled and thoughtful ones like Jaden, all had a certain level of recklessness built into their characters.

Nieve wasn't reckless. She never had been. She'd always made her money in a much more determined way.

She'd made her first profit when she was six years old, when they still lived in their big house and before her father had lost his job. He'd brought home a box of fun-sized chocolate bars as a treat for Nieve and Gail. Nieve knew how much each bar cost in the local convenience store, because that was where all the kids went to buy sweets. She sold them to the local children at a cheaper price. When Gail asked one evening where all the chocolate bars were, Nieve handed her the money instead.

'Those were a present from your dad,' Gail told her. 'He didn't bring them home for you to sell them.'

'It's better for me than eating them all,' she pointed out (reasonably, she thought, since Gail was always going on about healthy eating). 'And this way I can save up for things I really want.'

All through her childhood she'd come up with ways of augmenting her pocket money. She took neighbours' dogs for walks, weeded gardens, ran errands . . . all for a price. When she was older, she set herself up with a number of babysitting jobs too.

Her skills had come to the fore during transition year in school. This was the year in which students were freed from formal academic study but instead were meant to build life skills, learn about the wider world and get the work experience that would help them to make their choices about the subjects they wanted to take in their final two years at school. Nieve was placed in charge of one of the projects – to design and market a product and sell as many units as possible, thus making money for the school. The previous year's transition students had made key rings with the school crest as the fob. Nieve thought that key rings were passé and would only be bought by parents who felt sorry for them. She sat down with the girls in her group and said that they had to come up with something better than key rings or hairclips and that she expected them to have some ideas. The girls, Carol, Rosa and Darcey, looked back at her blankly.

Their blank looks weren't because they were stupid. Nieve's group was, in fact, known in the school as the Brainy Broads. This was because all of them were bright and all of them were considered to be far too studious for their own good. But none of them could think of anything more saleable than key rings and hairclips. The video was Nieve's own idea. It was called *How To Blag Your Way Through Your Exams*, and was a compilation of ideas to help you pass exams even with the bare minimum of work. Nieve was quietly confident that loads of people would buy a video which promised them exam success without working very hard and she insisted on charging a hefty price despite the doubts of the rest of her team. She offered to put some of her own money into the advertising in return for a proportion of the income. Surprised by her confidence, the others agreed.

The video was a massive success; the school made the most money on a transition year project ever, and Nieve cleaned up too. Almost everybody in the school bought the video, and they got orders from students in other schools as well.

It was Nieve's first commercial project. And it had been a resounding success.

She smiled at the memory. Then she logged on to her computer and began her random search of trades. At the same time she kept one eye on the electronic ticker that told her that her shareholding in Ennco had gone up another two per cent since opening and that her net worth had just increased by another few thousand dollars. Something which made her smile even wider.

# Chapter 4

The airport was, as always, chaotic early in the morning, the main concourse already crowded with long winding queues at check-in and the baggage drop areas. A businessman, computer bag over his shoulder and raincoat over his arm, banged into her, apologised brusquely, then hurried towards the security check looking anxiously at his watch at the same time.

Darcey could never understand how so many people at the airport always seemed to be in a rush. She had plenty of time. Punctuality had been drummed into her by her father, who insisted that being late was an unforgivable show of disrespect. He'd been talking about being late for meeting people, of course, but once it was ingrained in her consciousness, being late for anything was difficult – despite the fact that she rather thought there were worse ways of being disrespectful (and that her father wasn't exactly outside of the glasshouse when it came to it). Crazy, she thought now, as she keyed her flight number into the self-check-in console, how some things our parents tell us stay with us for ever. And bother us! Being late always bothered

Darcey, and she blamed her father for making her feel that way.

But it was thanks to him that she had plenty of time to negotiate the lengthy security queues and stop for a coffee and croissant in one of the airside cafés as usual. The café was crowded too, and the woman in front of her was tapping her foot impatiently as she waited for her coffee. When she finally got it, she drank it in two hurried gulps. When Darcey got hers, she took it to a table and sipped it slowly as she glanced through the paper. There seemed to be no more about the InvestorCorp takeover, which had dominated the business pages for the last few days. So far nobody from the InvestorCorp European office, based in Edinburgh, had been over to Dublin, although everyone was expecting to see the new owners any day now. Anna Sweeney had emailed Darcey, wondering and worrying again about the future of the HR function, while the conversation in the staff dining area (and, more importantly, in the privacy of the washrooms) was still all about what changes InvestorCorp might bring. Especially if the US people became involved.

The structure of InvestorCorp was different from Global Finance. The company had lots of offices around the world, including America, but its Scottish division was the biggest in Europe by virtue of the fact that the canny Scots had previously taken over ProSure, a major English investment firm. It was difficult, Darcey thought, to keep track of them all. It was no wonder that most people found business complicated. But the bottom line wasn't complicated. The Scots and the Yanks would come to Dublin soon. And that would change things for everyone.

Darcey took a deep breath as she thought about those changes, then finished her coffee and folded her paper. She left the café and strolled down to the gate. Most of the seats in the waiting area were already occupied, the majority by business travellers – almost all of whom were sharp-suited, laptop-carrying men tapping frantically at PDAs or talking on their mobile phones, despite the fact that it was only seven in the morning. They looked smart and self-important. Darcey wondered, as she glanced down at her silk navy suit and severe white cotton blouse, whether she looked smart and self-important too. Or did everyone who looked at her know that she really wasn't a business person at heart and was only faking it?

She never tried to do any work at the airport herself because she knew it would only end in disaster. Electronic equipment seemed to take an instant dislike to her. Her laptop crashed more often than it functioned and so the idea of taking it out and stabbing helplessly at it in public was too embarrassing to think about. Nevertheless, she always felt slightly out of place with her newspaper or her copy of *Newsweek* or *The Economist* (she would've preferred *Hello!* or *OK!* but that would've destroyed her image completely) when sitting beside people who frantically worked on the go.

Minette liked the image of a globetrotting executive-style daughter, although Darcey was at pains to point out that she only travelled around Europe and that – unlike in Minette's day – catching a plane wasn't a glamorous thing to do any more. In fact, given the ever-changing security restrictions, it was more like a nightmare.

'Oh, don't be ungrateful,' Minette retorted. 'You've done

well for yourself, and that's important. You came through everything as a winner. You showed them all in the end. And it's nice for you to get to these places first-class and for free.'

At which Darcey laughed and told her that Global Finance didn't get where it was by booking first-class travel for its employees – even if it was available, which usually it wasn't – and that she did actually work when she was away.

'But it's better than being stuck in an office,' Minette said hopefully. Darcey knew that her mother wanted to think of her as successful at something. 'And,' she added wistfully, 'you do stay in nice hotels.'

That part was true anyway. The company expenses allowed them to stay in decent places and Darcey was grateful for that. She'd stayed in some real fleapits in her time and it was nice to overnight in a hotel that provided shampoo and shower soap that was actually worth nicking.

The flight was called and there was the usual scramble to get on the plane. The man beside her closed his laptop and joined the queue. Darcey waited until it had thinned out a little and then boarded the plane, just about managing to find space for her bag in the crammed overhead bins.

Her seat was beside yet another computer-user. He kept the laptop on his knee, ready to start work again as soon as the plane had taken off, which Darcey felt was being too keen altogether! She settled back in her seat, closed her eyes and didn't open them again until the cabin crew started to push their trolleys along the aisle. She asked for a tea and sipped it, her eyes idly scanning the work the businessman beside her was doing. She wanted to point out to him that he'd put an incorrect formula in column D. But she didn't.

She unfolded the paper at the Sudoku page. By the time she'd completed the three different problems, the crew had finished the in-flight service and the plane was beginning its descent into Barcelona airport.

It was warmer in Barcelona than it had been in Dublin, and Darcey reflected that any job that allowed you to start the day beneath grey clouds but end up somewhere warmer and brighter was a good one. Her mother was right. Sometimes she spent too much time thinking about the things that had gone wrong for her instead of embracing all the things that had turned out just fine. And suddenly she felt the edge of gloom that had been with her ever since the InvestorCorp announcement start to lift.

She opened her diary to check on her appointment schedule. People were surprised when they saw her using an ordinary diary instead of a PDA or other electronic gadget, but she liked to actually write things down instead of committing them to electronic oblivion. And she loved her leatherbound diary, which somehow seemed so much more personal than a PDA.

She hopped into a taxi and gave directions to her first meeting, feeling herself relax even though she was already planning the structure of the meeting in her head. This was one of her favourite trips. She liked all of her Spanish clients and she thought that Barcelona was one of Europe's most effortlessly cool cities. Milan might beat it on style, she acknowledged, as they pulled up outside the tall building where Joaquin Santiago worked, but Barcelona surely had the edge when it came to sheer fun.

She'd had the most fun ever in Barcelona. It had been the last city that she and her friends had visited in their round-Europe gap year when they'd left school, and they'd been blown away by it. It had also been the only place where she'd struggled to make herself understood, and because of that, because they weren't all looking to her to sort things out as they had in France and in Germany and in Italy, she'd felt more of the gang than ever before. (But she hadn't liked not being able to speak the language, which was why she'd come back to Spain after college.)

She'd loved being part of a gang, though. At school, despite being categorised with the brainy ones, she hadn't really done gangs, preferring to stick to her closest friend. But Nieve was an altogether more gregarious person, and even though she and Darcey were best friends, she'd insisted that bumming around Europe would be better in a gang than by themselves.

It had been. And the best part of it all, at least as far as Darcey had been concerned, was that they weren't trying to prove anything. At school it had been about exams and doing well – about stretching the intellect, Miss Hargreaves had once told them. But in Paris and Frankfurt and Milan they didn't try to stretch their intellects. They just had fun.

One of the reasons that Darcey was so happy to have fun was that, because she was considered a bit of a smarty-pants, people expected her not to. All through her childhood, when he'd realised that she was exceptionally bright, her father had pushed her to do better and better academically. As a maths teacher, he was delighted at her ease with numbers. Her almost photographic memory was equally important. The language thing – well, he said, that was a given with Minette in the house. He told Darcey that it was essential that she didn't waste her gifts. That she had the opportunity to do great things. That she would be a success in life. And so, during her schooldays, he'd challenged her to work harder and harder and get better and better results. The only problem with this, as far as Darcey was concerned, was that nobody in school liked a smartarse. People were suspicious of anyone who seemed too clever for their own good. It was totally and utterly uncool to know all the answers. And it was only because the infinitely more popular Nieve Stapleton was her best friend that she managed to enjoy her schooldays at all.

School was hard. Not the work, that was easy for Darcey. But the people were more difficult. It was important not to be too clever or too stupid or too pretty or too unattractive. All these things marked you out. Darcey had never wanted to be marked out, but it was almost impossible when teachers relentlessly picked on her to answer questions or explain difficult concepts. She knew that most of the other girls hated her for it and she tried very hard to make herself inconspicuous in class.

But she hadn't been marked out during her gap year. She'd enjoyed herself. And as she stepped out of the cab on to the warm pavement of the Via Laietana, that sense of enjoyment came flooding back to her again and she walked into the Gaudí-designed building with a spring in her step.

Her meeting with Joaquin Santiago was a good one. She did what she was best at and extolled the virtues of his company doing business with Global Finance, pointing out how much money he'd both made and saved by working with them already. When she was finished, he asked her about the takeover and what that would mean.

'Nothing,' she said firmly, 'other than we will have greater resources behind us that will be of benefit to all of us. You included,' she added. 'As soon as I can give you more information on additional services, I'll be glad to come to see you again.'

She said the same things to the clients at her second and third meetings too, and to Francisco Ortiz, her final client of the day.

'And I will be glad to see you any time,' he told her. His dark eyes held hers for an instant.

'How is Inez?' She asked after his wife.

Francisco looked at her proudly. 'Pregnant,' he said.

'That's great news!' Darcey smiled at him in real delight.

He nodded. 'We are very happy.'

'Of course you are.'

His expression altered slightly. 'Of course, *we* could have been happy too.'

'No way,' she said quickly. 'You know that, Francisco. It was great and everything, but . . .'

'But you don't want to be tied down.' He repeated the words she'd said to him a couple of years earlier.

'Ah, Fran, you know that we were in the wrong place at the wrong time,' she told him. 'I was a mess and you deserved more. You deserved Inez. Besides,' she added, 'it was only a few weeks . . .'

'Great weeks, though.' His eyes twinkled and she blushed.

'Yes. Well . . .'

He laughed. 'And is there anyone for you, Darcey?'

'Oh, you know me,' she told him. 'Not a chance.'

He looked at her with affection, and she told him quickly that she had to go. He held out his hand and she took it. Then they exchanged a kiss on each cheek. Cerruti aftershave, she said to herself. It always reminded her of him. He'd been good to her and good for her, and it had been a time of intense passion. But never for ever.

'*Hasta luego*,' she said as she stood back from him.

'*Hasta pronto*,' he replied.

She left the office and didn't look back.

She didn't have any more meetings that day, but she did have dinner that evening with a potential new client. It was after one in the morning by the time she got back to the boutique hotel near the elegant Passeig de Gracía, where she'd checked in between sessions. It had been a nineteen-hour day and she was exhausted.

There was a half-bottle of Rioja and a glass on a silver tray in the centre of the low table in the corner of the room. She uncorked the wine and poured some into the glass. Then she sank into the red armchair and closed her eyes. As she sipped the wine and began to unwind, the thoughts that she'd so successfully pushed out of her head came rushing back in again. Thoughts of InvestorCorp. And, even more insistently, thoughts of the wedding invitation.

The most surprising thing about that was that it existed in the first place. She didn't know what was bugging her most. The fact that they hadn't got married before or the fact that they were going to now.

Nieve Stapleton and InvestorCorp. Two completely

separate parts of her life that she thought she'd put behind her for ever. But now they were coming back to haunt her. She couldn't quite believe that both of them were reappearing at the same time.

She'd known Nieve almost all her life. Nieve's parents, Gail and Stephen, had moved next door to Minette and Martin and their three daughters on the warmest, sultriest day of the year, which meant that the Stapletons were hot and frazzled by the time they'd finished unpacking and happy to see that Nieve had wandered up the street to the copse of trees at the end of the cul-de-sac where Darcey was sitting reading a book.

They were both seven years old.

'What'cha reading?'

Darcey hadn't even noticed the other girl until Nieve spoke.

'Why?'

'Maybe I could borrow it.'

'You mightn't be able to read it.' Darcey held her book close to her chest. 'And how do I know you'll give it back?'

'I'm good at reading,' said Nieve. 'I read lots. I've moved in to number ten. I didn't want to move. I left my best friend behind.'

Darcey heard the wobble in the other girl's voice.

'I live next door. In number eight.'

'So can I see the book?'

Darcey shrugged and handed it to her. Nieve took it and frowned.

'It's not in English.'

'It's French,' said Darcey. 'My mother got it for me when she was in Switzerland.'

'Then why isn't it in Swiss?'

'Because they speak French in Switzerland.'

'That's stupid.'

'I have this book in English too,' said Darcey. 'You could borrow that.'

'What's it called?'

'*Five Go To Kirrin Island*.'

'Read it already.' Nieve looked triumphant. 'Have you anything else?'

'Lots.' Darcey grinned at her. 'C'mon to my house. I'll show you.'

Whenever she looked back on it, Darcey thought that her sustained friendship with Nieve was down to the fact that they lived next door to each other and so saw each other every day. In many ways they were very different. But it didn't seem to matter.

Nieve was the smaller of the two, slender as a reed and deceptively fragile in appearance, with long blue-black hair that almost reached her waist and wide dark eyes that sometimes seemed too large for her heart-shaped face. She moved with the grace and poise she'd acquired from the ballet classes she attended every Saturday morning (until she decided that it was too much like hard work for something that would never be her career).

Unlike so many girls in school, Nieve's uniform fitted her perfectly, Gail buying it new at the beginning of every school year. Her poker-straight hair was always carefully tied back into a gleaming ponytail and secured with a stylish bobbin. Her books were neatly sheathed in see-through protective covers. Her pencil case was colour-coordinated with the pens and pencils inside. When she came into class she piled the relevant books and copies into a stack on her desk, the edges carefully aligned so that the heap was neat and tidy and unlikely to topple over even if one of the teachers brushed against them.

Nieve always looked the picture of innocence no matter what mischief she'd got up to, and it was generally agreed that if they were in trouble over anything, Nieve would be the one to do all the talking because she was ruthlessly persuasive and fiercely determined even while looking utterly angelic, and could make anyone believe anything.

Darcey was altogether sturdier, bigger-boned and a little overweight for her age, her fair hair hued with an assortment of honey colours and her blue eyes somehow more anxious and brighter than her friend's. She often told Nieve that they complemented each other. That Nieve's neat and tidy ways were a welcome contrast to her own sloppier lifestyle, in which her uniform was too long (and then later, when she had a sudden growth spurt, too short), her unruly hair fell in unmanageable waves around her face, and her books were never neatly covered but instead dog-eared with a well-thumbed appearance. Except for briefly during her princess period, Darcey had stayed well away from ballet classes – she lacked the necessary balance and elegance and, after she'd pirouetted into one of the other girls and knocked her over, giving her a black eye, both she and Minette agreed that the lessons were a waste of time.

Nieve was outgoing and confident about her schoolwork whereas Darcey hung back, even though both of them usually ended up in the same classes, studying the same subjects and getting the same grades. The teachers tried to push Darcey to do better but she hated the attention that being the best brought. Nieve, however, loved it. She was hugely competitive and liked getting the coloured stars that the teachers in primary school stuck in their exercise books. And she liked doing better than Darcey, because Gail often told her that Darcey McGonigle was an extremely clever girl and it was important not to fall behind her.

Darcey felt lucky that Nieve was her friend and she knew that being ahead was important to her. She also knew that Gail nagged her about her schoolwork and that it mattered to her that Nieve did well in class. So she didn't see any reason to compete. She was happy to let Nieve get better marks than her if it meant that much to her and if it kept them close. Tish and Amelie shared a special closeness as twins and Darcey had always felt excluded from that. Until the day that Nieve had moved in next door, Darcey hadn't been friends with anyone in particular. She'd always been afraid that they'd suddenly shut her out in the same way that Tish and Amelie did. But Nieve never did that. In fact Nieve seemed to want Darcey's friendship more than Darcey wanted to give it. But Darcey was OK with that. Sometimes, she thought, she felt closer to Nieve than she ever did to the twins.

The two girls treated each other's homes as their own. Minette was as likely to find her daughter's friend stretched out on Darcey's bed reading her comics, and later her teen magazines, as she was to find Darcey herself. Gail would often walk into the kitchen to find Darcey sitting on the scrubbed pine table swinging her legs, waiting for Nieve to come back from her music lesson.

They shared everything. Their toys. Their clothes. Their make-up. Even, on occasion, their boyfriends, though if it hadn't been for Nieve there wouldn't have been any boyfriends to share. That was the one area in their lives where Nieve was the undisputed winner.

Darcey didn't quite know how her friend did it, but Nieve seemed to attract boys without any appreciable effort. It really wasn't a question of looks – Nieve was pretty, but she wasn't exceptional. It was, Darcey decided, more to do with her personality. She made anyone she spoke to feel as if they were the most important person in the world, and boys seemed to like that. Darcey wasn't able to copy her. She thought that most of the boys in the neighbourhood were complete idiots.

Whenever Nieve was tired of a boy, she'd suggest he ask Darcey out instead. Darcey, she would point out, was a really nice person and it wasn't her fault that she was too clever by half. Also, she promised them, Darcey was an exceptionally good kisser. (This bit of information had been gleaned from an experiment that both girls had sworn to keep secret for ever. Aged twelve, they'd practised kissing on each other. Neither of them had particularly enjoyed the experience, but after she'd eventually kissed her first boy, Nieve had informed Darcey that she herself seemed to be a much better kisser and not half as rough.)

The boys dated Darcey but usually only once or twice. Her exceptional kissing skills would've kept them coming back for more, but she was the one who usually said no. Kissing was all well and good, she used to tell Nieve, but when they weren't kissing they'd have to talk, and she had no idea what to say to any of them.

'Just talk about normal things,' Nieve advised her. But Darcey only shook her head and muttered that there was nothing to talk about.

When they finally left school, it was Nieve who planned the round-Europe trip with the rest of the Brainy Broads, although Darcey, because of her language skills, was the one who did everything once they got there. It was Nieve who suggested, after college, that they do the trip again – only this time just herself and Darcey, since they'd already started to lose touch with Rosa and Carol, who'd gone to college in the UK. So they waitressed together in Paris, worked in a bar in Berlin and picked olives in Tuscany. Then they visited Darcey's relatives in Switzerland before heading off at Darcey's request to Marbella, where they managed to find jobs as au pairs to a couple of well-off families who had homes in the town. Nieve was hired by the wife of a wealthy international businessman who kept a yacht harboured in Puerto Banus and who simply wanted someone to keep their two children out of their way for the summer. Although they didn't pay well, their house, five kilometres from the beach, was stunning and they provided Nieve with a small jeep for getting around. Darcey found herself looking after four German children with impossibly good manners whose parents wanted them to spend a large portion of every day studying, which gave her a lot of time to wander barefoot on the beach and practise her Spanish.

Nieve had less free time, but whenever they could, they met up at the harbour and sat on the terraces of the bars and cafés, soaking up the sun and the atmosphere and wondering whether to stay in Spain for a little longer or go back to Ireland and get what Darcey mournfully called 'real jobs'.

'This is a lovely break, but I need to get back and make some serious money,' said Nieve forcefully one afternoon as they nibbled on tapas and sipped a local wine. 'There are so many business opportunities out there waiting to be grabbed and so many ways of making money and getting things that I feel guilty just sitting here.'

'I don't.' Darcey regarded her friend thoughtfully. She knew that Nieve liked having what she called 'material posses-sions'. In fact Minette had once called her Miss Want It Now. It was one of Nieve's greatest disappointments that her family wasn't loaded. They should have been, she'd once told Darcey furiously, if the company hadn't done the dirty on her father and made him redundant. If he'd been the kind of man to push himself forward more, then the Stapletons would've done much better in the world. And she, Nieve, would be the person *with* the au pair instead of *being* the damn au pair. As it was, her parents had thought themselves extremely lucky when Stephen had found a new job in a local garage shortly after moving in next door.

'Having things is nice, but being happy is better,' said Darcey mildly.

'Oh come on, Darce,' Nieve said. 'Cut the crap. These are the nineties, y'know. I swear to you the world is changing and now is the time to grab it with both hands. Which we certainly won't do by sitting on our arses in the sun.'

Darcey shrugged. 'I kinda like sitting on my arse.'

Nieve grinned at her suddenly.

'Sometimes you seem sadly unambitious for someone who's as clever as you are.'

'Oh, I know. And, like my dad says, it's a total waste of my God-given brain.' Darcey chuckled. 'You can research the best jobs and let me know what I should be aiming for. Meanwhile, I'll stick it out with the Germans!'

'What does Old Man Schroeder actually do?' asked Nieve.

'He's the MD of an engineering company,' replied Darcey carelessly.

Nieve traced lines on the red tablecloth with a cocktail stick. 'Max Christie is a financier,' she said. 'I don't exactly know what that means, but he seems to spend a lot of time talking about other companies having to downsize if they want to get anywhere.'

'Sounds like destructive money-making,' observed Darcey.

'Ah, get a life, Darce!'

Darcey giggled. 'I have a great life, thanks very much.'

'Maybe. But look at the lifestyle the Christies have!'

'So what?'

'You just don't get it, do you?'

'I do really.' Darcey shrugged. 'But in the end, all I want is to be happy. I don't need the possessions.'

'I could be happy with a house like the Christies',' said Nieve. 'And the yacht.'

'I'd be happy with another glass of wine.' Darcey drained her glass and grinned at her friend, who waved at the waiter.

'Not for me,' said Nieve. 'I've got to look after the kids this evening.' She ordered a sparkling water instead, and then looked at Darcey questioningly. 'By the way, I was wondering if you'd mind awfully lending me your necklace?' Her tone was apologetic. 'I'm going out tomorrow night and I need to make a bit of an effort. It's an opportunity to wear the new dress I bought last week. I just realised that I don't have any decent jewellery to go with it.'

'Going out?' Darcey enquired.

'Mmm. The son of the people next door. Tapas and beer. Nothing very exciting. But the first social event I've been at in weeks!'

'You've been to the open-air concerts with me,' said Darcey as she unfastened the gold necklace with its single diamond (a graduating gift from her parents) from her throat. 'Why don't you buy some cheap jewellery in the market?'

'I don't like cheap stuff,' said Nieve, 'and the earrings hurt my ears. I can only wear these studs. Thanks for the necklace, Darce. You're a pal.'

Darcey smiled. 'You're welcome. Hope it helps.'

'Ah, you know how it is,' said Nieve. 'Packaging, that's all. But the packaging is important.'

'Not at all.' Though her voice was solemn, Darcey's eyes twinkled. 'You know perfectly well, Nieve Stapleton, that it's what's inside that counts.'

They'd had this conversation a million times before.

Nieve laughed. 'Glitzy outside, glitzy inside.' She clipped the necklace around her own throat. 'I'll give it back to you next time.'

'No bother,' said Darcey. 'Enjoy yourself.'

'Oh, I will,' promised Nieve. 'You know I will.'

# Chapter 5

She might not have wanted many possessions, but over the last couple of years Darcey had acquired some. It was impossible to live in the city that Dublin had become and not feel the need to buy at least some of the glittering goods on display. The one thing she didn't have, however, was a car. She didn't really need one, living only a couple of miles from the centre of the city and being close to the Dart. Whenever she travelled around Dublin she took a cab, and when she wanted to go to Galway, as she did the weekend after her Barcelona trip, she usually flew. She always enjoyed the short journey: the commuter plane flew at a lower level than a jet, allowing passengers to see the broad tapestry of emerald-green fields below.

Amelie, darker-haired and more elfin than her sister but with the same sky-blue eyes, picked her up at Galway airport and drove her home. It was funny, thought Darcey, how she still thought of the three-bed semi as home even though she was very happy in her stylish city apartment. But home never changed – even when Minette decorated or bought new furniture, the same pictures hung on the walls and the same ornaments stood on the shelves, and it was always welcoming and secure.

'Hello, *cherie*.' Minette kissed her on both cheeks as she stepped inside. 'How was your trip?'

'Fine,' said Darcey as she hugged her mother in return.

Amelie sniffed appreciatively. 'Baking?' she asked.

'I made an apple strudel for Darcey,' said Minette.

'Crikey, you never do that for me.' But Amelie grinned at her mother and followed both of them into the warm kitchen. 'Oh, it smells good.'

'I know that Darcey doesn't eat properly,' said Minette. 'At least I can check on you and Letitia, but with Darcey I can't.'

'And you think me and Tish cook up apple strudels on a regular basis?' asked Amelie sardonically. 'When would we have the time? Aren't we both out slaving at the IT coal-face all day?'

'I know you and Tish work hard,' said Minette. 'Too hard sometimes. You shouldn't neglect your food.'

Amelie laughed. 'Not usually a problem for the McGonigle girls. Any chance of a slice?'

'Of course,' said Minette. 'I will make you some hot chocolate too.'

'I *do* so love you, Maman,' said Darcey warmly.

'It's your stomach talking,' returned her mother.

'I know,' said Darcey. 'But it's still love.' She grinned. 'I'll leave my bag upstairs.'

It was a shame, she thought as she always did when she was in Galway, that she didn't get home more often. But it simply wasn't possible. Despite the distance, they were a close

69

family. Except, of course, for their father. Darcey grimaced as she thought of him and his current wife, Clem, and Steffi, their eight-year-old daughter, her stepsister. Even though she told herself over and over again that she should feel some kind of connection to the little girl, she found it too diffi-cult. She'd met Clem and Steffi a few times but she'd never managed to lose the awkwardness she felt in their company. And she could never look at Steffi and consider her as a rela-tive. She knew that her attitude annoyed her father, but she couldn't help it. She didn't blame Steffi, though she certainly blamed Clem. Why shouldn't she when the woman had broken up a marriage, for heaven's sake? And more than that, her actions had impacted on Darcey's life and the lives of the twins too. There was no point in harbouring grudges now but sometimes that was easier to say than do.

By the time she came downstairs again, Letitia, Amelie's identical twin, although an inch taller, had also arrived at the house and was watching Minette cut slices of apple strudel.

'Here you go.' Minette proffered a plate as Darcey walked into the warm kitchen and sniffed appreciatively.

'Maman, you know that this is a heart attack waiting to happen?' Darcey took the slice of apple strudel smothered in whipped cream. 'As for the hot chocolate . . .'

Minette made her own hot chocolate from what she called her secret Swiss recipe, and which did, indeed, owe a lot of its richness to the blocks of dark chocolate she brought back every time she visited her own family in Lausanne.

'It's good for you,' said Minette robustly. 'Comforting.'

'*Très, très* comforting,' agreed Darcey. 'But not exactly good for the hips.'

Amelie chuckled. 'You don't have to worry. Tish and I were just saying earlier that you're like a rake these days.'

'Hmm, well, I have to work at it.' Darcey made a face at her sister. 'Remember the school photo? And remember the nineties?'

They all nodded. It would have been hard not to remember the shot of Darcey, aged thirteen, standing by the statue of Our Lady in the entrance hall to St Margaret's school, round and plump in her unflattering bottle-green uniform, her unkempt hair falling into her eyes and her green knee socks sagging around her ankles. Until then she had ignored all of the neuroses that the other girls in her class seemed to have about appearance and clothes and spots and weight, but from the moment she'd seen the photo she'd begun refusing Minette's practically irresistible sachertortes and creamy beef stroganoffs and exchanging them for salads and fruit juice. She'd even started taking PE in school again instead of sneaking off to study instead.

'Everyone relapses after a crisis,' said Amelie, who hadn't been thinking of the school photo. 'So the nineties don't count.'

'Hah! That's easy for you to say. You take after Dad. You're naturally thin.'

'Well, you've lost far too much weight,' said Minette sternly. 'You were never meant to be a sylph.'

'I'm not a sylph,' Darcey told her. 'I admit that I've gone to a size twelve from a fourteen this year, but that's not a bad thing.'

'I'm not sure.' Tish frowned. 'You're a bit Renee Zellweger post-Bridget Jones now, Darce. Too many cheekbones and not enough padding.'

'Give me a break.' Darcey looked at her family in irritation.

'*Bien*. No more about your weight. So instead, *cherie*, tell us about this takeover?'

Minette's voice softened and the twins looked at Darcey with some sympathy.

She shrugged. 'It hasn't made much difference so far,' she said. 'Some guys from Scotland came over and looked around, but everything went well.'

'No sign of Neil?' It was Amelie who put the question.

'No.' Darcey shook her head. 'Of course it might not have anything to do with him anyway. Or maybe he's moved on. Which is fine, obviously.'

'You don't talk to him at all?'

'There's no need. And I'm not talking about him now.' Darcey's voice was firm. 'Look, he was part of my life, but he's totally not any more, and if he turns up I can be adult about it and cope with it, but the chances are he won't so it doesn't bloody matter.'

Amelie, Tish and Minette exchanged glances.

'More than *part* of your life, Darce,' said Amelie gently.

'It was ages ago,' Darcey reminded her. 'It's irrelevant now and I really, truly don't want to talk about it.'

'Well then . . .' Minette paused and seemed to gather herself before continuing. 'On another subject entirely . . . what about the letter?'

'What letter?' Darcey kept her voice deliberately expressionless.

'The one from America,' said Minette. 'The one I forwarded to you.'

Tish looked at Darcey. 'You got a letter? From America? Not from – her?'

'It was nothing,' said Darcey. 'Not important.'

'*Cherie . . .*'

Darcey knew that she'd have no peace until she told them. 'It was a wedding invitation. She's coming back to Ireland to get married. Some castle somewhere. I don't remember. I don't know why in God's name she sent me an invitation. To gloat, I suppose. I'm not going.'

'You mean—'

'But I thought they were married already.'

Amelie and Tish spoke at the same time.

'Yes, well, so did I,' said Darcey. 'Look, it's irrelevant. I don't know why they didn't get married back then, nor do I care where or how they're getting married now. So let's leave it. That's all in the past too. A different past, obviously. But still nothing I particularly want to talk about.'

'Fair enough.' Tish nodded, though her tone was doubtful. 'We'll leave it. For the moment. If you're not going. She has a bloody cheek, though!'

There was another bout of silence. Darcey gazed into space, refusing to be the one to break it. Finally Amelie caved in.

'So if we're only allowed to talk about the present, Darcey – how was Barcelona? Any other nice trips planned?'

And for the rest of the night the discussion stuck with topics that all of them were comfortable with.

But when she was lying in her old bed (the one thing Darcey hated about going home was sleeping in a single bed again;

it was too narrow for someone who was used to five feet of sleeping space all to herself), she couldn't help thinking about the past. The problem with the past, she thought as she lay on her back and looked at the luminous stars that Martin had stuck on the ceiling when she was ten, was that it was always part of the present. You couldn't simply wipe things out and forget about them as though they didn't matter any more. And though she sometimes tried, more often she would try to pinpoint moments over the last ten years when events over which she had no control, or when she made the wrong choices, or when other people made choices for her – well, she would try to pinpoint those times and ask herself whether if she'd done things differently it would have turned out better for her in the end. But what would have been better? Because wasn't the truth of it that she was happy in her job and she was happy with her life, and even if both her mother and her sisters often told her that she had changed beyond belief (and not just because of losing a few stone in weight), well, wasn't it right to say that everything had turned out for the best in the end?

She wondered if her mother thought like that too. Whether Minette believed that, in her own life, things had eventually turned out for the best.

That was the moment, reflected Darcey. The day that Amelie had called her in Spain to tell her that Martin had walked out. That was the moment when everything changed, past, present and future.

She remembered the shock in her sister's voice as she told her of their father's desertion and then went on to tell her that Minette was having some kind of breakdown. That she'd locked herself in her bedroom and was refusing to come out. That she hadn't spoken or eaten since it happened and that the twins were worried sick about her.

'So you've got to come home,' Amelie said. 'We're at our wits' end.'

Darcey remembered shrieking at her sister that she should have called her sooner and that of course she was coming home straight away.

'I didn't phone because I thought it might be a storm in a teacup,' Amelie had protested. 'But when I realised that it wasn't . . .'

Darcey closed her eyes as she recalled phoning Nieve and telling her about it and half hoping that her friend, who had been so keen on the idea of coming home to find a job, would tell her that she'd chuck in her job and come home too. She'd been slightly surprised when Nieve had said that she was staying because she owed it to the Christies, but she hadn't had time to think about it very much because she'd managed to book herself on to a flight to Shannon and she needed to hurry if she was going to catch it.

It had all been so different to her excitement at coming away with Nieve in the first place. As the plane lifted into the air she felt a rush of anger at her father, who had precipitated the family crisis. But she'd never for a moment believed it wouldn't be resolved and that he wouldn't, eventually, come home again. In fact she'd half expected to see him in the house by the time she arrived.

But he hadn't been there.

Instead Tish let her in and quickly gave her the latest news.

'He says he's not coming back,' she told Darcey. 'He's "in lurve" with this girl. She's only two years older than me and Amelie, for heaven's sake. It's disgusting!'

'You've got to be kidding me.' Darcey was appalled.

'I wish I was.'

'I don't believe it. Not Dad.'

'You'd better believe it.'

'But . . .' Darcey didn't know what to say. Her father, solid and dependable, had left her mother for a girl who could've been her sister. It was too much to take in.

'Where did he meet her?' she asked eventually.

'At some damn teacher-training seminar . . . conference . . . whatever. I don't know. He got jiggy with her and now he's in love with her.'

'It's a fling,' said Darcey hopefully.

'It may well be a fling,' said Tish, 'but that doesn't make things any better for Maman.'

'No. It doesn't.'

'Her name's Clementine,' said Tish. 'Clem.'

'Have you met her?'

'No,' replied her sister. 'He's keeping her well away from us. They've run away to Cork. Apparently he's got a job in a private college there starting in September.'

'You're joking.'

'Of course I'm not bloody joking.'

'No. No. Of course you're not. It's just . . . I can't believe it.'

'Yeah, well, neither can Mam. Nor can Amelie.'

'I'd better say hello,' said Darcey, and walked into the living room.

Minette, who according to Tish had finally left her bedroom that morning, was curled up in an armchair in the corner of the living room, her eyes red and her cheeks blotchy. As soon as she saw Darcey, she burst into uncontrollable tears.

Darcey exchanged an incredulous look with the twins. None of them had ever seen their mother cry like this before. At a particularly poignant scene in a movie she would allow tears to roll down her face. And she'd cried when they went to the funeral of their dad's father, Gramps McGonigle. But that had been restrained crying, and Minette hadn't lost her composure even as she wiped her eyes. This was altogether different.

'She's been like this for three days,' said Amelie. She leaned over to her mother. 'Come on, Maman. There's no need to get upset like this. He isn't worth it.'

'Oh, but I thought he was!' Minette's voice shook and her accent, which she'd lost over the years, began to reassert itself again. 'I think he was the best man in the world. For him I leave everything. Everything! My country and my friends, and for what? To be left here?'

'There's nothing wrong with here,' said Tish. 'You love it here. You've lived here for twenty-five years, for heaven's sake!'

'It's all right for you, Letitia.' Minette sniffed. 'You have your life ahead of you. I gave up my life. Twenty-five years. She was only being born when I arrived here! And now I am destroyed!'

'Maman.' Darcey sat down beside her and put her arm around her mother's shoulders. 'You have a great life here. You know you have.'

'So good that you leave me?' cried Minette. 'That you rush to Europe and leave me just like your father!' And she started to weep violently again.

The twins sighed and Darcey looked at them helplessly. The woman in front of them was so different from the person they normally knew as their mother that they had no idea what to do.

All of their lives Minette had been there for them. They would come home from school to the sight of her in the kitchen and the aroma of freshly baking bread and scones; they wore the latest fashions thanks to her ability to copy any dress design and run it up on her sewing machine; and whenever any of them was hurt or upset she was always ready to comfort them with hugs and kisses. She was warm and loving and, as far as the three girls were concerned, a perfect mother. Nothing fazed her. Nothing upset her. Nothing, she used to say to them, is so bad that it can't be mended. Or, she'd add, if it absolutely can't be mended, then it gets replaced by something better instead. But now it looked as though she didn't believe a word of it herself.

'I'll make some hot chocolate,' said Darcey. 'That's got to help.'

She went into the kitchen and took down a block of the chocolate that was always in the cupboard. Then she heated it along with some milk in Minette's heavy-based saucepan, whisking it all the time before adding some vanilla essence and then pouring the concoction into the wide cups that Minette preferred. She sprinkled some cinnamon on top then put the cups on a tray and took it into the living room.

'Here,' she said. 'Drink this.'

Amelie and Tish took a cup each.

'Lovely,' said Tish. 'Have some, Mam.'

Minette shook her head.

'Come on, Mam,' said Darcey firmly. 'I've come all the way back from Spain to see you. I've made you hot chocolate. The least you can do is drink it.'

Minette was startled by Darcey's tone and she looked up at her youngest daughter.

'You didn't have to come home,' she said hoarsely.

'Of course I did,' said Darcey. 'You have the girls worried sick.'

'There's no need to be worried,' croaked Minette. 'I'm all right.'

'Obviously you're not,' Amelie told her.

'You haven't eaten in three days,' said Tish. 'That's certainly not all right.'

Minette pushed her lank hair out of her eyes. 'I'm not hungry,' she said.

'I can understand that,' said Darcey. 'But you always said that hot chocolate is food for the soul. And maybe you need some soul food right now.'

Minette looked at her youngest daughter. Their matching blue eyes met and held each other for a moment. She smiled faintly. Then she sipped the hot chocolate.

'You didn't whip it enough,' she told Darcey. 'And it could do with a little more vanilla.'

'I know,' said Darcey. 'But I wanted to get it to you quickly.'

'Thank you.' Minette uncurled herself from her hunched position in the armchair and stretched her legs out in front of her, wincing as the blood flowed back to her feet and set

79

off the tingling of pins and needles. She took another sip of the hot chocolate. 'Thank you,' she said again.

'Crikey, Mam, if I'd known all you wanted was a cup of hot chocolate I wouldn't have rung Darcey and made her rush back here,' said Tish.

'I would've come back anyway,' said Darcey hurriedly, seeing the glint of tears in her mother's eyes again. 'I wouldn't leave you all on your own.' She looked enquiringly at her sisters. 'Have either of you heard from Dad today?'

Minette looked at them too. 'Well?' she asked, her voice stronger. 'Have you?'

'He hasn't been in touch since he called the first night,' said Amelie uncomfortably.

'He just called?' Darcey looked incredulous. 'He didn't meet you or anything?'

Tish shook her head. 'He said it was all too raw and emotional at the moment,' she told her. 'He said he'd come and see us when things had settled down a bit.'

'For crying out loud!' Darcey put her now empty cup on the coffee table. 'Has he taken leave of his senses?'

'Yes,' said Minette. 'That's exactly what it is.'

'Did you know about her?' asked Darcey. 'Had you any idea? Or was this all a complete shock?' She pulled up a chair and sat down beside her mother. Amelie and Tish sat on the sofa opposite.

Minette pushed at her hair again.

'I knew something was wrong,' she said eventually. 'He was late at the school. Giving grinds, he said – extra tuition for some of the less able pupils. And he'd been made head of the maths department, so he was always going on about

80

having to go to meetings and things like that. Well, I could understand some of it. But not all of it. I just never thought . . . you never do think, do you?'

The girls stayed silent.

'And then he just told me.' Minette bit her lip and swallowed hard. 'He came home and he said that it was *fini*. I ask him what? He say us. He tell me . . . told me that he had met someone else and that he was in love.'

'That's what he told us too,' Amelie said.

'He said he meet . . . met . . . this girl at a conference and that he knew straight away. He said he was waiting for her his whole life. He said it was meant to be.'

'For crying out loud!' Darcey exclaimed. 'What in heaven's name's got into him? He was happily married for twenty-five years and now he's suddenly met the love of his life? After Mam? He's *fou. Loco. Verruckt.*'

'He said it was like a *coup de foudre*,' said Amelie scornfully.

'Yeah, well, he should have more sense than to believe in thunderbolts,' Darcey said. 'It's not like he's a teenager in love, after all.'

'It's a mid-life crisis,' said Tish. 'This girl has bowled him over and made him think of his youth or something.'

'I bowled him over once.' Minette's voice was bleak.

'Will you take him back?' asked Darcey abruptly. 'If he calls you in a day or two and says that it was all a mistake?'

Minette bit her lip again. 'I'm Swiss, not French,' she said. 'I don't believe in a *coup de foudre*.'

'But if he comes home and apologises,' said Tish, 'can you get over it?'

'I don't think he will,' said Minette. 'But if he does, then I will think very strongly about it.'

'In that case,' said Amelie, 'why don't you go and have a shower and get yourself back to normal so that if he does come back you won't look so dreadful.'

'Good idea.' Minette got up awkwardly from the chair. She looked at her daughters. 'Thank you,' she said. 'All of you.'

They hugged, holding each other close for a moment. Then she went upstairs.

'I really don't believe this,' said Darcey again.

'I think we'd better start believing it,' Tish said.

'Not before we go and see him,' Darcey said fiercely. 'Knock some sense into him.'

She looked so angry that Amelie giggled nervously. 'So long as you don't take that too literally,' she told her sister. 'You look like you could punch him in the face.'

'I might.' Darcey was thinking of Marbella and the life she'd left behind. 'You never know.'

She didn't punch him in the face, but the trip to Cork was futile. Martin left his daughters in no doubt that Clem was now the most important person in his life. It didn't matter that, at fifty, he was exactly twice her age. It meant nothing, he said. They were connected on a level that made a mockery of age.

The girls came home and told Minette that she would have to get over him. And they didn't try to stop her when she cried again.

# Chapter 6

Nieve liked travelling business class. It didn't matter that the flight to Vancouver only took a couple of hours, they were hours that she didn't want to spend back in coach, where she was bound to be sitting in front of the annoying child who spent his time kicking the back of her seat or whining about the fact that he was hungry or thirsty or bored and generally being a pain in the butt. She settled into her leather and upholstery seat with its additional leg-room and adjustable headrest, grateful that Ennco always sent employees business class and thinking to herself that there was no way that even when flying on her own account she'd ever bother with economy again. There was no need for her to save money on cheap seats. On cheap anything really!

Not everyone thought like her, she knew. There were people in Pueblo Bravo who, though loaded, trawled internet sites to find the best bargains in town and boasted of having saved a few dollars on their latest kitchen gadget or fashion accessory. There had been a time, of course, when Nieve looked for bargains as much as the next person. But she couldn't be bothered now. Her time was far too valuable to waste scouring eBay.

'More champagne?' The steward smiled at her and proffered a tray.

'No thanks.' She shook her head. 'Orange juice would be good, though.'

'Certainly, madam.'

They were always so much politer in business class too. Understandably, since there were fewer passengers to deal with and since most of them plugged in their laptops and started working as soon as the Fasten Seat-belts sign went out.

Nieve took the glass of orange juice from the steward. Would she have to give up business-class travel if and when she had a child of her own? The thought had only suddenly crossed her mind. If she never wanted to travel coach again, would she have the nerve to inflict a kid on passengers who had paid a premium for a child-free environment?

She had once been on a flight to Chicago where a father had brought his five-year-old son into the business section of the plane. She remembered her horrified feeling at the sight of the child. She remembered preparing herself for the inevitable moment when she'd have to tell the man concerned to shut his son up or leave. But in the end the kid had behaved impeccably and she'd forgotten he was there.

Our child would surely have equally impeccable manners, she thought, even as she wondered whether she truly was the sort of person who had the patience for children at all. But if she had the right kind of child . . . quiet and well-mannered . . . Maybe it wouldn't be so bad. She wasn't getting any younger, and having kids had always been on her agenda, but it had got pushed out further and further because other things seemed more important. She shrugged. Right now, other things still were.

She finished her juice and opened her laptop. She didn't really need to do any work, but she hated sitting there doing nothing, especially when the guy opposite her was immersed in a sheaf of papers, his red pen circling figures as he read.

You never know who your fellow passengers might be, she told herself. You might meet them sometime in the future across a boardroom table, and you wouldn't want them to remember you as the lazy woman they'd once seen on the San Francisco–Vancouver flight.

She opened a Word file on her laptop.

'Conference Timetable', she read, even though she knew the timetable by heart already. She didn't have to worry about this evening. The conference didn't start until the morning. So she had time to herself that she thought she might spend engaged in some retail therapy. She wanted to blow some of the Ennco share profit on something other than the wedding. She just wasn't sure yet exactly what.

But by the time she arrived at the hotel and got settled into her premier room with its wraparound windows and spectacular views, she didn't really feel like going anywhere. She kicked off her shoes and stretched out on the bed before picking up the phone. Her own voice answered, saying that they were currently unavailable to take the call but to leave a message. She hung up and dialled the cell phone number. But that went unanswered too. In the end she just sent a text message saying that she'd arrived and that she might call again later. But that right now she was going to chill out and relax.

Nieve's idea of chilling out was to go down to the health club, where she spent thirty minutes on the treadmill before getting into the pool (impossible to swim properly here, she thought, because the freeform shape didn't really lend itself to pounding lengths) and then taking a brisk shower and returning to her room. She ordered room service and ate her club sandwich while watching the business roundup on the TV. It was important to keep in touch with whatever was going on.

It was also important to Nieve to feel secure. Now she almost did. She would feel a hundred per cent safe when she could finally offload her stock and see the money tucked away in her bank account, and that was only a couple of months away. As she thought about the transfer of money into her account she smiled slightly and raised the glass of wine she was drinking in a toast to herself. I was right all along, she thought. Knowing how to look after myself. Staying one step ahead of the game. Grabbing my chances when they came.

She hadn't realised, of course, that the chance was being offered to her at first. It had been the day before Darcey had rushed home to Ireland. They'd met up in the afternoon for a drink – Darcey's German family had gone off for the day and hadn't needed her, and it was Nieve's afternoon off. She remembered sitting in one of the beachfront restaurants with her friend, watching the sun reflect furiously off the deep blue water of the Mediterranean Sea and enjoying the warmth of the gentle breeze as it wafted around her shoulders, but feeling impatiently that she should be doing something else. It wasn't that Marbella wasn't beautiful, or even that the Christies weren't reasonably decent people to work for, but this wasn't what she wanted from her life. She'd seen what people with real money had and she knew that she deserved to have those things too.

Darcey, though, hadn't seemed to think that way. It seemed to Nieve that Darcey would have happily stayed for ever on the Spanish coast, reading prodigiously and doing all the puzzles and crosswords in both the Spanish and English newspapers she could lay her hands on while keeping an eye on those German kids she was looking after. But it wasn't something that Nieve herself could do. And so she was still thinking about coming home to Ireland and getting a 'real' job when she left Darcey to her book and, ten minutes later, pulled up outside the magnificent inland house where she'd been living for the last few months.

It was surprisingly quiet inside. Normally she could hear the sound of the children shrieking around the swimming pool or clattering on the tiled floors of the house, but as she stepped inside, Nieve immediately sensed that they weren't there. She frowned. She knew they were supposed to be there. It wasn't her evening off or anything.

The gentle thwack of her flip-flops was muffled as she padded towards the kitchen. Whenever the children were missing or extra quiet, she normally found them in the kitchen. But this time all she found was a note from Lilith Christie which said that she'd taken Guy and Selina to a friend's house for the rest of the day and that the two children were going to sleep over there, so Nieve could consider this evening as her evening off instead of the following day.

'Stupid cow,' muttered Nieve as she crumpled up the note and flung it in the bin. 'Doesn't she know that I have a life of my own? She can't just switch my days on and off like that. And,' she muttered as she poured herself a glass of water, 'I can't believe she's actually got the kids somewhere without two hours of fuss and drama first!' She gulped back the water and then put the glass in the dishwasher. It was so bloody irritating, she thought, how the Christies seemed to believe that she was there to do whatever they wanted, whenever they wanted. The fact that she had plans for the following night was entirely irrelevant to them. She wondered whether Diego would be free tonight instead. She'd phone him and check.

A sudden noise startled her just as she was about to lift the receiver and she stood stock still. She'd thought she was alone in the house. The kitchen was pristine and so she assumed that Maria, who worked as the cook and house-keeper, had gone home. Max Christie usually played golf in the late afternoon and early evening. If Lilith and the two children were out, then there shouldn't be anyone else in. Although, she remembered now, the alarm hadn't been set. But that hadn't bothered her at the time because she'd expected someone to be home.

She hesitated. There had been stories of robberies in some of the high-profile houses in the area. Those robberies had usually taken place in the early evening. Surely that wasn't happening here. She tiptoed to the kitchen door and opened it slowly. If there were burglars in the house, she thought as she peeked out, it would be better to let them carry on. The Christies were insured after all.

And then she heard a noise that sounded like a giggle. It was coming from Max Christie's office. Burglars didn't giggle. But small children did. Had they come home and were messing around in Max's office? He'd go berserk if they were.

Her nervousness disappeared as she strode down the corridor and flung open the door. Then she stopped in stunned amazement. Max was sitting on his expensive leather swivel chair. Maria was sitting on his lap. Max was wearing a white shirt, his trousers at his feet. Maria wasn't wearing anything at all.

'Omigod,' Nieve said involuntarily as she gripped the door handle.

Max swivelled around on the chair. His eyes met hers. 'What the hell are you doing here?' he asked, while Maria buried her head in his chest as though it would make her invisible.

'Lilith changed my night in,' said Nieve, trying desperately not to look lower than his face. 'I didn't realise . . .' She whirled out of the door and fled from the house, her feet sliding from her flip-flops as she ran so that eventually she took them off altogether and held them in her hands as she hurried down the steps. She got into her jeep and drove down the road to a small bar, where she ordered a glass of wine and tried to gather her thoughts.

She hadn't thought that Max was unfaithful to Lilith. But then she hadn't really thought about Max and Lilith's relationship at all. And unfaithful probably wasn't the word Max would use about bonking the housekeeper. *Droit de seigneur*. The old-fashioned phrase learned at school came back to her. The right of the master to do what he liked with the servant. She wondered if Max Christie considered her a servant too. At which thought she gulped back the wine and ordered another.

It was dark by the time she returned to the house. The garden and pool lights had been switched on and there was a gentle glow from an upstairs landing window. Nieve took a deep breath and let herself in.

The alarm was still switched off. That meant, she supposed, that Max was still in the house. She wondered whether Maria had gone home.

She tiptoed up the stairs and into her room, wincing at the creak of the door as she pushed it open. Then she sat on the bed and exhaled slowly.

It was ten minutes before the rap at the door came. When she opened it, Max was standing there. He was now dressed in a pair of casual trousers and a polo shirt and he'd obviously had a shower, because she could smell the scent of the Fa shower gel that Lilith made her buy on her supermarket shopping trips.

He stepped into the small room and sat down in her only armchair. Nieve wanted to stay standing up but she didn't feel that she could. So she sat on the edge of the bed and looked at her employer thoughtfully.

'That was somewhat awkward,' he remarked. 'I didn't realise you were going to be here.'

'Obviously,' she said drily. 'Are you going to fire me?'

Her eyes hardened and she could see a sudden hesitation in his own look.

'Why would I do that?'

'I know too much,' said Nieve.

'You're exaggerating,' said Max. 'You know nothing.'

'I know that Lilith wouldn't be too pleased to think that you were having it off with the housekeeper,' she said with spirit.

'And she'd believe you?'

'Oh, I think so.' Nieve smiled slightly. 'Yes, I think she'd believe me.'

'So what do you want?' asked Max.

He's worried, she realised suddenly. He's afraid of me. Afraid of what trouble I could cause. The knowledge made her feel suddenly secure. And then suddenly anxious too. She needed to deal with this properly.

'I want a job,' she said eventually.

He frowned. 'You have a job.'

'A different job,' she told him. 'I can't help thinking that you'd prefer if I wasn't around. No matter how much I might promise not to say anything . . . well, you could never be sure.'

'I might not mind you saying anything at all,' said Max.

'You wouldn't be here if you didn't mind,' she pointed out, and he shrugged.

She cleared her throat. 'I want a job in one of your companies. I don't mind which. A good job. A responsible position. One that can make use of my skills.'

'We don't have a huge need for childminders,' he told her.

'Get a grip,' she said firmly. 'I'm not stupid, Max.' She'd never called him Max before. The Christies always insisted on being addressed formally. 'I have a business degree. I want to use it. I'm smart and intelligent and this job was just a gap-year kind of thing. I'm not a childminder and I never will be. I'm cut out for senior management eventually.'

His eyes widened slightly as she spoke.

'I thought a little extra in your pay packet this month might be enough,' he said. 'A leaving bonus.'

'I don't want to leave,' she said. 'I don't have another job.'

'But you just said that you have a degree and that you don't want to be a childminder.'

'I'll leave when I'm ready to leave,' she said.

'I think you're overestimating my concern about this. Lilith and I—'

'I don't think I am at all,' said Nieve impatiently. 'I'm asking you for a job, and that's not a bad offer if you think about it clearly. If I work for you I'm not likely to fuck it up by telling tales to your wife. I know I can be a good addition to whatever company you put me in. You're getting a good deal, Max. You should take it.'

'You're blackmailing me,' said Max curtly.

'No I'm bloody not,' retorted Nieve. 'If that was the case I'd be asking for money. I'm asking for a job. That's completely different.'

'And what if you're no good?'

'Then fire me,' she said.

He stared at her for a few moments, then nodded slightly.

'Give me two weeks to work something out,' he said. 'I'm trusting that you won't say something stupid to Lilith in the mean time. If you do—'

'Cut the melodrama,' she interrupted him. 'And I'll give you a week.'

She wasn't sure whether she saw the shadow of a smile crossing his face.

'Maybe you wouldn't be such a bad hire,' he said wryly. 'You're a tough cookie, aren't you?'

'You don't know how tough,' she told him.

Without the benefit of mobile phones, which were still too expensive to be owned by everyone at that time, she couldn't contact Darcey and tell her what had happened. And although she was pretty sure that Max would have allowed her to use the house phone (though normally she was restricted to just two calls a day, and she'd used them up by phoning both Diego and Darcey earlier), she knew that Darcey was probably still out and about somewhere.

It was the following day before she spoke to her friend. And then she didn't get to tell her anything, because Darcey had just heard about Martin's departure from the family home and Nieve knew that there was no point in talking to her about anything else.

The beep of her cell phone jerked her back to the present. She picked it up and looked at the text message.

'All nighter,' she read. 'Talk to you tomorrow. Have a great conference. Ax'

She deleted the message and went back to her computer.

The first session in the morning was Risk Assessment in Modern Markets. She had some questions she wanted to put to the speaker, but she wanted to make sure, one more time, that she hadn't missed possible answers in his last piece of research. It was hard work staying ahead of the game sometimes.

# Chapter 7

No sooner had she come back from her Barcelona trip than Darcey had to go away again – this time to Milan, where she did the same round of client meetings but where her dinner in the evening was with Rocco Lanzo, who had once been a Global Finance client but who had switched careers and now owned a speciality food store.

She arrived at the restaurant a few minutes after him and he was already sipping a glass of ruby-red wine when the waiter brought her to the table.

'Darcey.' He stood up and kissed her on the cheek. '*Ciao, bella.*'

She smiled. 'Hello, Rocco. *Come stai?*'

'I'm very well,' he told her. 'And you? You are looking lovely tonight.'

She smiled again. '*Grazie.*'

'But then you always look lovely.'

She laughed. 'And you always flatter me so well.'

'It's not flattery, it's the truth.'

She glanced at her reflection in the mirrored glass on the wall opposite. Her blonde hair was sleek and smooth, her blue eyes sparkled thanks to the eye reviver drops she'd used, and her newest cream blush had given a healthy glow to her cheekbones. She was wearing a low-cut turquoise dress with narrow shoulder straps and tiny Swarovski crystals beaded across the neckline.

'So tell me what's been happening in your life, *inamorato*?' she asked.

'Oh, the usual.' He poured her some wine just as the waiter arrived with two plates of pasta. 'I ordered for you. Pasta and then prawns to follow. That's what you always have here, no?'

'Yes.' She grinned. 'I'm far too predictable.'

'Not predictable enough.' He raised his glass. 'Cheers.'

'*Alla salute.*'

She liked Rocco, she really did. She liked all Italian men. They were so good at making women feel wanted and needed and gorgeous even if they did irritatingly chauvinistic things like ordering dinner for you. Nevertheless, they were a balm to anyone with a fragile ego, and Darcey knew that where men were concerned her ego was as fragile as a duck egg. She allowed Rocco to lead the conversation, talking about the success of the food store and then about movies he had been to and fashion shows he'd attended. Rocco's sister was a designer, though Darcey knew that his interest wasn't solely on Sofia's account. He was one of the most fashion-conscious men she'd ever met. Tonight he was dressed head to toe in Armani. It looked good on him.

'And so what will happen to your company now that the big bad wolves of InvestorCorp have broken down the door?' he asked after the meal, when they were sitting in the small bar of her hotel sipping cocktails.

'I don't know.' She shrugged. 'I hope it won't make a difference.'

'Maybe you will become a more important person.' Rocco grinned at her. 'And you won't have time to visit us in Milano any more.'

'I'll always have time for you,' she told him.

'*Molte grazie.*' He took her hand and kissed her fingers. With anyone else it might have appeared hackneyed and over-the-top. With Rocco it was just right.

'There is a bar in my room,' she told him softly.

'*Perfetto.*'

They took the lift to the fifth floor. He had unzipped the turquoise dress before they'd even closed the bedroom door behind them.

He left at one a.m. She kissed him on both cheeks and then on the lips and he told her to call him the next time she planned to visit Milan.

Once he'd gone, she ran a bath and lay in the warm scented water, watching the drips of condensation slide slowly down the white marble walls. Of them all, she liked Rocco best. Every man had his own special charm, of course, but Rocco managed to combine the best of them. There'd been four of them in four cities over the last four years. Francisco, Rocco, Jose and Louis-Philippe. Barcelona, Milan, Lisbon and Paris. She'd met them all on her business trips, Francisco and Rocco as clients, Jose and Louis-Philippe independently. Now that Francisco was married, she didn't have anyone in Barcelona any more. She hadn't looked for a replacement. She wondered whether she'd replace any of the others when they finally decided they didn't want to sleep with her any more. Or when she decided that she wasn't going to contact them whenever she visited. That was the thing. They never knew when she was travelling. She didn't have to contact them. She could assign Rocco to someone else and just let it go.

Part of her wanted to let it go. Part of her hadn't planned on sleeping with him tonight, but he'd been so lovely to her and made her feel so wanted – and God knows, she thought as she added some more hot water to the bath, it wasn't as though she was getting a lot of sex these days. There was no one in Dublin. No one in Ireland. The only times she slept with men was when she was on one of her trips. It was hardly the dynamic sex life that *Cosmo* preached was a woman's right!

Four men in four cities. Now three men. It worked because she was friends with them. Because they didn't want any more from her and she didn't want any more from them. She felt comfortable with them as friends. Of course it probably helped that she felt comfortable with them in bed too.

But it wasn't just the sex. She told herself that a number of times, because she had the horrible feeling that if anyone else knew about her four men in four cities that was exactly what they'd have thought it was. But it truly wasn't. Sex had a lot to do with it, of course. Sex with them was wonderful. But it wasn't the only reason. She liked having people who were waiting for her, who were there for her, who gave her what she wanted when she wanted and then left her alone. People she met infrequently so that, when they did meet, the intensity of their relationship, both physical and otherwise, was that much greater. And people with whom she didn't have to share the boring day-to-day things that dragged relationships into the doldrums. She liked having people that she would never fall in love with. Because, as she'd told Anna Sweeney, she didn't do messy love affairs. Not any more. This way was much better.

It might have sounded a bit bleak, she thought. But really it wasn't. It meant that she had someone to turn to in all those cities and it made her business trips that much more exciting. She'd had to be careful because of her business relationships too: she didn't want anything to end up in some sort of mess which would threaten her career. But she'd chosen well with all of them. She smiled wryly to herself. She was good with the casual relationships. It was the others that she had major problems with.

She got out of the bath and wrapped herself in an enormous white towel. Casual was good these days. Maybe the time had come to find new men to be casual with, because you couldn't stay casual with people you'd known for years. It became more than that, and she didn't want it to be more than that ever again. Casual was just about as serious as she ever intended to get these days. Casual supplied her every need.

She arrived back at the office the following afternoon. Her voicemail had fifteen messages and she had a heap of emails waiting for her attention. There were also a number of yellow Post-it notes stuck to her computer monitor. She plucked them from the screen one by one and left them in a neat pile beside her keyboard.

She rubbed her eyes. She was tired because, despite the intense sex and the warm bath, she hadn't slept well the previous night. She rested her chin on her hands, elbows on her desk, and closed her eyes while she thought about a technical problem one of her clients had raised with her and which she needed to resolve.

'Tired? Or bored? Or both?'

The words jolted her back from her thoughts and her eyes snapped open. It wasn't just the words, though. It was the voice.

'Hello,' he said.

She could feel her heart thumping in her chest and a pounding sensation in her head. Her mouth was suddenly Sahara-dry and she swallowed with difficulty.

'How are you?' he asked.

The man who'd spoken was standing directly in front of her, flanked either side by older colleagues. He was taller than both of them by a head and shoulders and younger by at least ten years. His eyes were the darkest blue and his hair soot-black without a hint of grey.

'This is Marcus Black,' he told her, indicating the man to his left. 'He's from the New York office of InvestorCorp. And this is Douglas Lomax, from head office in Edinburgh. And you already know me, of course. I'm with the Edinburgh office too.'

She moistened her lips with the tip of her tongue. 'Of course,' she said as she stood up and extended her hand. 'It's good to see you, Neil.'

'You too. It's been a long time.'

His handshake was firmer than she'd expected. She winced slightly as he held on to her for a second more than necessary.

'So,' said Marcus in his American drawl. 'Tired, bored, or both?'

'Thinking,' she said quickly. 'I don't do tired. And I'm certainly never bored.'

He laughed. 'Nice to meet you . . . Ms . . .' His eyes flickered between Darcey and Neil.

'McGonigle,' she said quickly. 'I'm the business development manager.'

'Darcey McGonigle,' said Neil.

'Ah,' said Douglas. 'Pleased to meet you, Darcey.'

'Good to meet you too,' she said. 'I guess we've all been a little concerned about how the merger will pan out.'

'Takeover,' Neil reminded her.

'Yes, indeed,' she said. 'Takeover.'

'You and Neil know each other already,' Marcus said. 'He's talked about you quite a bit.'

'Yes,' said Darcey quickly, wondering what he might have told Marcus. 'But it was – oh, nearly ten years ago.'

'It seems like only yesterday,' said Neil smoothly.

'Time flies,' she said. She looked at Douglas and Marcus. 'I'm really looking forward to working with you all,' she told them. 'I think that InvestorCorp has a lot to bring to the table here.'

'We sure do,' said Douglas. 'And I aim to open up new markets for you guys so that you can become twice as profitable as you are already.'

'Great.' Darcey beamed at him.

'You're too Europe-centric,' he told her. 'We'll be looking at that with our new business management team and we'll involve you in our thought processes too.'

'Great,' she repeated.

'I'll be joining you over here for a few months,' said Neil. 'I'm now director of new business worldwide. I was in the States with Marcus for a while before coming back to Scotland, but I'm going to base myself in Dublin while we look at a certain restructuring of our operations.'

'Restructuring.' Darcey felt her mouth go dry again.

'I'm sure you'll be an important part of it,' said Neil easily. 'We've had some amazingly good reports on you from the management here.'

He *would* be amazed, she thought, at the idea that people could think that she was good at what she did.

'Well, gotta keep moving.' Marcus smiled. 'Good to meet with you, Darcey, I'm sure we'll see each other again in the future.'

'You too,' she said.

The three of them smiled at her and turned away. They continued to walk through the sixth-floor suite of offices and she watched them surreptitiously all the time, while her heart began to return to a normal pace once more.

She really wished they hadn't seen her sitting there with her eyes closed. It looked bad no matter what she said about never being tired or bored. High-flyers like her were never meant to close their eyes. And trust Neil Lomond to make that comment about boredom. She cracked her fingers in frustration.

Her phone rang.

'You're back,' said Anna Sweeney. 'I'm ringing to warn you—'

'I know,' said Darcey. 'The InvestorCorp people. They caught me with my eyes closed.'

'Oh bugger.'

'I faked it,' said Darcey. 'Told them I was thinking. I doubt that I got away with it, but it proves I can be quick on my feet.'

Anna laughed. 'They're actually OK,' she told her. 'They were in my office for ages talking about staff and morale and all that sort of stuff. I gave you a good write-up.'

'They asked about me specifically?' Darcey's voice was a squeak.

'That Lomond guy did,' said Anna. 'First thing he wanted to know was if you were still working here. Said he knew you of old.'

'It was ages ago,' said Darcey wryly.

'An old flame?' Anna picked up the nuances in Darcey's tone.

'Not exactly,' said Darcey.

'Is he married? No, forget I said that.'

'Why?'

'I don't want to be the kind of woman that looks at a good-looking bloke and instantly wonders whether he's available,' Anna said. 'That's as bad as a bloke looking at a woman and instantly giving her marks out of ten. I want to regard men as equals, not prospective husbands.'

'Very noble,' Darcey told her.

'Is he?'

'What?'

'Married, you fool.'

'I don't know,' said Darcey.

'So maybe I can dream.' Anna sighed. 'I'll only allow myself to dream about one of them, and I might as well pick the good-looking one. He looks like good husband material. Though I have to think of father material too. It's very depressing.'

'The good-looking ones are hardly ever good husband material,' said Darcey drily.

'Hmm.' Anna sighed again. 'I suppose you're right. But it can't do any harm to hope. Anyway, how was Milan?'

'Not bad.' Darcey dragged her thoughts away from Neil Lomond and his possible married state. Strange, she told herself, that she'd never thought of him being married. It hadn't once crossed her mind. What sort of a person did that make her, she wondered, not to have even considered it? 'Good, in fact.'

'Glad it went OK. Would you like to come for a drink after work and tell all?'

'I'd absolutely love to, but I can't,' said Darcey. 'I've been away a lot over the last two weeks. I need to go home and wash my knickers.'

'So speaks the modern woman,' said Anna. 'Lunch tomorrow?'

'I'll give you a shout in the morning,' promised Darcey.

She replaced the receiver and rested her chin in her hands again. But this time she didn't close her eyes.

She was still in the office at eight o'clock that evening. She'd written up her notes on her client meetings and emailed

Customer Services with a solution to one of her client's problems, and finally she'd checked the figures for the amount of new business she'd brought in so far that year and felt quietly satisfied with herself. She picked up her bag from the floor and put it on her desk. But the sudden ping of the lift startled her and she knocked it over again, spilling the contents across the mushroom-grey carpet of the sixth floor.

'Shit,' she said as she chased after a lipstick that had rolled three feet away.

'Still here?' Neil Lomond stood in front of her and watched as she picked up the lipstick.

'Yes, I'm still here,' she said. 'But I'm on my way home.'

'Caught you in time, then.'

'No you didn't,' she said. 'I'm leaving. It's late.'

'Sure is,' he said. 'I remember you once saying that nobody in their right mind would stay in the office after six.'

'Perhaps I'm not in my right mind.' The words were out before she could stop them, but she tried to look nonchalant as she picked up a couple of Tampax that had also rolled across the floor in the spill and shoved them into her bag.

'Let me.' Neil began picking things up too. He handed over her set of keys and the small personal security alarm that she also carried in her bag.

'Worried about attacks?' he asked. 'From anyone in particular?'

'The company gave them to us,' she told him. 'Staff security and all that. It's nothing.'

He nodded, then leaned down again and picked up a card that had slid halfway underneath the pedestal beside her desk. He glanced at it as he was about to hand it to her, and then stopped and looked at it more closely, an astonished expression on his face.

She grabbed it out of his hand.

'Honestly,' she said, 'just because you've swanned in here as director of new business doesn't mean you can go around reading my personal things.'

'I didn't mean to,' he said. 'It was just that – well, it's a wedding invitation.'

'I'm glad to see your powers of observation haven't waned.'

'But for heaven's sake, Darcey! Aren't these the same people who . . . ?'

'Yes. Obviously they never bothered to tie the knot,' she said tightly.

'Correct me if I'm wrong, but . . .'

She shrugged. 'I made a mistake.'

He looked flabbergasted. 'Excuse me? You made a mistake?'

'I thought they got married,' she said. 'I don't know why they didn't.'

'I'm . . . I don't know what to say.' He stared at her. 'All the time when you were talking about them running off and getting married . . . all that commotion!'

'Them being married or not wasn't the issue,' she said.

'No. I suppose it wasn't.'

'Anyway, it's all water under the bridge now, isn't it?'

'Good grief! I never thought I'd hear you say that!'

'Well now you have.' She smiled awkwardly at him. 'So there. Can we leave it? It's all behind us, isn't it?'

'Sure,' he said. 'And – you and her? Have you rebuilt bridges?'

'That's asking a bit much!'

'So why did she invite you?'

'I asked myself the same question. Maybe that's why I'll go after all.' She shrugged. 'We'll see.'

'If you want my advice—'

'Neil!' She interrupted him. 'No advice. Thanks all the same.'

'You never could take advice.'

'Give over,' she said.

He nodded slowly. 'Maybe you haven't changed that much after all.'

'Believe me, I have. Don't I have a great career? Don't you think that means I've changed?'

He smiled faintly as she put the card back into her bag.

'Listen,' he said. 'I know it's nothing to do with me, but—'

'You're absolutely right,' she said firmly. 'So please, please don't try to get involved out of some sense of . . .' She broke off. 'What am I saying? You wouldn't really want to get involved. And you don't really want to give me advice. We're way past all that, aren't we?'

'Of course.' His voice was suddenly brittle. 'I wouldn't dream of interfering. And you're right. You have changed. There's something different about you.'

'Maybe I finally got some sense,' she said sheepishly. 'It took a while, obviously. But I'm sure you're glad to see it. And you're fine too, no doubt. You were always fine as far as I remember.'

'Darcey . . .'

'This is where I work,' she told him. 'This is where we both work now. I don't want to have any kind of personal conversation with you in the office. You know what that can lead to! We've done the personal, haven't we? Can't we just keep it totally, totally professional from now on? It'll probably be a bit of a shock to you, but I'm a very professional person these days. You won't have any problems in that regard.'

He stared at her.

'So, you know, let's just pretend that we're meeting for the first time and I'm totally embarrassed to have knocked over my bag in front of you, but you're a decent bloke from the new firm so it doesn't matter.'

He held up his hands. 'OK, OK, whatever you want. It's not like I was looking to open old wounds or anything.'

'Thanks.' There was relief in her voice. 'Everyone does stupid things in their lives, don't they? We don't need to let our stupid thing mess us up all over again.'

'No, we don't,' he said slowly.

'And you don't have to worry about my work,' she added. 'As you already said, you've had amazingly good reports about me.' A hint of anxiety crept into her voice. 'Do *I*?'

'Do you what?'

'Have to worry?'

'What would you have to worry about?'

'Restructuring,' she said flatly. 'That never sounds good.'

'I came up to leave a note on your desk to tell you that we're going to look at changing your brief. But you don't have to be concerned about your job, if that's what's worrying you.'

She sighed with relief. 'You could've emailed me.'

'True, but email is so impersonal.'

'So what do these changes mean?'

'We haven't decided yet. I'll need you to do a range of reports. I'll email those requirements to you. In the interim, you'll be reporting directly to me. Will that be a problem?'

She shrugged as dismissively as she could.

'You'll find I'm very easy to work for. And Darcey, as your boss I do have a sound commercial reason for hoping that your personal life is hunky-dory. I don't want my staff having nervous breakdowns over things that gave them nervous breakdowns in the past.'

'You're exaggerating,' she said evenly. 'And I've got my act together since.'

'I'm so glad to hear that.'

She thought he sounded sincere, but she knew she couldn't trust her judgement where he was concerned.

He nodded at her, smiled and walked towards the lift. Then he bent down and picked up a small packet from underneath a pedestal.

'Yours, I believe,' he said, and left another Tampax on her desk.

She was surprised he couldn't hear the grinding of her teeth as she watched him get into the lift. It was something she used to do in her sleep – for all she knew, something she still did, though it was a long time since anyone had said anything to her about it.

She zipped up her bag, switched off her monitor and slipped her jacket over her shoulders. Then she left the office, hoping that she'd seen the last of Neil Lomond for the evening.

She had. The only person who saw her go was the security guard, who wished her a good night. She nodded and began walking briskly towards the train station. She deliberately stopped herself thinking about personal things as she walked. Instead she thought about the reports for her clients and the success of her Barcelona and Milan meetings, and then, when she was safely sitting on the Dart, she opened her bag and took out the invitation.

Neil was right to be astonished at seeing it. After all, she'd blamed that relationship on so many things in the past. And now here was the proof that they hadn't even bothered to get married before now. That astonished her. And hurt her more than anything.

She'd already decided not to go. It wouldn't achieve anything. She was amazed that they'd even asked her. She worried that there was some ulterior motive. She certainly couldn't think of any reason why she would want to go and see the bitch walk up the aisle. But it had been nagging at her all the same. And now, looking at the invitation again, she wondered if she should go after all.

For closure.

She laughed shortly. Closure. Such an overused word. And what did it mean really? That you could forgive and forget? She didn't think she'd ever be able to do either. Seeing them together for the first time in years wouldn't make it happen. Would it?

She crumpled the invitation in her hand.

She hadn't wanted to open the envelope in the first place. Now she wished she'd left it in the bin. Or at least followed her immediate instinct and sent them a card with 'Fuck Off' inscribed on it. But that would've been petty and ridiculous, and she'd told herself (although it had been a long time before she'd actually believed it) that the best revenge wasn't in being petty and foolish but in getting on with your life on your own terms. She'd tried to do that, eventually. Sure, she'd had her problems, but so did everyone. It was just that hers had started with the person she'd least expected. Nieve.

# Chapter 8

Maybe she was being unfair blaming her problems on Nieve. That was the thing about identifying moments in the past; the benefit of hindsight meant that they took on a significance they really didn't deserve. In fact the problem wasn't so much Nieve as Darcey having to come home and be with Minette when she should have been in Spain and listening to Nieve's story about Max and Lilith Christie and discovering that Nieve was, after all, a much more self-centred and determined person than she'd ever realised before. And that she would do whatever it took to get what she wanted. It would, Darcey thought, have been very useful to know that. At the same time, it was hard to blame Nieve for using her knowledge of Max's indiscretion to get herself a job which was probably more senior than she deserved.

'Oh come on, Darcey,' Nieve had said later when Darcey finally got to talk to her on the phone about it and suggested, a little uncertainly, that she'd sort of blackmailed him into giving her the job. 'I might as well have got some benefit out of catching him with his trousers around his ankles!

What else was I supposed to do? Let him get rid of me from a bloody au-pairing job? Which is what he would've done. Much better that I got something out of the whole deal.'

Darcey knew that Nieve was right. After all, it wouldn't have been right for her friend to lose her job because she discovered her boss was having an affair with the housekeeper. But she also knew that she'd never have been able to face Max Christie down like that herself.

Of course, at the time it was all happening for Nieve, Darcey herself was blissfully unaware of it because she was back home in Ireland and dealing with the fallout of Martin's desertion. While Nieve was doing her corporate ballbreaking act, she was trying to persuade her mother that her life wasn't over just because Martin had left. It had been difficult at first. Minette had been totally gutted by Martin's infidelity and shocked because she hadn't realised it was happening. But she only cried for a day after the girls came back from Cork and told her that he simply wasn't coming home. She told Darcey that everyone had to get on with their lives, which was what she would do no matter how badly she felt about everything, and she insisted that her daughter go back to Spain if that was what she wanted.

It was. But Darcey still felt very guilty as she rang Nieve to say that she'd be coming back to Marbella soon. It was then that she learned about Max and Maria and about Nieve's demand for a job at Christie Corporation.

'So you can come back to Marbella if you like,' said Nieve. 'But I'll probably be going to London. That's where Max's head office is and he's going back there soon.'

Marbella on her own suddenly didn't seem so appealing.

And Darcey felt slightly happier at having had the choice taken away from her, almost forcing her to stay with Minette after all. She thought too that maybe it was time she did the same as Nieve and got a proper job. Even though she'd have to go about it in a more orthodox way. She had no idea what kind of job she wanted. Nieve had been right when she called her unambitious. Darcey didn't like pushing herself forward, and it seemed to her that choosing a career and wanting to be the best at it was somehow attention-seeking. She'd heard Nieve's dad talking about office politics and skulduggery and she simply couldn't bear the idea of being involved in things like that. Deep down she nurtured the idea of owning a small farm in Tuscany and living off the land. But that was just an idealised dream. Something for the far-off future, perhaps. Right now she was back in Ireland, and she had to find something useful to do. But the jobs market was dreary, the appointments pages sparse and the ads uninspiring.

Besides, she hated the idea of being tied down to an office job with office hours. She knew that Nieve was now working twelve-hour days so that she'd appear totally committed to Max Christie (and because everyone else in the company seemed to). Nieve said she didn't mind, that she was laying down the foundation for her future – a future, she said, in which she'd be even more successful than Max Christie himself. Darcey couldn't imagine ever spending twelve hours in an office because she simply couldn't imagine anything that would hold her interest that long. Even if there was the promise of an unspecified pot of gold at an undetermined time in the future.

Looking at the ads, her skills didn't seem to be hugely

practical. It was all very well being able to work out the square root of 1,864 in her head, but most people used calculators for that kind of thing. Speaking a clatter of languages wasn't a hell of a lot of use in Galway. If anything, speaking Irish would have been more useful to her, but like scores of other Irish children, she hadn't paid a lot of attention to it in school. She was still better at it than many of her contemporaries, but she was far more fluent in European languages.

She wished that she had a clear view of what she wanted from life, like Nieve. The trouble was that she seemed to have a clearer idea of what she *didn't* want to do than what she did.

After a few weeks of reading the ads and dismissing every single job as unsuitable (while Minette's lips got tighter and tighter with every one she rejected), Darcey went for an interview in a newly opened call centre company located in an office park a mere twenty minutes' walk away and which was looking for people with language skills.

'This is perfect for you.' It was Minette who spotted the ad and thrust the paper in front of her.

'Mam! It's just answering the bloody phone,' objected Darcey.

'You might start off like that, but if you're good you'll do well,' said Minette firmly.

Darcey knew her mother was right. After all, she couldn't sponge off Minette for ever. She read through the rest of the job ads and wondered why it was that she wasn't able to be a 'motivated self-starter'. She thought it sounded more like a car part than a person.

But she went for the call-centre interview in the modern new building overlooking the beautiful Lough Atalia. They seemed impressed by her languages and unfazed by the fact that her only work experience was in picking grapes and looking after small children. She hadn't even arrived home when they phoned back, and so she was greeted by Minette beaming at her and telling her that she'd been offered a job starting the following Monday.

A few weeks later, and unexpectedly as far as she was concerned, she was made a supervisor. She knew she was doing quite well in the job because she found talking on the phone to people easier than talking to them face to face, and she was quick at solving whatever problem they'd called about. Her languages had been a tremendous help too. Nevertheless, being a supervisor wasn't something she'd even thought about.

Darcey was surprised to find that she quite liked being the person in charge and that she was a good leader. She'd never been the leader before. It had always been Nieve. Perhaps, she thought sometimes, it had been a good thing, her having to come home and Nieve joining up with Max Christie. Nevertheless, she missed her friend's company, and – as she looked out of the window at the lowering clouds – despite the magnificent west of Ireland sunsets, she missed the blue skies and warm winds of continental Europe too.

But there were compensations. The social life at Car Crew was good, and she found herself going for drinks or to clubs with her co-workers at the weekends. It was a new experience for her. She realised that she was coming out from behind Nieve's shadow, and she liked it.

\*     \*     \*

The Car Crew girls were all looking for Mr Right, even the girls who said they weren't. Every man they saw was rated out of ten, every boyfriend was discussed, every nuance of getting and keeping a man was ruthlessly examined. Darcey reckoned that she learned more in the months with Car Crew than she ever had in her life before. She felt sure that if only she could actually meet a man, her new-found knowledge would mean that this time it would be different. This time she wouldn't be tongue-tied and stupid. This time she'd be able to act like a mature adult and have a proper relationship.

'Guys should be falling over themselves to go out with you,' Emma, one of the other supervisors, told her one day. 'And they would if you took a bit of time to look nice and didn't terrorise them by picking on them as soon as they opened their mouths.'

'I don't know what you're talking about.' Darcey looked at her colleague in surprise.

'You're a blonde!' cried Emma. 'A natural blonde. With blue eyes and perfect teeth.'

Darcey snorted. 'You're making me sound like a horse!'

'Yeah, well, you look more horse than human at the moment,' Emma told her bluntly. 'Get your damn hair restyled, buy some decent clothes, and for God's sake stop putting guys down before they even open their mouths. Not everyone is a walking bloody encyclopaedia like you, and that doesn't make them bad people.'

Darcey sighed, but conceded that Emma had a point. She was too impatient with people and too anxious to prove to guys that she wasn't a dumb blonde, and she knew that she came across stroppy and irritable even when she didn't want to be. So she tried to follow Emma's advice. She went to Galway's most expensive hairdresser to have her hair cut, traded in her denims and jumpers for some ridiculously expensive designer labels, and did her best not to criticise every man she met.

But despite the makeover and the clubbing, the late nights and the inexhaustible supply of advice from the rest of the girls, her Mr Right was nowhere to be found. It was her own fault really. Regardless of her best efforts she still wasn't good girlfriend material and she still found most men unutterably boring.

Then she met Aidan.

She didn't meet him in a pub or a club. She met him in the office. He worked in the IT department and he came to see her about a problem she was having with her computer. He strode across the room and everyone's eyes turned to follow him because, at six feet two inches, he was difficult to miss. He was, thought Darcey as he sat down in front of her, the most perfect man she'd ever seen before in her life. His hair was blond and spiky, his face tanned and his body muscular. His eyes were as blue as the ocean. He was dressed in jeans and a T-shirt. And he wore a small diamond in the lobe of his right ear.

'Hi,' he said in a gravelly voice and a soft Dublin accent that reduced her knees to jelly. 'I'm Aidan. What's the problem exactly?'

'It's not working.' She indicated her blank screen. 'And don't tell me to check that the monitor's switched on or that the cables are all connected properly. I've done that already.' She spoke more harshly than she'd intended and he raised an eyebrow at her.

'Take it easy,' he said. 'We ask those questions because ninety per cent of the time that's what the problem is.'

'Well I'm the other ten per cent,' she told him.

He grinned. 'Sure you are. OK, let's have a look.'

He tapped at her keyboard for a few seconds and then disappeared beneath her desk so that only his bum, encased in faded blue jeans, was visible. It was a nice bum. Darcey tried not to stare. But she couldn't help it.

'Right.' He emerged again and smiled. 'It's not your fault. It's the connection. You need a new cable.'

'Can you get one for me now?' she asked. 'I'm really busy today and I need to access my computer.'

'Well . . .' He looked doubtful. 'I'm not sure. It's very busy in IT too and I don't know if I've time to go through all those cables.'

'Don't be so silly.' She wished that she didn't sound so snappy, but she couldn't help herself. Part of her didn't want this guy to suspect that she fancied him (and that was based solely on his taut abs and neat bum, how pathetic!) and the other part of her was annoyed because she truly was busy.

'Just teasing.' He grinned at her. 'I'll be back in ten minutes.'

As soon as he got into the lift, Darcey grabbed her bag and hurried into the Ladies', where she pulled her brush through her hair and dabbed some lip gloss on to her lips. She wished she was the kind of person who kept an entire make-up selection in her desk drawer, because she couldn't help feeling that a bit of blusher and some mascara might be a good idea right now. But her collection consisted solely of the lip gloss (which she kept in her bag) and a concealer for the spots that occasionally broke out over her nose. No spots today, thank goodness, she thought as she sprayed herself with an almost empty Paloma Picasso perfume she'd picked up in Spain. Hopefully nothing would break out in the next ten minutes either.

It was nearly half an hour before Aidan returned, during which time she'd managed to lick off all the lip gloss and run her hands despairingly through her hair while she talked to a customer from Italy who'd run his hire car off the road in France.

'*Non si preoccupi*,' she told the client soothingly. 'Don't worry, *signore*. We will sort everything out for you. I will call you back very soon.'

She ended the call and looked up to see Aidan striding towards her desk again. God, she thought, her heart pounding, he's amazing. I wonder if there's the faintest hope in hell that he'd find me attractive. Then she saw the reflection of her tousled hair and gloss-less lips in her blank computer monitor and sighed.

He fitted the new cable and the monitor blinked into life again.

'*Molte grazie*,' she said. 'I mean, thanks.'

'You're the multilinguist, aren't you?' said Aidan. 'I've heard about you. Very impressive.'

'I don't see why. Lots of people here can speak different languages.' She frowned.

'But you speak them all.'

She shrugged. 'Not really. The main ones. But, you know,

times are changing. Someday we'll need people who speak Polish and Hungarian and Lithuanian and all sorts. I'll be a dinosaur with old European languages.'

He laughed. 'I love language.'

'Do you speak many yourself?'

'English,' he said. 'And Irish. My parents came from here and we spoke it all the time when I was a kid. I lived in Dublin for years, though, so I didn't speak it much there.'

'We didn't very much at all,' she admitted. 'I can speak it, of course, but I'm ashamed to say that I'm more fluent in French!'

'Ah, you know how it is.' He tweaked at the cable again. 'Nobody thinks it's important, so they don't remember it. But it's a lovely language.'

She smiled. 'You're right. Personally I think Italian is the nicest of them all.'

'Say something else in Italian,' he asked.

'Like what?'

'Anything.'

'*Tre persone su due non capiscono le proporzioni in matematica,*' she said.

'Huh?'

'Three in two people don't understand proportions in maths,' she told him.

'OK, I was thinking of something a little less . . . technical.' He grinned.

She thought for a moment. '*Non fidarti di una donna che si toglie tutto tranne il cappello.*'

He frowned. '*Una donna* is a woman, isn't it?'

She nodded.

He shook his head. 'I don't have a clue.'

'Don't trust a woman who takes everything off except her hat,' she translated.

He stared at her for a moment, then burst into laughter. Heads peeked up over the cubicle dividers.

'How d'you say: will you come out with me later?' he asked.

'Will you come out with me later sounds fine just the way it is.'

'Will you?'

'Me? With you?'

'Yes.'

'I'd love to,' she said.

'Excellent. How about eight o'clock? That bar near the Spanish Arch?'

'*Perfetto*,' she said.

'See you then,' he replied.


Whenever she looked back on it, she always thought that her first date with Aidan was the most perfect night of her life. It was the night when she got everything right with a man; the night when she knew that she'd been right all along to dismiss the other guys she'd met as being lightweight and meaningless. With Aidan, everything had simply fallen into place.

They'd gone to one of Galway's cheap 'n' cheerful restaurants where hot tomato topping from the pizza and warm buttery garlic from the bread dripped down her chin and covered her fingers and Aidan had laughed at her – but not at her, with her, so that she didn't care that she was making a mess of eating it and she didn't care that he was laughing.

And later, as they walked hand in hand through the winding city streets, stopping to throw money into the open guitar case of the busker who was singing ballads about love and loss, she told him why she was back in Ireland and the shock that her father's leaving had been for them all.

'Your poor mum,' he said sympathetically. 'Your dad – a bit of a shit?'

'I usen't to think so,' said Darcey. 'But obviously yes.'

Then he told her that his parents had split up when he was six and that his father had begged him to choose to live with him over his mother and that in the end he'd been shuttled between the two of them, one in Dublin and one in Galway, and it had all been horrible and stressful and he'd hated the fact that he was some kind of trophy they both wanted to keep.

'Maybe they loved you too much,' said Darcey.

'Nah, they loved themselves too much,' said Aidan. 'And each other not at all, unfortunately.'

She snuggled even closer to him, feeling the warmth of his body next to hers and knowing that the closeness wasn't just physical.

They walked all the way back to Darcey's house where, in the velvet darkness, he kissed her underneath the sycamore tree on the pavement outside. Although she'd kissed men before (even though it hadn't meant much at the time), Aidan's kiss was different. His lips, pressed against hers, opened her mind and her body to a new level of pleasure.

She wished, as her blood raced around her body and she trembled within his arms, that they were anywhere else but outside her family home in the suburbs. She wanted to be on a deserted beach with only the stars for light and only the gentle thud of the waves lapping on the shore as background noise, instead of the steady drum of traffic as it hurtled down the main road.

He moved away from her and his eyes met hers.

'Wow,' he said.

'Wow,' she replied.

'I think I love you.'

'I think . . . I think I love you too.'

'I'll drop by tomorrow, fix that computer of yours again.'

'It doesn't need . . . oh, yes, right.'

She didn't want him to go. She couldn't imagine a second in her life when he wouldn't be there. She rested her head against his chest and wondered what it would have been like never to have met him, never to have fallen in love with him.

'See you then,' he said, finally releasing her from his arms.

'See you.'

'In the morning.'

'In the morning.'

He put his arms around her again.

'*Oíche mhait, coladh sámh.*'

'Good night and sleep well to you too,' she said.

'*Sueños dulces.*'

She smiled and touched his lips with her fingers. 'I didn't know you could speak Spanish.'

'I can't,' he admitted. 'One of my housemates told me

124

that and I was always afraid it meant something like "you're an asshole", but I looked it up before I came out tonight.'

'*Sogni d'oro*,' she said softly.

'Sweet dreams.' He kissed her again. 'You're special.'

'So are you.'

She'd heard about people feeling as though they were walking on air. She didn't even feel her feet touch the ground as she walked back into the house. And although she didn't sleep a wink that night, she wasn't in the slightest bit tired when she got up for work the following morning.

She did, she supposed, feel a little bit guilty that she was so happy when she knew that, despite her assurances to the contrary, her mother was still miserable. The twins had moved back out of the house (they shared a rented apartment near the city centre) and Darcey was acutely aware that she'd come home to be there for Minette but that, thanks to Aidan, she was there less and less.

'I don't mind,' said Minette one evening when Darcey had stayed in (only because Aidan was working late at Car Crew – there was a systems problem and they wanted as little downtime as possible, so he wasn't pulling the plug on the technology until after midnight). 'You're entitled to your life, *ma cherie*.'

'I know.' Darcey smiled at her. 'Thing is . . . well, if this awful thing hadn't happened I wouldn't have come home and I wouldn't have met Aidan and . . . it doesn't seem fair somehow.'

'If something good has come out of your dad's bad behaviour, I suppose we should all be grateful,' said Minette.

'Oh, Mam.'

'I'm getting over it,' said Minette. 'I didn't think I would, but I am.'

'I still can't believe it happened. I thought he loved you.'

'I thought so too.' Minette grimaced. 'I guess I got complacent with him. I let myself go a bit. Perhaps that's why. I should have made more of an effort.'

'That's rubbish,' said Darcey angrily. 'Like it's all your fault that he behaved like a shit? Like he didn't let himself go a bit too? Like he didn't need to make an effort either? He's fifty, for heaven's sake. He's got a paunch. And grey hair.'

'He still managed to find a young wan, though,' said Minette gloomily.

'She was obviously blinded by the fact that he's older. It's a power thing. Not a body thing. And it won't last.'

Minette smiled. 'Maybe not. But I need to think about the body thing. I'm kind of plump. And I know I colour my hair, but I do it myself. I should go to the hairdressers and get it done properly. I should have spent more money on make-up and looking good and stuff like that. I'm forty-nine, not ninety-nine.'

'I still don't think it's right,' said Darcey mutinously. 'Why should you have to keep attracting him over and over while he never bothered to do anything himself? He married you. Surely that's enough.'

'Now you're being silly,' Minette told her. 'When he married me I was a slender thing with brown hair and good skin. Now I'm fat with grey hair and millions of those fine lines they keep telling us about.'

'You're not fat,' said Darcey heatedly. 'Sure, you put on weight. Everyone does. Everyone! You've had three kids, for goodness' sake. You can't expect to look like a twenty-five-year-old again.'

'But I don't look especially good for my age,' protested Minette. 'I'm not someone you'd look at and mistake for a thirty-year-old.'

'Yuck.' Darcey made a face at her. 'I don't want you to look like a thirty-year-old. You're my mother! You should look good for your age but not . . . not like competition!'

Minette laughed. It was the first time Darcey had heard her laugh since she'd come home. 'I won't be competition,' she said. 'But I need to do stuff for myself.'

Darcey nodded.

'So I'm joining WeightWatchers and I'm going to get my hair done properly, and if I ever see your dad again he won't recognise me,' said Minette. 'And I'm going to cut back on chocolate and pastries.' She sighed longingly. 'No more hot chocolate before going to bed.'

'Well, maybe that's good for both of us.' Darcey pinched more than an inch around her waist. 'I could probably do with giving chocolate and cream a miss too.'

'Do you want to come to WeightWatchers with me?' asked Minette.

'Maybe I will.' Darcey made a face. 'In the past I always felt that losing weight was all about attracting men. So I objected to places like WeightWatchers. I still think a bit that way. And I think it's wrong to do something just to attract men.'

'Why?' Minette looked at her curiously. 'You've had your

hair cut – and it's much better shorter. You've bought new clothes—'

'Yes, and that's because the girls at work said I should,' agreed Darcey. 'I know that they reckon it's the best way of getting a bloke. But I did it to look better for me.'

'Yet since then Aidan has turned up.'

'I know.' Darcey sighed. 'I so desperately don't want to be shallow and stuff, but it was because he was gorgeous-looking that I first noticed him. It was only afterwards that I liked him too. So I guess it makes sense the other way around too.'

Minette smiled. 'He's a nice boy,' she told her daughter. 'But you're still young. Don't go losing your heart to him.'

'I won't,' promised Darcey. 'My heart is perfectly safe.' But even as she said the words she knew that she was lying. She'd lost her heart already.

# Chapter 9

Ennco's stock price continued to rise. Nieve watched it as she sipped her tea the morning after the conference in Vancouver. As she looked at the on-screen ticker and calculated her net worth again, she was gripped with a sense of unreality, suddenly quite unable to believe that she, Nieve Stapleton, was the holder of stock options that had catapulted her into the more-than-a-millionaire class. It hadn't been a straight line of success, of course. It had started well and dipped dramatically, but she'd come through it all and she was a survivor. More than a survivor. She could give motivational speeches about seizing the moment and grabbing life with both hands, and people would listen to her because she was part of the mega-company that was Ennco and she was rolling in it. She'd played the game and won. She was living the dream. The American dream and the Irish dream and any damn dream that meant dollars and euros in your bank account.

She finished her tea and went out to the car. A couple of months and then she'd sell the stock and invest most of it in tracker bonds and good old safe-as-houses treasury bills, and the rest of it in some crazy leveraged fund that could hit pay dirt and double her money. And if she lost a bit of it in speculative trading, well, what the hell. She could afford it because she'd have a diversified portfolio and the gains should offset the losses.

Max Christie had taught her about diversifying her portfolio. Max Christie had taught her about getting rich a few months after he'd appointed her as his personal assistant.

She hadn't wanted to be his personal assistant, of course. That hadn't been the job she'd been looking for when she'd made her demands.

'A senior position,' she'd repeated.

'My PA *is* a senior position,' he told her. 'In fact it's one of the most coveted positions in the company. The previous incumbent was more highly qualified than you.'

'That wouldn't be hard,' said Nieve sourly. 'I did commerce at college. I'm no good at typing.'

'Daniel Weston had excellent keyboarding skills,' said Max calmly. 'I hope you'll bring yours up to speed.'

'Daniel?' She looked at him sceptically. 'Your PA was a bloke? I thought it was someone called Samantha Brooks.'

'Sam is my social organiser,' Max told her. 'She looks after my engagements and does, of course, liaise with my PA. My PA, however, looks after business matters. Daniel has now been appointed head of Christie's overseas division.'

'Oh.'

'So I'm keeping my word,' said Max. 'I'm giving you a senior position in the company. I expect you to keep yours.'

'It's not in my interest to do anything else,' replied Nieve.

\*   \*   \*

It was like opening a door into another world, a world she'd always wanted to be a part of. Although she'd seen the wealth and the lifestyle of the Christies in Spain, she hadn't really realised how much money they had. Nor had she realised what working in a successful organisation like Christie's could be like. And she certainly hadn't realised how important a figure Max Christie actually was in the world of business. She'd seen his name in the paper, of course. She'd seen tabloid stories about the extravagant party he'd thrown for Lilith's thirtieth birthday. (He'd hired Elton John to perform at it and – allegedly – filled the swimming pool with champagne.) But she hadn't quite appreciated how seriously he was taken as a businessman. She'd just thought he'd been lucky and got rich quick.

He'd changed her views on that on the way to a meeting in Amsterdam.

The flight was on his private jet. And they'd stayed at some incredibly exclusive hotel near Dam Square. A Daimler had picked them up to bring them to the meeting.

'How did you get so lucky?' she'd asked as they sped through the narrow streets to their meeting.

He'd glanced up from the papers he was studying.

'I don't do luck,' he told her. 'It was good judgement. And I don't do idle chitchat when I'm working.'

She nodded and kept silent.

'Buyouts,' he told her ten minutes later as he closed the folder he'd been going through. 'I buy companies, break them up and then sell the component parts.'

'Like Richard Gere in *Pretty Woman*?'

'Nothing like Richard Gere,' he told her tersely. 'I don't sleep with prostitutes.'

Sheila O'Flanagan

She kept her mouth shut. After all, Maria had been the cook and housekeeper. She didn't ever intend to refer to Maria, who had left the Christies' employment the day after Nieve had walked in on them but who had, apparently, got a job with an acquaintance of Max in Malaga.

'I don't need you to say anything,' he told her as they entered the two-hundred-year-old building where the business he intended to buy was headquartered. 'I just need you to take notes and nod whenever you think it's appropriate.'

The notetaking and nodding had gone well. Later that night, as she'd been lying on her bed wondering whether she should order room service for dinner or whether Max expected her to show up in the dining room downstairs, there was a knock at her door. He was there, holding a bottle of champagne and two glasses in his hand.

'They called,' he told her gleefully. 'They couldn't wait. It's a done deal and we are going to celebrate.'

She felt fuzzy after the champagne (Dom Perignon, and a particularly good vintage according to Max, though she didn't have a clue) and she knew she'd been a bit silly and giggly and not exactly how she wanted to be. It had suddenly occurred to her that he might want to sleep with her and she'd asked him straight out what his intentions were. He'd looked startled and told her that if champagne had that sort of effect on her, she shouldn't drink it. Their relationship, he told her, had been forced on him and it was a business relationship. But it might work out to their advantage because she was hard as nails and good at making men feel important. If he ever discovered that she'd tried sleeping with any of his clients or anyone in his companies,

132

he'd fire her on the spot. Nieve wanted to tell him that he was surely applying double standards. But the job was important to her and so she didn't. She said nothing at all as he refilled her glass and told her that they would clean up the European markets between them.

Obviously he didn't really mean that they'd clean up between them. He meant that she'd be there while he made the money. He started to invest in new technology industries, ones which hadn't made the grade yet but which he expected to do well in the future. He bought shares in Amazon and other fledgling dotcom businesses, and told her that he'd sell them before it all got too crazy. Run with your profits, he said. Cut your losses. When a stock has a big setback, get the hell out and look for something new. She'd remembered that a few years later when the modest holdings she herself had in technology shares started to decline in value. She managed to get rid of them all at a profit, even though it hadn't been as much as she'd hoped. But it had been enough to mean that she didn't have to panic when she was suddenly out of work because the company she worked for had gone bust.

The fact that she'd allowed herself to be seduced by the stock options made her realise that she hadn't learned as much as she'd thought from Max Christie, but none of that mattered now. She smiled as she thought about him. We were a good partnership, she thought, even though I wasn't as experienced as Daniel Weston. But I brought a touch of glamour to his meetings, and he liked that.

'Men are fools,' he told her once when the director of a middle European country had insisted on sitting beside her at a corporate dinner and had, inadvertently, told her much more than he meant to about his company so that, using the information, Max had been able to structure a much better deal for Christie's than ever would have been possible. 'You'd imagine none of us had ever seen a woman before.'

'You don't have enough of them in senior positions in Christie's,' she told him. 'All your directors are men. It's no wonder everyone starts panting when a female walks into the boardroom.'

'I don't like women in business,' said Max.

'Not even me?' asked Nieve.

'It's not the same,' he told her. 'You're my PA, not my rival.'

He was right, she knew, and yet the remark stung. She didn't want to be his rival but she wanted to think that she could be. She didn't want to have to work at it, though. She wanted to be like the heroines of the sex-and-shopping books she liked to read, who inherited family companies and a seat on the board. At the same time she knew that business was changing. You didn't have to be the top dog to make a lot of money. You just had to be in the right place at the right time. Being in the right place at the right time was what she wanted. Because, she realised, as far as she was concerned, it was all about the money. People could talk all they liked about job satisfaction, but if you weren't earning the big bucks then you were a fool. There was no job that was worth being paid a pittance for.

She wasn't paid a pittance as Max's PA but she was paid considerably less than Daniel had been. When she discovered this and pointed it out to Max, he roared with laughter.

'I told you before, Daniel was hugely qualified,' he said. 'You're nothing in comparison.'

'I have a business degree,' she said angrily. 'I get the work done, don't I?'

'Yes. But you don't add value to it in the same way as him,' said Max.

'Who cares!' she cried. 'You already know what you're going to do. Nothing I say will change your mind. And I bet nothing Daniel ever said changed your mind either.'

'You may not add value to the analysis side of things,' remarked Max. 'But you sure as hell make my business life seem like my home life sometimes. You're forever nagging me, just like a woman.'

'I don't nag,' she said. 'I point things out. I point out a lot more stuff than Weston! Sensible things like how you look more authoritative in a dark suit with a red tie than with a blue tie. And equally sensible things like the fact that buying a company that uses lead paint on its toys is a big, big mistake. You didn't spot that stuff about the paint. I did. I saved you billions. So don't say I don't bloody add value!'

'Millions,' he amended. 'And I would have noticed it myself.'

'Millions, billions. You didn't give any of it to me. Some show of gratitude that was.'

'You seem to think that whenever money is made here you should get some of it,' said Max. 'You're an inexperienced girl in her twenties, for heaven's sake.'

'Yeah, but the whole business model is going that way,' she retorted. 'What about your precious technology companies? These dotcommers you're buying into? They're all just kids. Younger than me. Guys, though – is that what makes the difference?'

'Talented, though,' he remarked. 'That does.'

'And I'm not?' She was really angry now.

'You have a lot of balls for a woman,' he told her. 'It's a pity you don't always have the brains.'

'Fuck off,' she said furiously.

He stared at her. 'You will apologise to me right away,' he said tightly.

She almost told him to fuck off again. But she didn't. She apologised instead.

Later that evening, after he'd gone to a meeting with a property mogul, she sat in her office just off his own and wondered what she could do to add value to her role as PA. She knew what he was talking about, of course, but she didn't want to admit that Daniel Weston had been better than her because he had a stupid MBA. She could get an MBA if she wanted. Though it would be a lot of hard work and she couldn't help wondering if it would really be worth it, because surely experience and common sense meant more in the end.

She wandered down to the third floor of the office building. Men and women were still at their desks, reading reports, analysing figures or preparing presentations for Max. Maybe I need to be a bit more like them, she thought. Maybe I need to stop thinking about the money and work harder. I like hard work really. I've lost sight of that a little bit over the last while.

She went back up to her office and looked at the pile of folders on her desk. They were full of information: briefings for Max, reports for him to read, accounts for him to look at – the results of what people down on the third floor were doing right now. And what she needed to do, instead of feeling hard done by that Max wasn't paying her as much as Weston, was to get her head around them and highlight the important parts for him so that he didn't need to waste his valuable time reading every word.

She pulled the first one towards her.

'Leveraged Property Fund', she read. 'Gearing up in Southern Europe.'

She yawned widely and opened it.

It was nearly midnight by the time she'd got through half a dozen reports, but she realised, somewhat to her surprise, that she could actually synopsise them pretty well and that there were a few points that needed to be emphasised in each one. She was highlighting a possible flaw in a South American utility deal when Max came into the office again. He looked at her in surprise.

'Still here?'

'Doing some stuff,' she said. 'You were right, Max. I need to work harder.'

He raised an eyebrow.

'Seriously.' She smiled at him. 'When I add value, you'll have no excuse for not giving me the big bucks in my payslip.'

He laughed. 'Here then,' he said. 'I have another meeting with these guys about their Côte d'Azur development tomorrow. This is a document prepared by their French counterparts. Have a run-through of it on my desk by the morning.' The folder he handed her was bright blue. She took it and glanced inside.

'This is in French,' she said.

'Huh?'

'French,' she said. 'The language they speak in France.'

'One day you'll cut yourself with that sharp tongue,' he said. 'What d'you mean it's in French? Isn't there an English version too?'

'Nope.' She held out the document.

'Oh, crap,' he said. 'I wanted to deal with that early in the morning.'

'Is it important?' asked Nieve. 'Aren't you heading off to Geneva tomorrow? They won't be expecting a response from you.'

'I wanted to deal with it before I go,' he said. 'They're talking to another consortium. I can take this deal or leave it, but I don't want to get into a bidding war and I don't want to underbid either.'

'So if I get an English translation to you before . . .' she glanced at the desk diary in front of her, 'before seven a.m., would that help?'

'D'you think you'll get someone at this hour?' he asked.

'Of course I will,' she told him confidently.

He laughed and said that if she managed to get the translated document to him before seven, and if he made a successful bid for the project, he would give her a ten per cent bonus on her salary.

'Right,' she said. 'You're on.'

Max went home, but Nieve picked up the phone and dialled Darcey's number. Minette answered.

'It's lovely to hear your voice, *cherie*,' she told Nieve. 'But Darcey is in bed. She has an early shift tomorrow.'

'It's important,' said Nieve persuasively. 'Can you get her for me?'

'Life and death?' asked Minette.

'Not quite,' Nieve admitted, 'but I know Darce will understand.'

Darcey didn't quite understand why her friend needed a six-page document translated over the phone in the middle of the night, but Nieve begged her to help. It was important to her career, she told Darcey, and if she got the promised bonus she would see that Darcey got something too.

'I don't want anything,' Darcey told her sleepily. 'Except to go back to bed. I'm knackered.'

'Were you out with your new man?' teased Nieve. She'd been both surprised and pleased when Darcey had first phoned to tell her about him. She found it difficult to think of her friend being totally smitten by anyone.

'Um . . . yes,' admitted Darcey (although she didn't tell Nieve that she was exhausted from the great sex that they'd had). 'So, look, can't this wait till tomorrow?'

'Please, Darce,' begged Nieve. 'It really matters to me now.'

'Oh, all right.' Darcey dragged herself into full consciousness. 'Go on, do your worst.'

Nieve put Darcey on speakerphone and tapped out the translation on her keyboard. It took over an hour, and every so often Darcey would moan that it was the most boring thing she'd ever heard. But Nieve insisted she kept going until the very end.

'*Merci beaucoup*,' she told Darcey when they finally completed it. 'You're a star.'

'Yeah, yeah.' But Darcey was pleased to have helped out in the end.

Nieve was even more pleased.

When she put the phone down, she couriered the document to Max's house.

Two weeks later she got her bonus.

# Chapter 10

'I have to go to Edinburgh,' Anna told Darcey as they ate lunch in one of the Italian restaurants near the office. The day was warm and the sun slanted through the plate-glass window, so that Darcey was squinting at Anna as she spoke. 'They've called me over to discuss the future of HR in Dublin.'

Darcey stopped pushing pasta around her plate and looked at her friend in consternation. 'They don't need to do that, surely,' she said. 'There's nothing wrong with HR in Dublin.'

'I told you.' Anna looked miserable. 'They want to consolidate everything over there.'

'They don't!' cried Darcey. 'There's a difference between the two companies. I know it's a takeover and that they're in the driving seat now, but that doesn't mean we'll lose our own ethos.'

Anna laughed harshly. 'You sound like a management consultant. Ethos! You know quite well that's corporate crap-speak.'

'Oh, come on.' Darcey looked at her encouragingly. 'Crap-speak maybe, but they've been OK to us so far, haven't they?'

'If OK means staying out of our hair, yes. But now it seems that they're prepared to get right on in there. Apparently Peter Henson is going to the New York office and we're getting a new MD. Neil Lomond is staying for a few months to work on new business, but we knew that anyway. Some other guy is coming over to work on new products and God only knows what other surprises they have up their sleeves.'

'Who are you going to meet in Edinburgh?' asked Darcey.

'Well, their HR guy, obviously,' replied Anna. 'I'm travelling over with Neil and that other Scottish bloke who's currently prowling around the office . . . The only good part of this deal is the idea of sitting beside Lomond on the plane.'

'For heaven's sake!' Darcey sniffed. 'You're not still thinking of him as some potential husband, are you?'

'You just never know.' Anna grinned at her. 'Come on, Darce, even you've got to admit that he's kinda hunky.' Darcey shrugged and Anna made a face at her. 'You prefer the overseas guys, don't you?'

'What d'you mean?' Darcey looked startled.

'Oh, Darce. You hardly ever go out with guys in Dublin, but I know you've been wined and dined when you go on your European trips. D'you keep your real lover stashed away in Milan or Barcelona?'

Darcey felt herself flush and Anna grinned.

'Don't tell me I've hit the jackpot!'

'No, you haven't.' Darcey recovered quickly. 'It's true that there have been one or two . . . flings . . . I guess . . .'

'Sure, why wouldn't there be?' asked Anna. 'There you

are, on your own in some lovely romantic city. Why wouldn't you hitch up with someone for a bit of harmless fun? Or fab sex. Whatever!'

Darcey grinned. 'I thought people might disapprove of me for that.'

'Why should they? I bet the InvestorCorp blokes have girlies stashed all over the place. Why shouldn't you have a man or two?'

'Because people don't really think that women just sleep with men for sex,' replied Darcey calmly.

'And do you?'

Darcey shrugged and made a face. 'Not entirely. I mean, the sex is fantastic and I love it and it's different, you know? Each of them is fun to be with. I wouldn't enjoy it if I didn't like them.'

'Each of them! How many are there?'

'There used to be four. Now there's three.'

'You are a dark horse, aren't you? And obviously hot stuff too.'

Darcey squirmed. 'Not really. It's all very casual.'

'What happens if you fall for one of them one day?'

'I won't.'

'Are you sure about that?'

'Absolutely,' said Darcey. 'I'm over and done with my falling in love thing.'

'Tell me about it.'

Darcey shook her head. 'That stuff is *so* not interesting.'

'I think it's totally interesting,' said Anna. 'We're friends, Darce. I never pry but . . . you know all about my hopeless relationships. Tell me about yours.'

Darcey looked at Anna thoughtfully. Then she opened her bag and took out the by now creased wedding invitation.

'This is probably the source of some of my relationship issues,' she said as she smoothed it out on the table in front of them.

Anna looked at the invitation and then at Darcey, her expression puzzled.

'What d'you mean?' she asked. 'Aren't you going to this wedding?' She leaned towards her friend. 'Do you have a secret past? Did you have a fling with him? Is that it? Doesn't she know about it?'

'Mmm.' Darcey left the invitation on the round granite table. 'It's not quite like that.'

'What then?' Anna looked at her expectantly. 'Tell me, Darcey. Whatever it is, it'll do you good to talk about it.'

'You think?' Darcey's smile was forced. 'I'm not so sure I want to talk about that arrogant cow, to be honest. But maybe it's time I did.'

She'd never really thought of Nieve as arrogant when they were younger. She knew that her best friend was self-confident and that sometimes her confidence meant that she appeared arrogant to both the teachers at school and her friends. Nieve was impatient with people who didn't see things as quickly as she did or who hadn't grasped a concept fully formed as she was able to do. But she was Darcey's best friend and the two of them stayed friends even when Darcey went home to be with Minette after Martin left, and even as Nieve's own career with Christie's continued to develop.

Darcey knew, because Nieve told her, that part of her fledgling success was due to her own help. She'd done a few more late-night translations for her friend, wishing that her calls didn't always coincide with the nights she was totally knackered to start with, but her tiredness didn't affect her ability to translate the words. Nor did it stop her from picking up two errors in the figures either. Nieve told her that Max had been very pleased when she pointed those out to him.

'Glad to be of help,' she said. 'Now any chance you could piss off and let a girl get some sleep?'

'Why don't you give up that crappy shift job and do something worthwhile?' asked Nieve. 'I could get you something with Max, I know I could.'

'Nieve – it's nearly midnight and you're still working! Whose job is crap?'

'I'm being paid for the crap-ness,' said Nieve.

'It's all about money now, isn't it?' Darcey sounded irritated. 'There's more to life.'

'Not in a bloody call centre.'

Darcey said nothing. The truth was that she agreed with Nieve about Car Crew. The work was becoming repetitive. But there were compensations. And the main compensation was Aidan Clarke.

It wasn't just that she'd fallen head over heels in love with him. It was that with Aidan, she was a different person. A Darcey McGonigle who laughed at life and at herself. A Darcey McGonigle who told him her deepest, innermost thoughts so that there was nothing that she hid from him. He knew that she hated being thought of as a smarty-pants but that she secretly enjoyed being quicker and brighter than most people around her. He knew that she hated her curly hair with a passion but that she equally hated the obsession that seemed to have taken over every female she knew with primping and preening and grooming themselves to within an inch of their lives. He knew that she'd felt left out as a child because Amelie and Tish were so close, and that she felt much, much closer to her best friend, Nieve, than she ever did to her sisters. He knew that, until he'd come along, Nieve was the only person she'd ever confided in. He knew almost as much about Nieve as he knew about Darcey, and told her that it was amusing to know so much about a girl he'd never met, although she sounded far too demanding for him. In Aidan's company Darcey felt completely relaxed. For the first time in her life she was thinking about a man as a friend and not just a boyfriend, and Aidan was now her best friend. Whenever she was with him she felt as though her life was complete. Before Aidan, all that mattered to her was knowing stuff. Knowing people was less important. Since meeting him, her views had changed. People were more important than facts. More important than anything. And Aidan was the most important person in her life.

Alone at night, she sometimes worried that she loved Aidan more than he loved her. She'd read once that in a relationship there was one person who loved and one person who let themselves be loved. She hoped that Aidan didn't just let himself be loved by her. She hoped he felt the same way.

When she was with him she had no doubts. He could hardly keep his hands off her, and she wasn't embarrassed by her slightly pudgy stomach or low-slung bum when she was with him. It was more than just the sex, though. It was everything. He was proud of her abilities and never made her feel too sharp for her own good (as one of her previous short-lived boyfriends had called her). Darcey thought that Aidan was the best boyfriend in the world and she wondered how on earth she had lived without him. But she still worried that her love for him was greater than his for her. On the nights that she didn't go out with him she stayed home with Minette and watched TV (or stayed home on her own when Minette went to her art class and her pottery class – she'd taken up evening classes to get herself out of the house and meet new people). But those nights Aidan went to the gym or met the guys in a pub for a few beers. He hardly ever stayed home alone. It bothered her that he was more sociable than she was, but she had to admit to herself that, despite the progress she'd made at Car Crew, she still wasn't the most sociable person in the world.

Then Emma Jones told her that she knew for a fact that Aidan was in love with her. Emma knew Conor, one of Aidan's flatmates (it was impossible not to know someone who didn't know someone else in Galway, Darcey often thought. You had to be really careful whenever you were out in case you said the wrong thing to the wrong person. One day it might become a big enough city for people to be strangers. But it hadn't happened yet), and Conor had told Emma that Aidan was thinking of asking Darcey to marry him. He'd sworn Emma to secrecy, which was why Emma had immediately confided in Darcey. According to Conor, Aidan was actually besotted with her, and the reason he went out every Wednesday and Friday with the lads was that he didn't want her to think that he was pathetically in love! But, he'd said, he was pretty sure she was The One. When he thought about being with her for the rest of his life, he felt comfortable.

Darcey had nearly fainted when Emma told her this. Until she'd met Aidan, she hadn't thought much about getting married at all. She'd had a horrible feeling that she was the sort of girl that blokes didn't really want to marry. She wasn't good at pandering to their egos. She didn't look fabulous even when she pulled out all the stops. And despite the redeeming fact that she was a good kisser and getting better in bed, she simply wasn't a man's woman. She knew that.

Yet Aidan Clarke wanted to marry her. It was the single most exciting thing ever to have happened to her – more exciting than getting the results of her Leaving Cert and seeing her photo in the paper the following day because she'd got the best results of anyone who'd sat the exam that year, and much more exciting than graduating from college with her unwanted commerce degree (she'd only taken it because that was what Nieve had been doing and because Martin had said that it would be more useful than wasting her time on pure maths). She told herself that she shouldn't be more excited by a man wanting to marry her than by doing well in her exams, but, she consoled herself, everyone wanted to be loved. It didn't make you less of a person just because you'd fallen for a guy and he'd fallen for you in return. The only slight niggle about the whole thing was that he thought life with her would be comfortable. She wanted him to think that it would be wonderful!

Emma hinted to her that Aidan was going to pop the question on the night of his birthday. Emma thought, but wasn't certain, that he'd even picked out a ring. Darcey was surprised by this, because she didn't think that Aidan would have chosen something without her there. But the idea of him going into a shop and buying her a ring was even more romantic than the two of them choosing it together.

She thought long and hard about the evening of his birthday. Knowing Aidan, he would probably want to take her to a fancy restaurant and present the ring to her during dinner. It would be the sort of expansive gesture that he liked. But she couldn't help thinking that when he did do it she wanted to be alone with him so that the moment could be hers to keep for ever. She didn't want anyone around to watch the most precious time in her life. She wanted it to be theirs alone.

Which was why, when Minette told her that she was heading off to Belfast to visit Nerys for a few days, days that included Aidan's birthday, Darcey decided that she would invite him to the house for a birthday dinner she would cook herself.

Darcey hoped that cooking for him would be a sexy sort of thing to do. She suppressed her doubts about letting him taste her cooking before he actually proposed because she knew that she wasn't a confident cook and she didn't want to scare him off. But fortunately he didn't love her for her skill with a frying pan. She'd often wondered, though, how she could be the daughter of a woman who could produce amazing dishes like coq au vin or the tenderest filet mignon accompanied by perfect vegetables and rosti without any seeming effort, when she herself was a serial toast-burner. However, since Aidan, Conor and Pat were utterly hopeless in the kitchen, she knew she didn't have much to live up to, and hopefully Aidan would think she was brilliant.

Her plan was to cook for him and give him the opportunity of proposing to her in intimate surroundings where, after accepting, they could make love together without the constant fear of being interrupted by Conor or Pat coming home from football or rugby or crashing around the flat after a few pints.

Darcey was surprised at how excited she was becoming about the whole thing. She rang Nieve to ask advice on the best way (in Nieve's opinion) to accept a marriage proposal, but she kept getting the answering machine on her friend's phone and it wasn't the sort of thing she wanted to leave as a message. It didn't matter, though. She spent the week practising different replies, and late at night would sit up in bed and write the name Darcey Clarke over and over again on the notepad which she kept in her locked drawer, before crumpling up the page in case actually writing the name before he asked her might be bad luck.

The week before his birthday (when she worried that he might pop the question early and ruin her planned night of passion and food) she trawled through Minette's recipe book in the hope of finding the perfect first meal to cook for the man who was going to be her husband. As she flicked through the pages she couldn't help wondering if she was being pathetically pre-feminist and downtrodden by wanting to do something so earth-motherish as cook for him. But she dismissed the thought. After all, if they had great sex afterwards, surely that was a *Cosmo* kind of thing to do? Maybe once she was engaged to him she'd devote equal time to both cooking and her career so that she could be one of those enviable women who had it all.

Minette's book wasn't a traditional recipe book because she more or less made up her own dishes as she went along, but the folder was full of cuttings from papers and magazines that she'd used to come up with her ideas, as well as notes for dishes that she'd devised herself. Darcey's plan was to choose a recipe that she could follow with ease and that would more or less cook itself while still looking fantastic. She was far too sensible to pick something difficult and complicated that would have her in a frazzle of nerves all night.

Nevertheless, it took her longer than she thought to find even a starter she could feel confident about. As she read through the various recipes she asked herself whether she wouldn't just be better off buying a ready-made meal in the supermarket and passing it off as her own. But that would be copping out, and she never copped out. So she clamped down on her ever-increasing doubts about the wisdom of doing this in the first place and eventually decided on a starter of duck with cranberries, which had the decided advantage of presenting the duck chopped and the cranberries mashed.

She'd already decided that her main course would be veal with Parma ham. This was something she'd seen Nieve cook in Spain a number of times, and Nieve had given her the recipe, telling her that it was practically foolproof. Nieve had always liked cooking; when she'd been smaller, she used to follow Minette around the kitchen asking incessant questions about what she was doing – Minette had often sighed and wished aloud that Darcey had taken the same interest as her friend. Darcey knew that Nieve had been given the veal and Parma ham recipe by Maria, the cook who worked for the Christies, and that it was absolutely gorgeous. Darcey felt that, even if she didn't get the recipe exactly right, she could fake it enough for Aidan.

It was the only part of the night she intended faking. She'd also bought a large quantity of aromatherapy candles for the undomesticated part of the evening. She'd chosen patchouli, palmarosa and sandalwood scents, which were supposed to enhance the sensual experience, and had splashed out on a very expensive massage oil which, according to the label, would transport them into higher planes of pleasure. Darcey was hoping that, following Aidan's birthday night, she would be able to tick 'yes' in the boxes of the quizzes that asked if you'd ever experienced multiple orgasms (though she secretly thought that she probably wouldn't need the massage oils and the candles – the engagement ring would do the trick).

She supposed that she had an unfair advantage in knowing Aidan's plans. But knowing them meant that she could turn this day into one of the most memorable of their lives. It was going to be perfect. She couldn't wait.

# Chapter 11

Years later, when Darcey saw Nigella Lawson doing her domestic goddess thing in the kitchen, she knew that was how she'd imagined herself cooking for Aidan. Totally feminine and nurturing while still being utterly sexy. Of course Nigella did have the advantage of looking fabulous. And of being a much better cook. But she was doing exactly what Darcey had wanted to do.

However, Darcey wasn't worried about her prowess in the kitchen that day. She was totally confident that she could manage to produce something edible even if it didn't quite match the glossy pictures in the recipe books. She also started the cooking preparations in plenty of time so that if she made a complete hash of something she'd have time to sort it out. And she comforted herself with the thought that if the worst came to the worst, the most romantic meal they'd ever had together was on that first night when she'd dripped tomato sauce down her chin and he'd wiped it off with the tip of his finger in the most sensual gesture she'd ever experienced. But she wasn't going to let things descend into a crisis. She was organised and ready to go.

By six, she was feeling good about things and had decided that she was her mother's daughter after all when it came to cooking. Following a recipe, she decided, was the same as following a mathematical equation. True, she'd made a bit of a hash of crushing the peppercorns with the pestle and mortar and had sent the entire thing skittering across the worktop and crashing to the floor with a thud which had smashed the bowl and left the floor covered in black pepper and shards of white ceramic, but she reckoned that if that was the worst that happened she was on to a winner. She swept up the debris and abandoned that part of the recipe, simply grinding pepper over the duck instead (wondering why the recipe had called for such a complicated way of doing things when surely everyone had a pepper mill). Some of these foodies were far too pretentious for their own good, she thought, as she made a mental note to buy her mother a new pestle and mortar. When the duck was safely in the oven, she took herself off to the bathroom and luxuriated in a hot bubble bath scented with oil she'd brought back from Marbella. She had everything under control. It was going to be wonderful. She drifted into a pleasant half-sleep, thinking of just how wonderful it was going to be and murmuring the name 'Darcey Clarke' over and over again.

A ring at the doorbell meant that she had to leap out of the bath and pull on her robe in a hurry, which somehow caused her to slip on the bathroom floor. She grabbed the towel rail for support. The rail, put up by Martin twenty years earlier, hadn't been designed for emergency situations. It came away from the back of the door so that she ended up sitting on the floor with tears running down her cheeks because she'd banged her lip against the side of the bath and bitten her tongue as she fell.

The bell rang again.

'All right, all right,' she muttered as she got up, gingerly dabbing at the corner of her lip, which she could feel swelling up by the second.

The bell rang again.

'Aidan.' She looked at him in surprise.

'Jeez, Darcey!' His eyes opened wide. 'What the hell happened to you?'

She glanced at the wall mirror. Her lip was now about twice its normal size.

'I banged it,' she said.

'Looks painful.' He reached out to touch it but she recoiled from him.

'I'm sure it'll be OK in a while,' she said apologetically. 'But it's really sore now. And I bit my tongue.'

'What on earth were you doing?'

'Getting out of the bath,' she said.

'Oh, shit. That's my fault, isn't it? I'm way too early. But the lads are watching soccer on the telly and you know I couldn't really give a damn about it. Suddenly it seemed a much better idea to come here.' His eyes crinkled at her and he leaned forward to kiss her on the cheek.

'Not your fault at all.' She turned her face sideways to him for another kiss. 'I wasn't paying attention and you know what I'm like. Miss Clumsy, that's me.'

'Ah, you're not really. And I didn't mean to interrupt your bath.' He stepped into the hallway and then sniffed the air appreciatively. 'Something smells good.'

She glanced towards the kitchen. 'I'm cooking for you.'

'I know you said you were going to, but deep down I thought we'd end up with beans on toast or a curry from the takeaway.' He followed her, his arms around her waist, as she walked into the kitchen and peered through the glass door of the oven. 'And you've started already? You really didn't have to go to any trouble.'

'It takes a lot of time,' she told him. 'Everything's fine.' And then she thought that she still had to take out the duck and shred it and let it cool, and she had to make the cranberry compote too, and she suddenly felt very pressurised. She'd planned to do all these things before Aidan arrived, so that if she did something really stupid (like breaking the mortar bowl) he wouldn't know about it.

'It smells better than the takeaway,' he told her. 'But then so do you.' His arms were around her and he was pushing the robe from her shoulders. 'I can't keep my hands – or my lips – off you!'

'Yeah, but keep them off *my* lips, will you,' she reminded him.

'Obviously,' he said. 'I know some people go for the fuller-lipped woman, but that's quite scary.'

'Thanks,' she said wryly.

'Oh, there are other places on you that I want to kiss, Mizz McGonigle.' Aidan pushed the robe a little lower. 'Thick lip or not, you're very, very desirable standing there all washed and clean-looking, with your face pink and your hair stuck to your forehead.'

'It's not, is it?' She made a face. 'I need to dry it. It's a total mess when I don't dry it.'

'I like you being a mess.' He kissed her again. 'And I like the idea of making love to you here and now.'

'In the kitchen!' She sounded scandalised.

'Hey, all the best movies have people making love in the kitchen,' he told her. 'It's definitely an erotic hotspot.'

She'd been feeling erotic herself earlier, but not now. Her lip was throbbing and her tongue still hurt too.

'I haven't finished cooking yet,' she told him.

His eyes twinkled. 'Who says you have to finish cooking?'

'Nobody. But . . . but . . . this is the *kitchen*, Aidan. My mother cooks in here.'

'So?'

'Well – you know . . .'

'Making love in the kitchen is absolutely the thing to do. Haven't you seen those movies where they get down and dirty on the worktop?'

She giggled suddenly. 'It's not that I don't want to . . . but it's *Maman's* kitchen! I think I have deep psychological scars about the idea of . . .' She giggled again. 'But I'll give it a try.'

He put his arms around her and drew her closer to him. He was right, she thought, as she ignored her stinging lip. The smell of the duck and the aroma of the spices were somehow heady and exciting, and she could push the thoughts of Minette slicing carrots and onions on this very worktop to the back of her mind, because what was going to happen on the worktop now was . . . She yelped sharply as she moved her bare foot on to a shard of ceramic from the mortar bowl that she'd missed sweeping up earlier.

'Shit!' she cried, hopping around the kitchen.

'What's wrong?' Aidan looked at her in surprise and then saw the blood dripping from her foot. His face whitened and his expression changed to one of horror. 'Oh, Darcey. Look, sorry. I . . . I don't do blood. It makes me dizzy.'

She could see that his face had gone very pale and she helped him to a chair, where he immediately put his head between his knees. 'Sorry,' he mumbled again. 'I feel such a fool.'

'No, it's fine. You're fine. Don't worry. And it's not that bad,' she added, although it seemed to her that she was spreading blood all over the place as she hopped the length of the kitchen floor. 'I just need a plaster.'

The first-aid box was in a cupboard at the other end of the room. By the time she eventually managed to stick a plaster on her foot, the floor looked like a scene from a horror movie.

'Sorted,' she told Aidan eventually.

'Sorry,' he said again as he lifted his head gingerly. 'Blood makes me sick. That's why I'm so hopeless at contact sports.'

'It's OK,' she said. 'But it's not a great start to your birthday dinner.' She sat on his lap. 'Perhaps I can fix that now.' She leaned forward.

'It's not that I don't want to,' he told her as he put his arm around her. 'Or that I won't want to. But I need a few more minutes to get myself back together. I know that blokes are supposed to be fine over blood and gore and stuff, but it really freaks me out. I fainted the one and only time I had a blood test. It was so pathetic. All these grannies were zipping by me with no problems whatsoever, and I was flat on my back. Very macho, I don't think!'

She chuckled. 'Never mind, you're still macho to me. I'll go upstairs. Dry my hair. Get dressed. Cook dinner. After that, you should be all right.'

'Thanks.' He smiled faintly at her and she realised that he really was very pale.

'Would you like some tea?' she asked. 'That's good if you've had a shock, isn't it? I suppose it must be good for people who've seen other people nearly bleed to death.'

'Don't say that,' he said tightly. 'Don't even joke about it.'

'OK, OK.' She got up from his lap.

'But tea would be nice.'

She made him some tea and dumped extra sugar in it to counteract his shock. He was still very pale when she gave it to him.

'I'm such an idiot,' he confessed. 'And a total wimp. You were so strong and determined, and you just wearing a robe! I'm impressed.'

She flushed and kissed him on the cheek. 'Thank you. Now I'll go and dry my hair and put on a bit more than the robe.'

'Not on my account.' He smiled wanly as she walked out of the room.

It wasn't a great start, she thought wryly. But things could only get better. Things *would* get better, and very, very soon!

As she stepped on to the first stair, she brushed against Aidan's jacket. She hesitated. Was there any chance whatsoever the ring was in the jacket pocket? Did she dare look? She stood on the step indecisively. Looking would ruin the surprise. And if the ring wasn't there – well, maybe that meant he wasn't going to ask her. Maybe Emma Jones was having her on. Darcey felt herself flush at the thought. But why would Emma do that? Emma was a friend. There was no reason for her to lie.

She had to know. OK, it wouldn't definitely confirm anything, because maybe he had the ring in the pocket of his trousers and not his jacket, but she couldn't walk upstairs without checking. Quickly she patted the pockets of the jacket. They were empty. She felt a bitter twist of disappointment engulf her. And then she thought about the inside pocket. She slid her hand into it and her fingers touched something small and square. Trembling, she took it out. It was a red box.

She didn't dare open it, did she? Was there some rule about bad luck and engagement rings? She didn't know. But she knew that she had to see inside. What if it wasn't an engagement ring at all? She'd feel like such a fool if he gave it to her and it was nothing more than a pair of earrings or something. Though why would he come to the house on his birthday (surely expecting a present from her!) with a jewellery box if he wasn't going to propose.

The voice of a sports commentator wafted from the living room, and she heard Aidan talking back to the TV in return. She had to open it. She just had to. She held her breath as she eased the lid open.

The ring was beautiful. He knew her taste. It was a delicate band of gold into which were set three diamonds that glittered in the light against their dark velvet backdrop. It was the most beautiful piece of jewellery she'd ever seen in her life.

Her mouth was dry. Mrs Aidan Clarke. Darcey Clarke. That was her future. The future she realised she wanted. She didn't want to be the girl who everyone found intimidatingly smart. She didn't want to be a career chick like Nieve. She absolutely and totally wanted to be Mrs Darcey Clarke and live with Aidan for the rest of her life. She swallowed with difficulty and closed the box, replacing it in the jacket pocket. Then she tiptoed up the stairs and into the bathroom.

The bath was still full of now tepid water and the bubbles had left a scum on the top. She didn't care. She pulled the plug and sat on the edge of the bath as the water emptied and tried not to laugh out loud with delight. He loved her as much as she loved him after all. She'd been wrong to doubt him. Now she had no doubts at all. Thinking of herself as Mrs Clarke (she didn't care about the whole feminist thing of keeping her own name – she definitely wanted to be known as Mrs Clarke), she felt that there were a whole range of new possibilities open to her. Or perhaps there weren't. It didn't matter. What mattered was that she had found the love of her life and he loved her too.

And, she thought fleetingly, as the last of the water gurgled down the drain, she was beating Nieve Stapleton to the altar. Of course it shouldn't matter that she was doing this. (Darcey did feel, this time, a touch of feminist guilt.) It wasn't a race to see who could get married first. But it was still nice to be the one to do it. She was getting a bit fed up with Nieve and all her bragging about her glittering career with Max Christie and the massive amount of money she was apparently earning. This time Darcey had something of her own to brag about. And she could prove to Nieve that there were, indeed, some things more important than money.

She got up from the bath and looked at herself in the mirror of the bathroom cabinet. Her lip was still swollen, although it seemed to be going down a bit now. Honestly, she thought, she was a desperate lump of a person sometimes.

She went into her bedroom and took out of the wardrobe the pretty new dress that she'd picked up at twenty per cent off in a tiny boutique off Shop Street. As she pulled it over her head, she allowed herself to daydream about her future with Aidan. Perhaps she'd change jobs, although she liked the idea of working in the same company as him for ever. But maybe it would be better not to. Perhaps she could find something more interesting. Or go back to college. Or start a family. She knew that he loved kids. So two children maybe. Not straight away, because they had a life to lead first, but they'd have children together. One of each. A boy named . . . Wolfgang, maybe, after her Swiss grandfather. They'd abbreviate it to Wolfie, though. You couldn't lumber an Irish kid with the name Wolfgang, but Wolfie was kind of boyish and strong. And a girl. She wanted a daughter too. She'd have to think of the right name for her – a name that conjured up brilliance but femininity, beauty and strength. She smiled. She wanted her daughter to be perfect. She supposed every mother felt that way. She gazed at herself unseeingly in the mirror for a few moments as she pictured Wolfie and her perfect daughter playing in the back garden. And then the doorbell rang and brought her back to the present.

Damn, she thought. If Amelie and Tish had called around

for a girlie evening, they could just leave straight away. She certainly didn't want the twins delaying Aidan's declaration of undying love and his handing over of the gorgeous engagement ring!

'Don't worry, I'll get it.' His voice floated up the stairs.

Darcey hesitated, then decided to give her damp hair a quick blast with the hairdryer before going down and getting rid of her sisters if necessary. They liked Aidan too and she could just see them settling down for an evening's gossip with him. But not tonight!

She skimped on the hair-drying, slapped on some perfunctory make-up and got dressed. Then she went downstairs, limping slightly because her foot still hurt. She opened the living room door and stood still, looking at their visitor with amazement. Not Tish or Amelie after all. The glamorous girl – when had she become so gorgeous? – smiled at her.

'Nieve!' Darcey exclaimed. 'What are you doing here?'

'Great welcome home that is,' said her friend drily.

'It's lovely to see you.' Darcey hugged her friend. 'I'm just surprised. You didn't call.'

'I wasn't expecting to be home,' said Nieve. 'Then things changed, so here I am. I got here earlier this afternoon. I was going to phone you, but then I thought, why not just surprise you?' She grinned. 'I didn't realise I'd be surprisingly you so literally.'

'It's OK,' said Darcey, who had recovered from the shock of seeing her friend. 'I'm thrilled you're back.'

'Aidan's been looking after me.' Nieve winked wickedly at her friend. 'Why didn't you tell me before how damn sexy he is?'

Darcey thought, for an instant, that Aidan was blushing. But he never blushed. She grinned.

'Ah, it's only because he's scrubbed up well tonight,' she told her friend. 'Most of the time he's a wreck.' But she took Aidan's hand and squeezed it to show she was joking.

'You look lovely too,' said Nieve. 'And you're wearing a dress!'

'*You* look absolutely amazing,' Darcey told her. 'A different woman.'

'Yes, well.' Nieve shrugged. 'I've glammed up a bit all right.'

More than a bit, thought Darcey, clamping down on an uncharacteristic spurt of envy. Her friend looked fabulous.

'And what a change,' said Aidan. 'I told her she looks a lot hotter now than in that photo of her you showed me.'

Nieve laughed.

'She's certainly changed more than me,' admitted Darcey. 'I guess I don't clean up as well.'

'Of course you do,' said Aidan loyally. 'You're stunning. I love the dress.'

Darcey didn't know whether to believe him, because although she usually wore a skirt and blouse to the office, she invariably wore jeans at home. The twenty per cent discount had swayed her into believing that she could be the sort of person who looked good in the girly, floaty dress with its pattern of red roses on the white skirt and bodice, and which the sales assistant assured her looked 'sweet'. She'd wanted to look sweet and vulnerable and romantic for Aidan so that he would feel ultra-masculine when he proposed to her, but deep down she didn't really think she was the kind of girl who could carry off sweetness.

Nieve was laughing. 'As you can see, I'm not a dress person either.' She waved at her figure-hugging jeans and tight red top which should have looked like a casual weekend outfit but somehow managed to appear incredibly sexy on her. Darcey wondered whether it had anything to do with the fact that Nieve's raven hair was now falling around her shoulders in big loose curls instead of hiding her face as it had done before; or whether it was that she was now Hollywood thin; or whether it was just that the red top and tight jeans were complemented by very high-heeled boots and discreet, but clearly expensive, jewellery, while Nieve's long nails (they'd never been long before; Nieve had bitten her nails, for heaven's sake!) were painted a colour that matched her top. Nieve looked grown-up, thought Darcey. And vampy. While Darcey herself was still just playing at being grown-up and was actually trying to look innocent.

As Darcey looked at her, Nieve opened her bag and took out a small box.

'What's this?' asked Darcey.

'Open it.'

Darcey lifted the lid and looked inside. The necklace with the tiny diamond that she'd loaned to Nieve before she left Spain nestled in a bed of cotton wool. Along with a pair of sparkling diamond earrings. She looked up at Nieve.

'I'm sorry about your necklace,' Nieve said. 'You headed off in such a rush that I didn't get to return it to you. And the earrings are a thank-you for all the translating work you did for me.'

'They're amazing,' said Darcey slowly. 'But you didn't need to do this, Nieve. I'm sure they cost you a fortune . . .'

'Ah, don't start that! You deserve them. I told you I'd look after you for all that work. And I can afford it.'

'Are you absolutely sure?'

'Of course,' said Nieve impatiently. 'Don't be daft, Darce! I bought them for you.'

'Well in that case, thanks very much.' Darcey took the necklace out of the box and fastened it around her throat. It was good to have it back. She'd thought about it from time to time, wondering when and how she'd ever manage to mention it to Nieve without sounding bitchy. Now she felt bad that she'd wondered if her friend would ever return it. She took out the plain gold stud earrings she'd been wearing and put in the diamond ones instead. They sparkled fierily in the light and made her feel equally bad about the nights she'd resented Nieve ringing her up with requests for help. But, she admitted, Nieve had paid her back in spades with such gorgeous jewellery, and they'd go wonderfully well with the ring still nestling in the box in Aidan's jacket pocket!

'So, are you back for a flying visit or what?' she asked as she secured the earrings while hoping that Nieve wouldn't hang around for too long. She wanted to catch up with her friend, but not tonight.

'Or what,' said Nieve.

'Oh?' Darcey looked at her curiously.

'I'm not working with Max any more.'

'Nieve! Why? I thought you loved it there. And you sure were climbing the greasy pole of success!'

'Yeah, well, it was all going great and Max was really

starting to trust me about everything, and there was this conference coming up when he was so bloody demanding and pushed loads of work on to me . . .' Nieve looked angry as she recounted her tale. 'At the same time we were working on a property deal . . . Anyway, I wanted to show him how on top of it all I was. I knew that one of the guys in the real-estate division had looked at the deal, and so one evening I accessed his computer and found his work on it and presented it to Max.'

Darcey stared at her. 'You stole someone else's work!'

'Oh, don't be so silly,' said Nieve impatiently. 'Jerome would've had to give me the file anyway in order for Max to see it. I just pre-empted it. Unfortunately there was a mistake in his bloody calculations! I should've checked them with you first, Darce! Max spotted the mistake. That wasn't the problem. The problem was that Jer met him that morning in the lift and told him he'd been doing work on the project but had corrected the mistake. So Max knew I'd lifted it.'

'Does that matter really?' Aidan shrugged. 'That's the sort of thing that goes on in big business, isn't it?'

'All the time,' agreed Nieve. 'It's a dog-eat-dog world. However, Max threw a bit of a wobbler and asked me how much else I was just lifting from colleagues and not giving them credit for. The annoying part is that this was the only time I'd ever done something like that. But at that point he decided that everything I'd ever done was suspect. He told me he was firing me.'

'Oh, Nieve, no!' Darcey was aghast.

Nieve grinned. 'It could've been worse. I told him if he

fired me I'd tell Lilith about him and Maria. I think he'd forgotten about that.'

'Lilith and Maria?' Aidan asked.

Nieve related the story of her discovery of Max and the housekeeper, and Aidan roared with laughter.

'I like it. I like the fact that he screwed her and you screwed him.'

'Aidan!' Darcey exclaimed.

'Chill out, Darce. It happens,' said Nieve.

'Well, I know stuff happens. It's just . . . you kind of think it happens to other people. Not to people you know. Whenever I think of you walking in on him and her and then having the nerve to threaten him afterwards – it just seems a bit seedy somehow.'

'If he hadn't been so stupid as to shit on his own doorstep I wouldn't have been able to do anything,' retorted Nieve. 'As it is, I worked really, really hard for him, and the truth is he never paid me as much as I was worth.'

'More fool him,' said Aidan.

'So what now?' asked Darcey.

'Now I have some time off before going to Jugomax California,' she told them.

'Jugomax?' Aidan looked at her questioningly.

'It's a start-up company in the States,' explained Nieve. 'One of his subsidiaries. An internet company selling toys and games. He thinks it's going to be huge. They're still working on the set-up details, but I'm on the payroll and I'll be heading there soon.'

'You've really fallen on your feet, haven't you?' said Darcey.

'Oh, hey, I'm doing well, but then that's always been what I wanted,' said Nieve.

'It's not just Jugomax, it's everything. Your job, your look, everything.' Darcey realised that she sounded envious, although she'd nothing to envy. After all, she was the one to have snared the gorgeous guy. She was the one who'd be wearing a fabulous engagement ring by the end of the evening. It didn't matter how great Nieve looked. Darcey knew that she herself was the lucky one.

Nieve chuckled. 'Ah, the look's not that fantastic. It's just a big change. You should've seen some of the other girls at Christie's. They'd really make you feel pea-green.'

'It's such a dramatic change, though,' said Darcey. 'You were never very interested in clothes before. You were kind of prim with your dead-straight hair – which, as you know, I always craved – and your neat skirts and tops.'

Nieve shrugged and then tapped her red nails against her thigh. 'Max made me do all this,' she said. 'He said that I was letting him down going to meetings and not being groomed and stuff. He was right. As soon as I got my hair done and my eyebrows plucked and lost a few pounds – well, it made a difference. People took me more seriously and they took him more seriously too. It's weird,' she added, 'how much appearances count. I was doing exactly the same stuff, but because I looked the part people believed in it more. Daft, but true.'

Darcey smoothed her own hair. 'Maybe a radical makeover is what I need at Car Crew to really get ahead.'

'But you don't want to get on at Car Crew,' objected Aidan. 'You're bored with it. You've said so a million times.'

He frowned. 'You told me you were thinking of chucking it in and trying something else.'

'Really?' asked Nieve.

'Maybe.' Darcey shrugged. 'I don't suppose anything I get will be as good as a start-up company in California.'

Nieve smiled. 'It's all what you make it,' she said. 'I bet you could make it really big in car hire if you wanted. If there's such a thing as making it big in car hire. I know that I want to make it really big in California.'

'Wow.' Aidan grinned. 'Determined or what?'

'She was always determined,' said Darcey. 'I remember at college—'

'Oh, no. Not college tales.' Nieve interrupted her. 'Look, Darce, I'd better go. I didn't mean to barge in and I certainly didn't think there'd be anyone here with you other than your mam. I wanted to say hello to her too.' She grinned. 'But of course I'm thrilled to have met you at last, Aidan. Sometimes when I've rung Darcey late at night she's just come home from seeing you, she sounds sooooo much like the cat that got the cream!'

'Nieve!' Darcey blushed flame-red and Aidan laughed.

'So listen, I'll head off. Why don't you give me a shout tomorrow?' said Nieve.

'Don't go.' Aidan put his hand on her arm. 'We were going to have dinner. You might as well stay.'

'Oh, I don't want to interrupt . . .' Nieve looked questioningly at Darcey.

'It's not a problem,' said Darcey slowly, although she couldn't believe that Aidan had asked her friend to stay. Surely he'd want to get rid of her too so that he could pop the question and they could celebrate together. 'It's Aidan's birthday. I'm cooking him dinner.'

'Is that your birthday present to him?' Nieve roared with laughter. 'You cooking for him! Aidan, don't you know that she's the world's worst cook?'

'I don't know about that,' said Aidan. 'There was a gorgeous smell earlier.' He sniffed and frowned.

'Oh, crap, the duck! I forgot to turn the oven off.'

Darcey hurried out of the living room and into the kitchen. She opened the oven door. The duck had caramelised inside the pot.

'Y'see,' said Nieve, who'd followed her.

'It doesn't matter about the duck.' Aidan peered around the door. 'I'm not crazy about it anyway.'

'Oh.' Darcey was taken aback. 'It doesn't matter. It was only the starter.'

'So what was for main course?' asked Nieve.

'Um . . . veal in Parma ham,' Darcey replied.

'*My* veal in Parma ham?' Nieve opened her eyes wide.

'Well, yes, your recipe.'

'In that case, let me cook.' Nieve smiled brightly at them. 'Why don't you two go inside and relax and I'll make dinner for you? It can be Aidan's birthday present from me. And it takes the pressure off you, Darcey.'

'I . . .' Darcey didn't know what to say. There was no doubt that the meal would be a million times better if Nieve cooked it. But it was something she'd wanted to do herself. It was her domestic goddess moment. She had a horrible feeling that with Nieve's arrival, the evening of romance was suddenly careering off in a different direction.

'Great idea,' said Aidan. 'Come on, Darcey. Let's sit down and have a drink and let your poor friend do all the hard work.'

'I don't know if . . .'

'Oh, go on,' said Nieve. 'It's not that often that I get a chance to do some cooking myself these days. If I'm not off at a business dinner with Max, it's takeaways and microwave meals for one. I'd like to cook.'

'If you're sure . . .' said Darcey doubtfully.

'Sure I'm sure,' said Nieve. 'Go on, get inside and relax. Let me do things in the kitchen.'

And Darcey simply wasn't able to say no.

They'd drunk a glass of wine each and Darcey had told him lots more stories about her escapades with Nieve by the time her friend came in with the food.

'This is fantastic!' Aidan looked at Nieve appreciatively as he tasted the veal.

'Darcey's mam taught me everything I know.' Nieve grinned back at him. 'She liked teaching me things. Darce never listened.'

Darcey shrugged. 'It was never my thing,' she said.

'So what was your thing?' asked Aidan. 'These days it's all languages and maths for you. Is there something else I don't know about?'

'Hey, – what more do you want?' Darcey didn't mean to sound cranky, but she couldn't help herself. Nieve's arrival had changed everything. Aidan seemed to be bewitched by her, hanging on her every word and paying her far too many compliments, and she'd managed to make Darcey feel both frumpy and inadequate thanks to her gorgeous new look and her incredibly good cooking. Darcey wasn't used to Nieve making her feel inadequate. And of course the meal was totally wasted on her, because she wasn't one bit hungry since all she really wanted from the night was her fabulous engagement ring!

'She was great when we trekked around Europe,' Nieve told him. 'Everywhere we turned up she chatted away, worked out the local currency and made things easy for us.'

'Most people speak English, though, don't they?' said Aidan. 'I mean, you can get by without languages now, can't you?'

'Not the places we went to,' Nieve told him. 'I would've been quite happy in the cities, but Darcey and some of the others had to do this trekking stuff to monasteries in the hills . . .' She grinned at her friend. 'We'd have been lost without her. Literally.'

'She's a great girl all right,' said Aidan.

Darcey glanced at him. His words had sounded forced and patronising, and he wasn't really like that.

'So when do you go to California?' Aidan asked Nieve.

'A few weeks.' Nieve sighed. 'I'll probably just about manage it without going spare, although my mother has me driven demented already.'

'You don't give her a chance,' said Darcey mildly.

'Oh come on!' Two pink spots appeared on Nieve's cheeks. 'You know what she's like, Darce. Nothing I do is ever good enough for her.'

Darcey nodded sympathetically. She liked Gail Stapleton, but she had to admit that she wasn't as easy-going as Minette.

Sometimes Darcey felt that Nieve's desire to succeed all the time was partly because Gail was always urging her to beat her best friend. Nieve had to work hard to get the grades that Darcey achieved without half as much effort, and Gail didn't seem to understand how difficult she sometimes made things.

'Anyway, she can't complain now,' said Nieve cheerfully. 'Off to the States with great prospects, and I'll tell you something, I won't be rushing back.'

'Ah, Nieve, don't say that. You'll miss us. We'll miss you.'

'Well, maybe.' Nieve grinned at her. 'Or maybe you'll chuck in that dreary old call-centre stuff and join me.'

'It's not that bad,' said Darcey defensively.

'But wouldn't California be a million times better?'

'Sounds bloody great to me,' said Aidan.

'I didn't think you were mad about the States,' said Darcey. 'I thought you were a Galway man at heart.'

'Oh, I am,' Aidan assured her. 'But California sounds so much fun. Eternal sunshine . . . Hollywood . . . Silicon Valley . . .'

'Silicon chests more like.' Darcey poked him in the ribs. 'You can forget about that right now, Clarke!'

Nieve chuckled. 'Yeah, maybe I'll get my boobs done when I'm there.'

'You wouldn't!'

'Why not?' Nieve tossed her head so that her hair clouded around her face. 'I've had everything done that's possible without resorting to surgery. Everyone does it there.'

'You're not everyone,' said Darcey. 'You're Nieve Stapleton and you don't need a boob job.'

'Chillax.' Nieve grinned at her. 'You do so rise to the bait sometimes, Darce. You need to lighten up a little.'

'I say that to her all the time,' agreed Aidan.

Darcey looked from one to the other. 'Give me a break.'

'Poor old Darcey.' Nieve leaned over and hugged her. 'Still a bit too serious for your own good.'

'And you're still a bit too damn flighty.'

The two girls looked at each other, a sudden spark of anger between them.

Then Nieve smiled at Darcey. 'Come on, Darce. We're not fighting, are we?'

'Of course not.' Darcey put her knife and fork down. 'Sorry. It's just – well, you look great the way you are. You don't need enhancing.'

'She's right,' said Aidan.

Nieve blushed. 'Thanks.'

'Listen, I'm just going to take some paracetamol.' Darcey pushed her chair back from the table. 'Back in a sec.'

'Are you all right?' Aidan sounded concerned.

'Bit of a headache,' she admitted. 'What with my lip, and my foot . . .'

'Huh?' Nieve looked at her quizzically.

'Long story,' said Darcey.

She tried not to limp back into the kitchen, but her foot was stinging like crazy. She opened the fridge door and poured herself a glass of water, then took a couple of pills. She reckoned that her headache had nothing to do with her lip or her foot but was simply the tension of waiting for Nieve to go so that the real business of the night could start. But the trouble was that Nieve seemed perfectly happy to stay, and Aidan wasn't trying to make her leave either. Darcey knew that he was far too polite to make Nieve feel unwelcome, but she wished she'd had the opportunity to tell her friend to leg it. She hadn't wanted to do anything so obvious as to try to get Nieve on her own, but surely she could see that she wasn't really wanted tonight? Although maybe not. Nieve could be incredibly thick-skinned sometimes!

Darcey finished the glass of water and went back into the dining room. Aidan and Nieve were laughing as she walked in.

'What's the joke?' she asked as she sat down.

'Nothing,' said Nieve cheerfully. 'We were just chatting about the problems of IT. I need to get up to speed on it, since Jugomax is an internet company.'

Darcey nodded and sat down. She joined in the conversation but was lost in the technical detail. She hadn't realised before how clued up Nieve had become. And she couldn't help but be impressed at how businesslike she could be. She could see that Aidan was impressed by the questions she was asking too.

It was after midnight before Nieve finally went home, promising Darcey that they'd have a gossipy lunch together very soon and catch up on all of their news. Darcey nodded enthusiastically at that. California and whatever else Nieve might have to tell her was all very well, but it would be truly trumped by her gorgeous diamond engagement ring.

After she'd gone, Darcey smiled apologetically at Aidan. 'She's great fun but a bit overwhelming at times,' she told him.

'I liked her,' said Aidan. 'I love her energy and her determination. I know I'm not really like that myself, but she makes me feel as though I should rush off to California tomorrow and become some kind of main IT man there.'

'She does have that effect sometimes,' agreed Darcey. 'She's good at getting people to do things they don't really want to do.' She left the room and returned a few moments later with a carefully wrapped box. 'I'm afraid it's past midnight, but happy birthday anyway,' she said as she handed it to him.

It was the latest Wolfenstein PC game, which he'd been wanting to get for ages.

'Thank you.' He smiled at her as he unwrapped the package. 'That's really thoughtful.'

'Well, you know I absolutely hate it and I think it's the goriest game in the history of the world,' she said. 'But you love it.' She chuckled. 'Though that's a bit rich for the guy who collapses at the sight of actual blood.'

'It's fantasy.' He grinned. 'I'd be too chicken to even load a gun in real life.'

'My hero.' She kissed him. He kissed her, avoiding her lip, and suddenly they were making love on the sofa, which, he told her afterwards, was the best birthday present ever. Then he brought her upstairs and they made love again. Afterwards, his arm across her, he fell asleep. But she lay awake for hours in the darkness, wondering exactly when he was going to give her the beautiful, sparkling engagement ring.

# Chapter 12

'So did you get engaged in the end?' Anna asked, as Darcey's voice trailed off. 'Obviously if you did you broke it off, but . . .'

'No. No, we didn't.' Darcey looked pained. 'She made an idiot out of me. She knew what she was doing and she did it anyway and she didn't give a shit.'

Anna looked at her sympathetically. Her friend had never before told her anything about her life prior to joining the company. Anna had guessed, because of Darcey's very uncommitted relationships, that she was wary of getting too involved with men, but she'd never realised that she'd almost got engaged. All the same, she thought fleetingly, it had been a long time ago. She was surprised that it still seemed to matter to Darcey, who was usually so unconcerned about ending relationships.

'He said nothing about the ring that night,' Darcey continued. 'Or the following morning. I got up early and tiptoed down the stairs to check that it was still in his jacket pocket. To check that it was real, to tell you the truth, because I still expected him to give it to me. But he didn't.

It was there all right, but he didn't take it out of the pocket.'

She hadn't known what to say or do. If he'd arrived with the ring he'd obviously intended to give it to her. But despite her dropping a ham-fisted hint about how she needed more jewellery to go with the necklace and the earrings that Nieve had brought, Aidan had simply smiled and told her that he was sure she'd collect plenty of jewellery in her lifetime. And then, after she'd made toast and coffee, he'd told her that he'd promised to meet Conor and Pat that morning because they were going to go to a local GAA match together, and would she mind awfully if he left her now? He'd call, he told her. Or see her in the office.

She'd known then that it had all gone wrong. He hated Gaelic football matches almost as much as he hated soccer. He hardly ever went to them. She wasn't able to comfort herself with the passion of their lovemaking of the previous night, even though she'd thought at the time that it meant everything was OK. He'd been going to ask her to marry him and he'd changed his mind, and the only extra ingredient in the equation was Nieve.

But Nieve hadn't done anything, had she? She'd looked amazing, of course, and flirted with him a bit, but it hadn't been serious. After all, Darcey reasoned, he'd made love to her after Nieve had headed home. He'd hardly have done that if he and Nieve . . . he and Nieve . . . what, exactly? What did she think had happened between her best friend and her almost-fiancé under her very nose? Nothing. She knew that. Nothing had happened, but somehow she'd managed to allow herself to become paranoid about the fact that he hadn't given her the engagement ring that night. Maybe he hadn't felt it was the right time after all. Maybe Nieve's arrival had taken the gloss off the romantic proposal he'd intended. Or maybe, she thought, suddenly and very miserably, maybe he hadn't intended the ring for her at all. Only that didn't make sense. Blokes didn't go around with engagement rings in their jacket pockets and not intend to hand them over to someone!

Darcey closed her eyes and thought back to the first kiss she'd shared with Aidan underneath the sycamore tree. A kiss that had been full of promise. And she remembered the good times they'd had together since then. Nothing had gone wrong between them. Nothing had changed. Despite the hollow feeling in the pit of her stomach, she was certain he'd call. But the phone remained obstinately silent, and when she rang him there was no reply. She thought about going over to the apartment to see him, but that seemed incredibly needy. She didn't want to appear obsessive. And there had been occasional times before when they didn't talk for a day or two. She was making a mountain out of a molehill, wasn't she?

The next time she saw him was at work on Monday. He smiled and told her that they'd had a real boys' day out and he was sorry he hadn't got in touch but he'd been totally the worse for wear and couldn't possibly have inflicted himself upon her in such a state. She asked him if he wanted to go and see a movie that evening, and he told her that he was working late. The tone of his voice seemed wrong to her. She felt the security of her relationship with him disintegrate a little further and the hollow feeling in her stomach deepen.

Emma Jones phoned to ask if congratulations were in order. Darcey didn't know what to say. In the end she told her that they hadn't made a decision, which caused Emma to whistle under her breath and tell her that if she let Aidan Clarke slip through her fingers, then she was a bigger fool than she'd thought. Darcey repeated that she hadn't made a decision and asked Emma not to talk about it. She wasn't at all confident that her colleague would stay quiet. The idea of everyone at Car Crew talking about her and Aidan and the engagement that hadn't happened made her feel sick inside. Because there was no way they'd get the wrong end of the stick like Emma and think that he'd asked her and she'd turned him down. Aidan wouldn't let that happen.

She called into the Stapletons' that evening, but Nieve had gone out – to meet with some friends, Gail told her, and Darcey had wanted to ask who were the friends Nieve had in Galway that she'd be meeting without Darcey? But she didn't. It was the next day before Nieve called around.

'He's cute,' her friend told her when Darcey asked straight out what she thought of Aidan.

'We're thinking of getting married.' Darcey blurted out the words.

'No!' Nieve's eyes widened. 'He's sweet, Darcey, but he's not really your kind of guy.'

'What on earth do you mean? Of course he is.'

'He wants to travel and do different things,' said Nieve. 'He's restless. He needs new experiences.'

'So am I. So do I.'

'Ah, Darce, you know you don't! Not really. You want to travel just to sit somewhere else with your crossword.

And you don't give a shit about a career; you're not in the slightest bit ambitious.'

'I usen't to be. But I think I've changed.'

Nieve said nothing.

'You don't believe me.'

'I don't think you're cut out for big business, that's all,' said Nieve.

'What am I cut out for?' demanded Darcey.

'I don't know,' said Nieve. 'I think you're a bit dreamy for real life most of the time. You could do so much more. I reckon you only use about an eighth of your brain.'

'Rubbish!'

'Hmm,' was all Nieve said in response.


Darcey felt as though she was living in some strange parallel universe. On the surface nothing had changed. But undercurrents swirled around her and she knew somehow that everything had. At the end of the week she went out for a drink with Aidan and asked him if anything was wrong between them.

'Wrong?' He looked uncomfortable.

'Wrong.'

'It's not you . . .' he began doubtfully.

'Oh shit!' She couldn't help it. She hadn't intended to cry, but the tears spilled from her eyes and down her cheeks before she could stop them. 'You're breaking up with me, aren't you?'

'Darcey, we're both young. It was never going to be for ever.'

'You told me you loved me. You made love to me! You—'

'Oh, come on!' His voice was firmer. 'People have sex. It doesn't mean undying love.'

'You told me you loved me,' she repeated miserably. 'And I thought we were going to get married.'

'Why would you think that?'

She couldn't tell him it was because Emma Jones had said so and because she'd peeked in his jacket pocket to see the ring. So she said nothing at all.

'I'm really sorry,' he said. 'There are so many things I need to do before I settle down. I can't . . .' He looked at her regretfully, and Darcey felt as though the bottom had fallen out of her world.

It had never hurt before. Breaking up with people had always been easy, because she'd never felt comfortable with them in the first place. But this was the worst thing that had ever happened to her in her life. How, she asked herself angrily, how had she ever had the nerve to try to cheer up Minette after Martin had left? It must have been so much worse for her mother, and yet she'd been completely unsympathetic. She remembered thinking that Minette just had to get over it. Telling her, in fact, to get a grip. But how did anyone get over a broken heart?

'Everyone thought we were getting engaged,' she said.

'Don't be daft. They couldn't have thought that. They were wrong if they did.'

But he looked at her uncomfortably and she knew that they hadn't been wrong. The ring had been in his jacket pocket, and it had been for her.

'Is it Nieve?' she asked abruptly.

'Of course not.' He sounded unconvincing.

'I don't believe you!'.

'It's not her fault,' said Aidan. 'It was just – meeting her made me think of things differently.'

'How?'

'Oh, Darcey, there's no need to go into all this.'

'Yes there is.'

'I can't help it if I've had to think a lot about what I want over the past few days. You should be glad of that. Glad that I'm not forcing you into making a terrible mistake.'

'Have you seen her since?' asked Darcey.

Aidan said nothing.

'Fuck you.' Darcey rarely swore, but she couldn't help herself. 'Fuck you, and fuck her too.'

'It was a long time ago,' Anna told her as she dipped some bread into the flavoured olive oil on the table in front of them. 'You can't still be nursing a grudge.'

Darcey turned the invitation over in her hand again. 'Not any more I'm not,' she agreed. 'But for ages afterwards I let it mess up my life. I know it sounds daft now, but I felt as though everyone was laughing at me, knowing that my best friend only had to come home and click her fingers for my nearly fiancé to lose interest in me. It was as though I'd been betrayed by the two people I trusted most in the world. And it seemed to me that all men were bastards and lots of women were pretty shabby too! My dad had cheated on my mum. The man I thought I was going to marry cheated on me. And my best friend was the one who happily destroyed my idea of happiness.' She smiled wryly. 'It sounds totally melodramatic now, I know. But back then it took over my life. I couldn't forgive her, you see. I couldn't forgive him either. And I thought that life was very, very unfair.'

'I didn't know about your mum and dad,' said Anna, 'but . . .'

'It's irrelevant really.' Darcey shrugged 'I suppose everything has some kind of effect on you. Dad moving out really bugged me at the time. I swore I'd meet someone better than him, but in the end I didn't. And I didn't deal with it very well afterwards. Instead of time being the great healer and all that bullshit, I got worse with every passing day. I thought about Nieve and Aidan all the time and I couldn't stop brooding. I kept picturing them heading off to the States, laughing at how they'd left me behind. Poor, silly Darcey who thought she was going to get married.' She made a face. 'I was thinking of them feeling sorry for me and I hated it! I hated both of them too. After talking to Aidan, I went to see her. She told me that she was sorry but he was the love of her life. He was supposed to be the love of *my* life! I said that to her and she just told me that I was lucky he'd met her instead because we would've been totally miserable together. She said she knew his type better than I ever would, that he needed a strong woman to bring out the best in him. Cheeky cow! I'm a strong woman.' She snorted. 'At least, I am now! All the same, it's a bit ironic, isn't it? He didn't marry me because of her, but he hasn't married her either. If it was such a great passion . . .'

'It can be a great passion and not end in marriage,' said Anna mildly.

'I know. I know.' Darcey nodded. 'It was just – he was

going to *marry* me. So it's not like he was against marriage. I just can't help wondering why he didn't marry her . . .'

She looked at the invitation again.

'People have all sorts of reasons why they do and don't do things,' said Anna. 'But you'd be crazy to go. What good would it do?'

'Closure?' said Darcey doubtfully.

'Closure is overrated. Besides, you said you're over it. Crikey, you should be. You've changed since then, obviously, because you have a great life now.'

'I know, I know. It's just . . . I can't help remembering it all. How I felt . . .'

'Darcey . . .' There was a warning tone in Anna's voice.

'Oh, look, it's not like I'm planning to do anything really stupid,' said Darcey. 'I've been thinking about it a lot. It might be good for me. I simply want to see them again. That's all.'

'Well then, go if you must, but I think it's a really bad idea,' said Anna. 'Weddings are emotional at the best of times, and what's the point in getting yourself into a state?'

Darcey laughed. 'I know. I know. But . . .' She sighed deeply. 'I haven't felt so . . . so . . . confused in ages. Sending me this invitation – she's messing with my head again.'

'Nobody's messing with your head,' said Anna firmly. 'Look, you have a good job and a great apartment and you've boyfriends wherever and whenever you want them . . . Hell, Darcey, women would kill to be you.'

'Maybe,' said Darcey slowly. 'Though I really don't know why.'

'That's because you can't step back and look at things

from another person's perspective,' said Anna. 'Not in your personal life anyhow. You're great at doing it professionally.'

'Obviously I'm better at my job than at my life,' said Darcey drily. 'Which is a laugh really, 'cos that's not how I expected it to be.'

'Ah, you'll be fine,' Anna told her. 'You always are.'

Darcey put the invitation back into her handbag.

'Absolutely,' she said, her voice steady again. 'Now what about you? You need to get your ducks in a row for your meeting in Edinburgh. Make sure that they know you're the hottest thing since sliced bread in the HR department.'

'My ducks *are* in a row,' said Anna. 'I was thinking, though, that if I seduced Neil Lomond when we got there, it might help.'

'You're not serious!'

'Probably not. But relying on being the best in the world at your job isn't always the way forward,' Anna told her. 'I'm thinking that womanly wiles might be much better. If only I had faith in my womanly wiles.' She pinched her waist. 'I *so* need to lose a few pounds, but I haven't been able to motivate myself to do it. Maybe if I set my sights on Lomond it might be exactly what I need.'

'He might not be available for seducing,' said Darcey. 'Have you found out whether he's married or not?'

'According to his personnel file, he's divorced,' Anna told her. 'Which is good and not good from my point of view. Not married is good. Baggage is bad. No kids, though, which is a plus. Mind you, I don't know if there's anyone in his life right now, but if there isn't . . .'

'You're not really interested in him, surely?'

'Why not?' asked Anna. 'Like I said, he's got the looks. Those eyes . . . and that smile.'

'For heaven's sake!' Darcey put down her fork. 'Get a grip, would you. He's not that great.'

'You're just saying that because he's come in as your boss,' said Anna. 'I know you, Darcey McGonigle. Always needing to be top of the pile. You resent him.'

'That's nonsense,' said Darcey mildly.

'Yeah, right.' Anna laughed. 'Tell me you're not the most ambitious person in the company. Tell me that your friend was completely wrong about you. Go on!'

'I'm not the most ambitious person in the company,' said Darcey easily. 'If I was, I'd be director of new business by now. Which I've somehow failed to achieve.'

'You see!' cried Anna triumphantly. 'I knew you were narked because Mr Sex-on-Legs came in as your boss. It's clouding your judgement.'

'It most certainly isn't,' said Darcey in amusement. 'But I see no need for him to be based here even for a couple of months when he could just as easily look after things from Edinburgh and leave us to our own devices.'

'Has he been interfering?' asked Anna.

'Not overtly,' admitted Darcey. 'But he's talking about a change in my client base, whatever that might mean. He wanted the reports from all my recent trips and he's demanded a business plan for the next year. So I emailed him the plan I'd already done and he emailed me back to say that there was plenty of room to add more to it. Made me feel like I was slacking.'

'You never slack,' Anna told her.

188

'I know. I'm just saying that's how he made me feel.'

'If you were any busier, you'd never be home.'

'I know that too.'

'Bastard,' said Anna.

Darcey peered at her through half-closed eyes. 'You don't really mean that, do you?'

Anna sighed. 'No,' she said. 'I still think he's the best thing that ever happened to the company.'

'Idiot.' Darcey picked up her fork and started to eat again.

'So give me the lowdown on him, since you obviously know something about him.' This time Anna looked at Darcey shrewdly. 'He did ask about you before.'

Darcey said nothing and Anna clicked her fingers in front of her.

'Hello? Earth to Darcey?'

Darcey swallowed her penne and took a mouthful of water.

'It's not important any more,' she said.

'But you do know him already.' Anna's eyes twinkled. 'You sidestepped the issue when I asked if he was an old flame, but you knew him in the past and I get the impression there was something. Since you're 'fessing up all about your love life, you might as well tell me if you had one of your overseas client one-night stands with him. I need to know if I'm thinking of seducing him myself!'

The sun was directly in Darcey's eyes and so she had to shade them with her hand to look straight at Anna. And then her mobile phone rang.

'Speak of the devil,' she said to Anna when she'd finished a rapid conversation. 'He's moved up the deadline for the reports I'm doing. Probably so's he can pull them to pieces before going to Edinburgh.' She pushed the remnants of her lunch away. 'We'd better go. I'll get the bill.'

She spent the afternoon working on the reports, an activity she thought was a complete waste of time. As far as Darcey was concerned, her job was about meeting clients and talking to them, not writing about it. Besides, she hated writing reports. She could draw up spreadsheets and graphs and provide plenty of statistical analysis to back up figures, but she was hopeless with words, and report-writing never came easy to her. All the same, she didn't want to give Neil any reason to fault her work. Not that he'd been able to do that so far. She'd bombarded him with information about her clients and her trips, and this was the last batch of it. She knew that he was just marking his territory by asking for so much from her. She'd seen it before with people who came into organisations. Sometimes they'd spend a while being nice to the staff before blitzing them with demands just to show who was in charge. Darcey didn't care. She'd got over the first feelings of terror about the takeover and about her job. If they wanted to fire her, then let them. She was a valued staff member. If Neil Lomond wanted to get rid of her, it would cost them. And he'd be doing it for personal reasons, not because she wasn't good enough.

Which might not necessarily stop him, she admitted to herself as she stretched her hands over her head. People always said that business wasn't personal, but they usually only said that when there was some kind of personal issue involved! Business, after all, was based around people. Sure, some decisions were made for solely corporate reasons. But many more were made because people didn't get on.

That's a nice way of putting it, she thought, flexing her fingers. Neil and I don't get on. Short and sweet. He's been appointed my boss and we don't get on. And they don't know about the past. Interesting that he's kept that particular piece of information from them.

She sneezed suddenly and sat up straight. She picked her bag up from the floor and took out a tissue. At the same time the wedding invitation fell out again. She shoved it into her desk drawer. She had to stop carrying it around like some sort of time bomb.

Her instant messaging pinged and the window opened on her computer screen.

'Can you drop into my office?' Neil's message said.

Her finger flew over the keyboard. 'Now?'

'Yes, now.'

'Our meeting isn't for another hour. I'm working on report number one thousand and two for you,' she typed rapidly. 'If I drop into your office now it may be delayed.'

'I can live with that.'

'Whatever you want,' she sent.

Neil's office was on the next floor up. She detoured into the Ladies', where she swirled some blusher on to her cheeks and touched up her neutral lipstick. Then she hurried up the stairs and tapped at the already open door of his office.

'Come in.'

He smiled at her and she felt her heart beat faster. There had been a time, of course, when Neil Lomond's smile had always made her heart beat faster and her legs turn to jelly, but that time had long passed. Like the time when Aidan Clarke had managed to make her heart beat faster and her legs turn to jelly too. The two men in my life, she thought, as she looked at him. Neither of whom I ever thought I'd see again. One who I believed was the love of my life. And one . . .

Aidan Clarke. Tall, fair and very attractive in an outdoors kind of way. Minette had once said they looked more like brother and sister than boyfriend and girlfriend as they walked down the road together. Neil Lomond. Taller but dark. More of a smouldering attractiveness. Anna was right. He was sex on legs. And nobody could have mistaken them for brother and sister. The contrast was too stark.

'Sit down,' he said. 'Make yourself comfortable.'

It was impossible to feel comfortable in the leather and chrome chair in front of Neil's desk. Darcey sat as still as she possibly could while her eyes flickered around his office, noting the world map with coloured pins representing different InvestorCorp offices and subsidiaries. She could see immediately that blue pins were the Global Finance offices. And yellow represented Global Finance clients. There they were: Dublin, Brussels, Milan, Rome, Paris, Marseilles, Madrid, Barcelona, Stockholm, Frankfurt, Copenhagen, Lisbon, Geneva, Amsterdam, Helsinki and Oslo. And newer clients in Moscow, Prague, Belgrade, Berlin, Ljubljana, Warsaw, Bucharest, Sofia, Tallinn and Vilnius. She'd been to all of those places. Met lots of really nice people. Brought back significant amounts of business for the company.

That was why Anna was right when she said that she was good at her job. Funny then, thought Darcey, how she always felt as though she was just winging it.

'Good business.' Neil had followed her gaze. 'But we're thinking of changing the balance between the InvestorCorp and Global Finance presence.'

She listened as he outlined changes that would mean the Edinburgh office taking over her client base. She said nothing but her mind was racing. He wanted to get rid of her after all. She'd been lulled into thinking that everything would be all right, writing reports for him, detailing her clients and the work she'd done, but in the end all he wanted was to let her go. She was surprised at how hurt she felt by that. But, ultimately, not surprised that he didn't want her in the company any more. It wasn't business. It *was* personal.

'We think that the InvestorCorp Edinburgh operation should focus on Europe,' he told her. 'The US looks after Canada, the States and Latin America. We want the Dublin operation to look after our Asian interests – Singapore, Hong Kong and Tokyo.'

'That's the biggest load of crap I've ever heard in my life.' The words were out of her mouth before she could stop them. 'Dublin is a million times more European than Edinburgh. For starters, we've been using the same currency as other member states for years. It's easy for me to get clients to deal with us. New York is probably more in tune with Singapore, Hong Kong and Tokyo. We don't have any experience in Asia at all!'

'Exactly,' said Neil. 'Europe is too easy for you. You sweep in and woo them in whatever language is necessary. Next thing you know, you've swooped up a bucketload of business and home you come. You've been very successful.'

'Amazingly successful, I think you said before.'

'You've done really well, haven't you?'

'I've worked hard.'

'I've seen your name in the business from time to time,' said Neil. 'And I'm glad you've done well. Though I was really surprised when I heard that you'd become involved in the industry again. I thought you were going to buy a vineyard in the south of France.'

'An olive farm in Tuscany,' she told him. 'And I was being ironic about it.'

'Ah. So . . . all those times you talked about living the simple life in the sun was complete bullshit?'

'There's no such thing as the simple life,' she said. 'Everybody wants it to be simple there but it isn't. Olive-growers in Tuscany worry about the crop. So do vineyard-owners in the south of France. Portuguese fishermen worry about the catch. Everyone worries about something.'

'And what do you worry about, Darcey?'

'Bringing in clients for Global Finance,' she replied promptly. 'I mean, of course, InvestorCorp.'

He leaned back in his swivel chair and regarded her thoughtfully. 'It's a radical change.'

'Not really,' she told him. 'I grew up, that's all.'

'And you think that's a good thing?'

'It certainly proved to be a good thing for the company,' she said spiritedly. 'Without me we wouldn't have made the kind of profits we made last year. Peter Henson might have had to drive a smaller Merc and go to less expensive restaurants.'

Neil laughed and then busied himself with the papers on his desk.

'InvestorCorp has a small client base in Asia,' he said. 'But we don't get anything like the kind of business we could out of them. It's not working from the US office. We think you might be able to develop the business instead. We're also looking at China as a growing market for us.'

'I don't speak any Asian languages,' she told him. 'Including Chinese.'

'It's not about languages, and you know that already,' he said quickly. 'It's about you being a good person to deal with.'

'But my advantage is being able to talk to people in their own language,' she pointed out. 'I know English will do perfectly well in most situations in Asia. So you're taking my natural advantage away.'

'Your advantage isn't the language,' said Neil. 'Your advantage is, as you already know – and amazing though it is to those who really know you – your advantage is yourself.'

She stared at him.

'When it comes to business dealings, you come across as completely sympathetic,' he told her. 'You make people confide in you. You're . . . you're the kind of person everyone wants to know. That's what everyone has said to me. And, of course, that memory of yours helps too. You can recall every part of a proposal, every piece of a deal.'

'I'm not in the slightest bit sympathetic,' she told him. 'Nobody in Global Finance confides in me.'

'That's what I would've thought too,' said Neil. 'We asked all the staff. Yes, people here are in awe of you, because they know you have an IQ of a hundred and forty-five or something.'

'A hundred and forty-four,' she said. 'I blew it on verbal reasoning.'

He smiled. 'But they totally respect you. They like you. And they think that you're one of the fairest people they've ever met. The reaction overseas is a little different. Everyone loves you there. They all think you're fantastic.'

'So you want to take all my clients who think I'm fantastic and give them to someone else. Then you want to palm me off on some poor sods in Hong Kong who probably have better things to do with their money.'

'There's a lot of money in Hong Kong,' said Neil. 'We think it could be a very lucrative market,' he added. 'Singapore is a big commercial centre where we haven't done as much as we should. Business in Tokyo is picking up. And, of course, China is obviously a huge prospect. We want you to start with Singapore and Tokyo, though.'

'Are you sure it's not just a question of you wanting me out of the way?'

'Why would I want that?'

'I wouldn't interfere in your life,' she assured him, 'if that's what you're worried about. I'm way past all that.'

He said nothing.

'I like Europe,' she continued. 'I don't like being told to hand over my work to someone else.'

'I understand that,' said Neil. 'We – InvestorCorp – understand that too.'

'My bonus is based on the business I bring in. It's good. Moving me might change all that.'

'I'm authorised to increase your basic salary as compensation for the fact that you'll be putting in extra work at the start,' said Neil. He scribbled a number on a piece of paper and slid it across the desk. Her eyes widened.

'Money isn't everything,' she said.

'But, like you once said yourself, it sure does help.'

'I didn't take this job for the money,' she told him, although she realised that she wasn't being entirely truthful. After all, it had been the offer of doubling her salary when she first joined Global Finance that had helped her make up her mind.

'Why did you?' He leaned back in his seat and looked at her thoughtfully.

'It was a new challenge.'

'Not the "I need a new challenge" routine?' He grinned at her.

She smiled slightly. 'Hey, you're the boss. I have to say things like that.'

'Not to me you don't.'

'No?'

'No,' he said firmly. 'You really don't, Darcey. And, you know, I'm glad you've got your life back together and you're doing well and . . .' He shrugged. 'I want to be able to work with you.'

'So are you telling me to go to Edinburgh and meet with people and tell them all about my European clients?' she asked. 'Is that what all these reports were really for?'

He nodded. 'I'm sorry if I misled you slightly. It wasn't my original intention, I promise. We hadn't decided on how we would deal with the client base at the start. But we do think that this is the best way. So I'd like you to draw up a schedule for Singapore and the rest. It'd be great if you could get out and meet a few people early on. Get a feel for the market. Within the next couple of months anyway.'

'I'll work on it.' She stood up. 'That's all?'

He nodded slowly. 'Just one more question.'

'What?'

'Have you decided whether you're going to that wedding?'

'Don't you think you're trespassing into the personal now?' She frowned.

'Don't.' He looked at her pleadingly. 'At least . . . not close to a business trip.'

She stopped frowning and smiled at him. 'It's not for ages yet. You don't have to worry about me cracking up with the clients.'

'I'm not worried about the clients. I'm worried about you.'

Quite suddenly there was a lump in her throat.

'I have to get back to my desk,' she told him hurriedly. 'Don't worry about me. I don't really think about it any more. As far as everything else goes, I'll let you know when I have things sorted out.'

# Chapter 13

Organising a wedding at long-distance was more complicated than Nieve had expected. She'd selected an Irish wedding-planner over the internet and had briefed her that no expense was to be spared on the extravagance of the event, but she found it difficult to stand back and let Happy Ever Afters take complete control of things. It would have been easier if it had been in the States, where she could've dropped in on the office and checked the venues and place settings and all those sort of things herself, but being five thousand miles away made life that much harder. And she wondered what on earth had possessed her to decide that getting married in Ireland would be a fun thing to do, when everything would have been so much easier in California.

Well, being honest with herself, she knew what had possessed her. She wanted to show off.

Until their decision to get married, she hadn't had the slightest desire or reason to go back to Galway, or even to Dublin, which everyone told her had become one of the hippest, most cosmopolitan and party-loving cities around. Quite frankly, Nieve didn't believe a word of it. No doubt the city and its people thought they were hip and cool, but there was no way Dublin could compete with San Francisco or New York or any of the major US cities she'd visited over the past ten years. Gail and Stephen, who'd come to stay with her a number of times, agreed that the States was great, but Gail always ended up saying that nothing beat Ireland. Nieve never believed her.

Happy Ever Afters was actually based outside Dublin, in the town of Rathoath. Nieve hadn't realised this when she'd booked them, and afterwards she'd been horrified, because Rathoath was surely just a sleepy village and what the hell would anyone there know about top-of-the-range weddings. But her mother had laughed when she said this and told her that every town within a fifty-mile radius of Dublin was now a city suburb, and that most of them were thriving with new businesses. Gail was sure that Happy Ever Afters was perfectly fine, although, she asked a little waspishly, what was wrong with a Galway company?

It was funny, Nieve thought, how the only person to ever really bug her about things was her mother. All her life, Gail had questioned Nieve's choices and her abilities – always pointing out that she didn't work hard enough, and that she needed to do better to keep up with the others in her class at school (especially Darcey McBloodyGonigle). In the end, Nieve thought triumphantly, she'd done it her own way, without any of Gail's nagging input. She'd left Darcey bobbing helplessly in her wake while she'd become the sort of person who could hire a wedding-planner and order them to create the day of her dreams. She'd allowed Gail to be involved too, to prove to her that she was the kind of daughter who could pay for the best. That she had become the best herself.

She knew that some people who knew about her and Aidan might have assumed that they'd already got married (and even divorced, heaven knows!). But it hadn't been the first thing on their agenda when they'd arrived in California.

She'd plunged headlong into her work at Jugomax, with twelve-hour days being the norm and most of them taking much longer than that, and she hadn't had the time to even think about marriage. Aidan, despite the fact that he kept telling her how great it was to be here with her, and how much she meant to him, didn't want to rush into things either. He'd suggested getting married that first year, a quick trip to Vegas to tie the knot. But the idea had been born of a bottle of Californian red on an empty stomach, and she knew he hadn't really meant it. Besides, they were too busy even for a trip to Vegas. She'd replied that she might marry him one day, but certainly not in a tacky hellhole. If and when they got married, she said seriously, their wedding would be the biggest social event of the year and would be a tacky-free zone. They joked about it afterwards, and he wondered aloud whether there was any need to get married at all, since things were going just fine the way they were.

She agreed, but there was a part of her that would have liked to get married sooner. She didn't say that this was because knowing him had ruined her relationship with her closest friend, and that, deep down, she felt the one thing that would validate their actions was getting married. She didn't really want to think about that too much, because she did feel bad about what had happened, even though she was as certain as could be that Darcey McGonigle and Aidan Clarke would never have stayed together, with or without her coming into the picture. Great as boyfriend and girlfriend. Hopeless as husband and wife. She'd been able to see that from the moment she met him. He thought he was in love with Darcey, but Nieve knew that he wasn't. He'd probably started out intrigued by her. Most men did. They wondered whether she was really as self-possessed and uninterested as she appeared. Clearly Aidan had found out that she wasn't. But the bottom line was that it had no future. He needed someone like Nieve herself. No question.

It was a pity, of course, that doing the right thing by Aidan had meant hurting Darcey. She'd never really intended to do that, but she had to admit to herself that it had been pretty much inevitable. She'd hoped that she'd be able to explain it to her friend, make her see that it was the right thing, but for once in her life, Darcey was cold and hard and stubborn, and Nieve couldn't talk her round.

Darcey had called to the house to confront her about it. Nieve had been out (with Aidan) at the time, and there had (according to her parents) been a bit of a scene, with Darcey demanding to wait until Nieve came home and Stephen eventually saying that they were going to bed and that she'd have to leave. She'd left, all right, but only as far as the porch, where she'd startled Nieve, who'd got out of the taxi that had pulled up to the kerb.

Nieve clearly remembered the sinking feeling in her stomach as her friend stepped out of the darkness and said her name.

'Oh. Darce. You nearly frightened the life out of me.'

'Nice evening?' asked Darcey. 'Enjoy yourself with my boyfriend, did you?'

'Come on, Darce,' said Nieve. 'There's no need to do this.'

'Do what?'

'Try to make me feel bad.'

'I doubt that anyone could make you feel bad, Nieve Stapleton. That's just not in your nature, is it?'

'I'm truly, truly sorry,' said Nieve. 'I know he meant a lot to you. But you've got to believe me when I tell you that I hadn't planned on anything like this happening . . . In fact I—'

'Fuck off,' said Darcey.

'Ah, I see we're going to have an intelligent, reasoned debate.'

'I can't believe you're doing this to me,' said Darcey. 'I did everything for you. In school, in college, at work. I helped you with your homework. I helped you with your projects. I helped you with your damn translations. And the thanks I get? You help yourself to my boyfriend!'

'Get some perspective,' retorted Nieve. 'We were *friends*. I helped you when we were in college too. I found boyfriends for you, for heaven's sake! I told them that you were a good kisser. It's not my fault none of them worked out.'

'So you decided to grab the one that did?'

'It wasn't like that,' said Nieve. 'Honestly it wasn't. There was just something . . . I knew it the minute I saw him. He knew it too.'

'He *loves* me,' said Darcey.

'I'm really sorry,' said Nieve again. 'But he doesn't. Not any more. It's him and me now and it's the real deal.'

'Don't you think you have plenty of other opportunities for real deals with available men?' demanded Darcey.

'Aidan *is* available,' said Nieve.

'We were going to get married!' cried Darcey.

'No,' said Nieve. 'You weren't.'

'Yes we damn well were,' said Darcey.

'He wasn't sure.' Nieve looked at her friend with a mixture of sympathy and regret. 'He thought he was in love with you, but he still wasn't a hundred per cent sure. Then he met me and he knew.'

'Yeah, right.'

'I didn't make him do this,' said Nieve.

'I hope you rot in hell.'

'Darcey, please!' Nieve had never spoken to her friend in such a pleading tone before. 'Please listen to me. I'm sorry this happened. I didn't mean for it to happen. But it has. And I don't want to lose your friendship over it. We've known each other for years!'

'You don't bloody know me at all,' snapped Darcey. 'I don't know why I was ever friends with you. And I don't want your damn fake apology.'

'I *am* sorry,' said Nieve forcefully. 'But I'm not lying. I didn't intend to steal him, you know. We both knew that what we had was something special. He's what I've been waiting for. He's the love of my life.'

'You shouldn't have let it become something special,' said Darcey. 'If you really were my friend you'd have backed off.'

'If you really were my friend you'd understand. And you'd

204

know that Aidan wouldn't simply let himself be stolen if he wasn't unhappy in the first place.'

Darcey had looked at her with real pain in her eyes then, and Nieve knew that this wasn't like the times when they had quarrelled before. Those arguments had been over silly things, like who was sexier, Pierce Brosnan or Colin Firth. This was different. This was the real deal, the end of their friendship. She'd never thought it would happen over a man.

She felt even worse afterwards when Gail had called her in the States to tell her that Darcey was devastated and that Minette was worried she had bulimia or some other eating disorder, because she would go days without food and then pig out on sachertorte and hot chocolate and her weight was going up and down like an inflating and deflating balloon. She'd been relieved to hear, eventually, that Darcey had headed off to London to work. She reckoned it meant that she'd finally got over it. She hoped so because, no matter what, Darcey had been her closest friend for years. But Darcey had never known a thing about men. Nieve did, and she knew without question that she and Aidan were made for each other. Aidan made her feel secure about herself.

Nieve wasn't a career-obsessed singleton who lived for her job. She was a career woman with a decent and attractive man in her life. She pretty much had it all, and she was happy about it. And so, over time, getting married became less important than the fact that they were living together and loving it, and that they really didn't have a whole lot of time to organise a wedding anyway. Besides, Aidan was working long hours in the Jugomax IT department.

'I knew that you were something special the very first time I saw you,' he told her one night when, as the only two left in the office, they were sitting on the floor of the IT room, their backs against the wall, drinking hot, strong coffee. 'The very second I opened the front door. You . . . you crackled with energy and positive vibes.'

'It was the same for me,' she admitted. 'But I have to tell you that it was nothing to do with your positive vibes or your sparkling personality or my faith in your technology skills. It was all to do with the fact that you were one of the sexiest men I'd ever seen.'

He laughed.

'No, seriously,' she said. 'And I've seen loads of them. When Darce and I were in Spain . . .' She broke off as he raised an eyebrow. 'Oh, don't worry. I didn't go through a string of them there,' she told him. 'But you could wander down to the beach at Marbella and watch them pose! Just think,' she added, 'if Darcey hadn't come back from Marbella because her father had left her mother, and if she hadn't taken that crappy job, she probably wouldn't have met you. And then *I* wouldn't have met you.'

'Have you been in touch with her at all since we've been here?' asked Aidan.

'I called once. She just put the phone down on me.'

'She'll get over it,' said Aidan uncomfortably. 'You can't go through life nursing a grudge. And you *are* best friends.'

Nieve winced. 'We *were*. But she can be very unforgiving. She only barely speaks to her father since he and her mother split up. I can't blame her for being mad at me but she has to face facts. Thing is, she's not always good at facing facts.'

Aidan himself still found it hard to believe that he was with Nieve and not Darcey. It was as though his entire life had been turned upside down in the briefest of moments. It had hit him the moment he'd opened the door and had seen her standing on the step, stunning and sophisticated and immediately taking his breath away. And as he'd talked to her while Darcey was upstairs, he'd found himself falling under her spell. She was wittier than Darcey, more fun, more cutting in her comments and simply more cutting edge too. She was the perfect package – a great body and a sharp mind – and the amazing thing about her was she didn't seem to give a damn about anything.

All through dinner (and how often did it turn out that a woman as gorgeous as Nieve Stapleton would also turn out to be able to cook to perfection?) he'd found himself falling more and more under her spell, so that suddenly he realised that he simply couldn't give Darcey McGonigle the diamond ring he'd so carefully selected for her. He couldn't believe how close he'd come to making the biggest mistake of his life. It wasn't, at that moment, that he'd expected to have a long-term relationship with Nieve. It was just that he'd been reminded that there were other women in the world besides Darcey, and that he was too young to make a commitment to her, no matter how much he cared.

A lucky escape, he told himself, as he reached for the wine bottle at the same time as Nieve, so that their fingers brushed off each other. More than lucky. Fate. And he believed in fate.

Nieve's fingers flew over the keyboard as she sent a list of questions to Lorelei at Happy Ever Afters. The venue had been booked, a private castle about an hour's drive from Galway. It had never been used for a wedding before, but Lorelei knew the owner and had managed to secure it for the Stapleton–Clarke wedding. This meant, she'd emailed Nieve, that they had the supreme advantage of not having their big day compared to any other at the castle, because it would be unique. Besides, she'd said, the usual selection of castles were getting passé. Far better to have found somewhere new. There were a number of rooms available for guests who wanted to stay overnight, and the castle staff would look after them.

Nieve was delighted with the castle. Lorelei had emailed her a video clip of it looking grey and forbidding but softened by the wonderful emerald-green meadows surrounding it and leading down to a silver-blue river that raced and gurgled over dark rocks jutting up from the riverbed. It would be, Lorelei wrote, an ideal location for stunning photographs, enhanced, she added, by the possible inclusion of the woolly sheep that grazed nearby. Nieve thought the castle was wonderful, though she couldn't have cared less about woolly sheep, but Lorelei hadn't sent her half enough information about the flowers and the caterers and the entertainment – Nieve wanted a really big name to perform at the wedding, that was what everyone who was anyone did here. She knew that she couldn't afford to hire someone really famous like Beyoncé (though she would have been amazing, and Nieve couldn't imagine how her Irish friends would have reacted to see such a star on stage!), but she was sure she could get someone well-known. Her wedding was going to be a celebration of everything – of her and

Aidan, of a triumphant return to Ireland, of proving to Darcey McGonigle that Aidan's leaving her had been the right thing to do and that being the brainiest girl she knew and laid back about it wasn't actually the way to go; you had to use your brains to get anywhere in the world and you had to make your own luck.

Darcey hadn't replied to her invitation yet. Always provided, of course, that she'd actually received it. Nieve had sent it to her old address because she'd checked that Minette still lived there. But the question was, would Minette have guessed it was from her and not passed it on? Nieve didn't think so. But she couldn't be certain. And even if Darcey had got the invitation, would she accept it? It was hard to tell. She might simply dismiss Nieve and Aidan as something in her past to be forgotten about. Again, Nieve didn't think so. She was pretty sure that Darcey would want to see them. She knew that she would be surprised by the invitation in the first place. And maybe she'd still be too angry to come. Nieve knew that Darcey could brood about things. But ten years! Surely not.

She'd invited her because she wanted to prove to her ex-friend that she and Aidan were the real deal. She wanted Darcey to see them exchanging vows. She wanted her to know that she hadn't simply lured Aidan away. That she'd been right when she'd told Darcey that Aidan wasn't right for her. She wanted to prove it all in front of her. She knew that Darcey might get the wrong end of the stick and think that in some way Nieve was trying to throw it all in her face, but she told herself that by now Darcey would have moved on. Well, of course she had. Hadn't Gail told her exactly how Darcey had moved on? So it surely wasn't any big deal for her to come. And it was a way of mending fences. Maybe Darcey wouldn't want to mend them. Maybe there was no need. But it was something Nieve wanted to do all the same.

She'd wanted to explain how she'd fallen for him that first evening, and how she'd tried not to be interested, but how she'd suddenly found herself calling him at Car Crew and asking him to meet her for lunch. She'd kept her request light-hearted and jokey, telling him that she needed to vet her best friend's boyfriend in daylight. He'd laughed at that and told her he'd meet her in a pub in the city, but that he was very short on time. They'd met at the pub, exchanged one look, and then he'd suggested that they go back to his apartment.

Nieve had never been totally taken over by lust before. But she had to have Aidan. She just had to. And so she wasn't thinking of anything or anyone (least of all Darcey McGonigle) when she lay on the crumpled bed in his apartment and allowed him to pull the clothes from her body. The sex was fast and furious and she'd liked it like that. Somehow she'd thought Aidan would be the slow, sensual type, but sex with him had been one of the least sensual yet most exciting moments in her life.

'I normally take more time over it,' he mumbled afterwards as they lay in each other's arms. 'But we're in a bit of a hurry, aren't we, and quite honestly I was short on patience. I think I wanted to do that to you from the moment I met you.'

'How much of a hurry?' Nieve's hand slid between his legs.

'A lot.' He groaned softly.

'Can you be just as quick at the second attempt?'

He rolled over so that he was on top of her.

'If that's what you'd like.'

'Absolutely,' she breathed. 'That's exactly what I'd like.'

She finished sending the email to Happy Ever Afters and turned her attention back to her work. She'd never been the sort of person who looked after personal matters in the office, but the wedding was a major project and she knew that Ennco wouldn't begrudge her a little downtime. Her eyes flickered towards the share price display. The Ennco price was down a few cents on the previous day, but that didn't worry Nieve too much. The entire market had slipped a little in value since opening; there were always days like this. The important thing was the long-term trend, and as far as she was concerned that was, quite simply, onwards and upwards. She wondered whether, if Jugomax hadn't collapsed in the late nineties, she'd now be earning anything like what was coming to her thanks to Ennco. She didn't think so. Even if she'd ultimately ended up as president or CEO of the firm, nothing compared to the buyout deal that she was getting now. People sometimes looked at the money paid to famous actors or singers or mega-selling authors, but the truth of it was that the real money was to be made in finance. And the best of that was that nobody else knew. It was quiet money. The sweaty masses, as Nieve liked to think of them, had no idea how much was splashed around by bankers and financiers and brokers. Which suited her perfectly. She liked being low-key in America. But she sure as hell was going to be high-key when she got home.

She opened her email account again: 'Please ensure that there are no yellow flowers', she typed. 'Yellow is my least favourite colour.' She hit send and smiled to herself.

Everything was going to be perfect.

# Chapter 14

$\text{D}$arcey liked watching TV at the weekend. She didn't have much time for it during the week because she was often late home or because she would sometimes join Anna and some of the other Global Finance people for a drink after work, but on Saturday nights she liked nothing more than settling down with a takeaway and a DVD. She had long ago decided that it wasn't boring and sad to stay in on her own on a Saturday night if she felt like it. So she switched on the TV, decanted chilli chicken on to a big blue plate, and settled in for some downtime.

She didn't start playing the DVD immediately because they were showing a programme on people who had moved to other countries to set up new lives. She was addicted to house-in-the-sun programmes and so she was perfectly happy to delay the DVD in favour of following the progress of a family who'd just bought a ruin in Tuscany and who wanted to turn it into their dream home.

Darcey knew the town of San Pietro, which she'd visited on her travels with Nieve, and remembered its narrow, winding streets and tall green-shuttered houses perched on a hillside overlooking the plains below. Why do they do it? she wondered, as she watched the family, who were currently living in a camper van outside the ruin, wrestle with the fact that the builders hadn't shown up for the third day in a row and the electricity wasn't working. And how can they make a decision to leave everything they know and move to a country where they don't speak the language and have no real idea of the culture?

She chased a fragment of chicken around her plate. She regularly joked about the Tuscan farmhouse with Anna Sweeney; now, looking at the blue sky and green fields of Italy, the red-tiled houses and the olive groves, she couldn't help feeling that maybe the non-Italian-speaking family (now struggling with the sewage system) had more get-up-and-go than her. And yet . . . and yet . . . she'd got up and gone herself, hadn't she? After the humiliation of Aidan going to America with Nieve, she'd decided to head off somewhere else too. She'd wanted to get away from the sympathetic glances of the people in Car Crew who knew that it had all gone horribly wrong for her. She felt as though everyone in Galway knew that she'd been dumped by Aidan Clarke in favour of Nieve Stapleton. She tried to tell herself that (a) most of them didn't know and (b) even if they did, they wouldn't care, but she couldn't help herself. She couldn't help feeling as though in some way she'd been marked out as a failure. Someone who'd lost her almost-fiancé to her best friend. She felt like an utterly hopeless case. She knew that she wasn't dealing with it very well. She knew that Minette was worried about her (she was binge-eating and piling on the pounds) but she didn't care. She knew that Tish and Amelie were concerned too, but she didn't want their sympathy. What would they know about it anyhow? she told herself miserably. The two of them had never needed anyone else.

Getting away from them all would help. At first she'd thought about going back to continental Europe, but instead she'd decided on London, where the pace of life was faster and where she wouldn't have time to obsess about what her life should've been like. She wanted to lose herself in work. Maybe even become a businesswoman like Nieve. (Though when that thought had crossed her mind she'd clamped down on it immediately. She didn't want to be like Nieve Stapleton. Ever.) But perhaps she could find some of the drive that had motivated Nieve and that had so attracted Aidan. Maybe going away would change whatever it was about herself that had made him prefer Nieve to her. Maybe then she'd understand it.

On the TV, another crisis had befallen the hapless Italy-lovers. They'd discovered that they had a lot less time than they'd previously thought to harvest the olives from the groves they'd bought. And so they were working in the middle of the night to bring in the crop. Darcey groaned on their behalf and rooted for them as they tried to knock the olives from the trees. But honestly, she thought pettishly, surely they should have researched it a bit more before they arrived?

The thing was, people didn't always do things the right way. They plunged in without thinking, hoping that everything would turn out OK. But of course it didn't. Rushing off to London hadn't been the rescue package she'd expected. That hadn't turned out the way she'd wanted either.

She finished her meal and put the plate into the small

dishwasher. She hadn't thought of any of this stuff in years. She resented the way it was all flooding back now. It didn't have the power to hurt her any more, of course, but it did make her feel sad about the way she'd wasted so much of her life in feeling hurt and not trusting anyone for such a long time afterwards.

The olives had finally been harvested and the family on the TV had brought them to the local press. Their plan was to bottle their own oil and sell it to the tourists. Darcey was sceptical. As far as she could remember, San Pietro was a tiny town and way off the tourist trail. The TV family had decided that it was precisely because San Pietro was off the beaten track that the tourists would come there. Darcey's doubts mounted, but it was hard not to hope that the family would come through in the end.

I might have been like them once, she admitted to herself as she poured herself a glass of wine. I might have thought that you can do things just because you want to, and that everything will work out in the end. But it doesn't. It didn't work out with Aidan, even though I was so madly in love with him. And, much worse, it didn't work out with Neil Lomond either.

She sighed regretfully as she thought of Neil. The truth was that it was only the wedding invitation that had made her think about Aidan and Nieve at all. She hadn't given them a thought in years. The real disaster in her life hadn't been that Aidan had fallen out of love with her. The real failure had been her relationship with Neil Lomond.

And she honestly couldn't blame Nieve Stapleton for that.

\* \* \*

Anna returned from her Edinburgh trip the following week and sent an instant message to Darcey to ask her to lunch.

'Working on business plan for client handover,' Darcey messaged back. 'Have meeting with Lomond this p.m. Won't be pleased if I skive off to lunch.'

'Thirty-minutes,' responded Anna. 'Just sandwich and coffee. See you reception 12.30?'

'Arm-twister,' typed Darcey. 'OK.'

She closed her instant message system and looked at the Word document on the screen again. She didn't know why she was doing so much bloody work for someone else. As far as she knew, nobody was writing out reams of information for her about InvestorCorp's Asian clients. She was going to go into all those meetings blind. But whoever took over from her would be helped enormously by all the information she was preparing. And so, unless they were incredibly inept, they would be able to replicate if not improve on the business she'd already brought in.

Oh well, she murmured to herself, I guess I just have to keep winging it and hoping for the best. They have faith in me, don't they? I just have to have the same faith in myself.

Anna was already waiting in reception by the time Darcey arrived, apologising for being late and explaining that one of her Polish clients had called just as she was about to leave.

'How's your Polish coming along?' asked Anna.

'I'll never be fluent, but at least I can say please and thank you.' Darcey followed her friend out of the revolving doors. 'Did you know that Singapore has four official languages?'

Anna chuckled. 'Bet you'll pick them up in no time!'

'Thankfully one of them is English. I can't honestly see myself becoming fluent in Malay or Chinese.'

'Tut, tut,' said Anna. 'Bang goes your Person of the Year hat-trick.'

Darcey laughed. 'It's all a plot by my jealous colleagues.' She pushed open the door of the Italian coffee bar. It was already quite full, because a lot of people in the Financial Services Centre went for lunch early, but they managed to find two stools at the granite counter that ran along one wall.

'What'll you have?' asked Anna.

'Tomato and mozzarella panini,' replied Darcey. 'And an Americano.'

Anna ordered the sandwiches and came back with the coffees.

'So,' said Darcey as her friend sat down beside her. 'How did the trip go?'

Anna beamed at her. 'Great,' she said, and Darcey could see the relief in her eyes. 'They're happy for a continued separate HR function here, although I will be reporting back to the HR guy there. But he's an absolute pet and I don't mind at all.'

'I'm glad,' said Darcey. 'I knew there was no need for you to panic.'

'Hard not to.' Anna sipped her coffee. 'And I know that if the worst came to the worst I could've got another job, but that would've been so disruptive, and I don't need disruptive in my life, thanks.' She made a face. 'It was bad enough having to go to Scotland. According to Mum, Meryl behaved like a demon while I was away.'

'You've never been away before,' said Darcey.

'No, but probably I should have done it more,' Anna told her. 'I realise that I've spoiled that girl rotten.'

'Ah, you haven't,' said Darcey as a waitress appeared with their food. 'She's a good kid really.' She picked up her knife and fork and cut into the panini.

'Well, probably,' conceded Anna. 'Still, I dunno how Neil Lomond might feel about her.'

Darcey coughed as a piece of panini went down the wrong way.

'You OK?' asked Anna as her friend dabbed at her eyes.

Darcey nodded and took a sip of coffee. 'What's the buzz between you and Neil?' she asked carefully.

Anna grinned. 'He's a really nice guy,' she told Darcey. 'But to be honest with you, Darce, whatever buzz might be between him and me rather depends on whatever buzz there was between him and you.'

Darcey said nothing.

'I asked him,' Anna told her.

'Asked him what?'

'About the pair of you—'

'Jeez, Anna!' Darcey interrupted her. 'That was a bit pushy.'

'I didn't ask him in a pushy way,' said Anna equably. 'We were at dinner and we were talking and the subject of you came up.'

Darcey nearly choked again.

'How?'

'He wanted to know how you fitted in. Whether you were happy here.'

'What!' Darcey's cheeks were pink. 'It's none of his business.'

'He was relaxed about it,' said Anna. 'Stop fretting. Anyway, in the course of the conversation I said that it seemed to me that you guys had known each other before. And he told me to ask you about it. So I am. After all, if I do fancy him a little bit, there's no point in thinking about it if he has unfinished business with you.'

'We don't have unfinished business,' said Darcey firmly. 'Whatever business there was between us is well and truly over, I assure you.'

'But there was something.'

'And he wouldn't tell you?'

Anna pointed her knife at Darcey. 'I kinda got the impression he wasn't entirely comfortable about it, and since I certainly don't want him to feel uncomfortable around me I didn't pursue it. So come on, Darce, what gives?'

'Oh well . . .' Darcey pushed her half-eaten panini to one side. She gazed unseeingly past Anna and at the sparkling water of the docks beyond. It had been a long time since she'd talked about it. The only people who knew or cared about her relationship with Neil Lomond were her family. And they thought she was over it. Which she was. She'd learned about getting over men after Aidan. She'd been much better, and much quicker at it, the second time around.

She'd met him in London.

She'd been lucky and found a nice place to live – a flat-share with three other girls in a large townhouse near Canary

Wharf, with glimpses of the river Thames from the bedroom window – and she actually had enough money to get by for two months before panicking. Helena and Gill, two of her housemates, worked in the City, and Darcey had told them that that was where she hoped to work too. She'd blagged up her experience with Car Crew when she talked to them so that she appeared to be a serious professional woman who would be a perfect tenant and pay the rent on time, but their main concern was that she'd be clean and tidy and look after her share of household chores.

They'd asked, too, about boyfriends, and she'd told them there wasn't anyone. That was the hardest thing she'd had to do. Say out loud to people that she didn't have a boyfriend when once she'd believed that she was going to have a fiancé. It didn't matter what people said about time being a great healer. Every time she thought about Aidan Clarke it was like a knife going through her heart, though she tried hard not to let them see that.

As soon as her accommodation was sorted out she went to see a job agency. It was bright and bustling and very busy, and Darcey thought it was a very businesslike place. She told them that she wanted to do something in finance (after all, if Nieve Stapleton could succeed by working for a financier, so could she!), and the girl nodded as though anyone could work in finance if they wanted to.

'I can set up an interview for you for this afternoon,' she told Darcey. 'An international bank.'

As she began talking about the bank, it seemed to Darcey that her voice was coming from miles away. She was talking about letters of credit and international trade, and using a whole heap of words that Darcey didn't understand, and she suddenly felt herself feeling more and more pressurised. It was all very well, she thought, to pretend that she was interested in banking and finance. But she wasn't hotshot businesswoman material. And the bankers would find that out. She didn't have the guts for a City job. She wasn't Nieve Stapleton after all.

'I'm not available this afternoon.' The words tumbled from Darcey's lips. 'In fact, I won't be available for at least a couple of weeks, maybe a bit more.'

'But you said . . .'

'I know,' Darcey acknowledged. 'Sorry about that. There are a few things I need to look after first. I'll – um – I'll call you again.' She got up and hurried out of the office.

She felt as though she was out of her own body and watching herself as she walked past Liverpool Street station. Outside she looked like a normal person. She'd spent a lot of time and effort trying to make herself look efficient for her interview with the employment agency, and so she fitted right in with all the other office workers walking by in their neat skirts and tailored jackets. She'd worn a navy suit and had loaded her hair with serum to keep it tidy and efficient-looking. Anybody seeing her walking down the street would think that she already had a job in one of the many banks in the area. She looked the part. But inside – inside, her stomach was churning. She couldn't be a businesswoman. She really couldn't. She couldn't even think about it. She'd had her chance at getting a good job and she'd blown it. She was an idiot. It was no wonder Aidan Clarke had left her.

Her stomach rumbled and suddenly she was back inside

her body again. And it was hungry, demanding food. Why, she asked herself dismally, am I not the sort of person who loses interest in food when I'm upset? Why do I eat twice as much when I'm stressed? Which is why this suit should be a 16, not a 14.

She stopped outside a sandwich bar. She had to have something to eat, even though it would make the tight waistband on the skirt seem even tighter. She went in and bought herself a roll, which was fresh and crumbly and immediately made her feel better. And then she saw that the sandwich bar was looking for an assistant.

I can't work here, she muttered. It's a bloody sandwich bar! I came here to get a decent job, not make sandwiches.

It was a nice sandwich, though. Herb chicken and low-fat mayonnaise with mixed pepper salad. When she'd finished, she licked the crumbs from her fingers and asked the manager about the job.

Barry Barnes looked at her warily. More often than not, students worked in the sandwich bar, and Darcey McGonigle most certainly wasn't a student. Nor did she look like an out-of-work actress or singer (he'd had a lot of aspiring performers working in the bar over the years). He weighed up the chances of her being any good, and then she'd smiled at him and said that the chicken sandwich had been gorgeous and the tarragon really brought the flavour out, and he'd been astonished that she recognised it. He'd also been captivated by the wideness of her smile and the sudden sparkle in her blue eyes. So he'd offered her the job even as he wondered what on earth he was doing.

She didn't regret accepting it, but she knew that it was

crazy. She wouldn't earn nearly enough to pay her portion of the rent in Canary Wharf, and she didn't want to be a sandwich bar assistant anyway. But she couldn't help herself. She told him she could start in the morning.

Actually she quite liked working in the sandwich bar. There was something surprisingly satisfying about doing something practical and getting to know the customers and not having to worry about anything at the end of each day. After two weeks she had them all sussed out and knew them by their order – the ham and Swiss on rye; the BLT bap; the chicken tikka wrap . . . and, of course, the girl who came in and dithered for ages before making the exact same choice every day – tuna and sweetcorn on brown, cut straight across and not diagonally as they normally did. She knew them all and got on with them, and surprised herself at how chatty she was with them. In some ways it was like talking to the clients at Car Crew, where she'd always been open and pleasant. Meanwhile Barry liked the fact that she was quick and efficient and the customers started coming back more often.

She noticed him on the third week. He ordered seven different sandwiches and a couple of oatmeal cookies.

'Hungry?' Her eyes twinkled as she handed him the carry-out bag.

'I'm buying for the team,' he told her defensively. 'We're brainstorming. If only we had a brain!'

He was buying for the team the second day too, although this time for six of them. One had cracked under the strain, he told her. Couldn't handle the pace. She handed him the sandwiches.

'Y'know, I didn't say anything yesterday because I was in a bit of a rush,' he told her. 'But you didn't ring any of those prices into the register. So . . . well . . . you might not be charging me the right amount.'

'You're Scottish, aren't you?' she asked.

'Aye, well . . .' His almost imperceptible accent broadened. 'Just because I'm in the big city disnae mean I cannae be thrifty.'

She laughed. 'It's the right price,' she told him. 'I knew you were in a hurry and it would've taken much longer to register them all. I did it afterwards; I'm not pocketing the money myself.'

'I wasn't suggesting you were,' he said. 'It's just . . .'

'You want me to go through them?' she asked. 'OK.' She listed each sandwich with its price and told him the total. 'See?' she said when she'd finished.

He shrugged helplessly. 'Fine. Whatever you say.'

'Ring your order in tomorrow and I'll have it made up for you in advance,' she said. 'You won't have to wait as long before getting back to the brainstorming.'

He did as she suggested the next morning and arrived at twelve thirty to pick it up.

'How's the brainstorming going?' she asked as she reached for the brown paper bag.

He made a face at her. 'Terrible. But at least the sandwiches are good.'

She laughed as she handed him the order.

'Aha!' He looked at her triumphantly. 'Gotcha! You're charging me twenty-five pence less than yesterday. But the order is exactly the same.'

She grinned. 'No it's not. You asked me to hold the peppers on the chicken salad. That's what saved you the twenty-five pence.'

'Bloody hell,' he said. 'Have you ever thought of working somewhere else? Where those adding skills might be even more useful?'

'Like where?'

And he told her that he worked with a life assurance company and that they were looking for people and he knew she'd be brilliant. He asked her to come for an interview and she laughed and said that she wasn't cut out for it, and he asked her to give it a try and looked at her so persuasively that she suddenly found herself saying OK.

She surprised herself by doing a good interview, not getting flustered or tongue-tied as she'd half expected, and when they offered her the job she accepted.

Barry was sorry to see her go. He told her that she was one of the best workers he'd ever had. She reminded him that she'd be only working around the corner and that she'd be back for sandwiches every day and would recommend the sandwich bar to everyone in ProSure.

And then she went back to the Canary Wharf house and wondered if she was going to become a businesswoman after all, and whether she'd be working with the nice guy who'd set it all up for her, Neil Lomond.

'And so?' Anna asked as her voice trailed off. 'You knew him in London. He got you a job. That's it?' She looked at Darcey enquiringly.

'Not entirely,' admitted Darcey.
'What then?'
Darcey looked at Anna uncomfortably.
'I married him,' she said.

# Chapter 15

Anna stared at her while Darcey picked at the edges of her panini. Eventually she looked up from the bread and shrugged.

'Darcey!' Anna was stunned. 'You . . . *married* . . . him. Neil Lomond is your *husband*? You've got to be kidding me.'

'Of course I'm not kidding you,' said Darcey mildly. 'Although obviously he's my *ex*-husband.'

Anna was speechless.

'I know. I know. I'm sorry.' This time Darcey herself was a little agitated. 'I should've told you before but . . . well, I kinda couldn't believe it myself when he walked into the office and . . .'

'You – you never said. You never talk about your former husband. I never thought . . . I couldn't have guessed . . .'

'No, well, it wasn't anything I needed to talk about,' said Darcey. 'It was a horrible mistake but it's in the past, over and done with, and I don't need to pick over the bones.'

'Well I can understand that you didn't particularly want to talk about your marriage, and that's fine, but . . . Darcey!

You should have said *something* to me. I'm your friend, for heaven's sake! You don't need to keep secrets like that.' Anna sounded hurt.

'I couldn't help it,' said Darcey. 'The first time you mentioned him you said he was cute or something and I just couldn't bring myself to say anything. It was silly. I'm sorry.'

'Is he a problem for you?' Anna looked at her shrewdly.

'Are you asking me as a friend or the HR manager?'

'Darcey McGonigle! Your friend, of course. I don't give a stuff about the company, but I do care about you.'

Darcey swallowed hard. 'I know you do. I . . . but you know me. I'm not great at talking about myself.'

'It's OK. I understand,' said Anna, although she was finding it difficult because she knew she'd never have been able to keep a secret like that. And she was still a little hurt that Darcey hadn't been able to confide in her. 'Please don't get me wrong, Darcey,' she added. 'But he's your boss. He used to be your husband. Doesn't it bother you? And doesn't anyone from InvestorCorp know this?'

'There's no reason for it to bother me, honestly.' Darcey's voice was steady again. 'I haven't seen him or spoken to him in years, so I'm not exactly devastated to see him now. The only thing that worried me was whether *he'd* have issues about it, but he doesn't seem to. And it certainly doesn't look like anyone from InvestorCorp knows. When Neil and I worked for the company it was called ProSure. Investor-Corp took it over in one of those merry-go-round shake-ups that happen in financial services. None of the InvestorCorp people were around when we . . .' She moistened her lips with the tip of her tongue. 'My one concern was that there were ProSure people who'd maybe know about us and they wouldn't be happy.'

'What wouldn't they be happy about specifically?'

Darcey made a face. 'Well, clearly the whole relationship thing,' she said uncomfortably. 'After all, there was a bit of history at ProSure.'

'What sort of history?'

'Oh, you know. We were married and working in the same company. When things started to go wrong it was kind of inevitable that it'd spill over into our working lives.' She shifted uneasily in her seat. 'And I suppose it was my fault, so . . .'

'Surely not all your fault,' said Anna supportively.

'Ah, y'know, it was.' Darcey sighed. 'I married the wrong man and I married him for the wrong reason, so I guess it was inevitable.'

'Don't tell me you were pregnant!' Anna's eyes opened wide.

'Would you get a grip?' Darcey said sharply. 'Of course I wasn't pregnant. I was just . . . um . . . well, before I met Aidan Clarke, my love life was hopeless. I guess I went back into hopeless mode afterwards – only worse, because he really and truly hurt me and I couldn't cope because Nieve was involved and that hurt me too. I swore to myself that I'd never trust a man again and I doubly swore to myself that I'd never have a relationship with someone I worked with again. And then I massively rebounded into Neil Lomond and forgot everything I'd ever said.'

\* \* \*

Of course she hadn't been thinking of rebounding with anyone when she'd walked into the company for her first day in the actuarial department. She hadn't been thinking of anything other than how life had a way of making things happen. Despite having chickened out at the employment agency and taking the job in the sandwich bar, she'd ended up in a financial company after all. What was more, she actually liked working in the actuarial department, even though she soon learned that the actuaries themselves were, according to everyone else who worked in ProSure, people who found accountancy too exciting, had the personalities of a damp paper bag and were therefore to be avoided like the plague. She'd laughed when they told her that. She told them she'd fit right in. But in fact she was starting to enjoy herself. The work suited her and she was good at it. Slowly she began to feel the pain and hurt that she'd carried around with her for the past few months start to disappear.

Nevertheless, she didn't throw herself into socialising with her new colleagues. She wasn't going to make that mistake again. And working with the actuaries meant that nobody tried to persuade her either, because they hardly even noticed her. But she gradually started to feel better, and the devastating pain of Aidan's betrayal subsided into a dull ache.

She knew that her life, commuting every day from the Canary Wharf house, spending weekends reading or doing puzzles in the newspapers and occasionally going out to the nearby wine bar with Jackie, her other housemate, wasn't the sort of life that would set the world on fire. But right now it was all she needed. The great thing about the girls in the house was that she didn't see them that often. Helena and Gill usually went back to their home town of Leeds for the weekends, while Jackie, a nurse, worked shift hours. It all suited Darcey perfectly well. Because ProSure was such a big company she didn't get to know everyone in the same way as she had at Car Crew. She did, from time to time, bump into Neil Lomond in the staff canteen and chat to him, and she also became friendly with one or two people in other departments, but generally she kept her head down and threw herself into her work.

And so it wasn't until December that she went out with any of them. And that was only because it was hard to avoid it, with a clatter of seasonal office lunches and departmental parties occurring almost daily, and people reeling into the office wearing fur-rimmed Santa Claus hats and singing 'Jingle Bells' as they rode up and down in the lift. The actuaries didn't bother with a departmental party, but the official company Christmas party was different. It was always attended by everyone.

'People think we're sad enough without not turning up at the staff do,' James Hutton told her. 'We always go. Though to be honest, it's not my thing.'

She smiled to herself at that. James Hutton was the same age as her, but clearly he was the person they had in mind when they talked about actuaries having a personality bypass. As soon as he opened his mouth to speak most people's eyes began to glaze over. But if even James made the effort to go to the Christmas party, Darcey knew that she couldn't miss it herself.

The girls at the house, who'd asked her about Christmas

at ProSure, were delighted to hear that she was going out. Gill said that they'd begun to wonder about her apparent lack of social life; Helen told her that the office party was an integral part of Christmas which couldn't be ignored; and Jackie commented ultra-casually that the party was the ideal time for a makeover.

'Oh look, I did that once before,' Darcey told her, remembering her efforts at Car Crew. 'But I relapsed. I'm not the type.'

'I'm not going to dignify that with an answer,' said Jackie, who was always impeccably groomed. She picked up the phone and dialled the local beauty salon.

'It's only a party,' protested Darcey feebly. 'There's no point in . . .'

'Look, I know you're an obsessed career woman,' said Jackie. 'But everyone needs a bit of glitz from time to time, and you'll get on much better if you take a few minutes to do your face every morning.'

'I'm not a career woman!' Darcey was shocked.

'With the hours you work?' Jackie looked at her sceptically. 'We all think you're nuts.'

How weird, Darcey thought, that they believed her to be a career woman just because she actually liked her job. Surely that simply made her a normal person who enjoyed what she did? Career women were different. They were like Nieve, scheming and plotting and stabbing people in the back.

She wished she hadn't thought of Nieve. She'd been doing pretty well at pretending the bitch had vanished off the face of the earth. She knew, because Minette had told her in a phone call, that Nieve was doing well in the States. Gail

Stapleton kept Minette informed as to how her daughter was getting on. The two mothers hadn't fallen out over what both agreed was bad behaviour by Nieve. Gail defended her daughter by saying that these things happened and that Darcey would get over it; Minette responded by talking up Darcey's job in London, which made Gail tell her about Nieve's success in return – but as neighbours they both felt they had to stay civil to each other; although Minette couldn't help feeling relieved the day Gail told her that she and Stephen had bought a new home near Oughterard and would be moving there shortly. But whenever Minette mentioned Nieve, Darcey felt a hot rage take over so that her stomach cramped into a knot and her head started to throb.

'Even if you're not a totally committed career woman, you need a decent bit of slap,' Jackie said. 'And you absolutely must dress up for the party. I'm not letting you out of the house until you give in.'

So she did, even though she told them that it was a complete waste of time and money. She didn't do glamorous. It wasn't in her nature.

All the same, she left the office early on the day of the party (much to James's astonishment) and turned up at the beauty salon to fulfil her duckling-into-swan destiny. As she approached the double glass doors and saw the incredibly beautiful receptionist inside, she almost chickened out. But she didn't, and spent the next couple of hours being pampered on a grand scale and gently lectured about the importance of looking after her skin and her hair. That afternoon was the beginning of her lifelong addiction to hair serum and GHDs.

By the time they'd finished with her, her blonde frizz had been smoothed and glossed, her face had been made up so that her eyes appeared bluer and her lips fuller and, for the first time since she was about seven, she was wearing nail varnish. Darcey didn't bite her nails, but she wore them very short, so the salon had given her French polish tips to lengthen them. She was fascinated by them and kept waving her hands ultra-casually in front of her, although she wondered how easy it would be to use a keyboard with acrylic nails. She blinked a couple of times as she stared at her reflection in the mirror. If she'd looked like this a few months ago, she couldn't help but wonder, would Aidan Clarke have left her for Nieve Stapleton after all?

Jackie, Helena and Gill were all thrilled by her appearance. And they were even more thrilled when she slipped into the dress she was wearing for the night: full-length green velvet with a low-cut V-neck and equally low-cut back.

'Crikey,' gasped Helena.

'I should've bought decent shoes,' said Darcey regretfully. 'I never thought of them.'

'You're the same size as me, aren't you?' asked Gill. 'Five?' Darcey nodded.

'You can borrow my party pair,' said Gill. 'They'll work with that dress.' She disappeared into her room and returned with a pair of black suede shoes with a small velvet bow at the toe. 'See, perfect.'

'I can't borrow your shoes!' exclaimed Darcey.

'D'you have veruccas?' demanded Gill.

'Ugh, no!'

'And you're wearing stockings, aren't you?'

Darcey nodded.

'Well, then. No probs.'

'Um . . . well . . . thanks.' Darcey slipped on the shoes. They fitted perfectly.

'Now, Cinderella,' Helena giggled, 'you shall go to the ball.'

Darcey laughed and waved goodbye to them. And then she set out for the party.

The hotel was already crowded when she arrived. She was glad that she'd given in and spent hours at the beauty salon because every single woman in the company had been stylishly transformed, and it would have been a disaster if she'd turned up, as she'd originally intended, in her five-year-old little black dress and having done her hair herself. She would have felt terrible. As it was, she felt great. She walked to the bar and ordered a glass of wine. It had been a good year for the company which, as a result, had provided a free bar. By the time dinner was served most of the employees had got themselves into the Christmas spirit, and Darcey, who'd never really been much of a drinker, knew that three glasses of Chablis had taken the edge off her natural reserve and made her feel more outgoing and relaxed than she'd been in ages. Which was why, as she walked back from redoing her lipstick and saw Neil Lomond sitting at a table on his own, she sat down beside him.

'How's it going?' she asked.

'Good grief.' He looked at her in astonishment. 'Darcey?'

'Who else would I be?' she asked.

He sat up straighter. 'You look completely different.'

'It's the Christmas party,' she said dismissively. 'I got dressed up.'

'You look great,' said Neil. 'I like how you look normally, but tonight you've got the wow factor!'

She laughed. 'Gee, thanks.'

They looked at each other in silence for a moment.

'And listen, Neil, thanks again for getting me the job.'

'You know, you thank me regularly for that.'

'I'm not good with casual conversation. I tend to repeat myself.'

'Well, I'm glad you like actuary-land.'

'I love it.'

He grinned at her. 'Saddo.'

'I know. It's awful, isn't it? At this stage in my life the most important thing should be clubbing on Saturday nights or something, but I really do like struggling with actuarial tables more.'

'Even more sad than I thought. And so untypical. Especially for a natural blonde.'

She punched him gently on the shoulder. 'We're not all thick, you know. And it might not be natural.'

Neil raised an eyebrow and she felt herself blush.

'I desperately want to make a joke about finding out, but I'm afraid that might be considered harassment,' he said.

'Dead right,' she said, straight-faced.

'I'm sorry.' But he didn't look in the slightest bit contrite. 'I'd like to harass you a little bit.'

'Neil!' Darcey felt her face flush.

'Well, not harass you,' he said quickly. 'Just . . . I've a soft spot for blonde, blue-eyed girls with fabulous complexions who put me in my place – and you sooooo did that at the sandwich bar over the cost of the order.'

'I just told you how much it was,' she protested, aware that her cheeks were still pink.

'It was the way you did it,' he said.

'I hope you're joking.'

'Of course I am.' He smiled at her. 'Actually, I just knew that they were looking for people in actuarial who had even a faint grasp of arithmetic. I'm good pals with the head of that department. He's always complaining that the junior staff are numerically illiterate.'

'Lots of people are,' agreed Darcey. 'They're afraid of numbers. I don't know why. I like numbers. I like the logic of it. And the certainty.' She hiccoughed gently. 'Oh! Excuse me.'

'That's OK.'

She took a deep breath and held it.

'Does that work for you?' he asked.

She scrunched up her nose.

'How long can you hold your breath for?'

She made a face at him.

'Do y'know that you're going all red? And it's clashing with your dress.'

She released her breath in a puff and giggled. Her hiccoughs had gone. Neil was laughing too.

'Yes, it works,' she said. 'But I simply can't clash with my dress!'

'Excellent,' he said. 'Want to dance with me?'

'Why not?'

It was only as he led her on to the dance floor that she

realised their conversation had been the longest non-work-related conversation she'd had with a man since Aidan. And it was only as he put his arm around her that she realised what a nice guy Neil Lomond was.

'And so?' Anna looked at her impatiently. 'What happened?'

'He was lovely,' said Darcey. 'He was attractive and nice and he seemed just the guy for me. But . . .' She faltered. 'I couldn't really believe in it. I kept thinking something would happen – he'd find someone else and it'd be over. Besides, it wasn't the same as what I'd felt for Aidan. And so I thought that Aidan was the one I should really be with. I thought that maybe I should have fought for him. Not given in to Nieve the way I did.'

Darcey rested her brow in her cupped hands as the memories rushed back.

'Darcey? Are you all right?' Anna's voice broke into her thoughts.

'Sure.' She shrugged. 'I wasn't really in love with Neil, just the idea of being in love with him. Of having someone madly in love with me. We got married in Gretna Green shortly after we met.'

'Jeez, Darcey . . .'

'I wanted to marry him. I felt . . .'

'What?'

'That if I didn't, someone else would.'

Anna looked at her with sudden understanding. 'Just because your first real boyfriend ran off with your best friend doesn't mean that you have to marry the second in case he runs off with someone else too.'

'Oh, I know that now,' said Darcey quickly. 'But I didn't then. I felt that getting married was really, really important. Nieve and Aidan were married – or so I thought – and I reckoned that getting married myself would . . . would . . . make me feel OK about it all.' She shook her head helplessly. 'Thing was, he was up for it too. He wanted to be married to me. I honestly think he loved me.'

'And why didn't you love him back?'

'Bottom line? I don't think I was over Aidan at all. I felt cheated out of him, you know? I wasn't able to love someone else.'

'Oh, Darcey.'

'I know,' said Darcey. 'I behaved just as badly as Nieve in the end. I married him and I didn't love him and it was a horrible, stupid and unfair thing to do. I don't blame him for how things turned out. It was all my fault.'

She hadn't worried about how things would turn out at first. When they'd returned to work after their wedding at Gretna Green (chosen because Neil confessed to always having wanted to get married there) and after the furore of their becoming an item and getting married all within the space of a couple of months (Minette had tried to hide her anxiety about it, but Darcey knew she wasn't entirely happy, even though she liked Neil) she was sure that she'd eventually forget about Aidan Clarke. They rented an apartment a couple of tube stops from the office; they went into work together, they came home together and sometimes they lunched in the staff restaurant together too. Darcey reckoned that they must be crazy about each other after all to spend so much time with each other.

She asked him every day whether he was happy and whether he loved her, and she told him every day that he was the only person in the world for her. She went to cookery classes so that she could be confident with a range of home-cooked meals for him, even though he told her that he was perfectly happy with takeaways. She chided him, saying that they were fine as treats but not every night, warning him about cholesterol and blood pressure and telling him that she would always look after his best interests.

He used to laugh and call her his little perfectionist, and he'd make her laugh too. And she would always be relieved that, even if they argued, they could laugh about that too.

She was delighted when he was promoted within the client relationships department. He worked hard and deserved the promotion, but it meant that he often had to work longer hours and travel more, usually to places in Europe that she knew and remembered from her travels with Nieve and with the Brainy Broads. She envied him because she thought it would be nice to go to all those places again, not as a tourist but as someone with a different reason to be there. She wished him luck any time he went away, and hated being alone. She was surprised at how bad she was at being on her own now, given that she'd never had any real problem with it before. Every time she went to bed by herself she would pull Neil's pillow under the covers beside her and hug it close to her body, struggling to sleep in the absence of his rhythmic breathing beside her in the bed.

'It's you, not me who should be going on these trips,' said Neil one evening as he packed an overnight bag for his flight the following day. 'Your French is so much better than mine and it does so shock them when you can understand every single word they're saying.'

'Yes, but you know what to say to them.' Darcey handed him a neatly folded shirt (ironed by Neil, who was much neater and better at housework than her).

'You'd be good at that.' Neil stopped packing and looked at her. 'You seem to remember everything about our product range just by reading it once. And then you're good at explaining things. I know most of the time you prefer to scrabble around with your numbers and stuff, but actually, when you get talking, you're quite good.'

'Gee, thanks!'

'No, I mean it. It's kind of astonishing how good you are with people in the office. You seem to have a flair for talking about the business and making them feel at ease with it. And that's odd, because . . .'

'Because what?' She handed him a pair of socks.

'Well, because you're not so . . . so open at home.'

'What on earth does that mean?' she demanded.

'Just that you seem to be better at talking about finance than about feelings.'

Her eyes narrowed. 'What feelings do you want me to talk about?' she asked.

'Oh, I'm just being silly.' He grinned at her. 'I'm going away and I want you to throw your arms around me and tell me that you love me.'

'Of course I love you.' She hugged him. 'Of course I do.'

'Good,' said Neil. 'Because you're the only girl in the world for me.'

In the office the following day she bumped into Ricky Calvin, who worked with Neil.

'I thought you'd gone to Paris,' she said in surprise.

'Not this time. Didn't Neil tell you?'

'I didn't ask,' she admitted. 'He's on his own?'

'No,' said Ricky. 'Jessica's gone with him.'

'Jessica? Jessica Hammond?' She looked at him in surprise. 'But she's only been in the company a wet week. What's she doing going on trips to Paris?'

'Oh, Jessica's fast-tracked for the top,' said Ricky wryly. 'And why wouldn't she be? She's smart and good-looking and she knows exactly what she wants. To be fair, though, she does have experience. She worked in client relations in another company.'

'Still.' Darcey looked thoughtful. 'It's a big move for her.'

That evening, Neil phoned to say that they were spending another night in Paris. And even though he gave her the perfectly rational explanation that one of their clients hadn't been able to make the meeting but had asked if they could do it the following morning instead, Darcey was conscious of a sudden thread of anxiety beginning to unravel inside her.

'I was insanely jealous,' she explained to Anna as her untasted coffee cooled in front of her. 'Off-the-scale jealous. I kept thinking that if she was fast-tracked for success, she must be the sharp career woman that I simply wasn't. She was the new Nieve Stapleton, and if she wanted Neil she'd just go after him. Which I kinda assumed was what she was doing on that extra night in Paris.

'So when he came home I quizzed him incessantly about every second of every hour of the trip. Eventually I asked him straight out if he was having an affair with her. He was furious with me – asked me exactly why it was I didn't trust him. I said he was a man, wasn't he, and was therefore intrinsically untrustworthy.'

'Oh dear,' said Anna.

'He was really hurt. I see that now, of course, but I didn't back then. And because I didn't feel able to talk to him about Aidan and Nieve and explain why I was so irrationally jealous, things just festered between us.'

Darcey pushed her coffee cup away from her. 'It all came to a head one evening when they were working late and I was at home watching a TV movie. In the movie, the manager of the office was having an affair with his secretary and they were getting down and dirty on his desk. Somehow I got the idea that Neil and Jessica were . . . well . . . you know I have damn-all imagination of my own, but seeing the TV made me think . . . Anyway, I went back to the ProSure building, stormed into his office and accused them of having an affair.'

'Darcey!'

'They both looked at me as though I was completely bonkers. They were checking through some figures and of course there was nothing going on at all. He told me to go home and she could hardly keep the smile off her face. I was humiliated. But, you know, so was he.'

\*   \*   \*

She closed her eyes as she remembered it. She'd walked out of the office and gone home just as he'd demanded, ashamed and embarrassed at her overreaction and wondering what on earth had happened to her. She'd always been a logical person before, but somehow she was totally unable to think logically now. She sat alone in their apartment and wondered how it was that she seemed unable to have a trusting relationship with her husband, who had never given her any reason to believe he'd be unfaithful to her.

It was very late by the time she heard Neil's key in the lock. She felt a sense of relief, because she'd thought that maybe he wouldn't come home at all.

'I am *not* having an affair with Jessica Hammond,' he said as he walked into the living room. 'I have never been unfaithful to you. I love you very much. But you've got a big problem about something and you're taking it out on me.'

'Maybe,' said Darcey.

Her admission stopped Neil in his tracks. 'Tell me about it.'

She'd had a lot of time to examine her feelings and her behaviour while sitting at home waiting for him. So she told him all about Aidan Clarke and Nieve Stapleton and her sense of betrayal by both her best friend and the man she'd loved. And she told him that she was struggling to believe that it wouldn't happen again.

'I'm not this guy,' said Neil angrily. 'He sounds like a complete shit and not deserving of a moment of your thoughts. Darcey, I love you. I married you.'

'Yes, but what if you get tired of me and someone better

comes along?' She looked at him unhappily. 'Jessica Hammond is beautiful and smart.'

'You're beautiful and smart,' said Neil.

'Don't lie to me.'

'Darcey, you're lovely. I love you. And you know that you're smart.'

'Clever, perhaps,' she admitted. 'That's totally different. I'm not . . . I'm not work-smart. And, be honest with me, Neil, I'm not beautiful either.'

'I'm tired of this.' He looked at her in frustration. 'I love you and I married you, but you don't seem to believe me.'

'I do.' She leaned forward and rested her head in her hands. 'I do. I'm sorry.'

'Hey, don't be sorry.' He put his arms around her. 'It's fine. We're fine. We just need to work it out a bit.'

'Yeah,' she said. 'That's all we need to do.'


'So didn't you kiss and make up?' asked Anna. 'Didn't you try to work it out?'

Darcey nodded. 'But then it happened again. Y'see, I couldn't really believe that someone as great as him had fallen for me, no matter what he told me. I'd completely lost my sense of perspective and was just waiting for it all to go horribly wrong.'

'Darcey, that's crazy.'

'I know. I know. I even knew it at the time. But it was like someone had pushed the self-destruct button on me. And then – well, it was bad enough when I'd stormed into the office the first time and it was only Jessica, but I did it again. He was at lunch in a local pub with Melinda

McIntyre from our new business division. What I didn't realise was that she was informally interviewing him for a job. Anyway, I'd gone to the pub with a couple of the actuaries because we'd finished a particular project and this was our very exciting way of celebrating. When I saw them there I went over to them and demanded to know what they were talking about and why they were sitting together so cosily in the corner. When he told me to get lost, I upended his plate on his lap!'

'Crikey.'

'I was fired.' Darcey heaved a sigh. 'Not surprisingly. And they told him that if he ever wanted to get on in business, he'd either have to ditch me or see that I got psychiatric help.'

'And he ditched you?' Anna looked incredulous.

'He tried so hard to help me,' Darcey said sadly. 'He really did. But I was beyond help at that point. I refused to talk to anyone about it, but I was caught up in my own world where every man was a cheating bastard and every woman was a total bitch. He couldn't cope with it in the end and I don't blame him one bit.'

'Whew.' Anna gazed at her friend and Darcey grinned lopsidedly.

'Afraid of me now?'

'No,' said Anna. 'How did you get over it all?'

'I headed back to Ireland and told my mother what had happened and that Neil had filed for divorce, and she freaked out and said that I might have behaved really badly but he was a shit to leave me,' Darcey told her.

'Hum.'

'And I told her that I didn't actually blame him for leaving me but, yes, I did seem to have problems. I told her that I hadn't really loved him in the first place. That I married him – well, to get back at Nieve and Aidan. She was utterly horrified at that. She told me that I was a bad person. Of course then she immediately said that she understood and that I wasn't really bad, just upset. But she was right the first time. I was horrible and I behaved appallingly. So I ended up seeing someone and getting a bit of counselling so that I could put it all into perspective. But not until after I'd sat at home for three months comfort-eating so that I ballooned in weight and turned into this hideous lank-haired, dull-eyed blob who was a million times more unattractive than before.'

'You're being hard on yourself,' said Anna.

'It wasn't until Tish and Amelie started being hard on me that I jolted out of it,' Darcey told her. 'Maman felt that feeding me up was a good thing because I was like a rake when I got home. I hadn't eaten for ages. It was the one time that being miserable put me off my food!'

Anna exhaled slowly. 'I didn't know any of this. I'm supposed to be your friend, but you didn't tell me.'

'It's not something I wanted to revisit,' said Darcey. 'Truth is, I'm fine now. Anyway, I did a lot of talking through my issues, as they like to say, and then I decided to head to Dublin to get a job. Only thing was, I didn't want a permanent job. I wanted to be a temp so that I couldn't get involved with anyone in the company. It seemed to me that I'd had to leave two jobs because I'd got involved with people there, so I didn't want to do it again. And I didn't want to be in a position where I'd get really interested in the job or be seen as a career woman. Only I got over that in the end.' She laughed. 'Lured by the money, I guess. Anyway, I'd changed. I realised that there were other things in life besides looking for happiness in the wrong places. And I eventually got over all of it. Although I do worry that one day someone from management will find out that I was a complete whacko.'

'There were extenuating circumstances,' said Anna.

'Oh, come on!' Darcey shook her head. 'Loads of girls have relationships that break up and they don't just marry the next available bloke who comes along. Loads of girls get married and don't suspect their husband of having affairs with every woman he meets afterwards. Most girls are actually in love with the man they marry. I was just crap at all that. Like Neil said once, I have better relationships with square roots and algebra than with people.'

'You're fine with people!' Anna disagreed with her. 'Darcey, you're the business development manager, for heaven's sake. You meet people all the time.'

'Ah, yes, but I don't get involved with them,' said Darcey. 'That's the difference.'

'What about your occasional guys?' asked Anna. 'Your continental fuck-buddies.'

Darcey made a face at her. 'That's a really horrible expression,' she said. 'If true. And yes, I sleep with them because I enjoy it, but I don't have relationships with them.'

'Which is why you never hang on to a man?'

'I'm not cut out for it,' said Darcey. 'There's some kind of DNA thing missing. I don't do good relationships.'

'You're older now,' said Anna. 'And wiser. Maybe it's time to start.'

'Just because you know you're crap at something doesn't mean you'll ever be any good at it,' Darcey told her. 'I'm out of the relationship business and I'm happy that way. And so if you want to go ahead and seduce Neil Lomond, that's perfectly all right by me. He deserves someone good. He deserves someone like you.'

Anna looked at her thoughtfully. 'Are you sure you're totally over it all? I mean, if you're upset because of this wedding invitation, if Neil being here is getting to you . . .'

'It's unsettling,' admitted Darcey. 'It's bringing it all back. But it's not a big issue. I promise you.'

Anna nodded slowly. But Darcey could see that she wasn't entirely convinced.

# Chapter 16

Nieve liked celebrating her birthday. Each year, as the day fell, she thought about the highlights of the previous twelve months and set herself goals for the coming ones. This year it was easy. The highlight, without a doubt, was the Ennco buyout. She hadn't yet decided on what her goal for the next year would be. It would be difficult to top the seven-figure dollar payout she was due to receive.

'Perhaps you should set up a business of your own,' suggested Courtney Crane, one of the group of friends who'd met Nieve and Aidan at Buck's Diner to mark the occasion. 'You sure have the balls to go it alone, and . . .' she looked around at the other people in the iconic Woodside restaurant with its kitsch diner decor, which had become a Mecca for geeks and venture capitalists alike, 'you could hook up with someone here to get you going.'

Nieve laughed. 'Perhaps. But it would have to be something I really cared about.'

'Difficult,' said Aidan easily, 'given that the thing you care most about is yourself.'

There was an edgy silence at the table and their friends

looked at each of them uncomfortably. But Nieve roared with laughter again.

'That's so not true,' she told him. 'I care more about you than anything else. Didn't I buy you a new Prius to prove it?'

Relieved chuckles echoed around the table and Aidan grinned at her.

'Of course you did.' He leaned towards her and kissed her on the cheek. 'And I didn't mean that to sound as if you were an egotistical bitch. I just meant that you look after number one.'

'Well, hey, if I don't, who else will?' she demanded. Her question embraced everyone at the table and each of them nodded in agreement. It was all very well, they conceded, to work for a generous company or to have high-minded ideals about how life should be, but you always had to remember that no matter what they said publicly, everyone else was looking after their own interests and you had to protect yourself first.

'How are the wedding plans coming along?' asked Mischa Jewell. 'I can't wait to be part of the Irish event of the year.'

'It's going to be great!' Nieve detailed the plans so far and Mischa and Courtney, who were going to be brides-maids, nodded in agreement with them.

'I just love the sound of that castle,' said Mischa, who'd Googled it and had been enchanted by the rolling coun-tryside and lowering skies. 'And the restaurant for the rehearsal dinner sounds just peachy.'

'I hope so,' said Nieve. 'I haven't been there before, but Lorelei, my wedding-planner, assures me that it's top notch. I worry a bit because it is, as we say, in the absolute arsehole of nowhere, but apparently there are all sorts of decent restaurants in out-of-the-way places.'

'And we're staying in a real Irish castle,' cried Courtney. 'I can't wait.'

'I hope it's OK.' Nieve looked a little worried. 'You can never be too sure about these damn castles. Everyone expects something like Dromoland – you know, famous faces enjoying luxury living in a completely renovated setting – but I have a horrible feeling that some of them trade on the fact that it's a castle and forget about the home comforts a bit.'

'Maybe that's what you should do with your money,' said Mischa.

'Buy a castle?' Nieve laughed.

'And run it like a luxury hotel,' suggested Courtney.

'Can you really see me doing home-cooked breakfasts in the mornings?' demanded Nieve.

Her friends laughed.

'Now that you mention it – absolutely not,' Mischa conceded. 'Anyway, it all sounds utterly fabulous and I'm so looking forward to it. Hope the Ennco share price recovers a bit so that you can pay for it all!'

Nieve made a face. The markets had been going through a bit of a downturn over the past couple of weeks and the Ennco share price had traded steadily lower, eroding some of the profit that she hoped to make. But by the time she'd be able to sell them – a couple of weeks after the wedding – things would undoubtedly have recovered again. She certainly wasn't going to worry about a few thousand dollars, although, she acknowledged, better in her bank account than someone else's. Still, no point in getting in a heap about it. She'd spoken to both The Bear and The Stuffer about the likely market trends for the coming weeks, and they'd both agreed that there was a good chance of a rebound once the next set of economic figures was out of the way. Neither of them was too worried, which comforted Nieve immensely, since The Bear, by his very nature, always looked on the pessimistic side of things.

'I can't believe I'm thirty-four,' she exclaimed as her food – the hot Dungeness crab with melted Cheddar that she always ordered at Buck's – was placed in front of her. 'It seems like only yesterday I was twenty-four.'

'And you haven't changed a bit,' Aidan told her.

'Thank you.' She beamed at him.

'So here's to the next thirty-four years,' he said, raising his glass, 'especially since they're so full of options.'

It was later that night, when they were curled up together in the swing-chair on the veranda of their timber-framed house that she asked him what he thought those options were. He'd been talking more and more about the future lately, and now, with the sounds of the cicadas in the pine trees behind them and a warm breeze wafting across the garden, she wanted to know what was on his mind.

'Oh, I haven't pinned down specifics,' he told her. 'Like Courtney said, maybe you want to open a business of your own.'

'It's a possibility. As long as it's not a B&B in Galway! We could make good money if I pick the next big thing.'

He nodded, although she could see that he'd simply

thrown out the comment and it wasn't something he really wanted to happen.

'But that's not what you want me to do.'

He set down the frosted margarita that he'd blended earlier and looked at her.

'No. It's not.'

'What then?'

'We're going home,' he told her. 'And maybe it's time we stayed there.'

'What!' She looked at him in astonishment. 'Are you out of your mind? Stay in Ireland? Why?' She shook her head. 'Besides I can't. I've got to stick with Ennco for six months under the terms of the deal.'

'But after that we could go home. This . . .' he gestured to embrace the veranda, the house and garden and all of Palo Alto, 'this isn't home. This is – this was the dream. We've done it. Now maybe it's time to go back.'

'This *is* home,' she said fiercely. 'It's not a dream. It's reality. I've worked bloody hard for us to get here and you're saying that it's not enough!'

'I'm not saying that,' he told her. 'I'm saying that since you've now hit the jackpot, maybe we can afford to live a little. Go back home, buy a nice house in Galway, do our own thing there.'

'For crying out loud, you wanted to leave,' she protested. 'You were the one who said that Galway was a jumped-up backwater village. Why on earth would you want to go back?'

'Because sometimes it's so frantic here,' said Aidan. 'The money-making ruthlessness of it all. The long hours. The fact that all we care about is whether we have more and bigger and better and . . .' He shrugged. 'There has to be more to life.'

'Haven't you read the reports on Ireland now?' she asked acidly. 'The capitalist centre of Europe. You think life's going to be any different in Galway?' She snorted. 'It'll be exactly the same, only bloody colder.'

He laughed. 'Maybe you're right. But, sweetheart, don't you think it's time for us to look at our priorities? As a family.'

'We are,' she said. 'We're getting married.'

'I know,' he said patiently. 'But there's more to a family than just the two of us.'

She looked at him uncomprehendingly.

'Nieve – what about children? We did say, didn't we, that we'd have children some day.'

'Sure,' she agreed dismissively. 'But there's plenty of time.'

'I don't want to sound ageist and everything on your birthday,' he said, 'but you're thirty-four. It gets harder.'

She looked at him angrily. 'What are you saying? That I'm washed out and old?'

'Of course not,' he said. 'You know I don't think that. But if you really do want kids, hon, it's something that we should be factoring into the equation now.'

Nieve said nothing. She was bitterly regretting having initiated the conversation and the direction it was taking. Aidan was right, she'd agreed on having children. She did want them. Eventually. On her own terms. When she was ready. She knew all that claptrap about her biological clock, but she felt as good as, if not better than she'd done when she was in her twenties. She had the energy. She could afford to wait.

'Before it was all about work,' said Aidan, thinking it would be better to get away from the topic of children. 'Now you've got the rewards, why can't work take a back seat?'

'I'm not the only one with a career here,' she said. 'What about you?'

'Oh, look, I'm doing OK, but it doesn't matter as much to me. I'm not as driven as you and I haven't landed the big bucks either. I'm too lazy for that. I know that everyone thinks IT people earn a fortune here, but not doing what I do.'

'You earn good money,' she said.

'Sweetheart, what I make is nothing – nothing – in comparison to the payoff. How could it be? My career, anything I want to do, is irrelevant.'

'No it's not,' she said obstinately. 'When we came here first you said that you got a great buzz out of the whole industry. I know it went pear-shaped for a while, but you like what you do. I can't believe that you want to throw it all away.'

'Sure I like what I do. But it's a job. Yes, I might tinker around with software just for the fun of it. But not to make money. Because you've made the money. There's no need for me to try to compete with you. But there's no need for you to compete with yourself either. You can afford to step back.'

'If I step back now, what will happen to my career?' Nieve looked at him blankly.

'Hon, you've got everything you wanted out of your career,' he pointed out. 'We could live – a tiny bit downsized maybe – but still we could live on the interest of the share sale.'

'Oh, come on, our lifestyle would be crap by comparison!' she said fiercely. 'A few million isn't what it used to be, you know. Besides, I haven't achieved everything. I want to prove myself.'

'You *have* proved yourself.' This time his voice was impatient. 'God Almighty, Nieve, how much more do you have to do?'

She got up abruptly from the swing seat so that Aidan had to grab hold of the armrest to prevent himself from falling out of it. He watched as she walked through the neatly tended garden and stopped beside the elaborate marble fountain they'd had installed the previous year.

She was still beautiful, he thought, as she stepped into the glow of a garden light. Her face was smooth and unlined and her dark hair still tumbled around her shoulders in the careful disarray of curls that had so disarmed him when he'd first seen her over ten years ago. She still had the same restless energy and force of personality that had drawn him to her, that had made Darcey McGonigle suddenly seem so insignificant beside her. And that was what he loved about her. He loved the way she swept him along with her, never once complaining that he should do more or be more than he was. She'd said to him once that he was her rock. That with him beside her she could blaze her way through life, knowing that he would always be there for her. But he couldn't help feeling that it was impossible to live life at full throttle for ever and that surely now it was time for them to ease back a bit. He'd thought that getting married would be the beginning of a new phase in their lives. Now he was beginning to wonder whether he'd misjudged things after all.

She called the shots. How could that not be when she was the one with the real earning power, when she was the one who'd made all the right decisions, and when she was the one who'd steered them successfully out of the mess that had overwhelmed them after the technology disaster? They'd been laden with debt then because of the big house they'd bought on the expectations of bigger money that had never materialised. Those days they'd sat in Buck's, shellshocked along with so many other people by what had happened to them. But she'd picked her way through it all and managed to find the job outside the industry that had turned it all around. And all the time being optimistic and determined and never letting him allow the tentacles of despair to wrap themselves around him. Because he had been despairing. All those qualified people looking for jobs. And he was only one in thousands. One who didn't have the same skills as many of the others. One who was better at fixing things than creating things. It had been a nightmare. He knew that the whole thing had both scared and scarred her. And he knew that she wanted to feel secure. But there was no way, with the great Ennco deal behind them, that they wouldn't be secure for ever. He just had to make her see that.

He got up and walked over to her.

'I'm sorry,' he said. 'I didn't mean to pressurise you.'

'Didn't you?'

'No,' he said. 'I do want a family, I have to admit that. But I don't really mind whether we live here or in Ireland. I guess I was just keyed up over the idea of being there again.'

'There'll be children,' she told him. 'I promise.'

He kissed her on the cheek and put his arm around her. 'I know,' he said. 'And I bet you'll be just as brilliant at being a mother as you are at everything else.'

Later that night, as Aidan lay sleeping, Nieve pushed back the oyster silk comforter and slid out of their enormous bed. She tiptoed into their plainly decorated home office, where she switched on the computer and looked at the Ennco graph. Aidan was right, she thought as she looked at the line with its massive upward spike and with only the tiniest of downward movements on it reflecting the last few weeks. They were totally secure. They could afford to have a family and she could afford to be a stay-at-home mother.

She leaned her head against the razor-thin screen. She'd hoped that organising the wedding would divert Aidan away from the whole question of babies and families, which she knew had been at the back of his mind for the past few months, but if anything it had made him worse. She knew that there was an age issue. She wasn't stupid. But she just didn't feel ready yet. She'd seen friends, once committed career women like herself, succumb eventually to the tyranny of talcum powder and school runs and being on the PTA. These weren't the sorts of things she was interested in. People said it was different when it was your own kids, but she couldn't see how she could juggle her career and a family. It wasn't fair on your colleagues when you skived off for family stuff.

But she wouldn't have to do everything, would she? She could afford a nanny or an au pair, couldn't she? And the thought made her grimace, because she'd suddenly remembered being the Christies' au pair and how often she'd wanted to get away from those bloody demanding kids! Despite what Aidan said, would she be a crap mother? Had she been a crap au pair? After all, she'd lived for her time off, when she could get away from the house and meet Darcey at the beachfront bar for a drink.

Would Darcey and Aidan have had kids together before now? The sudden thought shocked her. She hadn't thought of them together ever since she'd first slept with Aidan and known that there was no way he was going back to Darcey. But now she couldn't help wondering. If they'd married each other after all, would Nieve have been proved wrong by them staying together and having children together and making it all work out?

No, she thought. They wouldn't. She was quite certain of that.

She still hadn't heard back from Darcey about the wedding, which surprised her. She'd expected to receive a reply even if it was a regret. She could certainly understand Darcey not coming, but there was no way she wasn't going to invite her.

She leaned back in her chair. Aidan was hoping that Darcey wouldn't come and had flipped when he realised Nieve had invited her.

'What if she freaks out?' he'd asked, and Nieve had had

to say that if Darcey was in freak mode she wouldn't come. Why would she want to make a fool of herself? Aidan had muttered that he simply couldn't understand why she'd asked Darcey at all and Nieve had murmured something about showing that there were no hard feelings. She didn't say anything about wanting to prove something to her former friend. She didn't think Aidan would understand that.

Would she lose him if she put off having children any longer? Nieve nibbled at the tip of her finger. She truly loved him; he made her feel clever and in control of things. She liked knowing that she could depend on him to turn up at her business functions and wow everyone around him because now, at thirty-six, he was even more attractive than he'd been when she'd first met him. She didn't want to lose Aidan. He was hers. But she had to have a strategy for keeping him.

She logged off the computer. The first part of the strategy was getting the marriage under her belt. Then she had to persuade him that the children would come. And the third part of the strategy was making sure that he was happy while he was waiting.

She'd always been able to keep him happy. She'd always known which buttons to press. That was why she'd been the one to ask him to marry her. She'd always said she'd marry him when she'd achieved her dream.

But, she wondered as she sat in the darkness of the room, would it be a good idea to consider a pre-nup first? Just in case things went horribly wrong in the future?

# Chapter 17

Darcey arrived at the airport with even more time in hand than usual, because she wanted to get through security as quickly as possible and have her morning coffee in peace without bumping into Neil Lomond. They were travelling to Edinburgh together that morning so that she could make her presentation to the relevant people there, and Neil had originally suggested picking her up at her apartment.

'I'm getting a cab from Sandymount,' he told her. 'It's only a short distance away.'

'You'd be much better simply heading across the toll bridge,' she replied. 'Don't worry about me. I'll be there on time.'

She didn't want Neil to come to her apartment even if he decided to wait outside in a taxi. In fact she wasn't entirely comfortable about travelling with him to Scotland, despite her assertion to Anna that his being in the company didn't bother her at all. She didn't relish the idea of sitting beside him on a plane and worrying that at some point the conversation would shift to personal things. She didn't want to discuss anything personal with her ex-husband who, she felt, was still pissed off with her (not that she could really blame him). And as she'd murmured the words 'ex-husband' to herself, she realised that she still couldn't quite believe that she had both married and divorced the man who now had influence over her career. Somehow her life with Neil seemed to have taken place in a parallel universe where she'd been a very different person. She couldn't imagine getting upset over a man these days.

She organised her own cab to take her to the airport and having completed the check-in, she strode towards the security gates, a striking figure dressed in a black leather coat over a black cashmere top and tailored black trousers, her golden hair slicked back into a tiny bun at the back of her head. Her computer case, carried over her shoulder, was pillar-box red.

'Darcey!' She heard her name through the buzz of the crowd and whirled around. Neil was a few feet behind her. She frowned.

'Gosh but you walk fast,' he said as he caught up with her. 'Work out these days, do you?'

'Not especially.' She wished, no matter how much she had managed to put it all behind her, that she felt more at ease with him.

'You ready for today?' he asked.

'That's a silly question,' she responded mildly as they joined the queue. 'Haven't I been wasting my time on this presentation for weeks?'

'It's not a waste of time,' he told her. 'Your expertise is important.'

'I guess so.'

God, I sound petulant, she thought. I don't want to sound like this. I want to be upbeat and cheerful and an asset to the company and not like some raw recruit straight out of college. I need to focus!

But working and travelling with Neil was all so freaky, she was finding it difficult to cope. It was usually the other way around in these type of situations, she thought. The employee would fall for the boss and everyone eventually would live happily ever after. It shouldn't be that the employee had already divorced the boss and was having to prove to him that she wasn't a complete flake any more. She groaned inwardly. She'd never really been much good at getting things right. And she didn't think anyone believed in happy ever after these days.

'Coffee?' suggested Neil. 'I could really do with a cup.'

'You're here very early,' she remarked as they walked towards the café.

'I can't help it,' he said. 'I hate being late.'

Yes, she remembered that. She remembered thinking at the time that it was something that should keep them together, a shared belief. But in the end it was one more thing that drove them apart. Because every time he had been unavoidably late, she'd been convinced he was seeing another woman, and every second that went by made her get angrier and angrier at his probable infidelity.

God, I really was messed up back then, she thought as she put her espresso cup on her tray. I'm glad I've got through it all now. I'm glad that I don't overreact to things any more and I'm glad that I don't need to have a man in my life to make me feel worthwhile. I'm just sorry that Neil was in the wrong place at the wrong time. Because he was a decent bloke and he didn't deserve the hard time I gave him.

'Still drinking that rotgut?' he asked as she took her espresso to a recently vacated table.

She smiled faintly. 'Depends. Sometimes I take the herbal tea route, but it was late when I got to bed last night and I need the boost.'

'You don't look like someone who's had a late night,' he remarked.

'It's make-up,' she told him. 'Hides a multitude.'

'You look great. And you do seem . . . so much better,' he said.

'Oh, look.' She swallowed back the coffee in one gulp. 'If you're going to keep harping on about the past, then this trip will be a complete nightmare. I'm fine, thanks, not that there was anything wrong with me really. I'm just not the sort of person who should be married. Of course I'm sorry that things didn't work out, but it was good while it lasted. I get the feeling – and I don't blame you – that you're trying to needle me in some way, probably because I did mess up your life for a while, but there's really no need to go back over all that stuff again. And it's been years. So can we just get on with things?' The words had tumbled out in one breath.

'Sure,' he said after a moment's silence. 'That's all I ever wanted.'

'Me too,' she told him. 'And – you know, I really do hope that our past doesn't interfere with our work now.'

'Nothing I want more than that to be the case,' he agreed. 'Would you like to share this Danish?'

She shook her head but he cut it in half anyway. And she was suddenly engulfed by a feeling of unexpected regret that it hadn't worked out between them. If she'd met him now – older, wiser and harder-hearted – would things have turned out differently? She took the piece of Danish from him. Probably not. She still wouldn't have fallen in love with him. She was pretty sure that she'd never fall in love with anyone ever again. She simply didn't know how.

The weather in Edinburgh was unexpectedly balmy. Darcey shrugged off her leather coat as they left the airport and felt her spirits lift as they drove to the InvestorCorp building in Edinburgh Park, although she was also conscious of butter-flies in her stomach. Her presentation was on her laptop computer. She knew that if anything was going to go wrong it would be with the laptop, and she dreaded that moment of horror when she'd realise that technology had let her down again. She didn't know what it would mean if things didn't go to plan with the board of InvestorCorp. Would they decide that she wasn't good enough to take over the Asian business? Or was that a poisoned chalice anyway? She'd thought about it the previous night as she'd gone through the presentation for the hundredth time before going to bed. InvestorCorp wanted control of her best clients. They'd given her a whole new set-up to deal with. If she failed, they could simply let her go while having all the information necessary to deal with the Europeans. Perhaps that was the ultimate plan. Perhaps – and this thought had first come to her at three in the morning, causing her to sit up in bed, her heart racing with sudden anxiety – perhaps that was what Neil Lomond had being working for all along. His revenge on her for being a demented, jealous wife who'd humiliated him not once, but twice, in front of his colleagues.

She'd broken into a sweat at the thought then. She realised that she was perspiring very slightly now. She brushed her damp forehead with the tips of her fingers.

'So,' she said, after Neil had introduced her and she was standing in front of a group of conservatively dressed men. 'The Global Finance, now the InvestorCorp, European client base. Let me talk you through it.'

She double-clicked on the PowerPoint icon on her computer. Nothing happened. She felt the prickles of sweat on her back. She double-clicked again. The computer screen went blank.

'I think it's switched itself off,' said Neil. 'Are you OK for battery power?'

'Should be,' she said, although she had no idea because she hardly ever used the laptop and she couldn't remember the last time she'd charged it.

'I have a lead,' he said, opening his briefcase. 'You might want to try it.'

'Thank you.' She smiled at him as she took it, but deep down she was hoping that it wouldn't work. That the reason the computer had shut itself down wasn't to do with anything as stupid as the battery running out.

She powered it on and it started up. And this time when she hit the PowerPoint presentation, the slideshow opened.

\*　　\*　　\*

'You've already done a great job in Europe,' Michael Banks, one of the senior managers, told her when she'd completed the slideshow and they were standing around the highly polished walnut table in the boardroom flicking through the hard copy of her presentation. 'The numbers are really impressive.'

'Oh, well . . .' She shrugged. 'I do my job.'

'We'll be looking forward to seeing more of the same from the new territories.'

'I hope that happens.'

Shit, she thought as soon as the words were out of her mouth. That sounded so lame. As though she wasn't confident of success. As though she wasn't up for the challenge.

'No bother to you.' Neil was suddenly at her shoulder and his voice startled her. 'You're a whizz at it.'

'Oh, I know I can do it,' she said quickly. 'The challenge will be great. I guess I'm a little sorry to be leaving some of my best clients in other people's hands.'

Neil chuckled. 'They have a lot to live up to.'

'Thanks for your vote of confidence,' she said.

'I have complete confidence in you,' he said as Michael excused himself and went to speak to another colleague.

'Do you?'

'Of course. The numbers don't lie. Though . . .'

'Though what?'

He lowered his voice slightly, 'I have to admit that I'm really surprised you've become so . . . businesslike. And so determined to do well. You used to be a bit scathing about success before.'

Her eyes twinkled at him. 'As far as I remember, I

269

complained that women had to be cold and calculating to get to the top. It was true then. I don't know how true it is now.' She half smiled. 'Still true, probably. I know I've done OK, but that's kind of despite myself. I'm not really a go-getter, not someone who wants to get to the top.'

He grinned. 'Still hankering after the Tuscan farmhouse instead?'

'Oh, I don't know.'

'It's a nice dream.'

'Just a dream,' she said. 'My future's with InvestorCorp and I'm happy with where I am in the company.'

'Really?' He raised an eyebrow.

She frowned as he turned away from her and murmured something to one of his colleagues. She turned to face the opposite direction herself. He was still being supportive and nice. But a sudden thought had struck her. What if his niceness was just a front? What if he actually hated her? What if he wanted to some day humiliate her the way she'd humiliated him?

She listened carefully as the board members discussed the company's future prospects during lunch. She'd heard these conversations a million times before: half-genial, laden with power-struggling undercurrents, everyone with a hidden agenda.

'Why did you choose to go into Business Development?' asked Neil suddenly. She stared at him. He was at the opposite end of the table and he'd had to raise his voice so that she could hear him.

'Pardon?'

'I know you were originally involved in actuarial work,' he said. 'What made you change?'

Shit, she thought. That's a loaded question. He's trying to trip me up over this.

'I was offered the job.' She smiled tightly at him.

'Seems a strange move. From numbers to people.'

'Not really,' she told him. 'It was just how things panned out. And it was my language skills that swung it for me. Perhaps if Global Finance had been looking for an actuary, I might have gone down that road instead.'

'Well, we're lucky to have your experience.' Gordon Campbell, the CEO, who hadn't said much until then, added his voice to the conversation. 'It's great to have someone who has talents in a number of areas.'

'Oh, I'm sure you have plenty of those already,' she said quickly.

'But I think you might be one of our most versatile employees,' said Neil.

'Well, thanks.' She knew that she should be telling them that she was absolutely brilliant, but she always felt uncomfortable with praise. And she still couldn't figure out whether Neil was a friend or a foe in the boardroom. Which was very, very worrying indeed.

'A good day,' he said as they flew home that evening. 'You did really well.'

'You were building me up like nobody's business,' she remarked. 'For a while anyway. If I make a complete hash of it you'll look like a fool.'

'You won't make a hash of it,' he said. 'You'll do fine. And the board thinks you're a great asset too.'

'Why do you care?' She turned to him, frowning. 'Why does it matter to you what kind of asset I am to the company?'

He looked at her in silence for a moment. 'Because I'm your boss,' he said. 'It matters that my staff are seen as competent and capable. Especially when we're making radical changes. Especially when my budget has been made a good deal more difficult for the coming year. I want them to know that I have people who can do the job.'

'I see.' Her voice was thoughtful. 'And leaving me out of the equation, do you think you have people who can do the job?'

'I hope so,' he said. 'I know that the Edinburgh team is good. I don't know much about Dublin.'

'You're afraid.' Realisation dawned in her voice. 'You're afraid that I'll be useless. That somehow we've faked the figures or that I wasn't responsible for any of the good things in Global Finance. You want your own people dealing with Europe and you're sacrificing me on the altar of new markets.'

'That's complete nonsense,' he told her. 'Everyone says you're great. I asked.'

'But you think you know better. Because you know me.'

'I can't lie and say that I wasn't surprised when I realised you were with the company,' he admitted. 'And when everyone talked so highly of you. But I'm not surprised that you're competent. Only that you pulled it all together.'

'You still think I'm bonkers,' she told him.

'That's your expression, not mine,' he said mildly. 'I never thought you were bonkers. But I did think you had some very real issues to deal with. And I'm sorry I didn't realise it before we got married.'

'So am I,' she said honestly. 'It's a pity things didn't work out, but . . . *c'est la vie*. Everyone makes mistakes.'

'I rushed you into it,' he said. 'That was the mistake.'

'Can we agree that both of us were young and stupid and it's behind us now?' she asked.

He nodded. 'And can we agree that we don't hate each other and we're not going to do anything to fuck up each other's careers?'

'Absolutely.'

'I'm glad that's sorted.'

She chuckled suddenly.

'What?'

'You didn't tell anyone there about us. They don't know.'

He shifted uncomfortably. 'There was no need. They'd have worried about the consequences of the relationship on our ability to do the job.'

'So . . . is this keeping shtum for your sake or mine?'

'For both our sakes,' he told her. 'I won't blab if you don't.'

She nodded and then shrugged. 'Anna Sweeney knows.'

'Oh.'

'You did tell her to ask me,' Darcey pointed out. 'So she did and I told her.'

'Um.'

'She's the HR manager,' said Darcey. 'She's good at keeping secrets.'

'I liked her,' Neil said. 'I think she'll be discreet.'

'She liked you too.' Suddenly there was an amused glint in Darcey's eye. 'She thinks you're handsome.'

'Well I think she's very attractive.'

'Good news for both of you so,' said Darcey as she took a newspaper from her bag and started to read.

# Chapter 18

Darcey sat at her desk and flicked through the web pages of the companies she'd lined up as prospective customers for her Singapore trip. Although she was more anxious than she wanted to let on about it, she was beginning to feel a sense of excitement at the thought of going into a new market. It would be a totally different experience to hopping across to Paris or Milan, but ultimately very satisfying when the business started to come in. Results might take some time, she thought, as she looked at the information in front of her, but it would be great to bring in new business from a place that had been so underdeveloped by the company before. And it would be equally nice to visit somewhere completely different. The InvestorCorp people were right about one thing. Europe was easy for her. It was time to get out of her comfort zone and push herself again.

An email alert distracted her from her assessment of the Lotus Financial Corporation as a potential client. She opened the message.

'Table Quiz,' she read. 'All staff. Friday 16th. Wright's

Howth. 8 p.m. Submit your name or table of six.' The message was from Anna.

Darcey grinned. Table quizzes had been Global Finance's standard bonding experience. Anna must have decided, or been asked, to do something to bring everyone together after the disruption of the InvestorCorp takeover. In the last couple of weeks a few more people had joined the company from the Edinburgh office and Douglas Lomax had taken over from Peter Henson as MD while Peter had been sent to Chicago.

She finished her work on Lotus, then picked up the phone to call her friend and ask about the quiz.

'Oh, Douglas wanted us to do something,' Anna told her, 'I suggested it. You know how it is here, everyone is so bloody competitive they always come to the quizzes, and it has the added advantage that it means they're not spending the entire night propping up the bar.'

Darcey laughed. 'If you think our colleagues can't do quizzes and prop up a bar at the same time, you're sadly mistaken.'

Anna laughed too. 'True. But at least this way we're pretending to be doing something interesting too. Anyway, the prizes are great. The Scots aren't being stingy! An overnight in the K Club with a round of golf thrown in for the winning table. Dinner for two at Patrick Guilbaud's for the runners-up. And a bottle of champers for third place. Plus a few spot prizes throughout the evening.'

'I'd better come second then,' said Darcey, 'given that I'm utterly hopeless at golf.'

'Oh, we can substitute a spa treatment for the golf,' Anna

assured her. 'Always provided you manage to do better than last time.'

'Last time I was on a crappy table,' protested Darcey. 'We didn't have anyone who knew anything about sport and there were far too many questions on bloody football.'

'I'll get them to throw in a mental arithmetic one just for you,' said Anna.

'Ha bloody ha.'

'Dunno why you're wasting your time talking to me about it,' Anna said. 'Better you go and try to find yourself a decent table.'

'Actually, better I answer my phone,' said Darcey as it started to ring. 'Talk to you later.'

She'd expected the call to be from one of her clients, but in fact it was from John Kenneally, in the accounts department, asking her to be on his quiz team. Darcey got on well with John. He reminded her a little of James Hutton, with whom she'd first worked when she'd gone to London, although with more personality and with a razor-sharp mind.

'If we don't win I'll eat my financial printout,' he told her. 'I'm going to get Sally from reception – she's brilliant on soaps and movies and stuff like that; I've already nabbed Walter and Dec from Investment Management – music and sport; and Laura from the support team who's good on current affairs. I'm the literature person and you're general knowledge and any of those mad paper-and-pencil rounds that require screwed-up thinking.'

'Got it sewn up then, have you?' she asked in amusement.

'I play to win,' he said. 'I want the best team. Besides,

I have my heart set on the K Club. I've never played golf there and I really want to.'

'Right,' said Darcey. 'Count me in.'

'Don't forget to read the newspapers too and remember the names of people and places,' warned John. 'They always throw in stupid questions about quirky stories in the papers, and you're good at remembering them.'

On the Friday of the quiz, Darcey went home a little earlier than usual, changed into a pair of faded jeans and a plain white T-shirt and then took the Dart from Grand Canal Dock to Howth. It was ages since she'd been out on a Friday night and she told herself that being a happy singleton was all very well but she truly did need to socialise in Dublin a bit more.

By the time she arrived at the bar it was already a heaving mass of InvestorCorp employees, scrimmaging to get their drinks and secure their places at the tables that had been dotted around the room. There were fifteen tables, which meant that most of the staff had turned up for the evening's entertainment.

Darcey ordered a beer then looked for the rest of her team members. They found themselves a table conveniently placed close to both the bar and the scoreboard. Unfortunately, John hadn't been able to get Sally, who'd been approached by a rival team first. He'd substituted her with Thelma, who worked in the IT department and who, he said, was nearly as good.

'What d'you mean, nearly?' said Thelma as she sat down. 'I know more about TV than anyone else in the company!'

'Is that a good thing?' asked Dec.

'When it comes to quizzes, yes.' Thelma looked accusingly at him and he held up his hands in mock surrender.

The team at the table opposite them arrived and Neil Lomond, catching Darcey's glance, waved at her. She nodded at him, noting that Sally from reception was on his team. She wondered who'd tipped him off about her!

Anna grabbed a microphone, welcomed everyone, reminded them that the night was meant to be good clean fun and told them it was tough if they didn't like the answer to any question because she was in charge and her decision was final.

'Right,' she continued. 'Let's start.'

The teams wrestled with the questions, arguing among themselves as to what was the world's most popular non-alcoholic drink (it turned out to be coffee, much to the disgust of Darcey's team, which had plumped for water), or the name of the actress who'd said she was as pure as the driven slush (Tallulah Bankhead; the team got that right), or the winners of the 1970 World Cup (Brazil; John knew that one). After half the rounds had been played, Anna called for a break. At that point Darcey's team were three points behind Table 9, which was being captained by Neil.

'We have to pull up our socks and beat them,' said John grimly. 'Grind them into the ground.'

'John!' Thelma looked surprised. 'You're going over the top a bit, aren't you?'

'Yeah, but that Lomond guy has me driven demented looking for all sorts of financial reports ever since he got here. We want original Global Financers to win, don't we?'

'Of course we do,' said Walter. 'No way Lomond's going to get our round of golf.'

'Too right,' said Dec.

The girls exchanged glances.

'I forgot how competitive you blokes can get,' complained Thelma.

'Hell, I don't want to be beaten by Neil Lomond either,' said Darcey firmly. 'John's right. Let's get ourselves a drink and then focus!'


'It's very tense, isn't it?'

Darcey had gone to the bar to get the drinks for the team when Neil came up behind her and spoke.

'That's the original Global Finance people for you,' she told him without turning around. 'We do so love our quizzes.'

'I got the answer to one wrong in the last round and I thought they were going to lynch me,' he said.

Darcey smiled. 'Which one?'

'The nine handmaidens of Odin,' he said.

'Our Walter knew that,' she told him. 'He says that "The Ride of the Valkyries" is one of his favourite pieces of music.'

'Are you enjoying yourself?' asked Neil.

'Sure I am.'

'You're doing surprisingly well.'

'Excuse me!' She turned and frowned at him but her eyes were dancing with amusement. '*Surprisingly* well?'

'I didn't think this was your kind of thing.'

'Neil, I seem to remember you once telling me that I had the most appalling amount of useless information in my brain of anyone you knew,' she told him sweetly. 'I can't remember what you were nagging me about at the time, but I do remember you saying it.'

'I never nagged you.'

'You were always nagging me,' she said. 'You must remember – about applying for that quantitive analysis job, or joining the chess club, or—'

'You'd have been great at that job,' he said.

'Actually, I'd've been crap,' she said. 'It's not really my thing. And I'd've been crap at chess too.'

'Probably.' He grinned. 'I seem to remember you always made some mad moves with your queen, leaving your poor king undefended.'

'He's a man, he should've been able to look after himself.' She laughed as she picked up the tray of drinks. 'Now I'm going back to my table, and we're gonna whip your sorry ass.'

'Would that make you feel better?' he asked, his voice suddenly serious.

'About what?'

'About everything.'

Her eyes narrowed. 'I feel fine about everything,' she told him. 'I don't need to beat you for that.'

'No, you probably don't.' His tone was stark and she looked at him curiously. But then he smiled at her and winked, and she smiled briefly in return.

As she went back to the table, she was conscious of his eyes following her. She was still thinking about him as Anna read out the next question, so that when they started arguing about what Pascal was famous for, it was a while before she realised what the question was about. At which point she told them that they were barking up the wrong tree with their insistence about him having something to do with computer languages, and that he was the person who'd first realised the importance of a particular mathematical concept originally developed by the Chinese.

'Are you sure about that?' John was sceptical because it had taken her so long to come up with the answer.

'Absolutely.'

When the answer was given out, she was the one getting pats on the back, because their table was the only one to get that right and they were now within one point of Table 9.

'Don't let all the good work slip away from us,' John said as Anna started on the picture round. 'Take your time.'

They did well on the picture round, and on the following rounds too, so that by the end of the quiz they were tied for the lead with Table 9.

'Sudden death,' announced Anna theatrically. 'A play-off for the K Club or Patrick Guilbaud. Both prizes I'd like anyway, so no bloody big deal if you ask me. Except for the fact that it's for the honour and glory of becoming the inaugural InvestorCorp Quiz Champions, and we all know just how important that is!'

Table 6 looked across at Table 9. Neil stared directly at Darcey. She looked impassively back.

'Question one,' said Anna. 'Who founded the city of Singapore?'

All eyes on Table 6 turned to Darcey. 'You're going there,' said Laura, unable to keep a note of envy out of her voice. 'And I know you, you'll have done your research.'

Darcey grinned and wrote the answer down on the sheet of paper.

'Both correct,' announced Anna when the two tables had handed their answers up. 'Sir Stamford Raffles. A bit easy that one, because even I knew the answer.'

By the end of sudden death, the tables were still tied. The rest of the staff were getting stuck into the social part of the evening, but the tension was high between tables 6 and 9.

'I've conferred with my fellow judges,' said Anna. 'And we've agreed that since the teams are still tied, it should be a sudden death head-to-head. Tables 9 and 6, choose a person to answer the next question for you.'

'Darcey,' said John before she could say anything.

'Oh, please, no!' she cried. 'It'll be something about movies or singers and I won't know the answer. Thelma should do it.'

'They're doing the weird-and-wonderful type of question, Darce,' said Walter. 'That's your forte.'

She groaned.

'We're all decided. It's up to you.'

John pushed her out of her seat and she walked up to Anna. From Table 9, as she'd somehow expected, Neil Lomond took up a position on Anna's other side. The director of human resources smiled edgily at them both.

'Darcey McGonigle versus Neil Lomond.' She cleared her throat. 'I'll ask you alternate questions. Best of three. Toss for who goes first?'

'Heads,' said Darcey as Anna flipped the coin.

'Tails,' said Anna. She looked at Neil. 'Your choice.'

'I'll go first,' he said.

Anna took a card from the pile.

'On what day of creation did God make the sun, the moon and the stars?'

Neil grinned and answered without hesitating. 'The fourth.'

'Correct.' A roar went up from Table 6. Anna looked stern. 'Darcey. Which number president of the US was George W. Bush?'

Darcey closed her eyes and began counting. Learning the names of the US presidents had been something her father had once made her do to train her memory. But there had been a few more of them since then.

'Forty-third?' She wasn't confident.

'You're right,' said Anna, while Table 9 erupted with joy. 'Neil. Who was the Greek goddess of Victory?'

'That's too easy!' cried Thelma. 'Everyone should know that by now!'

'Nike,' responded Neil, and Anna nodded. 'Darcey. What are the caves at Lascaux famous for?'

Darcey sighed with relief. 'Prehistoric paintings.'

'Two-all,' said Anna dramatically. 'Neil. Your final question. Illustrated on its logo, the product Marmite is named after a French word meaning what?'

It was as though she'd suddenly been hurtled back in time. Darcey was standing in the kitchen of their London home, looking into the cupboard. She was asking Neil why on earth there was a pot of Marmite in there. It was disgusting, she said. Nobody could possibly eat it.

'I love it,' he'd responded. 'I was practically brought up on it at home.'

'Well, it might be called after a cooking pot, but it's nothing I'd put into cooking,' she'd retorted.

'Ah, yes. But you don't cook.' And he'd grinned at her then and kissed her on the back of the neck.

She opened her eyes and realised that Neil was looking straight at her. And she knew that he was remembering too. She waited for him to give the right answer.

'Sauce,' he said.

Darcey looked at him in complete astonishment.

'I'm sorry,' said Anna as Table 6 groaned collectively. 'The answer is cooking pot.'

Neil shrugged.

'Darcey. To win the quiz for Table 9. What is the meaning of the word hypocaust?'

She looked at Neil again. She couldn't win this quiz because he had deliberately given a wrong answer. And it had to have been deliberate. There was no way he could have forgotten their conversation, because after kissing her on the neck he'd wondered aloud what it would be like to smother her with Marmite and lick it all off. She'd laughed at that and said she wouldn't dream of being slathered in revolting gunge, but if he had a better choice of foodstuff . . . It had been during the summer and he'd suggested ice-cream instead. There had been a tub of Häagen-Dazs cookies and cream in the freezer. It hadn't ended up being an erotic experience because they'd laughed too much as the ice-cream melted on her body. But it had been fun. She'd thought then that maybe she did love him. But she'd been wrong. It had been great sex, though.

'Darcey?' repeated Anna.

She looked at the people at her table. John's face was anxious. Laura was giving her encouraging signs. Thelma's eyes were closed. Walter and Dec both had their fingers crossed.

'Underfloor heating,' she said abruptly.

Anna looked surprised. 'Correct.' Table 6 erupted in joy while the Table 9 competitors consoled each other.

'Well done,' said Neil.

'Yes, well done,' repeated Anna. 'I didn't think you'd get the last one.'

'Dredged it up,' said Darcey.

Neil held out his hand. 'Congratulations.'

She frowned as she took it. 'You knew the answer,' she muttered as Anna thanked everyone for coming along. 'Marmite. When we . . . you must have remembered . . .'

'Remembered what?' He was still holding her hand.

'I . . .' Her eyes searched his but she could see nothing behind them. 'Marmite. And Häagen-Dazs.'

'Sorry.' He let go her hand and shrugged. 'I don't know what you're talking about. Admittedly I once lived on the stuff, but that was a long time ago.'

She nodded slowly. 'Sure. Of course.'

'So well done,' he said. 'You'd better go back to your table. They want to congratulate you. And I'm sure John Kenneally is thrilled about his golf.'

John was ecstatic. He hugged Darcey with delight and said that he didn't know whether beating Lomond or winning the golf was better. The girls bubbled with excitement about the spa treatments. And Darcey smiled at them all, relieved she hadn't made a mess of the last question yet feeling incredibly flat about the win.

She felt her phone vibrate and took it out of the pocket of her jeans.

'It's me,' said Tish.

'Hold on.' Darcey moved outside the bar, where it was quieter. 'What's up?' she asked, shivering slightly in the cool evening breeze.

'You're not going to believe it,' Tish told her abruptly. 'It's ridiculous. But Dad's back.'

# Chapter 19

Of the two hundred people they'd invited to the wedding, one hundred and seventy-six had accepted. That included all of their Stateside friends, who were busily planning their trips to Ireland and trawling the internet for information about Galway and the surrounding area. Nieve knew that Gail was hopping with excitement over the whole thing and she copied her mother in on every email to and from Happy Ever Afters so that she was kept in the loop. She always found it much easier to be friendly with Gail from a distance. Her mother had gone to see the castle and had emailed Nieve to say that it was the most perfect venue ever and that people would be overwhelmed by the beauty of it all.

As well they might, thought Nieve, as she looked at the list on her computer. She was going to a huge amount of trouble to ensure that the setting was as fabulous as it was possible to be, providing a choice of main courses for the meal with vegetarian and halal options, and ordering Newbridge Silverware mementos for the selected guests who'd been invited to the rehearsal dinner. She'd chosen little heart-shaped lockets for the women and arrow cufflinks for the men. Lorelei from Happy Ever Afters had suggested them to her and Nieve knew that the guests would love them.

She scanned through the list of names again. She'd managed to track down Rosa and Carol from the Brainy Broads and they'd accepted her invitations to both the wedding and the dinner. Rosa had replied in a breathless email, saying how great it would be to see her again and how wonderful it was that she was doing so well, and that she'd always known Nieve would make it big because she'd been so brilliant, and it was great that she was getting married too now . . . It had gone on and on and Nieve had felt exhausted just reading it. She hadn't remembered Rosa being so exuberant. Carol had sent a handwritten card in her beautiful neat script, accepting the invitation with thanks. Rosa was coming with her husband. Carol was coming on her own.

Her computer beeped and Nieve closed down the invitation list and looked instead at the Ennco graph price. She beamed widely. The Bear and The Stuffer had been right. The economic statistics had come out a few minutes earlier and already the stock market was moving ahead again, Ennco with it. Soon the price would be back to the original level and, hopefully, through it. Nieve had to admit to herself that she got a greater buzz out of watching the increase in the share price than dealing with the wedding stuff. But, she assured herself, the wedding was just one day. The profits from the sale of her shares would be for ever.

She stretched her arms over her head. Even though she

hated the thought of being away from the share price ticker, it would be nice to have a break. One month away from the office was the longest she'd ever taken, and she was both looking forward to it and dreading it in equal measure. Aidan, on the other hand, couldn't wait to have a month off. He had all sorts of plans for travelling around Ireland and then heading off to Europe for a while. Completely chilling out, he told her. Doing the whole backpacking thing that so many people had done but which they'd never given in to because they'd been too busy with Jugomax. He was convinced, he told her, that a month of the simple life would be good for her. She didn't know why he thought that. She reminded him that she'd already done the backpacking thing with Darcey and that he should know her too well to imagine that she would actually enjoy staying anywhere other than five-star hotels with Egyptian cotton sheets, marble bathrooms and broadband connections in the rooms.

Ten years, she reminded herself. We've been together that long and it's a hell of a lot longer than loads of people have been married. We might like different things but we do know each other. We'll combine the backpacking and the five-star hotels. We won't make a mess of it. We love each other.

She clicked on to her guest list again. One hundred and seventy-six. But no Darcey McGonigle. Not even a response from her. She was annoyed that her former best friend hadn't even bothered to reply.

'Hi, Nieve.' Murphy Ledwidge, one of her colleagues, strolled into her office. 'How's it going?'

'Pretty well.'

'That's our department, always on top of things,' said

Murphy cheerfully. 'Hey, did you see that we made *Business-Week* this week?'

She shook her head.

'Big profile on our chief and his team. Compliance got a mention too. They said that it was well run and regulated under the stewardship of one of the industry's leading women.'

'Really?' Nieve looked pleased.

'Yup. You'll catch it on their website.'

'Nice to see us backroom boys getting a mention,' Nieve said.

Murphy laughed. 'Yeah, 'cos it's usually only when something goes wrong that they talk about the compliance team.'

'Don't worry, there'll never be a problem while I'm in charge,' she told him confidently.

'How're the wedding plans coming along?' he asked as he shuffled some papers on the desk in the corner of the room.

'An eighty-eight per cent confirmation rate,' she told him. 'It's gonna be great.'

'I hope so.' She grimaced. 'The wedding-planner totally seems to know what she's doing, but there are so many bits and pieces and something's bound to go wrong . . .'

'I know.' Murphy grinned at her. 'But that's half the fun.'

'You're joking,' she said. 'You know I don't allow things to go wrong!'

'Here, maybe,' he agreed. 'But you gotta lighten up a bit, Nieve. You're looking tired and you've got big circles under your eyes.'

'No I haven't.' She peered at her reflection in the burnished steel of a filing cabinet.

'It's stressful,' said Murph. 'And I bet you're on to that company every day. Let them get on with it.'

Nieve smiled. 'I guess.'

'Anyway, me and Duke are really looking forward to it. We've bought green velvet suits.'

'You haven't!' She looked at him in mock horror.

'Absolutely,' he confirmed. 'Hey, it's Ireland. My name is Murphy. The least I can do is wear green.'

'Most Irish people don't,' she told him. 'I have a feeling you're going to be horribly disappointed in the auld sod.'

'No way,' he said. 'I've been doing some digging on my ancestors, and apparently I might hail from Tipperary. Is that far from the wedding?'

'A couple of hours,' she told him.

'No distance.' He looked pleased.

She smiled at him. Murph was always so innocently enthusiastic about things. She wondered when it was that she'd lost the enthusiasm for doing something for its own sake, not because it made her more money.

'We're going to spend four days tracking down the relatives,' he told her. 'Then I'll be back to look after your empire.'

'It's not an empire,' she said.

'No, but I know you hate to leave it.'

'I worry,' she said.

'The place won't fall down just because you're away,' he told her. 'Honestly.'

She laughed. She loved Murphy. She really did. He always cheered her up.

Her computer beeped and she turned her attention back to it, noticing a transaction that had been input incorrectly.

She was still dealing with it when Paola Benedetti tapped at the door of her office. Paola was a couple of years younger than Nieve and not unlike her in appearance – a tall, dark-haired woman who dressed well and always made the most of her looks. Paola worked in the compliance department too.

Nieve looked up, taking in the fact that Paola looked tired, and that the bump from her five-month pregnancy was becoming more and more apparent.

'Yes?' she said.

'I'm really sorry.' Paola sounded nervous. 'I had a call from Freddie's school. He's just been sick. I need to get there.'

Nieve regarded her colleague thoughtfully. As far as she could recall, this was the second time in a month that Freddie Benedetti had been sick at school and Paola had asked for time off to bring him home.

'Is there an ongoing medical problem with your son?' she asked.

'Not at all,' Paola said emphatically. 'He's just going through a phase. Growing a lot. It's nothing to worry about, but obviously I really need to get him home.'

'We're running a trade diagnostic at the moment.' Nieve glanced at the computer screen. 'It's not terribly convenient.'

'I do understand that,' said Paola. 'Obviously I'll work the hours to compensate for it.'

'The thing is . . .' Nieve tapped her pen against a file on her desk, 'you do seem to need a lot of time off.'

'This is my son,' said Paola. 'I need to be with him.'

'It's not fair on other people,' Nieve told her. 'We work as a team. You need to be a part of that team.'

'I am,' said Paola fervently. 'I really am. This is just unusual, Nieve. It doesn't normally happen.'

Nieve sighed. This was what bothered her about people with kids. This was why she wasn't ready for it herself. She regarded Paola with ill-disguised irritation.

'If you have to go, you have to go.'

'I'll make up the hours,' Paola repeated.

'Of course you will,' said Nieve.

Nieve was home late because she'd spent some time checking the incorrect transaction and making sure it wasn't linked to anything else. Then she'd had a coffee in the staff rest area, where she'd been surprised to see Mike Horgan, the company CEO, sipping a latte as he flicked through a magazine. She'd greeted him and he'd smiled at her and asked her how things were going, and she'd told him that it was all fine. She mentioned the *BusinessWeek* piece and he smiled complacently, then asked her about the plan she was drafting up to monitor certain transactions more effectively. She told him that she'd had a number of meetings with Harley, the chief financial officer, and that she hoped to have something for him soon. He nodded and thanked her and said that he knew she'd had a lot on her plate lately, what with getting things in shape for the flotation, and that she deserved a nice break back in Ireland. She said that she intended to have a good time and commented that it was good to see the share price going up again. Mike chuckled deeply and said that it wasn't half yet of what it was going to be. And that if she stuck with them she'd be a very rich lady indeed. The conversation with Mike had left her feeling good about herself and good about Ennco, and she was in a sunny mood as she walked into the house.

Aidan was sitting in the living room, his feet on the coffee table alongside an empty pizza delivery box and a can of Bud. *The Simpsons* was showing on the HDTV.

'Sorry I'm late,' she said. 'I was talking to Mike Horgan.'

'And how is the Mighty Mike?' asked Aidan.

'Mighty,' she said. She looked at the empty pizza box. 'Anything for me?'

'I thought you were on a mad pre-wedding diet,' he told her. 'Correct me if I'm wrong, but wasn't your comment at the beginning of the week that you were going to be on a strict salad regime from now on?'

'Yeah, but I expect support,' she told him. 'The smell of that cheese is driving me crazy!'

'I have better ways to drive you crazy.' He grinned at her.

'Not till after I've had something to eat.'

Aidan got up from the sofa and pushed her gently into it. 'You relax,' he said. 'I'll make you one of my famous club sandwiches.'

'That'd be nice.'

'What's more, I'll bring you an ice-cold beer from the fridge.'

'Now I'm getting worried,' she said. 'What's with all this pampering?'

'It's simple, honey. You've been working harder than ever and trying to do all the wedding stuff too . . . You're looking tired.'

Nieve stifled a sudden yawn. 'I am tired,' she admitted. 'Much as it pains me to say this, I'm starting to look forward to our month off.'

'Excellent.' Aidan's voice floated in from the kitchen. 'I'm hoping that you're finally getting some sense on the whole slow-down-and-smell-the-roses routine.'

'Maybe,' she called back. 'The thing is – I like the idea, I'm just not so sure I'd be good at the practice.'

She leaned back into the sofa and propped her feet in the space recently vacated by Aidan. She smiled as she watched the cartoon, and wondered what it would be like to be an average-Joe family like the Simpsons. Or like Rosa, whose email had gone on to talk about her husband of six years and her three children. Nieve had already forgotten the husband's name and she found it hard to imagine Rosa with three children. There had been an incident when they were younger, which Nieve only vaguely remembered, in which Rosa had once left her brother on the bus because she'd had her nose stuck in a book and hadn't even thought about him when she was getting off. And this was the person who now had three kids of her own! Nieve thought that people should be tested for competency before they were allowed to have kids.

Carol's standard acceptance card hadn't mentioned children, but on the basis that she was coming to the wedding on her own, Nieve was hopeful that she was still single and child-free.

'Here you go.' Aidan put a plate with an overfilled sandwich on the table in front of her. Then he eased the tab back on another Bud and handed it to her. She glugged some back happily.

'I so love that ice-cold taste,' she remarked.

He grinned at her. 'You're so upmarket in other ways, aren't you, but you do like your beer!'

'Sod off,' she said amiably. 'At home a beer is the only thing. Out and about – it has to be wine.'

'You got some mail today,' he said, after she'd had another mouthful.

'Oh?'

'Two more accepting our wedding invitation.'

'Really?' She looked vaguely annoyed. 'They were supposed to have replied by last week.'

'One is from an aunt of mine who's been living in Wales and has clearly lost all sense of time and space,' said Aidan. 'The other . . .'

Nieve heard the change in his tone.

'It's from her, isn't it?' She held out her hand. 'Give it to me.'

He passed her the envelope. The card inside was small and neat.

'Darcey McGonigle will attend the wedding of Nieve Stapleton and Aidan Clarke' was all it said.

'She took her sweet time about it,' muttered Nieve. She turned the card over and looked at it. 'No email address or phone number.'

Aidan shrugged.

'So she's coming on her own,' continued Nieve. 'Still useless with men, obviously.'

'Just because she's coming on her own doesn't mean she hasn't got a boyfriend,' pointed out Aidan. 'She did get married, after all.'

'And divorced.'

Aidan looked anxious. 'I really wish you hadn't invited her.'

'You were hoping she'd say no.'

'Of course I was,' he said. 'Look, even if the break-up had been the most amicable thing in the world, there's something a bit odd about asking . . . well, my old girlfriend along.'

'Oh, get over it,' said Nieve as she replaced the card in the envelope. 'She was my best friend and I want her to know that I didn't just run off with you to get at her. And I'm not getting all soppy and sentimental or anything, but I'd kinda like her to be there. Anyway, she'll be fine. She was always a sensible person at heart and we've all grown up since then.'

Aidan nodded but he felt uncomfortable. It was all very well to talk about being grown-up, but sometimes he still felt like a kid of seventeen in an adults' world. And he simply couldn't imagine what it would be like to be face to face with Darcey again.

# Chapter 20

Darcey's first instinct when she got Tish's phone call was to rush back to Galway to find out what on earth was going on, but she knew it was far too late to do anything about it that night. She stood indecisively at the door to the pub and wondered why it was that her father had the ability to do the most unexpected things. He'd always seemed such a sensible man when she was a little girl. But clearly he was an emotional disaster area.

She moved closer to one of the outdoor heaters and allowed its radiant heat to warm her shoulders. Honestly, she thought, he screws up our lives by leaving, and God knows what sort of mess he's going to create by coming back. And she frowned because she couldn't quite believe that Minette would actually take him back. Not after so many years. It didn't make sense. She might have wanted him back at one time, but she'd long since got on with her life. And so had Martin. He'd forged a new one with Clem and Steffi, and Darcey couldn't get her head around the idea that for some reason he thought he could just pick up on the old one again. For heaven's sake, at this point he was practically a stranger!

'Here you are!' John and Thelma came out of the pub. 'We were looking for you. Didn't think you'd be out here with the smokers.' John shook a cigarette from the carton in his hand and lit up.

'My phone was ringing,' explained Darcey. 'I needed a bit of peace and quiet.'

'Well done on that last question,' said Thelma. 'You're a quiz demon, aren't you?'

'Only sometimes,' replied Darcey.

'The expression on Lomond's face when he got that question on Marmite!' John laughed. 'You could almost see him wondering what on earth the stuff was.'

Darcey said nothing.

'Anyway, I'm really looking forward to that game of golf,' John told her. 'And it's always good to stuff the opposition.'

'Why don't you like Neil?' asked Darcey.

'Too full of himself,' responded John promptly. 'Too quick to think he knows all the answers. And too bloody demanding.'

'I think he's rather cute,' remarked Thelma. 'Lovely eyes.'

John snorted.

'I'm not the only one to think so,' said Thelma defensively. 'Sally agrees with me. Mona McCutcheon is cracked about him and Mylene Scott fancies him too.'

'For heaven's sake!' cried Darcey. 'Don't tell me half of the women in the company seem to have fallen for him.'

John snorted again.

'But he seems to be making a move on Anna Sweeney,' Thelma continued. 'He was smiling at her in a very come-to-bed way.'

Darcey laughed. 'A come-to-bed smile?'

'Yeah, well, nobody would waste a smile like that on you, Darcey McGonigle,' said Thelma. 'They'd know better. But Anna's just lapping it up.'

'Hmm, well. Maybe I'll go and see for myself,' said Darcey.

Thelma grinned. 'Don't tell me you secretly fancy him too.'

'As if,' said Darcey, and walked back into the bar.

Thelma was right. Neil and Anna were sitting beside each other in a corner of the bar and Anna was leaning towards him in a way that gave him an uninterrupted view of her cleavage. But it wasn't her breasts (great though they were, Darcey thought enviously) that Neil was actually looking at. He was engaged in eye-to-eye contact with Anna, talking rapidly while she smiled at him and nodded every so often in agreement with whatever he was saying. The conversation looked intimate, excluding everyone else.

Would it work out for them? wondered Darcey. Was there the faintest chance? They both deserved someone nice. Anna especially. She was a great working mother, fantastic with Meryl and determinedly putting her first despite the fact that she tried very hard to appear high-profile and always available at work. It hadn't been easy for her. And Neil – well, he was a decent guy too. He'd wanted a family of his own. There'd been no chance of a family with Darcey. With Anna, it was ready-made.

She looked around the bar for another couple of minutes. Suddenly she didn't want to stay. Nobody was watching her. She slipped into her jacket and walked out into the night.

\* \* \*

The following Monday, Anna rang her to find out where she'd disappeared to and Darcey told her about the phone call from Tish and said that she hadn't felt like hanging around. She said that she was heading over to Galway on Friday evening to see exactly what the situation was. Anna had agreed that the whole idea of Martin turning up at the house was utterly bizarre, but cautioned Darcey against getting involved.

'I have to get involved,' said Darcey. 'He really hurt her and I can't stand by and let him do it again.'

'What makes you think that's going to happen?' asked Anna.

Which was a fair point, Darcey had to admit. Minette was a different woman to the one who had been so badly treated by Martin. But still, it was easy to say you wouldn't let yourself get hurt; not quite as easy to avoid it.

So the following Friday night, as she walked up the garden path and rang the doorbell with her special ring to let Minette know it was her before putting her key into the door, Darcey told herself that she wouldn't lecture her mother about whatever was going on. And that if her father was there she'd be mature and adult about it.

But Minette was on her own. Darcey kissed her on both cheeks before heading into the living room and curling up in an armchair opposite her. She didn't want her first words to be a question asking where her father was and whether he'd gone home to Clem and Steffi, but she was having a hard time not asking all the same. Then Minette told her. He was out but he'd be coming back later. And Darcey felt herself bristle.

'How could you?' she demanded. 'He was a complete shit.'

'Don't use words like that about your father,' said Minette.

'You used worse,' Darcey told her.

Minette nodded slowly. 'I know.'

'Why is he here? What happened?'

It was strange, thought Darcey, as Minette began to speak, how it was that her mother confided in her more than in the twins. Every day that week she'd called Tish or Amelie but neither of her sisters had any more information other than that Minette had told them that Martin was (at least temporarily) staying in the family home. It wasn't that she and Minette were so very close, Darcey mused, but they clicked in a way that neither of them did with the twins.

The problem, according to Minette, was that Clem had had an affair. A younger man. At this, Darcey pursed her mouth into an 'I told you so' expression. It didn't surprise her in the least that Clem would find Martin too old for her now. It might have seemed glamorous and exciting to steal an older man ten years ago; and it might be true that most men of sixty would now consider themselves to be relatively young, but a twenty-five-year age gap could still matter.

'And she's pregnant,' said Minette.

'You're joking!' Darcey's eyes widened.

Minette sighed. 'Not by your dad. The man she was having an affair with. He's another teacher. Clem met him when she took some kids on one of those adventure sport week-ends.'

'Jeez, that woman is a menace on those courses,' remarked Darcey. 'That's how she nabbed Dad too.'

'She had to tell him. It was obvious that the timing was all wrong for it to be his. And the other man doesn't want to know.'

'I know I asked but I can't help feeling that I'm getting far too much information about my father,' said Darcey.

'*C'est la vie*.' Minette shrugged.

'So why's he here?'

'He doesn't know what to do. He needed some time to think and he didn't want to be with her. He didn't want to throw her out either, not . . . well, he couldn't, could he? He's very upset. His doctor has diagnosed mild depression—'

'Yeah, I guess I'd be mildly depressed all right if I was him,' interjected Darcey.

'And so he's off sick from work. He wasn't sure where to go.'

'For God's sake, Maman!' Darcey looked at her mother impatiently. 'He's nothing to you any more. You're divorced! Why on earth would he come here?'

'He called me,' Minette told her. 'He was staying in a hotel and he called me and I said he could stay here for a while.'

'OK, now it's you who's officially cracked.'

'There's nothing going on between us,' said Minette. 'I'm just helping him out.'

'He's the man who walked out on you!' cried Darcey. 'Who dumped you for a girl young enough to be my sister! Why should you help him out this way?'

'I feel sorry for him.'

'That's utter nonsense,' Darcey said. 'He's using you like he did before.'

Minette said nothing.

'Oh, look, I'm sorry. I don't mean he always used you before. It's just – he's taking advantage of your good nature.'

'Maybe I don't mind my good nature being taken advantage of,' said Minette. 'Maybe it's nice to be needed.'

'He doesn't need you!' cried Darcey. 'He could manage. He's managed for the past ten years! He's like all men. Manipulative. Out for themselves. Untrustworthy. Ready to take advantage of any weakness.'

Minette looked at her daughter thoughtfully. 'Is that what you really think?' she asked. 'About all men?'

Darcey sighed. 'OK, so I'm generalising a bit. But not much.'

'I'm sorry if that's how you feel,' said Minette. 'And I'm sorry that you have had such bad experiences that you should think of all men the same way. Because it's not the case. If you think it is . . . then it's no surprise that your marriage failed.'

'We're not talking about my marriage here,' said Darcey. 'We're talking about yours! I'm not the one letting an ex-husband back into my life and my home.' And quite suddenly she was extremely glad that Neil Lomond hadn't called at her apartment the day they'd travelled to Edinburgh together.

'*Cherie*, I'm not letting him back into my life or my home,' said Minette. 'He is an old friend who, yes, I believe behaved badly but who is now going through a hard time himself. And I will give him some comfort for that. You've got to think of what it is like for him to find out that his wife – a woman he loves – has been seeing another man and is going to have his baby. That's not a good thing for a man of any age. And your father is an older man. So there isn't a lot of future for him in terms of finding someone else to settle down with and build a family with and do all the things he thought he had with Clem.'

'He had them all with us.' Darcey couldn't keep the sadness out of her voice. 'He was perfectly prepared to walk away from that.'

'You're right,' agreed Minette. 'And I don't forgive him for it. But I won't leave him living in a hotel and worrying about what he's going to do – and worrying about Steffi too.'

'You're a more generous person than me in that case,' said Darcey.

Minette sighed. 'No. Not more generous. Just . . . older.'

'Tcha!' Darcey made an impatient gesture. 'Look, would you mind if I spent the night at the twins' place? They asked but I said I'd call here first. I can't stay if he's here. I truly can't.'

'It's fine by me,' said Minette.

'I'll call them.' Darcey stood up. 'I respect your decision, Maman. I really do. But please don't let your heart rule your head.'

'Don't worry,' said Minette. 'Like I said to you before, I'm Swiss. Not French.'

'I don't think it matters what nationality women are where men are concerned,' said Darcey ruefully

As she picked up the phone she heard the sound of the front door opening. Minette got up and walked out of the room, and as Darcey spoke rapidly to Tish, she could hear the murmur of voices in the hall. She replaced the receiver and the living room door opened.

Her father looked older. Greyer, both in his hair and in his face. Darcey could see misery in his eyes too. She wanted to think that he deserved it, that it was payback time for the pain he'd put the family through, but she suddenly felt sorry for him.

'I'm heading off to the twins' place now,' she said. 'Dad, I'm sorry that you're having a bad time.'

Both her parents looked at her in surprise.

'Thanks,' said Martin.

'Maman, I'll call you again soon.'

'I look forward to it, *cherie*.' Minette kissed her on both cheeks.

Martin looked at her for a moment. Then Darcey shrugged and kissed him on both cheeks too.


She went out for a drink with Tish and Amelie, thinking that it was nice to socialise with them for a change. They strolled to a bar that had once been a comfortable pub where the locals had nursed a pint all night, but that had since been renovated and remodelled into a modern glass and marble building offering food and late-night music. It was heaving with the Friday night crowd.

The three sisters ordered a bottle of wine and bagged a recently vacated high granite-topped table, perching themselves on three moulded but slightly uncomfortable steel barstools.

Darcey related, for a second time, her conversation with Minette and then told them that she'd seen Martin before she left and that he looked terrible.

'I couldn't feel angry at him any more,' she admitted.

'Though I wanted to. And Maman is practically a saint for having him there!'

'I feel sorry for her, though,' said Amelie. 'She probably feels obliged to help out.'

'It's Steffi I feel sorriest for,' said Tish as she topped up her glass. 'After all, we were adults when he left. She's only a kid.'

'I'm afraid he'll twist Maman around his finger and sucker her into letting him stay,' said Darcey. 'And you know that sooner or later she'll end up in his bed.'

The other two made faces of disgust. But they agreed. There was no way that Minette and Martin could live in the house and not end up sleeping together.

'I wanted to shake her,' added Darcey. 'All this talk about forgiveness. He's a stranger to her now for all that he was her husband. I know it's hard on him, but why should she even consider letting him through the door?'

'What about you?' asked Tish idly. 'If Neil Lomond knocked on your door and asked you if he could spend a night because he was in some kind of trouble, what would you do?'

Darcey paused with her wine glass at her lips. Then she took a sip and replaced it slowly on the tabletop.

'I'd tell him to sod off,' she said finally. 'And I'd mean it.'

The twins exchanged glances, but it was Tish who spoke again.

'And has he turned up?' she asked. 'At Global Finance?'

Darcey looked at her in surprise. Neil's presence at the firm was so familiar to her now that it didn't even occur to her that her sisters didn't know about it.

'Yes,' she said ultra-casually. 'Of course we're called InvestorCorp since the takeover. But him being there doesn't impact on me much. Besides, I think he's dating one of the other girls.'

'Oh, wow, Darce!' Amelie winced. 'That's got to hurt.'

'We're divorced,' said Darcey. 'So it shouldn't.'

'But even so . . .'

'It's a bit . . . weird,' she admitted. 'The girl he's interested in, Anna, is one of my friends.'

'Darcey . . .' Tish started to speak and then faltered.

'What?'

'Another one of your friends with another one of the men in your life?'

Darcey laughed. 'This is different. In fact I'm happy for them if they're together. She's a lovely person and he's . . . well, he's probably going to be great with the right woman and so . . . I don't mind. Honestly.'

'But don't you have any feelings for him at all?' asked Amelie.

'Hell, girls, we've just said that Maman shouldn't have any feelings left for Dad!' Darcey exclaimed. 'Why should you think I'd have any left for Neil? And in our case he didn't even leave me for a kid half my age!'

Tish laughed. 'That's true.'

'So you're OK about it?' Amelie still didn't sound convinced.

'Totally,' said Darcey. 'But,' she added, knowing that it would effectively change the subject completely, 'what I'm not OK about is stupidly accepting Nieve Stapleton's wedding invitation.'

'Wh-at?' Both of them looked at her in astonishment.

Darcey was a little astonished at herself. She hadn't intended to reply to the invitation at all. It had hung around in her desk drawer until one day when she'd taken it out and looked at it and realised that the RSVP date was the following day. And she honestly didn't know what had made her go out and buy a card and send it off. But she had. Almost as soon as she'd let the envelope drop into the postbox she'd regretted it. She'd even thought about sending another card saying that she couldn't in fact come, but then she thought that would make her seem indecisive and a bit flaky. What was worse, she'd accepted the invitation to the rehearsal dinner too. That was to be held in a small local restaurant after the rehearsal at the church and would be, according to the letter that had been attached to the invite, an informal get-together of the out-of-town guests plus some old faces. Darcey wasn't sure who the old faces would be – school or college friends, she supposed – but the whole thing brought her out in a rash every time she thought about it.

All I have to do is back out, she told herself. It's no big deal. And yet she knew that she wasn't going to be able to.

'It's a train-wreck,' cried Amelie when Darcey explained it all to them. 'What were you thinking?'

'She was thinking that she's strong enough to go along to this thing and hold two fingers up to the cow,' said Tish.

Darcey looked at her gratefully. The twins had been initially supportive when they'd heard about Nieve and Aidan, but they'd fairly quickly told her to pull herself together. She'd never let them know about the engagement ring in Aidan's pocket, the one he'd never given her.

'Y'know, we're not exactly a lucky family when it comes to love,' remarked Amelie. 'There's Ma, tied up in knots over Dad. And you tied up in knots over Aidan . . . with the small added tangle of Neil lurking around in the background. And us!' She shrugged theatrically. 'We're a two-for-the-price-of-one deal.'

'Good God, surely not!' Darcey was startled.

'Not literally.' Tish grinned. 'But the twin thing – it messes up our relationships. I know it shouldn't but it does.'

'Does either of you want to get married?' asked Darcey.

'One day, I suppose.' Amelie sighed. 'But neither of us is good at hanging on to a man long enough for that to happen.'

'You're right so,' said Darcey glumly. 'We're useless.'

She slid off the barstool and went to the Ladies' where she watched younger, prettier girls make themselves look even more glamorous as they redid their make-up in the huge mirrors that lined the walls. How did other women do it? she wondered. How did they pick the right guy? How did they know he was the right one for them?

As she walked back to the table a few minutes later she felt a hand on her shoulder and heard a man's voice say her name. She turned around and was face to face with Denis Wade, who'd worked with Aidan in the IT section of Car Crew.

'Denis,' she said as she recalled his name. 'How are you?'

'I'm great,' he said. 'But you – you look amazing.'

She laughed. 'Thanks.'

'No, seriously,' he said. 'Very stylish.'

'Thanks,' she said again. 'You're looking good yourself.'

'I'm working in a computer software company now,' he said. 'Great pay and conditions. Plus there's a gym on site so we can work out there. How are you doing? I heard you'd gone off to France or Germany or something.'

'London,' she told him. 'But I'm back now.'

'Well, look, if you're ever at a loose end . . . if you'd like to meet for a drink or anything.'

She smiled. 'That's really nice of you, Denis, but I'm actually living in Dublin. I'm just here for the weekend.'

'Just my luck.' He grinned at her. 'All the good ones have something better to do.'

'Just somewhere else to be,' she said. 'It was lovely seeing you again.'

'You too,' he said. He took out his wallet and handed her a card. 'If you need to contact me,' he said, 'this is my number.'

'Gosh, well, thanks,' she said.

She walked back to the table with a grin on her face.

'Y'see,' she told the twins as she put Denis's card down in front of them. 'No need for me to hanker after any of the men in my past. I can get one just by walking into a bar. So maybe not useless after all!'

'Our sister the siren,' said Tish, and the three of them dissolved into giggles around the table.

# Chapter 21

Nieve had used the same law firm ever since she'd come to California, and, although the company specialised in business law, she made an appointment to see her attorney anyway.

Three different firms shared the same L-shaped building on North California Boulevard, but Judd Bryant, the firm she used, had the best offices, located in the short side of the building with gently rustling trees just outside the window, something which made all the clients feel a little less pressured as they sat in the open reception area and waited for their high-priced attorney to show up.

She'd been sitting there for less than five minutes, flicking through *USA Today*, when Corr Bryant strode through the opaque glass door and smiled at her.

'Nieve. Always a pleasure.'

She smiled in return. Corr was a great lawyer. He was tall and broad-shouldered, always impeccably dressed in tailored suits and crisp white shirts with expensive cufflinks, and he radiated both comfort and confidence.

She followed him along the short corridor to his office,

where he tilted the blinds to shut down the glare from the sun and offered her coffee from the espresso machine on a maplewood cabinet.

'I bought it last year,' he told her as he made himself a cup, although she'd declined, asking for water instead. 'I love my coffee!'

'D'you sleep at night?' she asked.

He laughed. 'Like a baby. But then that's because I don't worry about things. What about you, Nieve? Why do you need me?'.

Corr had worked for her during her Jugomax time and had helped her to deal with the massive fallout of the company having to file for bankruptcy. He'd made her feel as though this was something that had happened because of the business world and not because of anything to do with her part in its management or because she was in some way a failure. These things happen, he'd said. You gain experience. Life goes on. It's not the end of the world. But it had seemed like that to Nieve. She couldn't believe that Jugomax, for which she'd spent hours helping to draw up a really good business plan, and which had real products to sell, had gone to the wall in the same way as the thousands of speculative internet companies with nothing behind them. She'd been horrified at the suddenness of their fall, the abrupt way in which the banks had pulled their support, and the immediate downgrading of Jugomax to nothing more than another fly-by-night dotcom company. At first she'd tried to be blasé about it, in the same way that the CEO of the company, Richie Jefferson, appointed by Max, was being blasé about it. She'd thought that she could shrug it off too, but in the end it really hurt when the banks pulled the finance and Richie just didn't bother to show up one morning. She'd been the one to call Max, who told her that he wasn't going to put any more money into Jugomax either.

'Maybe we're ahead of the game,' he'd told her in the phone call in which he let her know that it was all over. 'But this was just a diversion on my part. If it worked, fine. It hasn't. Equally fine.'

'What about me?' she'd asked. 'What about me and Aidan and the rest of the staff?'

'I did what you asked.' And this time his voice was cool. 'I gave you a job and I gave you your chance and it's not my fault that you blew it. And if you come to Lilith now with stories of housekeepers from Spain – well, she'll just think that you're a disgruntled employee and she'll give them the attention they deserve. Which is none.'

'You're glad it's all gone wrong!' she'd cried. 'You never wanted me to succeed.'

'Bullshit,' he'd retorted. 'You're playing with my money out there. Of course I wanted you to succeed. But I'm equally pleased to see the back of you, Nieve, because, quite frankly, you're a bitch.'

Funny how that always had the power to hurt her. She wasn't a bitch. She knew what she wanted and she went all out to get it, but that didn't make her a bitch, did it, only a person who had goals. She was fed up with people thinking that just because a woman had a plan she had to be a bitch.

She put a lid on her thoughts and looked at Corr, who was emptying a narrow sachet of sugar into his coffee.

'I'm hoping you can give me some advice,' she said.

'Hey, looking forward to it.' He grinned. 'Are you going to set up on your own again? Use that Ennco money?'

She looked at him in surprise.

'I can't believe that you're going to stay with the brokerage. Not now,' he said. 'Everyone's intrigued to know how you guys are going to spend your loot.'

She laughed. 'Not really. We're small fry.'

'Small fry?' He laughed too. 'No you're not.'

'Thing is, in business anyone who isn't worth billions is small fry in this country,' she said.

'You might be right,' he agreed. 'But you're all going to do pretty well all the same. So what is it?'

'I'm not setting up my own company,' she told him. 'At least, not yet.'

'Shame. I can offer you advice on dealing with the money, though,' he said. 'Not that you need it.'

'It's partly about the money,' she said slowly. 'Sort of personal, really.'

'Not generally my area of expertise,' said Corr.

'I'm getting married,' said Nieve.

'Congratulations.'

'And I'm wondering about a pre-nup.'

'Ah.' Corr nodded slowly. 'I see. And who's the lucky man?'

'Aidan.' She was surprised he'd asked. Corr had met Aidan a number of times.

'So . . . you're wanting a pre-nup for a marriage to the guy you've lived with for – what, eight, nine, ten years?'

She made a face. 'I know, I know. And it's not that I

want a pre-nup, it's just that I was thinking about it and suddenly it seemed that there's so much money involved, and . . .' She sighed. 'I love him. I really do. But then the most solid of marriages seem to break up these days, and I don't want to lose all my hard-earned cash if we do.'

'Understandable,' agreed Corr.

'I feel terrible about it,' she admitted. 'He's been nothing but brilliant to me but . . .'

'You have to cover all the bases. I know. Like I said, this isn't my area of expertise. I'm a business law expert. But hell, Nieve, it's a difficult situation. Put it this way, if you weren't getting married and you split up and I was advising him, I'd be going after your sorry ass for palimony.'

'I know,' she said.

He moved the computer mouse on his desk and clicked it a few times. The printer whirred into action.

'These are the details of the person I'd recommend to you,' he told her as he took the sheet of paper from the tray and handed it to her. 'They're really good on the whole family law thing.'

'Thanks.' She took it from him, folded it, and slid it into her bag.

'Everything OK between you and Aidan?' he asked.

'Perfectly,' she said. 'I'm trying to be careful, that's all. It's a lot of money, and . . .'

'. . . And Aidan would piss it all away given half the chance.'

'Corr!'

'You said that to me about him before. That he was hopeless when it came to business and hopeless when it came to money.'

She nodded. 'He is. Y'know, when we came to the States first I thought he wanted all the same things as me. He talked the talk. But when it came down to it, he didn't walk the walk. He was happy with enough to get by plus a little bit extra. He didn't want to shoot for the stars. Once Jugomax was up and running, he wanted to do things for fun. He doesn't understand the concept of driving things forward and looking for the main chance. The whole idea of striking it rich doesn't bother him.'

'Maybe he doesn't think money is important.'

'Oh, come on!' Nieve laughed.

'I know it shocks you to think like that, because it shocks me too.' Corr grinned. 'Some people are content with less. You and me, Nieve, we're never content. There's nothing wrong with that, but not everyone understands it.'

'I know,' she said. 'Sometimes people make you feel bad for wanting to succeed.'

'Does Aidan make you feel that way?' he asked. 'Because – not that I'm one to offer you relationship advice – maybe if he does, it's not a pre-nup you need to be thinking about.'

'Normally he doesn't,' said Nieve. 'It's just that he thinks we should chill out on the Ennco money and I think we should use it to make more. I don't think there's anything wrong with that. Nobody should make me feel bad for wanting that.'

'Certainly no one in America should.' He grinned at her.

'Yeah, but we're in California,' she reminded him.

He chuckled. 'We might have our fair share of bleeding hearts,' he told her, 'but deep down we're all the same. Money matters.'

'Y'see, I know that.' She smiled back at him. 'And that's why I want to make sure that I keep what's mine no matter what happens in the future.'

'Talk to Bartlett Hobbs,' he told her. 'They'll look after you. I'll ring Leeza Bartlett and tell her about you.'

'Thanks, Corr.' She stood up.

'And if you do decide to set up something of your own, don't forget to give me a call.'

'I won't,' she promised.

She walked out of the offices and into the car park. The sun glinted off the roof of her red Acura. A part of her felt disloyal to Aidan for visiting the lawyer. But a part of her told her that she'd been sensible. That true love might conquer everything – and it had for them – but that it was always as well to be prepared for the future. Because you never knew exactly what the future might hold.

When she got home that evening, Aidan was already there. He'd fired up the barbecue and the smell of hot charcoal greeted her as she walked through the house and pushed open the back door. I'm a cow, she thought. I've been thinking of the worst that can happen, but he's always been the best.

He was sitting on a lounger and reading a book. Beer was chilling on the low table beside him.

'Charring meat?' she asked.

'I thought it would be nice,' he told her as he closed the book. 'It seems ages since we've done this and it's a lovely evening.'

'Sure.' She kicked off her high-heeled shoes and slid her

stockings from her legs. She would much have preferred to go bare-legged when the weather was warm, but Ennco frowned upon bare-legged women. Despite having lived in the States for a long time, Nieve couldn't quite understand why most women preferred to wear stockings or tights (and she hated the way they coyly spoke of pantyhose!) when it was so much nicer to wear neither. She sat on the spare lounger and buried her toes in the dusty grass.

'So how's things at the money farm?' asked Aidan.

'Share price is up,' she told him.

'How about this?' he suggested. 'As soon as you get the cash, we take a year off and cruise around the world.'

'I can't do that,' she said. 'In the same way as I can't immediately up sticks and move to Ireland. There's a golden handcuff. We have to stay with the company for a minimum six-month period after the deal.'

'They've tied you in pretty good, haven't they?' complained Aidan. 'You can't sell the shares yet, and even when you do you can't walk away.'

'They don't want us all to walk away,' said Nieve. 'It's quite reasonable really.'

'Yeah, but you're not at the cutting edge. You're not a trader. You're just supervisory staff.'

'Supervisory staff?' She looked at him impatiently. 'It's a bit more than that, Aidan. It's making sure that everything that goes on in Ennco is done by the book. So that we don't have an Enron-like disaster. Sometimes I don't think you realise just how important my job is. They mentioned me in *Business Week* this week, you know.'

'I'm sorry, I'm sorry,' he said hastily. 'I was paraphrasing.'

'I'm still insulted.'

'Ah, get over yourself.' He got up. 'I'm going to put the burgers on the barbie.'

He walked into the kitchen and came back with the meat patties, which he took over to the barbecue. Nieve watched him for a moment, then crossed the garden and stood beside him.

'Sorry,' she said.

'You need to relax a bit more, hon.' He flipped a burger then glanced at her. 'So what's Ennco's strategy for the future?'

'Grow bigger and better.'

'And what then?'

'Oh, God, I don't know.' She looked at him, tension in her face. 'What's with all this "business is evil" crap you're coming out with lately? I'm not stupid, Aidan. Every time we have a conversation it's all about chucking it in and making babies, isn't it? I thought there was more to us than that.'

'There is,' he said seriously. 'You know there is. And, sweetheart, I don't want to make you do things you don't want to do. I just want to point out the options.'

'You never stop pointing out the options!' she cried. 'Every bloody day turns into some kind of hippy-love-in-versus-corporate-suits conversation. This is meant to be a good time in our lives but you're making me feel totally pressurised. As though the wedding wasn't enough pressure in itself.'

'I'm not trying to pressurise you.' He put down his barbecue fork and wrapped his arm around her. 'It's truly not that I want to mess with your choices. I want you to be happy. I do love you, you know. I just don't want you all burned out and wondering in a few years "is that it?"'

She leaned her head on his shoulder. 'I swear to God I won't wonder that.'

'If the wedding is too much pressure – well, who's to say we have to get married?' Aidan said softly.

She stepped away and stared at him. 'I thought you wanted to get married. Have you changed your mind?'

'Don't be daft. But, sweetheart, I want it to be a happy occasion, not something that sends you into stress overdrive. So, you know, if it's not making you happy . . .'

She swallowed hard. 'I *want* to marry you,' she said. 'I've wanted to for a long time.'

'Then let the wedding-planner do what she's paid for and stop stressing out.'

She nodded slowly. The thing was, she kind of liked stressing out. He knew that. So why wouldn't he want her to be stressed now? Why would he be making ridiculous suggestions about calling everything off? She shivered, then leaned her head on his shoulder again. But she was still stressed.

# Chapter 22

The weekend before her first trip to Singapore, Darcey got into a panic about her wardrobe and took the afternoon off to go shopping. Although summer warmth hadn't quite made it to Dublin yet, the shop windows were already filled with soft floaty dresses in floral patterns and pastel colours, while strappy sandals had taken over from sturdy shoes and boots. Darcey wandered up Grafton Street and wondered what it would be like to buy a floaty floral dress again. She hadn't bought one in years. In her mind, floral dresses were associated with the horrible evening when she'd thought she was getting engaged but didn't. After that experience her wardrobe had changed for good. It hadn't ever been very feminine in the first place – she'd always preferred jeans and T-shirts to skirts – but since that night she'd shied away from anything overtly pretty and, with very occasional exceptions, her daytime wardrobe consisted almost entirely of black or beige suits for work and faded denim jeans which she wore with black or beige tops at weekends. The only colour she added was through her accessories, and that very occasionally.

She wasn't looking to change from black or beige – after all, the colours meant that she never had to worry about anything clashing – but she wanted to buy something more lightweight for the Irish summer and she also needed something appropriate for a city where the humidity level was always high. She was certain that the office buildings in Singapore would probably be freezingly air-conditioned, but her experiences in Europe during the summer told her that as soon as she stepped outside into the warmer temperatures she'd dissolve into a perspiring puddle.

She wandered into Brown Thomas, where she walked past the displays of pastel shades and the racks of more vibrant summer oranges and lemons (which she knew would look awful on her anyway) and eventually found a perfectly acceptable linen suit in her favourite biscuit shade which she promptly bought along with half a dozen crisp white blouses. It wasn't exciting, she knew. But it was safe. Then she went into the shoe department and selected a pair of high-heeled Marc Jacobs shoes to go with it. Darcey liked expensive shoes. Naturally she didn't buy them in girlie colours either, but she did like high heels because she thought they made her ugly ankles look a lot slimmer. The result, though, was that walking in comfort was sometimes not an option. And of course there was always the possibility of sprawling across the pavement when her feet went from under her. She'd got over the everyday clumsiness of her childhood, but she knew that she still wasn't a graceful person. However, the Marc Jacobs were supremely comfortable and well worth the extravagant price tag to make her ankles look thinner and her legs longer and more elegant.

'We have them in purple too,' said the assistant, who had noticed Darcey's satisfaction as she looked at herself in the mirror.

'Oh, no, these are fine.' She'd chosen a tan pair with an embroidered detail in fine gold thread. Glitzy enough, she thought. They're for business after all.

She walked out of the store, its distinctive carrier bag swinging in her hand, and collided with someone walking in.

'Sorry!' she gasped.

The tall brunette, also toting a selection of carrier bags, apologised too and then frowned.

'Darcey? Darcey McGonigle?'

Darcey nodded and her eyes flickered in recognition.

'Carol Jansen?'

Carol beamed at her. 'I just don't believe it,' she said. 'It's great to see you.'

'How are you keeping?' Darcey moved out of the doorway and the two women stood on the pavement outside the shop. 'You look fantastic.'

'Thanks,' said Carol. 'I lost a bit of weight.'

'Well, not that I would've mentioned it . . .'

Carol had always been heavy at school and permanently on diets that never seemed to work.

'I had a baby,' she told Darcey. 'And then afterwards I reckoned that I could add the weight I'd put on during my pregnancy to my overall meaty proportions or I could get rid of the lot of it. I decided to get rid of it all.'

'Suits you,' said Darcey.

'Hey, you've undergone a bit of a change too,' Carol

told her. 'You've lost weight as well, and I just love the hair.'

'Thanks. It's high-maintenance, but a girl's gotta do what a girl's gotta do.' Darcey laughed.

Carol grinned. 'Where would we be without beauty products? Not that you need them, you always had great bone structure.'

'Thanks, but you know that's complete horseshit,' said Darcey.

'No, really,' protested Carol. 'I always envied your cheekbones.'

'You did?'

Carol nodded.

'I didn't know. But it's nice to hear.'

'Are you busy?' asked Carol. 'Would you like to have a quick coffee and catch up?'

Darcey instinctively glanced towards her watch, and then lowered her arm without looking at the time.

'Sure I would,' she said.

They walked around the corner into Wicklow Street and found themselves a window table in a small café, where Darcey ordered a cappuccino topped with cinnamon and Carol asked for a mint tea.

'OK, that's far too healthy,' complained Darcey.

'It's the slimline lifestyle,' admitted Carol. 'I'm a bit of a calorie-head now, but it works for me.'

Darcey tipped some sugar into her coffee and tried not to feel guilty about its possible effect on the size of her hips.

'Do you see any of the old gang?' asked Carol. 'I lost touch with everyone when I went to college in England,

and I don't get back to Galway much these days. Nor can I be arsed to go to any of the reunion things I hear about. I'm actually in town shopping for an outfit for Nieve Stapleton's wedding. I thought it might be fun. I presume you're going too?' Her eyes dropped down to the carrier bag. 'And if that's an outfit, you'd better let me see it so's we don't turn up in the same gear.'

'Oh, no, this isn't for the wedding,' said Darcey, who was wondering if Nieve had invited all of their old friends to the damn event. Would entire years of old class and college friends show up? 'Although I suppose I should be thinking about it.'

'I'm not great at getting dressed up,' said Carol. 'But I feel that I've got to for this. The invitation was so flashy and I've always wanted to see that castle – there was a piece in the *Sunday Times* about the restoration work they did there that was fascinating. As well as which, I do a bit of freelance journalism these days. I might be able to write up on it.'

'You were always the literary one.' Darcey grinned.

'Hardly literary. I do stuff for the housing pages. And other stuff.' She looked slightly embarrassed.

'I don't think I've ever seen your name on anything,' said Darcey, 'but then I guess I don't really look.'

Carol lowered her voice. 'I keep it quiet. I'm Ask Sam.'

Darcey looked at her blankly. 'Ask Sam?'

'In a tabloid. The *Irish*—'

'Oh, the agony aunt?' Darcey asked in astonishment.

'Hard to believe. But yes.'

'I've heard about you. You're madly popular.'

'Yes, well, always better at dealing with other people's problems than my own.'

'You have problems?' asked Darcey. 'You were always very together, I thought.'

'Hell, Darce, we all have problems!'

'True,' admitted Darcey. 'What are yours? Or d'you not want to say?'

'Oh, I managed to mess it all up after I graduated,' said Carol. 'That was when I got pregnant.'

Darcey looked at her sympathetically.

'It's fine,' said Carol. 'She's a great kid.'

'If she's anything like you, I'm sure she is,' said Darcey loyally.

'Luckily she does seem to have inherited some of my genes.' Carol's voice was grim. 'Her father's Tommy Brennan. Remember him? From Audubon Road? He went to the same college as me in the UK. Honest to God, you'd think that having headed away from Galway I'd manage to hook up with someone else, but no, it had to be Tommy Brennan.'

Darcey recalled the dark, brooding youth who had always seemed a little dangerous to them (mainly because he smoked incessantly and wore black leather biker gear all the time).

'Ah, he wasn't a bit dangerous,' said Carol. 'Underneath it all he was quite ordinary. Too ordinary. When he heard I was pregnant he insisted on "doing the right thing". I married him and I was bored out of my mind. We got divorced a couple of years ago.'

'Gosh, I'm sorry to hear that.'

Carol shrugged. 'These things happen. He met someone else anyway. He's getting married the day after Nieve.'

'Oh.'

'Who cares,' said Carol lightly. 'Me and Julie are better on our own. She reminds me a bit of you, Darcey. A total perfectionist.'

'I'm not . . .' Darcey stopped and giggled as she saw the expression in Carol's eye. 'Well, maybe a bit.'

'So what have you been up to?' asked Carol.

'I work in finance,' said Darcey.

'No big surprise there. You were always great with numbers. We always thought you'd have a fantastic career.'

'Did you?'

'Oh, yes. Rosa and I would talk about it. She used to say that one day the light would come on in your head and you'd stop pretending that you weren't interested in being good at things.'

Darcey felt her cheeks burn and Carol laughed at her.

'You so just wanted to be average,' she said. 'I hope you're something big in the city.'

'Not really.' And then Darcey shrugged. 'Well, actually, I suppose I kind of am. They're sending me off to Singapore next week for business.'

'Y'see!' Carol beamed at her. 'Lucky thing. I'm delighted for you. Is that what you're shopping for?'

Darcey nodded.

'Well don't forget to take time out and buy loads of lovely stuff while you're there. I know it's an electronics paradise, but I did a piece a while back about getting tailor-made clothing over there. Fabulous. You should do that for Nieve's wedding. You'd look lovely in a hot pink or fuchsia.'

'Not quite me.' Darcey laughed. 'But I'll think about it.'

'Do, absolutely. And that way I'll know we won't be wearing the same thing. Listen, are you bringing someone along on the day? If you're not, we could go together.'

'Um . . .'

'Oh, but of course – you got married, didn't you?' exclaimed Carol before Darcey had a chance to reply. 'I heard about that from someone.'

'You did?'

'Can't remember who told me.' Carol frowned.

'We divorced,' said Darcey.

'Jeez, we're not doing too well, are we?' asked Carol. 'I mean, there were four of us in that gang. Two of us are divorced already! D'you have kids?'

Darcey shook her head.

'People will say that's a good thing because of the mess that going through divorce is, but to tell you the truth, Julie is my life. She's brilliant – you'd never think her dad was that tosser! I was thinking of bringing her along as my partner, but then I thought that if the whole gang was going to be there, she'd be a bit sidelined. Besides, I got an invite to the rehearsal dinner the night before, so obviously I'm staying over. I presume you did too. D'you know who else is coming – Rosa, I guess. How about Millie Smith, and that other girl, Lindsey what's-her-name . . . ?'

'No,' said Darcey. 'I – well, I kinda lost touch with Nieve, so I don't know anything at all about it.'

'That's a shame,' said Carol. 'You two were inseparable at school.' She frowned. 'Wasn't there some bust-up? I vaguely remember someone telling me something . . .'

Darcey was surprised Carol didn't know what had fractured the friendship between herself and Nieve. She'd spent so long thinking that all her friends were talking about it, it hadn't occurred to her that some of them had been too busy living their own lives to bother.

'I'll tell you another time,' she said now. 'Long-ish story. But the bottom line is, I haven't spoken to her in years, so I was a bit surprised to get the invitation, to be honest.'

'And is there someone in your life to bring along?'

Darcey shook her head. 'No one special. I thought about bringing someone just for the company, but if you're on your own too – well, it might be better fun.'

'Absolutely,' said Carol. 'We'll have a laugh.'

'Yeah. We will.'

'I always have a laugh at weddings.' Carol looked cynical. 'All those dewy-eyed moments and you know it's probably all going to end in tears.'

'Not for Nieve,' said Darcey. 'You know her, always falls on her feet. Besides, she's been living with him for years.'

'Really? And now they've decided to tie the knot? I wonder what made them finally take the plunge.'

Darcey shrugged.

'Anyway, it'll be fun to see her again.'

Darcey tried to make her smile look genuine.

'So I'll see you there. And look, we should keep in touch.'

'Yes, we should,' agreed Darcey. She took a card out of her bag and gave it to Carol.

'Business Development Manager,' read Carol. 'I'm impressed.'

'Ah, would you stop! There's nothing to be impressed

about. Bottom line – I'm a divorced wage slave with a messed-up life.'

Carol chortled with laughter.

'Don't you worry about your life,' she said as she drained her mint tea. 'I'll solve it for you in front of our millions of readers!'

'Gee, thanks, just what I need. The whole world knowing that I'm a dope.' But Darcey smiled too and then headed out of the café and back down Grafton Street.

She stayed late in the office the night before her trip. She didn't really need to stay late at all, but she wanted to go through the material she'd prepared one last time and make sure that she had included every possible piece of information, as some of the products and services offered by Investor-Corp were new to her. It was totally unnecessary, because she remembered it all perfectly well, but she couldn't help herself checking. And she also wanted to make sure that her laptop was fully charged and that she'd remembered to put the cable in the carrying case for it too. Her phone also needed to be charged, but she planned to do that overnight.

She'd thought that perhaps Neil would drop down to see her during the day and ask her if she had everything she needed, but he hadn't been in touch and Minette was the only person who'd called to wish her good luck with the trip. Darcey had filled her mother in on all the changes in the company since the takeover, and Minette was pleased and proud on her behalf. Darcey didn't say that she was still a little bit worried that Neil Lomond might conceivably be setting her up for a fall, and Minette merely remarked that it was nice to think that despite everything they'd gone through, she and Neil seemed to have a good working relationship. Surprisingly adult, she said, and Darcey had retorted that she might be being adult about it but she hadn't allowed him to live in her apartment while he was house-hunting, and had Minette got rid of Martin yet? Minette had replied that she would be the one to decide when Martin should leave the house and that it wasn't really any of Darcey's business. At which Darcey had apologised and told her that she should, of course, do whatever she thought best, but that honestly the whole Martin thing just wasn't good news.

'Worry about yourself,' said Minette sharply, and Darcey had backed away from the subject of her father and mother.

Please let me not mess it all up, Darcey murmured under her breath as she zipped the computer into its case and made sure that her out-of-office message was activated. Please let me get loads of brilliant business and repay everyone's faith in me.

She walked through the empty office and waited for the lift. She never minded being in the building on her own, although she knew that plenty of the other staff – both male and female – disliked it. Anna said that she always thought about horror movies and being stalked by some lunatic with an axe when she was on her own, but Darcey laughed at that and remarked that she didn't have enough imagination to visualise it. Although now, with only the muted clicking of the electronic equipment making any sound, she conceded that it was just a little bit unsettling. At least it wasn't dark. That would have freaked her out. Total darkness was her only phobia, but the lights at InvestorCorp worked on a sensor, which meant that they came on and went off depending on where people were in the office so that no one was ever unexpectedly left without light.

She stabbed at the lift button again and heard it whirr up to the sixth floor. The ping of the bell echoed around the silent office. She stepped inside, pressed the button for the ground floor and glanced at her reflection in the mirror. She should've got her hair cut, she thought, as she tucked it behind her ear. She'd meant to do it the day she bumped into Carol Jansen, but meeting her old friend had put it straight out of her mind. Perhaps she could get it done at the hotel in Singapore.

She was still fiddling with her hair when the lights went out.

She stood still, frozen in horror. Then the lift shuddered to a halt, causing her to stumble and fall to the floor. She knelt, immobile, feeling the rapid beat of her pulse in her throat while she waited for the lights to come on again.

They didn't.

She realised that she'd clamped her eyes closed and she opened them cautiously. There should be an emergency light, she thought as she tried to make out anything in the almost total blackness. It's so silly that there isn't an emergency light. Her breath was coming in quick gulps and she told herself to calm down. But the rational part of her mind was being harried by her irrational fear of the dark.

She listened for the sound of anything happening, but the silence was as total as the darkness. Her heart was beating even faster and she could feel herself beginning to shake.

'It's a power failure,' she said out loud, the sound of her own voice bouncing off the walls of the lift. 'It's not that serious.' She put out her hand and felt for the lift phone. She had no idea where it was connected to, but she hoped someone would answer the call.

Only she couldn't see what number to call in the darkness. And anyway, the phone line seemed to be down too. She knew that she was on the verge of panicking. She could feel tears prickling her eyes. She took a deep breath and let it out very slowly.

Then she thought of her mobile phone and she scrabbled around in her handbag before her fingers curled around the clamshell Motorola. The light from the keyboard when she opened it was extremely welcome, but the signal was weak. So was the charge. But enough, surely, to contact someone. Anna, she thought, who would be able to find out exactly what was going on and would help her. She pressed the speed-dial number and heard it ring.

'Hello?'

'Hi, Anna!' she said, and the phone went dead.

It seemed twice as dark with the phone off. Darcey took another deep breath and powered it up again. She hit redial, conscious that her hand was shaking even more now.

'Hello, Darcey?'

The phone went dead again. Darcey nearly screamed with frustration. And she was beginning to feel claustrophobic in the darkness of the lift. If the power didn't come back on, what was she going to do? Nobody would come near the building until the morning. There was a security firm, she knew, but they just checked outside the premises from time to time. Nobody would be walking around inside.

Think this through, she told herself as calmly as she could. For the phones and the power to go it has to have been some major fault. That will get fixed. If the power comes back on, the lift will start to work again. And so will the phone. I might only be here a couple of hours. And the worst that can happen is that I'll be here overnight. I won't run out of air overnight.

Except my flight to London to make the connection is at eight in the morning. And my suitcase is at home. And I've stuff to do. And I don't like this one little bit!

To her horror, she felt the earlier threatened tears flood her eyes and she sniffed loudly. If only there was light. It wouldn't be so bad if the lights came back on.

The laptop, she thought suddenly. The fully charged laptop. If she switched it on, at least she'd have some kind of light. She took it from the bag, sat down on the floor and powered it up, feeling a comfort from the normally irritating start-up chime.

If only we had wireless internet in here, she thought, I could email Anna and she could sort things out. Or the emergency services. She was stuck. It was dark. And she wanted to go home. That was an emergency, wasn't it? She wished she'd charged her phone at the office, or brought the lead which connected it to her computer. That might have given it enough of a charge to make a call. It was extremely frustrating to be surrounded by different means of communicating with people and not be able to use any of them.

She got up and picked up the lift's phone receiver again. But it was still dead.

It was half past ten. She had a horrible feeling that whatever had happened and whatever steps were being taken to fix things, she was still going to be stuck in the lift for hours. And she'd miss her flight and the whole Singapore trip would be thrown into complete chaos, because every second of her time was accounted for. Instead of going down in the annals of the company as the woman who'd revitalised their Asian client base, she'd be forever known as the stupid cow who'd got stuck in the lift and missed the most important business trip of her career.

Not expecting anything of it, but feeling that she had to try once more, she switched on her phone again. It suddenly occurred to her that she might have better luck with a text message. She managed to key in that she was stuck in the office and hit send before the phone went dead again. Maybe it had gone to Anna. Maybe not. She could only hope.

She slid into a seated position, her back against the wall of the lift, and rested her head on her knees.

It was nearly an hour later when she thought she heard something. She'd spent the time playing solitaire and then looking through her computer files and reading through the analyses of business that she'd brought into Global Finance over the past few years. She'd also done her best to ignore the fact that the bottle of Coke she'd drunk earlier at her desk was making its presence felt.

Now she strained her ears to catch the sound again. Despite

her lack of imagination, she'd suddenly wondered if something cataclysmic had happened when she was in the lift, something much worse than a power cut. A bomb, maybe, which had taken out a chunk of the city. It seemed far-fetched, but then so had events like 9/11. What if there had been some kind of terrorist strike? What if she was the only person in the area left alive? She managed to clamp down on thoughts that she told herself were pure hysteria, but the niggling worry remained. And so she wasn't prepared to shout in response to a possible noise until she knew exactly what it was.

'Darcey!'

It was her name. And it was Anna Sweeney's voice, coming from a distance. She felt relief flood through her.

'Anna! I'm here.'

'Darcey!'

'Here!' she cried as loudly as she could. 'In the lift.'

'Hold on.' The voice was silent, and then she heard Anna say her name again, and this time she was much closer.

'Anna, I'm in the lift. It's stuck. I think it's between the fourth and fifth floors.'

'Don't worry,' said Anna. 'We'll sort it out.'

'It's dark.' Darcey heard the tremble in her voice.

'You poor thing. Really, don't worry. We're calling the emergency services to get you out.'

'Oh, good.'

'Are you all right in there?'

'Yes. But I'd rather be somewhere else.'

'We'll get you out soon. Honestly.'

'What happened?' asked Darcey.

'A digger,' explained Anna. 'You know where they're doing some work outside the offices right now? It cut through the power lines and took out half of Dublin 1.'

'Hey, Darcey, are you all right?' Darcey recognised Neil Lomond's voice and she grimaced.

'Yes, I'm fine,' she said.

'The fire brigade is on its way,' he told her. 'They'll get you out.'

Bloody hell, she thought. Why does he have to be around to see me make a fool of myself?

'Are you OK in there?' he asked.

'Well, it's not exactly five-star,' said Darcey. 'But I guess I can cope.'

'Think of it like the opening sequence in *Speed*,' Anna said. 'Only not as bad!' she added hastily.

'That's very comforting.' Darcey felt some of her spirit return.

She heard Neil laugh.

'I bet you would've been great driving that bus too,' he said.

She laughed too, although she realised that she was shaking again. 'Probably.'

It was half an hour later that Anna called to her that the fire brigade had arrived and she heard the sounds of activity outside. And only a few minutes after that before the doors of the lift were prised open and a flashlight beamed in at her.

'You're almost on the fourth floor,' said the fireman. 'We'll just haul you out, love.'

'Here.' Darcey closed her laptop and put it back into its case before handing it and her handbag up to him.

'We're more interested in getting you out than anything else,' he said.

'I need that stuff,' she told him. 'It's important.'

'Come on then.' He held his hand out to her and helped her out of the lift. Another arm steadied her as she stumbled.

'Thanks.' She looked into Neil Lomond's anxious eyes.

'Are you all right?' he asked.

She nodded, suddenly utterly unable to speak and thankful for Neil's firm hold around her. It was oddly familiar, and very comforting.

'Oh, Darcey!' Anna, who'd been standing beside another fireman, flung her arms around her. 'I'm so glad you're OK.'

'It was nothing really. I'm grand, no bother.' Darcey slid out of Anna's embrace even though she was still trembling.

'What on earth were you doing in the office at this hour?' demanded Neil.

'It wasn't this hour when I got into the lift,' she retorted. 'It was just before ten.'

'Honestly, Darcey. Hanging round the office at ten and you supposed to be heading off to London early in the morning. Are you cracked?' asked Anna.

'What happened with all those cut-off phone calls?' asked Neil. 'And then your text was very cryptic. We thought at first it was some kind of joke.'

'My mobile needed charging and the signal in the lift was crap,' said Darcey. She heaved a sigh. 'Anyway, all's well and all that sort of stuff. It wasn't that bad really.' She clenched her fist so that nobody would see her hand shaking.

They followed the firemen and the security company key-holder out of the building. Anna held on to Darcey's arm. Neil walked the other side of her, but he didn't put his arm around her again.

The entire area was still enveloped in darkness, although candles flickered in the windows of some of the apartments and of the nearby bar.

'Want a drink?' asked Neil.

Darcey nodded. 'I think I could do with one. But I desperately need to use the bathroom first.'

When she returned from the Ladies', Neil and Anna were sitting at a table, drinks in front of them. Anna had ordered a glass of wine for Darcey.

'Cosy,' Darcey remarked. Then she took a large gulp of wine.

'Candlelight is nice,' agreed Anna. 'Are you sure you're OK?'

'Of course. I wasn't there that long, and I knew that sooner or later everything would be fine.'

'You're so cool about it,' said Anna. 'I'd have been going nuts.'

'I didn't feel cool at all,' admitted Darcey. 'I'm very glad you turned up when you did. But at least I had my computer with me. I was able to do a bit of work, and that distracted me.'

'Darcey McGonigle! Please tell me you weren't working while you were stuck in the lift!' Anna looked at her in mock horror.

'I didn't do much,' said Darcey. 'I was too worried about when someone would find me to concentrate.'

'I'd have been freaking out about the possibility of being stuck there for the whole night,' said Anna.

'That wouldn't have happened,' said Neil. 'The power would have come on eventually.'

'I knew that,' Darcey said. 'I was more worried about making my flight in the morning.'

'Are you OK to go?' Anna asked. 'I mean, you've had a shock, and—'

'Of course I am,' said Darcey quickly. 'Don't be daft, Anna. I'm fine. It's all set up. I'm sorry I worried you, but it was lucky you were around. I thought you'd be at home.'

'Neil and I had some business we needed to discuss,' said Anna. 'So we came here. We were just about to leave when you rang.'

'Oh.'

'I was worried about you when I got your message and Neil thought that maybe you couldn't get out of the building because the doors are electronic.'

'I didn't think you'd be stuck in the lift,' he said.

Darcey raised her glass to them. 'Well, thanks for being here.'

'You're welcome,' said Anna.

'It wouldn't have done my position much good if your dehydrated corpse was discovered in the morning,' added Neil. 'Not great for staff morale.'

Darcey laughed, then Neil's own mobile began to ring.

'Excuse me,' he said, and got up from the table.

Darcey turned to Anna and raised an eyebrow.

'Things to discuss?' she enquired. 'In the pub? On a Monday evening?'

'Hey, I like to keep it casual.' Anna grinned. 'And so does

he.' She looked at her friend. 'I was right about him. He is kinda sweet.'

'I know,' said Darcey. 'That was what got me at the start.'

She shivered again. And she wasn't sure whether it was because she was reliving the terror of being stuck in the lift on her own, or the sudden memory of Neil's arm holding on to her tightly afterwards.

# Chapter 23

At the same time as Darcey was being helped out of the lift in Dublin, Nieve was in a meeting with Ennco's chief financial officer. Harley Black had one of the nicest offices in the building, a large corner room with floor-to-ceiling windows on two sides, luxurious dark blue carpeting on the floor and an enormous rosewood desk in the centre. There were plenty of strategically arranged green plants around the room, and expensive modern art on the walls – which also held plasma-screen monitors, TVs, and five clocks showing the time in various world locations. Harley's office had a small bar too, although he himself never touched alcohol during the working day. Nieve didn't drink during office hours either and, as she sat in one of the comfortable leather chairs and talked to Harley about the finances of Ennco, she sipped a double espresso instead. Lately she seemed to be feeling constantly exhausted and she needed the caffeine hits to keep her going. The espresso made her heart race and her hands shake a little, but she knew that it also sharpened her mind.

'Everything's looking good,' said Harley as he flicked through the folders of spreadsheets in front of him. 'We're on track with our filings and with our ratios, and unless any of your traders have managed to cook the books on your watch, Ennco is in great shape.'

Nieve allowed her annoyance to flicker in her eyes. 'The traders are under control,' she told him. 'There's nothing wrong with my area. You're the one who needs to be sure that all those quarterly loans are paying back like they're supposed to and that you've dotted all the i's and crossed all the t's!'

'Relax,' said Harley. 'Of course they are. Anyway, the auditors were happy enough, they didn't find anything.'

'I wasn't expecting anyone to find anything,' commented Nieve. 'God knows we have enough systems in place.'

'And we have enough people who're smart enough to get around them,' said Harley.

'None of my people,' said Nieve calmly.

'You put far too much faith in your end of things,' said Harley. 'But I suppose you don't need to worry about the traders so much when the big money is in corporate finance. Did you look at the returns from those guys last year?'

'What about the hedge funds?' she countered.

'They had a piss-poor twelve months,' he returned.

'Yeah, last time. But up till then they were the engine driving this business, so get your head out of your ass, Black.'

The two of them glared at each other, and then Harley laughed.

'You fight like a tiger for your people,' he said.

'So do you.'

345

'Would you ever give it up?'

Why did people keep asking her that? Nieve wondered. Nobody asked the guys whether they'd consider giving up their jobs, but they seemed to think it was fair game to ask a woman. Even a woman as dedicated as she was.

'Only to set up something of my own,' she said.

'Are you thinking of it?'

She shrugged. The truth was she didn't know whether she was thinking of it or not. Maybe Aidan was right when he said that the time had come to ease back a bit. But she was afraid of easing back. She couldn't imagine what it would be like not to be tense about something.

'There's a bit of a rumour going round that a few of the guys are thinking of setting up a fund management operation of their own.'

She shrugged again. That was always an occupational hazard of working in the markets. Sooner or later everyone realised that they could make more money working for themselves than for a company. So that was what they did, upping and leaving the firm where they'd made their names and trying to take the best clients with them.

'We can't leave yet,' she said easily. 'We're golden-hand-cuffed.'

'Yeah, but you can get the background work done,' said Harley.

Her eyes narrowed. 'Are *you* thinking of it?'

'Not me,' he said. 'Mike and I are in this together. He's loyal to me. I'm loyal to him.'

'Are you trying to find out about other people?' she asked. 'Sniff out possible defectors?'

'We need to know,' he said. 'People might think it's a good thing to leave this firm. But it isn't.'

'It's not on my radar at the moment.' Even if it was, she thought, I'd hardly tell you.

'It's important for the share price that we don't lose good people,' said Harley. 'Mike wants the team to stay together even when people can do their own thing.'

'In that case, the best thing he can do is make this a place where people want to stay,' said Nieve. 'Hey, Harley, it's a good place to work anyway. We all know that.'

'It's different when it's a public company,' said Harley. 'It's important to toe the line, to keep with the company mood.'

'What's all this about?' She stared at him and felt a sudden tug of unease. 'Is there something wrong?'

'Of course not,' he said. 'I just want to make sure that nothing *does* go wrong.'

'You do your job, I'll do mine, and nothing will,' she said as she stood up.

He grinned. 'Mike likes you,' he said. 'He thinks you're a hard worker.'

'I am.'

'He has plans for you.'

'He does?'

'So stick with us. What you've got now is only the beginning.'

She went back to her own office and backed up her computer files. She'd just finished when Paola walked in, looking anxious. Nieve sighed. Paola's constant nervous look freaked her out; she couldn't bear the other girl's hesitant nature. And it seemed, too, that she'd expanded enormously over the last few weeks, because her bump was in the office before she was.

'I'm really sorry,' she began.

'What now?' There was resignation in Nieve's voice.

'Nothing major. But my appointment with my ob-gyn has been rearranged. I'll be out tomorrow morning instead of tomorrow afternoon. I thought that would suit you, actually.'

'Sure. That's fine.'

'Well, OK,' said Paola. 'I'll see you later. I'm off to lunch now.'

Nieve glanced at her watch. 'A bit late for lunch,' she remarked.

'I worked through,' said Paola. 'I had stuff I needed to finish.'

'You can't skimp on your food,' said Nieve sharply. 'You're pregnant. You have to eat properly.'

Paola looked surprised.

'I'm not having you say that your baby has problems because you didn't have enough time to go to lunch,' Nieve told her. 'Make sure you organise yourself better.'

'It's nothing to do with my organisation,' said Paola. 'It all depends on the trades.'

Nieve shrugged. 'Whatever. Just – you know, look after yourself.'

'I will,' said Paola, and walked out of the office.

When she'd closed the door behind her, Nieve leaned her chin in her hands and sighed. She wished she could deal with pregnant women better, but she simply couldn't. Her mind didn't work that way. She would have to be nicer to Paola. She just didn't know if she could.

By later that evening she'd forgotten about Paola, but her earlier conversation with Harley Black kept running over and over again in her head. There had been something strange about it, something slightly off key, but she couldn't put her finger on what it was. It was as though Harley was both flattering her and warning her, and she couldn't see why. She wondered about the whole aspect of people jumping ship from Ennco once they could sell their shares. Was there a possibility of wholesale defections? She didn't think so, but she wasn't sure. Nobody had come to her with some other opportunity. People had asked, but only, like Harley, about setting up on her own. Nobody had suggested that she might like to set up in partnership with them. Not that she would anyway. The idea of starting a new company and trying to build up a client base was far too much like hard work. And the thing was, despite the long hours and the fact that she did work hard at Ennco, it wasn't as stressful as she sometimes let herself imagine. That was because she knew everything – the people, the systems – back to front. She could sleepwalk her way through Ennco. The only pressure was the pressure she put on herself. And she could stop doing that if she wanted. Although she didn't.

Aidan knew that something was bothering her because she couldn't sit still while they were watching the TV movie she'd claimed she wanted to see.

'Maybe I should go through the accounts,' she said

thoughtfully after she'd explained to him that her conversation with Harley had left her feeling uneasy. 'Maybe there's something there that needs checking.'

'Hey, Harley's the accountant, isn't he? If there's something needs checking, he's the one to do it.'

'Not on his side,' she said. 'Mine. Maybe one of the traders has done something and it's popped up somewhere, only I've missed it.'

'How likely is that?' he asked.

'Not very.'

'So chill out.' He put his arm around her. 'Chill out and forget bloody Ennco and forget Mike Horgan and Harley Black and all of those damn suits, and think instead about the great day we're going to have soon.'

She slid into his arms. 'You're right. Harley is the one who needs to check things. And it's in his interests that everything is kept under control. Besides,' she shrugged, 'he's a brilliant chief financial officer. It's not my job.'

'Exactly,' said Aidan. 'Now, c'mere. Let me see if I can't remind you why there are more important things in life.' He unhooked her bra with one hand.

She giggled. 'These are the times when I know why I ran away with you,' she said.

But later that night, as they lay side by side in their huge bed, she allowed herself to think again about Ennco's accounts and Ennco's future. It doesn't matter, she thought, as she stared into the darkness. I've got what I want out of it. If the company stops making oodles of money it shouldn't really matter to me.

And yet it did matter. She'd been with one company that

had failed and she certainly didn't want to be with another. But Ennco wouldn't fail. Ennco was huge and profitable and strong and Ennco had made her very, very rich.

She punched the pillow and snuggled down beside Aidan, who put his arm around her and told her to go to sleep. Still later, though, while Aidan was sleeping (why is it I do so much work when he's sound asleep? she asked herself), she got up and logged on to her computer again. She looked through the trades and the profits and she couldn't see anything wrong. She could, of course, spend even more time going through each individual trade, but that would take days, and deep down she was pretty sure that there wasn't a problem, because she knew she would have noticed it already. She wished, though, that she was as intuitive with numbers as Darcey McGonigle. If there was something, no matter how trivial, she knew Darcey would have spotted it. The woman seemed to have some kind of homing instinct when it came to figures. In school and college she'd always been able to guess the answer before having to work her way through the question. And although she never wrote down the guess as her final answer without doing the work, she was invariably right.

Nieve had burned her bridges with Darcey even though she'd asked her to the wedding. But right now she wished they were still friends. Not just because of the Ennco figures. But because she needed to talk to someone. About Ennco. About Aidan. About everything. If Aidan had been any other man in the world, she could have talked to Darcey about him. About the pre-nup that Leeza Barrett had drawn up but that Nieve hadn't been able to ask Aidan to sign. About having kids. About taking time out to smell the roses – Darcey had been good at that! She wouldn't, of course, have said anything useful. But just talking to her would have helped.

But more than her worry about the personal things, Nieve truly wished that she could ask Darcey about the Ennco numbers. Just to be a hundred per cent sure that everything was OK. The thing was, whenever Darcey had had a bad feeling about something, she'd generally been proved right. Nieve knew that she herself could get into a panic about nothing at all. Not that anyone knew she was panicking. Not that she would ever let them know.

It's fine, she told herself as she logged off again. I haven't cocked it all up. I know I haven't.

She opened her desk drawer. The replies to her invitations were neatly bundled together. She looked through them all again.

A few weeks, she murmured. A few weeks and she'd be seeing people she hadn't seen in years. It had all seemed great when she'd started to organise it. But now she was beginning to wonder whether it would be so great after all. When she looked at the cards she remembered people as they were. But people changed. She'd changed. There was no reason to imagine that everyone else hadn't changed either.

They wouldn't be rich, though. That was the thing to hold on to. No matter who they were, no matter what they'd done, they wouldn't be rich. And when it came down to it, having money was the most important thing in the world. Regardless of whatever claptrap people spouted about love, it was money that really mattered.

# Chapter 24

Darcey groaned when the alarm went off the following morning. She knew she'd only been asleep for an hour at most, but she'd finally fallen into that very deep sleep that so often happens just before it's time to get up. It was the kind of deep sleep she would have liked earlier in the night after she'd finally flopped into bed following her ordeal in the lift. Both Anna and Neil had offered to accompany her in the taxi back to her apartment afterwards, but she'd shaken her head and told them that it wasn't necessary, that she was perfectly fine now, thanks, and that she was going straight to bed. But before she headed for the bedroom she made herself a mug of hot chocolate (instant, so not as comforting as Minette's) and mentally checked off the contents of the suitcase that she'd packed the previous night, while waiting for the feeling of helplessness that had engulfed her in the lift to pass.

When she'd finally crawled beneath the downy duvet (despite the fact that it was a warm night and she didn't really need to bury herself under the covers) she found herself quite unable to sleep. She got up then and turned on the bathroom light, aware that it was the darkness of her bedroom that was bothering her. It wasn't really all that dark because the glow from the street lamp outside penetrated her sheer curtains and bathed the room in a faint yellow light, which she usually found vaguely comforting; but that night it wasn't enough for her. And so she turned on the bathroom light and left the door ajar so that she didn't feel suffocated by the darkness.

But she still couldn't sleep. She kept thinking of how scared she'd really been in the lift and wondering what on earth would have happened if Anna and Neil hadn't shown up, although most of her thoughts were about the disaster that missing her flight might have been. And whenever she thought about the flight, she thought about the fact that she really and truly needed to go to sleep now but couldn't. And she'd pummel the pillow and wrap the duvet around her once more and try desperately to think of something else but fail miserably, so that her thoughts returned again and again to the events of earlier.

It was fortunate that Anna and Neil had come to rescue her. And she was pleased that her friend and her boss (it was actually quite hard to think of Neil as her boss, but she was getting used to it) seemed to like each other so much. Anna was very likeable, though. And a really good friend.

At least, Darcey told herself in the semi-darkness, I've got better at picking my friends and my lovers these days. My continental relationships worked out just fine, and Anna is a million miles away from the sort of person that Nieve Stapleton was.

Thinking of Nieve banished all hope of sleep. She pushed

the duvet from her shoulders, slid out of bed and retrieved the crumpled wedding invitation from the living room table. Accepting it had been mental. But perhaps going along with Carol would make it . . . well, not fun, it could never be fun . . . but not a nightmare either. She knew that going was crazy. But not going would be even worse. And (she finally admitted it to herself) she desperately wanted to see Aidan again. She wanted to see what he was like, because somewhere deep inside she felt as though she had unfinished business with him. She wanted to see him and discover that she wasn't in love with him any more. Although there was a part of her that was very, very afraid that maybe she was.

She got back into bed and eventually drifted into a half-sleep punctuated by dreams in which she and Nieve or Aidan or Anna or Neil were stuck in a plummeting lift eating black olives as it hurtled downwards. She would jerk into wakefulness just before the lift crashed into the ground and her heart would be hammering away in her chest so that it was impossible for her to get to sleep again.

She didn't know why it was that she'd managed to finally fall asleep properly just before it was time to get up. She felt it was a mean trick of her body and mind to play.

However, she was ready and waiting, looking fresh and rested in her dark trouser suit and plain cream T-shirt when the taxi arrived. She had her usual coffee at Dublin before getting her connecting flight to London, where flying business class meant that she could relax in one of the lounges away from the crush of other travellers. Although she felt slightly guilty at the sudden bout of cosseting, she also found herself starting to relax and the memories of her hours in the lift beginning to fade. And because her mind was now focusing on her business trip instead, she was also able to forget Nieve and Aidan and the fact that she had voluntarily decided to go and see the love of her life get married to another woman.

It was a thirteen-hour flight to Singapore.

Darcey occupied herself by watching a selection of comedy videos and then an in-flight DVD (*Lost in Translation*, which she hadn't previously seen and which she hoped wouldn't be an indication of her own business trip); and by reading the book she'd bought in the airport (although reading wasn't exactly the right word; she'd bought *Problems from the Maths Olympiad* and was working her way through them) while also gorging herself on the business-class food. The combined effects of the movie, the food and wrestling with the maths problems – as well as her broken sleep the night before – eventually made her eyes start to close. She'd once read that airlines turn up the heat on long-haul flights to send the passengers to sleep. She wasn't sure whether it was true, but she knew that she was tired now. She fiddled with the controls until she'd reclined the seat as much as possible, stretched out on it and pulled a blanket over her. She was asleep within five minutes, and despite a bout of turbulence over the Indian Ocean she didn't wake up until the cabin staff announced their descent into Changi airport.

Her bag was one of the first to appear on the carousel and she pounced on it with delight before making her way through to the arrivals hall, where a driver was supposed to be waiting for her. She saw her name on a board held up by the driver and followed him outside into the soupy, humid air.

The sky was faint blue with banks of white and grey clouds that hinted at rain. Darcey felt beads of perspiration break out on her forehead in the few moments she had to wait before getting into the chill of the air-conditioned car.

The driver kept up a continuous stream of conversation as he drove her towards her hotel in the financial district, talking proudly about the growth that the city had seen over the past years and the good job the government had done to keep it clean, safe and prosperous. Darcey, who was used to cab-drivers in European countries snarling about the inefficiencies of government bureaucracy, was amused by her driver's apparent contentedness. She was even more amused when he slowed down to allow a car from another lane of traffic to cut in front of him. If anything made her realise that she was experiencing a different culture, it was the behaviour of her driver.

Will I meet someone here? she wondered suddenly as they drew closer to the tall towers of the financial district near the harbour. Will I replace Louis-Philippe or Rocco or the others with a man from Asia? Will I get seduced by the beauty of this city in the same way as I've been seduced by other cities before?

Will I get the job done?

That was the most important thing. Bringing back the business for InvestorCorp. It was her biggest single challenge. And she didn't want to fail.

The hotel foyer – minimalist cream marble tiles with a square fountain in the centre – was bustling with people. Darcey felt big and clumsy as a group of small and elegant Singaporean women walked by her, dressed in black suits with white blouses, their dark hair neatly pulled back from their faces. They were tiny, she thought. And beautiful. And she was a hefty lump by comparison!

'You're on the twentieth floor,' said the hotel receptionist (another petite and elegant woman), handing her a coded key card. 'I will show you to the elevators and your luggage will be brought up to you.'

She led Darcey to a bank of lifts and pressed a button. Darcey stepped inside and then swallowed hard at the memory of her last experience in a lift. Although it was only twenty-four hours ago, it seemed a lifetime away, yet the whole idea of being in a lift again suddenly made her shudder. But fortunately this one had glass walls and Darcey felt confident that even if she got trapped in it she would at least be able to see outside. She comforted herself with that thought until they reached the twentieth floor and she was able to get out again.

Her room was beautiful, with spectacular views across the harbour and the city.

I am so lucky, she told herself, as she stared across the water, to have a job that allows me to come to places like this. I'm a success. I've done well. What more could anyone possibly want?

She made herself a cup of green tea and, as she waited for it to infuse, a knock at the door signalled the arrival of the porter with her luggage. She drank the tea wrapped in a hotel robe, sitting beside the window and thinking to herself that, great though the European trips had been, this was surely something completely different and exciting. She hoped fervently that she'd manage to bring in the same kind of business as she'd done in Europe, and briefly visualised a possible moment of glory as Person of the Year again, with Neil Lomond having to make the award.

It was a lovely thought. And it was only half an hour later, when the empty tea cup fell from her hand and woke her, that she realised she'd fallen asleep in the comfortable chair, dreaming about it.

Her first meeting was at ten o'clock the following morning in one of the myriad glass towers that punched skywards through the heavy air. Darcey wore the biscuit-coloured suit she'd bought for the trip with one of her crisp white blouses. Although, as she stepped into the humid air and felt the inevitable beads of perspiration immediately break out on her forehead again, she wondered just how long the blouse would actually stay crisp.

But, as she'd suspected, the office buildings were heavily air-conditioned. And she managed to maintain her cool and her composure despite the fact that the offices of her first meeting were on the twenty-ninth floor of an impressive circular building and the lift was almost identical to the one in the InvestorCorp office. She held her breath as she was whisked upwards but she was perfectly calm by the time she met her prospective clients. After a slightly difficult start when she didn't know exactly at what point the pleasantries had finished and she was supposed to get down to business, she began her pitch.

They listened to her impassively as she spoke about her company and its products and she began to feel slightly panicked at the polite nods but lack of questions. She was also slightly disconcerted by the fact that they got into a huddle at the end of her presentation and began talking among themselves, but she was pleased when they agreed that InvestorCorp had some interesting products that they might consider.

The mid-meeting huddle happened again at her second appointment (nineteenth floor, not too bad, but she wished she could stop worrying about suddenly being plunged into darkness; she knew the chances were remote!), and at her third, so she realised that this was something that happened as a matter of course here. And quite suddenly she began to feel comfortable with what she was doing and comfortable with the people she was meeting and very comfortable with the beauty of the city.

Her fourth and final meeting of the day was in yet another business tower. She was looking forward to it now, in tune with what she was doing and how to deal with the people she was meeting. She wondered why it was that she could speak so easily and so fluently to complete strangers when she seemed to get tongue-tied and say the wrong things so often to people she knew.

The head of asset allocation at Asia Holdings was English. Although she now felt comfortable with the Singaporeans, it was a little easier to talk to someone whose culture was the same as hers, with whom she could make small jokes and not be met with a blank face. She relaxed into her presentation as she extolled the virtues of InvestorCorp.

Jason White was easy to get on with. He knew what he wanted from her product line and he also knew the right questions to ask about the way they managed their business. He told her that he'd briefly dealt with the company in the past when he himself had been working in London, but that he hadn't renewed the contacts when he'd transferred to Singapore. However he was happy to do so now. He reckoned that it could be profitable for both of them.

Darcey nodded, pleased with the good response that she was getting and pleased that every meeting she'd had had been so positive. She was still nodding when he asked if she'd like to have dinner with him that evening.

'Oh, good,' he said. 'I was afraid you'd have plans.'

She was suddenly unsure whether the invitation was supposed to be business or pleasure. Not that it mattered, she thought, but it would be useful to know.

'I'll book a table,' said Jason. 'A nice restaurant on the Esplanade. Do you want me to pick you up?'

She shook her head. 'I'll meet you there.'

He scribbled on a business card. 'Here's the address. It's not far, but get a cab.'

She nodded again.

My first full day, she thought. Four meetings and a dinner invitation. Damn, I'm good!

The restaurant was near the water's edge, with a stunning view of the lighted tower blocks behind Singapore's iconic Merlion statue which spouted water into the harbour.

'I'm so glad you came.' Jason was already at the table

when she arrived. 'I was afraid you'd be jet-lagged and have fallen asleep.'

'I did,' she confessed as she sat down opposite him. 'Which is daft because I slept fairly well last night. But when I went back to the hotel and lay on the bed for five minutes and, next thing I knew, it was time to leave. Sorry if I'm a bit late.'

'Fashionably.' He grinned at her. 'A mere ten minutes.'

'I'm not normally,' she told him.

'D'you know, I kinda guessed that. You seem far too efficient to be late for anything.'

She made a face. 'I like being professionally efficient. Being personally efficient just sounds too control-freaky.'

'Not a bad thing,' he told her as a waitress handed them menus. 'Now, what are you going to have? You can't leave Singapore without tasting chilli crab. And they do the best in the city here.'

It was an enjoyable evening and the crab, as Jason had promised, was fantastic. He told her a lot about living and working in the city, the up sides and the down sides, talking about the things he missed about London and the things in Asia that compensated for them. He was divorced, he told her, and had come to Singapore after his wife had left him. 'She thought I worked too much,' he observed wryly. 'I thought I was doing the right thing, building a good life for us. But she complained that I was ignoring her. I can't help feeling that it isn't possible to get it right for women. They want a good life but they also want love and commitment and partnership and discussion and us being there all the time.'

Darcey grinned as he said this. 'And men want that old thing about a cook in the kitchen and a whore in the bedroom,' she pointed out. 'Then as soon as our boobs and butts start to go south, they look for someone new.'

He laughed.

'Do you have a girlfriend here?' she asked casually.

He shook his head. 'I was going out with a Singaporean girl for a while,' he told her. 'I cared for her a lot but in the end it didn't work out.' He sipped his beer. 'It's a great life, it really is, but it does sometimes get a bit lonely.'

'I can understand that.'

He signalled for the bill. 'I feel that all this sounds like I'm leading up to asking you back to my apartment,' he said as he signed the credit-card slip.

'It does rather.'

'And?'

'I had a really busy day today,' she said. 'Despite my catnap earlier I'm still a little tired. I really don't think I'd be much fun.'

'You look to me as though you'd be masses of fun,' he said.

She smiled and got up from the table. He slid his arm around her waist as they walked out of the restaurant and along the Esplanade.

'It wouldn't be a good start to our professional relationship if I slept with you,' she told him as she moved away from his hold.

'I know,' he replied. 'But it'd be a great start to our personal one.'

She walked alongside him in silence. She'd wondered if

she would meet someone in Singapore, and she had. Jason was nice. She could have a long-distance relationship with him and know that he was here for her whenever she came back . . . a friend in the city, she told herself. Someone to have fun with. Someone to sleep with. But not someone to fall in love with. That's not a problem, she told herself. I don't want to fall in love with anybody. But, she thought, she didn't really want to sleep with him for the sake of it either. Not now. Not yet. She didn't know when.

'I can't come back to your apartment,' she said as they arrived back at street level. 'I really enjoyed dinner, and I like you very much . . .'

'But?'

'I'm not quite ready for this,' she told him. 'I know it'd be a one-night thing with no strings, and it's very, very appealing, but – right now it's not what I want.'

He nodded. 'Tomorrow, perhaps?'

'Oh, Jason, I don't think so.' She smiled wryly. 'I enjoyed tonight, I really did, and I like you a lot. But not this trip.'

'You intend to come back?'

'Of course.'

He grinned at her. 'It could've been fun.'

'I know.' She looked at him. 'And maybe . . . well, who knows? Just not now. I'm sorry.'

'Don't be. I'd rather you were honest.'

'I hope I haven't destroyed any chance of you guys doing business with us?'

This time he laughed. 'No! Your pitch was good. We'll be in touch.'

'Thanks,' she said.

She raised her arm and flagged down a taxi. When she got back to the hotel, she sat for an hour by the window of her room, gazing unseeingly over the glittering lights of the city, before eventually going to bed alone.

Once again she couldn't sleep. She kept thinking of Jason White and wondering what on earth had possessed her to turn him down, because he was an ideal . . . she didn't want to use Anna's awful term, fuck-buddy, but he totally was. So why, she asked herself, why didn't she want some casual sex with a great guy? What was she looking for now? A real relationship or something? She snorted at the thought. That wasn't going to happen. She knew that. She should've gone to bed with Jason. She was far too awake for sleep. At least some fun sex would have helped!

The next day was filled with meetings too, and in the evening she went to dinner with a group of people from one of the companies she'd spoken to. They had a fun evening at the bustling area of Boat Quay followed by drinks in Molly Malone's Irish pub. The Singaporeans had been delighted at the thought of bringing her to an Irish pub and she'd been amused by the fact that wherever they were in the world her countrymen managed to open one! But it was a good laugh and she felt as though she was really connecting with everyone she met. She knew that there was a lot of innate cultural politeness in the Singaporeans, but she also felt as though she was getting on with them too, so that it wasn't just about face and saying the right thing at the right time, it was also about trust and understanding.

The next day was her final one in the city, and she had

only one meeting, which again seemed to her to go really well. Afterwards, on the advice of everyone she'd met, and to celebrate the fact that she was confident about bringing in new business, she took herself off to Orchard Road to shop.

It was just as well, she thought later as she stood outside one of the street's many malls, that she hadn't come here earlier. She'd have completely lost the plot. One of her new contacts, Melanie, had told her that the national pastime of Singaporeans was shopping, and Darcey could now see why. She looked at the displays of designer shoes and handbags and felt herself change from professional businesswoman to girl let loose in a sweetshop. Her eye was caught by a pair of shoes on a display. They were deepest purple, with a tiny pink ribbon at the toe and very high heels. A matching soft leather bag with an appliqué detail was arranged beside it.

Darcey had turned down the idea of a less vivid pair of purple Marc Jacobs in Dublin. And the heels on these were much higher than she'd usually wear. But there was something about the shoes that made her go back and look at them again, even after she'd walked past and told herself that they weren't her style.

Somehow with the different light and a whole array of new colours, scents and sounds around her they seemed a perfectly acceptable purchase. They would go with the plain but elegant dress she'd bought a few minutes earlier in the Prada store. Darcey didn't normally buy designer dresses because her body wasn't the right shape. But this dress had fitted almost perfectly and she'd wanted something identifiably expensive to wear to Aidan and Nieve's wedding.

If, of course, she actually went. She reminded herself that she was still unsure about it and very wary of her own motives. The previous night, as she'd lain awake, she'd decided that there were three reasons why she wanted to go. The first was that she didn't want Nieve to think that she was still too caught up in past feelings not to (or maybe think that she was somehow *afraid* to). The second was that she needed to know how it would feel to see Aidan again. And the third was that she wanted to see his reaction to her. (Though, she added to herself, God knows why. If he simply ignored her she'd be hurt, yet what the hell could he say to her that she wanted to hear?) Anyway, she told herself as she handed over her credit card, whatever happened, whether she went or not, there was no harm in buying the shoes!

She emerged from Takashimaya half an hour later with the dress in one bag and the shoes in another, as well as a gorgeous multicoloured bag in soft leather, wondering how she'd managed to talk herself into buying things so out of character and when, in her normal Dublin life, she'd ever get around to toting multicoloured bags and wearing purple shoes with pink ribbons.

Back in her hotel room, after she'd finished most of her packing, the phone rang and the receptionist in the hotel spa reminded her that she had booked a treatment in thirty minutes' time. Darcey zipped her suitcase closed and then pulled on her bathing suit. She wrapped herself in a robe, slid on towelling slippers and left her room for the end-of-trip treat that she'd been looking forward to ever since she'd booked it. She reckoned it would do her good to get on the flight in a state of pampered bliss. The spa was only five floors up, so she avoided the lifts – even though she was almost over her phobia now – and walked up the stairs instead.

The spa was warm and restful, soothing Asian music mingling with the scent of aromatherapy oils and the gurgle of the fountain in the reception area. Darcey (with a renewed sense of her gawky lumpishness compared to the serenity and elegance of the therapists) allowed herself to be whisked away to a room where she was exfoliated and massaged, then her skin rubbed with oils and creams until she felt as though she was floating on a bed of essences. She wondered, dreamily, whether she couldn't persuade Anna Sweeney to install a therapist in the InvestorCorp offices to offer massage therapy to stressed-out employees. She hadn't realised that she was feeling stressed, but she was feeling so relaxed right now that she knew she'd certainly been a good deal more tense when she walked through the door of the spa.

She was dreading going outside and rejoining real life again, but she had a little more time to herself first as the therapist brought her to a quiet room for additional relaxation. Comfortable lounge beds were arranged in a circular pattern around the large flickering candles that were the only source of light, and Darcey lay down on one of them and closed her eyes.

Before she knew it, she was asleep again.

She didn't wake, as she had done the last few nights, with a startled jump. After thirty minutes of dreamless sleep her eyes flickered open and she was instantly awake. She still felt utterly chilled out but she didn't feel in the slightest bit tired. In fact she felt marvellous. She was definitely going to get Anna to organise massages in the office when she got back!

She walked out of the reception area, smiled at the chic receptionist and turned back towards the stairs. She was thinking that she had time for a leisurely lunch before heading off to the airport (and wondering which of the hotel's speciality desserts she'd indulge in) as she reached out for the handrail. She didn't quite know what happened next, but somehow she managed to miss the top step. She gasped as her foot slid out of the towelling slipper and, as she made a vain attempt to grab the handrail, she knew that no matter what she did she was about to fall head over heels down the flight of stairs.

She wasn't sure which part of her was hurt most, her pride or her body. Her pride was a strong candidate as she lay on the landing, winded, wondering how on earth she'd managed to end up in a heap like this and thinking that she'd been right to feel enormous and clumsy in Singapore because that was exactly what she was. But, as she tried to sit up, she realised that it might actually be her body which was hurt the most. The pain that shot through her arm was excruciating and she yelped before breaking out into a cold sweat. She told herself that she'd be all right in a moment, that she'd had a shock and that it wasn't such a big flight of stairs, so if she took things slowly she'd be fine. But then she looked at her hand and realised that it was already beginning to swell up and that she wasn't able to move her wrist.

I couldn't have, she muttered under her breath. I couldn't have been so stupid and so clumsy as to have broken it, could I? Not here. Not now. Very gingerly she touched the swollen area, and yelped again.

No point in staying here, she told herself. I need to get up and get it treated. But as she tried to stand she realised that as well as an injured wrist she'd also managed to wrench her ankle, because as soon as she tried to put weight on it she crumpled in a heap again.

This can't be happening to me, she gasped, as she took some deep breaths. I'll be fine in a minute. I just need to take it slowly.

She sat in a huddle at the bottom of the stairs, her robe pulled around her, and tried not to cry. She wasn't sure at this point whether she wanted to cry because of the agony of her wrist (and the secondary agony of her ankle) or because her successful trip looked like ending in a kind of ignominy. Or because she was sitting in the stairwell of a five-star hotel wondering whether she'd ever manage to get back up the stairs to the spa again.

She was starting to get cold. She shivered slightly and pulled the robe tighter. And then she told herself that she couldn't stay here because nobody used the stairs and it might be ages before anyone came along. She simply had to move. But even the smallest movement was incredibly painful.

Eventually, though, she got to the point where she was sitting on the bottom stair itself. Instead of trying to stand up, which she doubted she could do at that moment, she bumped herself upwards, step by step, until she reached the landing. Then, slowly and still painfully, she managed to haul herself into an upright position and pull open the door to the twenty-fifth floor.

The therapist looked up in horror as Darcey hobbled into the reception area cradling her injured left wrist in her right hand. She immediately rang for a doctor, then helped Darcey sit down in one of the comfortable armchairs, while getting a stool for her foot and telling her to elevate it right away.

'I'm sorry, I'm sorry,' repeated Darcey over and over as different therapists fluttered anxiously around her, wrapping her in soft yellow blankets and offering her cups of jasmine tea. 'It was my fault. I slipped. I'm so stupid.' And as she wiped away the tears that were unaccountably beginning to roll down her face, she wished fervently that she wasn't once again the centre of attention over something silly.

Dr Tay was calm and professional. He looked at Darcey's wrist and ankle, told her that he thought she might have broken one and sprained the other, and then made arrangements for her to be brought to the local hospital as quickly as possible.

Everyone at the hospital was calm and professional too. They arranged for both her wrist and her ankle to be X-rayed, although the young nurse told her that she'd be very surprised if she'd broken both of them. But what an unfortunate thing to have happened, she said. It was true, wasn't it, that sometimes the simplest things caused the most trouble.

Darcey waited for the results of the X-ray, trying to persuade herself that the pain in her wrist was definitely subsiding now and that she'd probably be able to walk out of here if they gave her some painkillers, telling herself that it had been as much about shock as anything else. And then, as she looked at the clock on the hospital wall, she realised that she'd have to be walking out of here very soon or she'd be late for her flight.

She'd persuaded herself that everything would be OK when the doctor reappeared with her X-rays and showed them to her.

'Good news and bad news,' he said cheerfully. 'But mostly good news. Your ankle is badly sprained but it's not broken and should be fine once the swelling has gone down, although you need to keep the weight off it for a couple of days. Unfortunately, though, you've fractured your wrist. It's not the worst break I've ever seen, but I would suggest that we perform a minimally invasive surgical procedure which will give you better healing time and prospects than a traditional cast. You'll have to wear a plaster splint for about ten days and then switch over to a lightweight plastic one.'

'How long will it take?' she asked.

'To heal? It's a slow enough process, unfortunately, but you'll get a range of motion very quickly—'

'No, to do the job,' she interrupted him. 'I'm supposed to be at the airport in half an hour.'

He smiled at her. 'That's not going to be possible,' he told her. 'As I said, it's a surgical procedure. We have to make an incision in your wrist and insert a screw. You will have to forget about the flight for a day or so.'

'Oh, but . . .' She looked at him anxiously.

'There is some pressing reason for you to be back in . . .' he glanced at his notes, 'Ireland again?'

There wasn't really a pressing reason, she supposed. Other than the fact that she had a lot of work to do.

'It's just . . .'

'You need to have this set now,' said the doctor firmly. 'If we do not do this now there may be problems for you in the years ahead.'

'Of course,' she said. 'I know it has to be done. I . . .' She sighed. 'Better get on with it, so.'

Darcey lay on the hospital trolley and stared at the ceiling. A few days ago she'd been worried about going down in InvestorCorp annals as the person who'd got stuck in the lift. Now it looked like she'd be remembered as the person who'd come back from Singapore with her arm in a cast. *I'm such a dope,* she thought glumly.

There was no problem in holding on to her hotel room for another couple of days. The staff couldn't have looked after her better, fussing over her to make sure that she was comfortable and had everything she needed. But all she really wanted was to return home as quickly as possible. She needed to make sure that all the arrangements for her potential clients were in place so that if they called to do business with InvestorCorp they'd be able to execute it without any problems. And she wanted the comfort of her own apartment and her own things around her.

She phoned Anna Sweeney, but got through to her voicemail, and so she left a message simply saying that she'd had a minor accident and had rearranged her flight for a few days later. She told Anna not to worry and not to bother ringing back as she'd probably be asleep.

The doctors had given her painkillers, and although the day after her return from the hospital her ankle was still painful and her wrist was throbbing underneath the cast, the pills made her feel as though the pain was coming from a distance. She lay on top of her hotel bed but knew that she wouldn't be able to stay awake to watch the TV she'd switched on. She felt as though she'd come halfway around the world to spend most of her time asleep!

It was after midnight when the phone jolted her into wakefulness. She blinked a couple of times and realised that the chambermaid had come into the room while she was sleeping and had switched off the TV, closed the curtains and switched on one of the room lamps. There was a card beside the bed saying that she should call the director of guest services if there was anything at all that she wanted. She peered blearily at it as she picked up the phone.

'I'm sorry to disturb you, Miss McGonigle,' said the receptionist. 'But there is a gentleman at reception who is from your company and who asked me to see if you were awake.'

'From InvestorCorp? Here? Now?' Darcey was astonished.

'He is Mr Lomond,' said the receptionist.

'Oh.'

'He has checked in to the hotel,' the receptionist continued.

'Right,' Darcey said. 'Well, I guess you can send him up.'

'I will have him escorted,' said the receptionist. 'You should sit still and not move.'

Darcey smiled to herself. 'OK, thanks.'

She replaced the receiver and reached for her bag, which was beside the bed. She pulled out a brush and ran it through her hair, although she knew she had to look an absolute fright by now. She wished she could see herself in the mirror, but it was out of sight of the bed (apparently a mirror reflecting the bed was bad feng shui, and they were into good feng shui in the hotel – not that it had done her much good!). But what the hell, she thought. Neil had seen her before just after waking up. What difference would it make this time?

There was a tap at the door and she called out that it was OK to come in.

'Your guest, madam,' said the bellboy.

'Hi.' She looked apologetically at Neil, who seemed mesmerised by her splinted wrist and strapped ankle.

'What the hell happened?' he asked as walked into the room and sat down on her bed.

She explained it to him, wishing that she'd been mugged or run over or something rather than having to admit that she'd been coming back from a spa treatment. It sounded as though she'd been lounging around on company time and fallen over because she hadn't been paying attention (which, in fairness, was actually what had happened).

'So do they think you'll need more done to it when you get home?' he asked.

She shrugged. 'Hopefully not. My wrist isn't badly broken. The doctor says that everything went really well, although it'll be a while before it's good as new. Fortunately it's my left arm, so I can still do lots of things.'

'What about your ankle?'

'Only sprained,' she told him. 'Apparently it'll be black and blue before long, if it isn't already.'

'Why weren't you looking where you were going?' he asked.

'Oh, you know me!' she replied. 'I slipped. I know that it's the sort of thing that happens to me on a regular basis, but it really wasn't my fault.'

'I didn't mean to imply that it was,' he said mildly. 'You're having a bit of a rough time of it, aren't you, what with getting trapped in the office lift and now flinging yourself down the stairs.'

'Normally my business trips work out perfectly well,' she told him. 'Normally I don't get stuck in lifts either.'

'Maybe I'm a jinx,' he told her.

'Maybe you are.' Her voice was suddenly flat. She squeezed her eyes shut and then opened them again.

'C'mon, Darcey.' He leaned towards her as though he was going to put his arm around her, and then changed his mind. 'It'll be fine.'

'I know. I know.' She sighed and then looked at him curiously. 'Why on earth are you here?'

'You're an employee,' said Neil. 'You were away. You had an accident. I came to see if everything was all right. It wasn't entirely clear from your message to Anna what had happened. We were worried about you.'

'There was no need to worry,' she said. 'You could have just called to check.'

'You told Anna not to call you,' he reminded her.

'On the first day,' she said. 'I was a bit woozy when I left that message. Honestly, there was no need to come all the way just for me. I could've managed on my own.'

'Darcey, just because you *could* manage on your own doesn't mean you *should*.'

She felt a sudden lump in her throat.

'The cost of your trip will put a dent in my budget.' The words were a million times harsher than she meant them to sound.

He frowned. 'Do you really think like that these days?' he asked. 'Do you honestly look at everything and everyone in terms of budgets and work?'

'Isn't that how InvestorCorp looks at it?' she asked. 'Shouldn't that be how you look at it?'

'I'm – I'm – OK, I'm not your friend,' he said, 'but I *am* someone you know even though I work for the company. And I'd like to think that someone would've come out if anyone who worked for us had an accident like this, and made sure everything was OK. If Anna had come you'd have appreciated it.'

'I do appreciate it,' she confessed. 'Honestly I do. And it's not that I want to pretend that I don't know you and that you don't mean anything to me. It's just . . . oh, I guess I like to think I'm doing a good job, and this kind of thing . . .' She looked up and smiled ironically at him. 'I suppose it's better than you having to get me out of jail for smuggling hash or something.'

'Don't even joke about it,' he said.

She looked rueful. 'Joking's all that's left at the moment.'

He nodded absent-mindedly and then looked at her curiously. 'Do I?' he asked.

'Do you what?'

'Mean anything to you? You said that it's not as if I don't. Does that mean I do?'

'Jeez, Neil, I loved you once.'

He raised an eyebrow. 'I thought you said that you'd never actually loved me.'

'You know what I mean.' She pinched the bridge of her nose. 'I thought I did. I was wrong. I know that. But it doesn't mean that I don't . . . that I didn't . . . oh hell, Neil – I've never got over feeling guilty about you.'

'Right.'

'And so I feel bad about the fact that perhaps for some crazy reason to do with us once having been married you came all the way out here when it wasn't really necessary.'

'You're a gas woman,' he said. 'You overanalyse everything.'

'Don't forget I'm on drugs at the moment,' she reminded him. 'My brain isn't properly in gear.'

'OK. I forgive you.'

'How's Anna?' she asked suddenly.

'Fine,' said Neil. 'Like I said, a bit worried about you.'

'Tell her that I'm bruised but not beaten.'

'I will.' Neil grinned.

'She's a really nice person,' said Darcey abruptly. 'Don't mess with her.'

'I'm not messing with her.'

'She's my best friend. I don't want her hurt.'

'Why would I hurt her?' he asked. 'Look, I'll leave you alone now. Try to get some sleep and I'm sure you'll be able to come home with me soon.'

'Are you staying?' She looked at him curiously. 'To come home with me?'

'Of course I am,' he said. 'You don't think I came all the way out here to return empty-handed, do you? Give me a break.'

She looked at him.

'Bad choice of words,' he conceded, and she couldn't help but smile.

# Chapter 25

Actually, thought Darcey a couple of days later, as they were driven on a buggy through the airport concourse, it was wonderful to have someone to look after things for her. Normally she preferred doing everything herself and in her own way, but having both an injured wrist and an injured ankle was incredibly restricting. She couldn't put much weight on her foot, nor, because of the splint, could she use crutches. So despite her assertions of being perfectly able to cope, she knew that it would have been a nightmare on her own.

Neil was fantastic. He dealt with everything so that the only thing she had to worry about was settling herself in her seat on the plane. And when the stewardess came through the cabin with glasses of champagne for the passengers before they took off, he made sure that she took one.

'Though what are we actually celebrating?' she asked as he clinked his glass against hers.

'I read your reports. You did a great job and I'm sure we'll get loads of business. So here's to finally getting home.'

'I *am* sorry.' She sipped the champagne cautiously. 'Dragging you halfway round the world like this.'

'Ah, it made me feel quite important rushing to rescue you.' He grinned at her. 'And accidents happen to the best of us.'

'Oh, I know,' she agreed. 'But lately lots of silly accidents are happening to me. Getting stuck in the lift and falling down the stairs were both stupid. I'm just a clumsy fool.'

'You have your moments,' he agreed. 'Remember that night when we went to Covent Garden and you tripped over the cobblestones—'

'And I broke the heel of my only decent pair of shoes and ended up flat on my face,' she interrupted. 'And I had to go home in my bare feet. In the rain! How could I forget!'

They both laughed at the shared memory. But quite suddenly Darcey felt uncomfortable about it and she turned away from him to look out of the window. The plane bumped slightly as it was pushed from the stand and the stewardess came around to collect their glasses.

Darcey picked up a copy of *Newsweek*. She'd wanted to buy a gossip magazine at the airport, but with Neil beside her, and remembering that he was her boss after all and that she should make some effort to appear businesslike to counteract her broken wrist and sprained ankle, she'd gone for *Newsweek* instead.

Neil took out a copy of an Andy McNab SAS action novel. Darcey wondered whether he secretly dreamed of being an action hero. She didn't know what Neil's secret dreams were. She'd never found out what he really wanted from life. Was being the worldwide director of new business the height of his ambitions? Or did he have a completely different heroic aspiration?

I guess he turned out to be my hero this time, she thought in sudden amusement, coming halfway around the world to rescue me. Even if I didn't really want to be rescued.

She leaned back in her seat as the plane gathered speed and finally took off. Being rescued, though, meant thirteen hours sitting beside her ex-husband. And that wasn't something she was really looking forward to, no matter how nice he'd been about it.

She was afraid that thirteen hours with him would mean a forced intimacy that would inevitably end up with them talking about the past. But he spent a lot of time reading his book and playing video games on the console attached to the seat and ignoring her completely. The only time they talked was when they were eating. The stewardess had kindly chopped Darcey's glazed turkey breast into bite-sized pieces for her so that she could eat it more easily. She chewed on the meat and tried to think of something to talk about.

'Have you met Meryl yet?' As she spoke, Darcey winced. She had no idea what had made her ask Neil about Anna's daughter. Perhaps Anna hadn't even said anything to him about her yet. She'd have to sooner or later, of course, but maybe she was waiting for the right moment.

'No,' said Neil.

'Anna's great with her. A fantastic mother.'

'I'm sure she is.'

'No, really.' Darcey wanted him to know how much her daughter meant to Anna. 'She went through a really tough time with her but she kept it together well.'

He frowned. 'I thought Meryl was about eight. You weren't working with Global Finance then. You wouldn't have known what it was like for Anna.'

'Oh for God's sake, we're women, we talk.' Darcey looked at him impatiently. 'We share things.'

'I didn't think you were into that very much,' he remarked. 'Girlie gossip, that sort of thing. Sharing stuff regardless. It wasn't your thing.'

'Anna and I share,' she said firmly. 'We can be completely gossipy when we want.'

'Really?'

'Yes.'

'Is she a girlie girl then?'

Darcey chuckled. 'Sometimes.'

'Because you're not really. I mean,' he added hastily when she looked curiously at him, 'you work at it sometimes, when you get made up and everything, but it's not really your thing, is it?'

'Nope.'

'I like Anna,' he told her. 'But getting involved with people in the office isn't always a good thing.'

'One bad experience,' said Darcey. 'Don't let it put you off for life.'

'I've generally steered away from office romances all the same,' he told her.

'So . . .' She hadn't wanted them to talk about themselves, but now she was curious. 'Has there been anyone else serious?'

'Mmm. Her name was Megan. I nearly married her.'

'Oh.' She was surprised. 'So why didn't you?'

He looked thoughtful and took his time before replying.

'I want it to be exactly right the next time,' he said. 'I want to be sure. And with Megan I just wasn't completely certain.'

'I understand that,' she said.

'So what about you?' he asked. 'Any chance?'

She shook her head. 'It's not on my list.'

He said nothing. She wriggled in her seat.

'You OK?'

'Yes, I am. But I think I'll get some sleep as soon as they take away the tray.'

'Good idea.'

'Thanks,' she said suddenly.

'For what?'

'Coming out to get me. I know I said I could've done it on my own, but . . . I couldn't. So thanks.'

'You're welcome,' said Neil as he picked up his Andy McNab book again.

It was evening in Dublin when their connecting flight from Heathrow finally touched down. By now Darcey was feeling utterly drained and her wrist was throbbing insistently. Neil, who said nothing about the dark circles under her eyes or the pain lines etched on her face, told her he'd accompany her back to her apartment. This time she didn't feel that she could say no, even when he paid the taxi-driver and told her that he'd help her with her luggage before going home. She knew that it would be stupid to refuse – churlish and unfriendly too. Neil had been an absolute rock and she couldn't throw all that back in his face just because she had a bit of a thing about him being in her apartment.

She unlocked the door of the building while he wheeled her small (but bulging) suitcase inside.

'You should've brought a bigger case,' he remarked.

'I try to travel light,' she told him as she pressed the button for the lift. 'But I couldn't help buying stuff.'

As they got in, she squeezed her eyes closed and then, almost immediately, opened them again. Neil, who'd noticed, grinned at her.

'It'd be the straw that broke the camel's back if we got stuck in this one,' he told her.

She smiled slightly. 'The thing is, I wasn't totally phobic about lifts after that happened. I knew it'd only take a short time to get over it completely. If I'd got into the damn hotel lift, none of this would've happened.'

'I didn't realise you were claustrophobic,' he said.

'Not normally,' she corrected him. 'It's the dark I don't like.'

'I didn't realise you had a thing about the dark either.' He frowned.

'I don't really . . .' She looked at him uncomfortably as the lift stopped at her floor. 'It was after we broke up I had trouble with it.'

'Oh.' He followed her out of the lift and down the short corridor to her apartment door.

She unlocked it and pushed it open. She hobbled inside and Neil followed her again. He looked around in surprise.

'It's very neat,' he said as she opened the curtains on the living room windows.

'Excuse me?'

'Neat and tidy,' he told her. 'It's amazingly neat and tidy. Our place was never like this.'

'It's easy to keep it tidy living on my own,' said Darcey.

Neil laughed. 'You were the one that couldn't put anything away at home,' he reminded her. 'As I recall, I used to go nuts looking for my socks and stuff.'

'Just because I wasn't exactly God's gift to washing and putting away,' she retorted.

'No, no, you shoved things in the washing machine all right,' he said. 'Though fairly frequently with the net result of them all turning pink or blue because you were hopeless at sorting it properly. But if you remember, you used to leave it all drying on radiators for days so that everything was kind of solid by the time you'd finished.'

'So I'm not domesticated,' said Darcey. 'So what?'

'But you are, that's the point!' he cried. 'This is like a show house.'

She grinned at him. 'I always tidy up before I go on a trip,' she said. 'You haven't seen it in its usual state.'

'I hope not,' he said. 'I'd hate to think that you've changed beyond all recognition. It was enough of a shock seeing you in the first place.'

'Why?'

'Your hair, your clothes, everything!' he exclaimed. 'Darcey, you have this whole businesswoman look that's absolutely amazing. Quite honestly, you took my breath away.'

'Don't be silly,' she said uncomfortably. 'I'm not that great-looking.'

'It's not a prettiness thing,' he said. 'It's a – a confidence thing. When I first set eyes on you in the office you looked so confident just sitting there . . .'

'My eyes were closed,' she said.

'That's the point. You were sitting there with your eyes closed but you didn't look like you were sleeping or anything. You just looked – confident.'

'Well I'm glad you got the right impression,' she told him, 'because I was worried you hadn't.'

'There was no need to worry,' he told her.

'Why? You guys were the big hotshots coming into town and buying out our little company. We were all worried we'd lose our jobs.'

'I certainly wasn't going to come into the company and fire you,' he said.

'I'd have thought it would have been pretty easy to do.'

'You'd have taken me to court for unfair dismissal. And you and me, we've had our day in court already.'

She shrugged. They hadn't actually had a day in court at all. Their divorce had been quick and easy, helped by the fact that there were no children and neither of them wanted anything from the other.

'Would you like a cup of coffee or anything?' she asked, breaking the sudden uneasy silence.

He shook his head. 'I'd better get going.'

She nodded. 'Thanks for everything. I mean it.'

'You're welcome,' he said. 'Don't come rushing into the office. Take a few days off.'

'I'll go to my own doctor tomorrow,' she promised. 'After that, we'll see.'

'Darcey, it can't be easy getting around with your ankle like that,' he told her. 'And you already tried to kill some poor woman at Dublin airport with your splint.'

'She got in the way.' Darcey grinned. 'Look, we'll see what the doctor says. I'll phone Anna and let her know. But I do want to fill out the paperwork for the Singapore people. I'm really hopeful about them. Especially Asia Holdings.' She flushed slightly at the memory of Jason White. Perhaps if she'd taken him up on his invitation back to his apartment, she might have spent her last day there too instead of falling down the hotel stairs.

'Don't worry about the paperwork.' Neil hadn't noticed her blush. 'You've emailed all the relevant information already. I'll look after it.'

She hesitated.

'It's not like I'm going to nick your clients,' he pointed out. 'We'll know where they came from.'

'I wasn't worried about that,' she said. 'It's my job, that's all.'

'Would you stop obsessing and take some time out, for heaven's sake,' he said. 'Even if you hadn't decided to throw yourself down the stairs, it was a tiring trip.'

'Um, well, I guess so.'

'OK, then. I'm off.' He picked up his own cabin-sized bag. 'I'll see you in the office.'

'Right,' she said. 'See you in the office.'

The apartment seemed very quiet when he'd gone. She manoeuvred her suitcase into the bedroom and opened it on the floor. She looked sadly at the purple shoes. Her foot wouldn't even fit into the shoe now, so as killer footwear for Nieve and Aidan's wedding they were off the list. She'd be lucky if she could fit into anything other than a pair of trainers. And she certainly wasn't going to go to the social event of the year wearing a pair of trainers! So maybe she would have to back out of it after all. Which would probably be a relief all round.

There was no point in thinking about it now. And she didn't have the strength to unpack either. She closed the lid and pushed the case under the bed. Unpacking could wait. Laundry could wait. She was going to make herself a cup of tea. And she was finally going to sleep at home.

# Chapter 26

The doctor, more or less as she'd expected, told Darcey to take it easy for a few days and to rest her foot as much as possible. Normally she found it difficult to take it easy, but she was by now utterly washed out both from her trip and from the constant ache in her ankle and her wrist. So she rang the office and spoke to Anna, who commiserated with her on her accident, told her to stay home for as long as necessary, and said that she'd call around to see her the following evening.

'I thought I'd got over falling flat on my face,' said Darcey glumly as she and Anna sat in the living room of her apartment eating the sushi takeaway that Anna had brought and sharing a bottle of wine. 'I don't even bump into the corner of desks in the office as much as I used to. But what with the lift incident and now this, I'm beginning to wonder. And of course I was like an elephant beside all those gorgeous Singapore girls, who looked like a feather would knock them over!'

'The lift was a pure fluke. And falling down the stairs could've happened to anyone.' Anna echoed the words that Neil had said so many times, and Darcey snorted.

'Well, it could!' repeated Anna.

'I know that. I just wish it hadn't happened to me and that Neil hadn't felt the need to rush over to Singapore to see if I was OK,' she said. 'It made me feel like some kind of helpless damsel in distress being rescued by the boss. Especially as I was actually quite glad to see him.'

'Douglas told him to go,' Anna said.

'Oh.'

'But Neil would've gone anyway.'

'You think?'

Anna nodded. 'He was very worried.'

'He was great, to be honest. I'd forgotten how organised he can be.'

'Organised? Neil?'

Darcey nodded. 'He used to drive me nuts because he was so neat and tidy. He folded socks, for heaven's sake! And whenever he was going on a business trip he spent ages checking things out to make sure that everything was OK.'

'Sounds like you,' remarked Anna.

'I don't fold socks!' Darcey looked at her in disgust.

'But you do the business travel research.'

'That's just good work practice.'

'I think maybe you picked it up from him.'

Darcey shrugged. 'Maybe. I saw him go off on enough trips without me.'

Anna's eyes narrowed.

'Oh, come on, Sweeney!' cried Darcey. 'I told you the history. He went on trips. Without me. But they were business trips, I accept that now.'

'If you'd accepted it then, d'you think you would've divorced him?'

'How the hell do I know?' demanded Darcey. 'It was ages ago. I've changed. I'm sure he's changed.'

'D'you ever think of getting back with him?'

'For heaven's sake!' Darcey looked at her friend impatiently. 'We're *divorced*. We have been for years. That generally means not even wanting to set eyes on the other person again. I know, I know.' She held up her hand as Anna opened her mouth to speak. 'We have to see each other for work and I guess we're dealing with it pretty well, all things considered. But just because some couples don't rip each other's faces off in the courts doesn't mean that they secretly want to get back together.'

'I just wondered,' said Anna. 'You're getting a bit het up, aren't you?'

'No, I'm not!' said Darcey hotly.

Anna gazed at her thoughtfully. 'Are you *sure* you don't have feelings for him still?'

'The only feelings I have are of total embarrassment that my trip went haywire and he came out at all.'

Anna was silent.

'Are *you* in love with him?' demanded Darcey after a few seconds.

'I like him a lot.' Anna refilled their wine glasses. 'He's a really nice person.'

'Yes,' admitted Darcey. 'He is. And not that it matters, but I hope you make a go of it. You deserve each other.'

Anna laughed. 'Oh, Darce, you really haven't got a clue, have you?'

'About what?' Darcey looked at her defensively.

'Ah, nothing,' said Anna as she reached for her glass of wine.

The following day Darcey took the train to Galway. She'd called Minette and told her about her accident and her mother had instantly insisted that she come home for a few days.

'You can't possibly manage on your own,' she said firmly, and Darcey couldn't disagree with her. It was almost impossible to take a shower and keep her splint dry. It was totally impossible to manage her hair (she'd gone to the hairdressers to have it washed and dried that morning and was wondering exactly how much she was going to spend in hairdressing bills over the next few weeks). And everything else was a real chore when she couldn't use her arm properly. Plus the fact that even walking was still difficult. So the idea of going home and allowing Minette to take care of her was very, very appealing. But she didn't want to stay with her mother if her father was still there.

'He isn't,' said Minette mildly.

'Oh?' Darcey had spoken to Amelie the previous night and her sister had been sure that Martin was still at the family home.

'He went today. We'll talk when you get here,' said Minette.

So Darcey packed a weekend bag, caught a cab to the train station and got on the Galway train. There was more leg room on the train than on the small commuter plane that flew to Galway, and she felt like she needed the space.

Minette picked her up from the station and clucked anxiously at the sight of her strapped ankle and wrist.

'You said a bit of a fall,' she said. 'But look at the state of you! And there are dark circles under your eyes.'

Darcey hadn't slept well the previous night and the train journey had been more jolting than she'd expected. Right now she had a headache, her ankle was throbbing again and her wrist itched irritatingly beneath the splint.

As soon as they got home, Minette told her to stretch out on the sofa while she made her a hot chocolate.

'Oh, Maman.' Darcey took the mug from her mother. 'It's so gorgeous and comforting, but you know that it's a real minute-on-the-lips-lifetime-on-the-hips drink.'

'You need it,' said Minette firmly. 'And don't start talking to me about saturated fats and all that nonsense. Drink it and enjoy.'

Darcey sipped the creamy chocolate and felt her tension headache disappear. There was something deeply satisfying about being at home with Minette fussing over her, as she'd done all those times when Darcey was a little girl and had fallen off walls or out of trees, or come home battle-scarred from a scrap in the schoolyard. She sighed contentedly, snuggled into the cushions that Minette had propped behind her and pulled the light blanket she'd left around her. The great thing about being at home was not having to think. Not having to worry about getting something to eat or whether there was fresh milk in the apartment . . . Just knowing that her mother was there to look after her made her feel a million times better.

'*Bien, cherie.*' Minette smiled at her. 'Now tell me what happened.'

Darcey related the story, praising the skill, professionalism and care of everyone who'd looked after her.

'But it must have been difficult travelling home.' Minette frowned. 'It's not easy at the best of times.'

Darcey, as diffidently as she could, mentioned that Neil had come to collect her.

'Your Neil?' Minette was astonished.

'Not *my* Neil,' insisted Darcey. 'He only came to Singapore because he's my boss. Besides, he's seeing someone else now.'

'Tcha.' Minette shook her head. 'This is not necessarily a good thing.'

'What isn't?' demanded Darcey, feeling her headache start to return.

'That he is getting involved,' said Minette.

'He's not.'

'Are you sure?'

'As sure as you are that Dad has left and isn't coming back.' Darcey looked at her defiantly.

'Of that I am very sure,' said Minette.

'Then I'm sure that Neil is not getting involved.'

Minette's eyes narrowed.

'For God's sake, Maman!' Darcey frowned at her mother, then drained her mug and put it on the table beside her. 'That was lovely. Thank you. Now forget about Neil, which I assure you is not an issue, and tell me about Dad.'

Minette allowed her eyes to relax as she told Darcey that Martin had decided to go back to Cork and have discussions with Clem about their future.

'But is there a future?' asked Darcey. 'She's pregnant with

another man's child. It's hardly a good basis from which to move on, is it?'

'That's what your dad and I talked about,' said Minette. 'He wanted to know about forgiveness.'

'I bet.' Darcey sounded disgusted.

But Minette told her not to be so hard-hearted. He'd walked out on them, she agreed, but he did truly love Clem. And he was gutted at the thought of not seeing Steffi every day.

'He wasn't so damn worried about us!' cried Darcey.

They'd been grown up, Minette reminded her. It wasn't as though they saw him every day anyway. And of course it had all been wrenching and horrible at the time, but the truth was that she was happy now. Maybe it wasn't what she'd expected, but she was content with her life.

'So why let him back into it?' asked Darcey.

'I didn't,' replied Minette. 'Look – like I told you, he was down and miserable and very, very unhappy. How could I turn him away?'

'You're crazy, you know that? He probably thought you were thrilled to have him back.'

'If he did, I very quickly made him realise he was wrong,' said Minette. 'But I don't think so. He was too consumed by his own unhappiness to care.'

'He's still a selfish bastard,' said Darcey.

Minette shrugged. 'Better for him to leave here with some plan for the future and feeling better about things than being a miserable selfish bastard, no?'

Darcey laughed. 'Sometimes you're too good.'

'No, no.' Minette smiled at her. 'But sometimes practical.'

She picked up Darcey's empty mug and took it into the kitchen. Darcey heard her rinse it under the tap before putting it in the dishwasher. 'Besides,' she added when she came back into the room again, 'Martin was an important person in my life for a long time. I know it probably seems odd to you, but I don't hate him any more and I don't care that he left. I wish it had been different, but when he came to me and he was so unhappy, I had to help him.'

'Yeah, well, you're more charitable than me,' remarked Darcey.

'Years of practice.'

'Do you miss having someone in your life?' asked Darcey curiously.

'Do you?'

Darcey stared at her mother.

'It's not the same thing at all,' she said. 'I'm younger and I'm out at work all day and I have a social life. I have the chance to meet other people if I want to. I have men in my life, Maman. Just not in Ireland.'

'I have a social life too,' Minette reminded her. 'I don't spend all my time sitting around on my own, you know.'

'I'm sorry. You're right. Knowing you, it's probably a better social life than mine!'

'I would like to see my children settled,' said Minette gloomily. 'Not one of you is married.'

'Marriage isn't bloody everything.'

'I know.' Minette sighed. 'But it would be nice all the same.'

The next morning dawned hot and clear and suddenly very summery. Darcey and Minette sat in the back garden for a while before Darcey said that she was feeling restless. She hadn't walked anywhere in over a week, she said, and the inactivity was doing her head in.

'You travelled back from Singapore and then came to Galway,' Minette pointed out. 'You've hardly been inactive, *ma petite*.'

'Inactive enough.' Darcey wriggled her arm. 'And this thing is driving me demented.'

'Come inside and I'll blow it with the hairdryer for you.'

Darcey nodded and hopped into the house, where Minette blew cold air from the hairdryer underneath the plaster splint.

'Oh, that's sooooo good.' Darcey groaned with the pleasure of it and Minette laughed.

'We need to do something to distract me,' Darcey told her. 'I have an idea but I'm not sure how you'll react.'

Minette raised her eyebrows. 'What idea?'

'I want to visit a castle,' said Darcey.

'Which castle?'

'The one where Nieve is getting married.'

'What!'

'It's an hour's drive from here,' explained Darcey. 'In the town of Rathfinan. I'd like to see it and the town.'

'Why?'

'I accepted the wedding invitation,' explained Darcey. 'Although I was never sure about going. Then . . .' she looked sheepishly at her mother, 'I bought shoes in Singapore which were so great I thought I should go because I'd look wonderful in them. Now, with what's happened, I don't think I can possibly go. I'll hardly do myself justice tramping up in my Reeboks! But I'd like to see it all the same. Maybe decide then.'

'You don't need to see anywhere to know that going to this wedding is decidedly not a good idea.'

'Neither was letting Dad stay in the house,' responded Darcey. 'But you dealt with it. I – well, I might need to deal with this.'

Minette sighed but she didn't object any further. And so an hour later she helped Darcey get into the little red Punto and they set off down the road.

Darcey had to consult the map to find Rathfinan, which was north of Galway and well off the beaten track. Driving along the minor road, with the windows down and the scent of freshly mown grass drifting through the car, she remembered days years ago when Martin had driven them to little-known places in the country where they ran free in the fields and picnicked beneath wide, leafy chestnut trees. Sometimes they went as a family but more often Nieve came too, sitting beside Darcey in the back seat of the Ford Cortina, both of them chanting 'Are we there yet? Are we there yet?' because they knew it irritated him so much.

Had Nieve picked Rathfinan Castle because it reminded her of those days? wondered Darcey, as she told Minette to take the next turn left. Or had it been a completely random choice?

Minette pulled up outside the gates of the castle. As castles went, it was small but impressive, an oblong silhouette raised against the skyline, with crenellated walls and a square turret at each corner. The grounds were generally flat, without many trees, and a small river ran though them and behind the castle building. Once again the air was heavy with the scent of freshly mown grass.

'It looks lovely.' Darcey peered through the iron bars of the gate. 'I can just see it with a marquee or whatever on the lawns and Nieve looking gorgeous in her wedding gear.'

'It doesn't seem to be open to the public,' observed Minette as she pushed on the gates.

'They're electronic. We can't open them,' observed Darcey. 'Pity. I'd like to get a sneak preview.'

'Why?'

'I don't know,' said Darcey. She tugged at the gates futilely. As she did, she noticed a man walking across the grounds. It looked like he had a shotgun across his arm.

'Oh *merde*,' she said.

'We're not doing anything wrong,' said Minette.

'Yeah, but he might be the sort to shoot first and ask questions afterwards.'

'Don't be silly. This is the twenty-first century. And we're in Ireland, not Texas.' Minette stood her ground while the man walked closer to them. He appeared to be in his fifties or early sixties, with a traditional tweed cap on his head, although he was wearing a plaid shirt and jeans and a pair of worn trainers.

'Can I help you?' he asked pleasantly, though Darcey's eyes were drawn only to the gun.

'I'm sorry if we disturbed you,' she began.

'Disturbed me?' There was real amusement in his eyes. 'You hardly disturbed me. It's not as though I could hear the noise of the gate from the house, is it? I was walking through the grounds and I saw you.'

'Well, for maybe distracting you,' amended Darcey. 'We were just looking.'

'There isn't much to see.'

'No. Not with the gates closed,' said Minette. 'But my daughter is coming to a wedding here in a couple of weeks and we just wanted to check it out.'

'Ah, Stapleton and Clarke,' he said.

Darcey wondered why it was that hearing somebody else say their names made the whole idea of the wedding a good deal more real than anything else.

'Yes,' she said. 'Stapleton and Clarke.'

'And which side are you?' he asked. 'Stapleton or Clarke?'

'Good question.' She grinned lopsidedly. 'I know them both.'

'I'm interested to meet them,' he said. 'There has been such a list of demands . . .'

'That sounds like Nieve,' agreed Darcey.

'They want flowers.' He looked at the wide expanse of green grass behind them. 'In the grounds. This isn't really a flowery castle. It's an ordinary castle.'

Minette laughed. 'How can any castle be ordinary?' she demanded.

He laughed in return. 'To me it is. We've been here for years and I guess it's just a home to us.'

'You mean you live in a castle and you're not a pop star or something?' asked Darcey. 'Are you big in business?'

'The castle is my business.' He scratched the back of his head beneath his cap. 'Do you want to come in and have a proper look around?'

'Could we?' Minette was thrilled.

'Sure.' He pressed on a keypad and the gate slid open.

'Welcome to Rathfinan Castle. I'm Malachy Finan.'

'Oh my God,' said Darcey. 'Is this your ancestral home? Has your family been here for generations?'

'As a matter of fact, no,' he replied. 'We chose this castle because of the name.'

'Nice coincidence.'

Minette and Darcey walked through the open gate.

'Are you sure you'll be able to get as far as the building?' He looked at Darcey's injured ankle.

'I'll walk slowly,' she said.

'I'll do my best to take it easy,' Malachy told her.

'I'll walk with you. Darcey can follow,' said Minette. 'My name is Minette McGonigle, by the way. Darcey is my daughter.' She nodded at Malachy and then at Darcey and headed towards the castle.

Darcey walked behind them, straining to catch all of what Malachy was telling her mother. That he'd been involved in property development and had made a good living out of it but that he'd grown tired of it. That the castle had come up for sale and that he and his two brothers had thought it might be an interesting project. That they'd taken out loans to buy it and that, after a lot of renovations, the castle was now a popular choice for business conferences. They had, she heard him say before they got too far ahead of her to be able to catch their voices any more, adapted some of the castle rooms for conferencing and they usually had an event every two weeks. So it was a business proposition as well as a family home. But this was the first wedding they'd agreed to. It wasn't really their thing. It probably wouldn't be again, she heard him say faintly. It was far more trouble than a conference.

This is lovely, she thought, as she walked slowly through the slightly damp grass. So peaceful and beautiful without being too fairy princess. She could see why Nieve had chosen it. It would have been the sort of place she'd chosen herself.

Except, of course, she hadn't chosen a place like this. She'd gone along with the Gretna Green wedding with the reception in a small bar instead. And she supposed that hiring Rathfinan Castle wouldn't have been in her price range anyway. She didn't know how much it cost to rent a castle but she had a feeling that it wouldn't come cheap. Typical Nieve, she thought. Typical over-the-top Nieve.

Minette and Malachy were waiting for her at the entrance. She upped her pace a bit, even though it made her ankle ache, and caught up with them.

'You OK?' asked Malachy.

She nodded.

'Want the grand tour?'

She nodded again, although being honest with herself she would have preferred to sit down and rest. But she followed them through a maze of downstairs rooms, which included the huge hallway with its vast open fireplace, the enormous dining hall, and various other rooms of differing sizes. Each had been painstakingly renovated and stylishly decorated to take advantage of its unique character. Finally they reached one which opened directly on to an outdoor area of flagged paving stones at the back of the castle. There were a number of wrought-iron tables and chairs set around it, and Darcey looked longingly at them.

'Would you like to rest?' asked Minette.

Darcey nodded.

'I'll get you some cushions,' said Malachy. 'We're not running a conference at the moment, which is why they're all inside. Hang on a minute.'

He left Minette and Darcey standing outside, looking across the beautifully tended garden towards the river.

'It's fabulous, isn't it?' remarked Minette.

Darcey nodded.

'But it'll be Nieve's day,' said her mother. 'And you don't really want to be here for that.'

'Oh, I don't know.' Darcey smiled at her. 'It might be a bit of fun. Carol Jansen's coming, remember her?'

Minette nodded slowly. 'Nice girl. Good with words. Very smart.'

'We were all smart,' said Darcey. 'Only it sure seems like Nieve was the smartest of us by far.'

'She was a user,' said Minette, and Darcey looked at her in surprise. 'Of course she was.' Minette's cheeks had flushed pink with anger. 'She used you to get her great job in the same way that she used you all through school. And then she was dishonest with Aidan under your very nose.'

Darcey sighed. 'I know. I can't forgive her for that. But I should blame him more. After all, as she said to me, he allowed himself to be stolen.'

'He was weak,' said Minette. 'Like so many men. You're twice the girl she'll ever be and he was a fool to let you go.'

'Thanks.' Darcey smiled fondly at her mother. It was nice to have someone so completely on her side, even though Minette's sudden vehemence had surprised her. Her mother had never spoken much about Nieve before. But maybe that was because Darcey hadn't allowed her to.

Malachy returned with some deeply padded cushions, which he put on the patio chairs. 'I've asked Andrea to bring you some tea,' he said. 'If you'd like anything else, just let her know. She's my sister-in-law and works here too.'

'Thank you very much.' Darcey sat down and stretched her leg out in front of her. 'But really, you needn't have bothered. We're taking up a huge amount of your time.'

'I don't mind.' He smiled cheerfully at her. 'I like showing the castle off.' He turned to Minette. 'Ready for some more?'

Minette nodded, and the two of them went back inside. Darcey closed her eyes and enjoyed the warmth of the sun on her face.

It was hard not to think about coming to the wedding now that she'd seen the castle. She wanted to come. But she wasn't sure whether her reasons for wanting to come had changed at all.

'Tea?'

Darcey was jolted out of her thoughts by the arrival of a tall woman around her own age, carrying a tray with a silver teapot, silver jug and sugar bowl and china cup and saucer.

'Thank you.'

Andrea slid the tray carefully on to the table. She was stunningly beautiful, with porcelain skin, dark blue eyes and dark hair pulled back from her face. She was much younger than Malachy, and Darcey wondered how old his brother was and whether he'd had any trouble in getting such a beautiful woman to be his wife. But men with power and money never had a problem attracting women. Which made it all the more gut-wrenching that Aidan, with no power and no money, had managed to attract Nieve Stapleton, who had always wanted both. Darcey had secretly been quite sure that Nieve would eventually prise Max Christie from Lilith's arms. But maybe Max was actually smarter than Nieve after all.

She still didn't know how she felt about the fact that Aidan and Nieve hadn't bothered to get married before now. Somehow that made it all the more insulting and hurtful. When she'd thought about them over the last ten years it had always been as a married couple. She'd wondered too if they'd had children. Aidan had been keen on children; he liked kids, even though when they'd talked about it themselves the idea of them had been at some point in the future. Maybe they did have children, of course. Maybe they'd be there on the day, perfect replicas of either Nieve or Aidan. She didn't know. She didn't know anything and she wanted to know everything, and that was why she wanted to come to the wedding.

'Hi, honey.'

Minette and Malachy had walked back on to the patio area. Minette sat down beside Darcey.

'It's just gorgeous,' she said. 'Beautifully restored and absolutely *fantastique*. The bedrooms are wonderful and, best of all, they have good plumbing too.'

Darcey laughed.

'Would you like to stay here the night of the wedding?' asked Malachy. 'There are rooms reserved for guests, but not in your name. If you want . . .'

'I don't think so,' said Darcey quickly.

'But if you come to the wedding it's a good idea,' said Minette. 'Then you don't have to worry about getting a taxi back to Galway at some crazy hour of the night. Maybe you could stay over for the rehearsal dinner too?'

'I'm sure someone will give me a lift home,' said Darcey. 'Both nights.'

'The offer is there anyway,' said Malachy. 'It's not a problem either way.'

'Thanks.' Darcey nodded. 'Maman, we'd better get going. We've taken up enough of Mr Finan's time.'

'No rush,' said Malachy. 'Minette, would you like some tea?'

And when Minette said yes, Darcey realised that they would be there for a lot longer.

'You were flirting,' Darcey told Minette on the way home two hours later.

'Me! Don't be ridiculous.'

'Maman, you were very continental and your accent was a million times more pronounced than usual and you *flirted* with him.'

'Tcha.' Minette shrugged and then grinned. 'So what if I did? I haven't in years! It was fun.'

'Is he available to be flirted with?' asked Darcey.

'*Oui*,' said Minette. 'He's not married. Never married. The two brothers live in the castle also and they are both married. One of their wives is Andrea who brought the tea. The other's wife works in a law firm in Galway. They are both involved in the business. There are grown-up children also involved.'

'And they all live at the castle?' asked Darcey.

'Lorcan, the older brother, and his wife live in a lodge in the grounds,' said Minette. 'Phelim, the younger, and Andrea live in the castle. But it's a big place. They don't bump into each other that much.'

'I'd find it very suffocating,' said Darcey primly.

Minette chuckled. 'I flirted with him but that's all. You're rushing ahead a bit, *ma petite*. But then that was always your problem.'

'Very funny.'

'No, seriously.' Minette coasted up to a set of traffic lights and looked at Darcey. 'You wanted to marry Aidan. You wanted to marry Neil. You are not happy to live the here and now. You always want more.'

'Not these days.' Darcey thought of Louis-Philippe and Rocco and Francisco and Jose. And Jason White in Singapore. 'I've changed. Completely.'

'Only because you've had to,' said Minette. 'But it is not how you are inside. Inside you are always wanting . . . something more.'

'Inside I am actually wanting something to eat,' said Darcey. 'The lights are green, Maman. Get a move on. I'm starving.'

Minette snorted and put the car into gear. But she kept throwing sidelong glances at Darcey, who was staring straight ahead, an impassive expression chiselled on her face.

# Chapter 27

Their plane landed at Shannon airport to a glorious summer's day of clear blue skies and warm southerly breezes. Nieve was amazed that Ireland was putting on such a display of warmth and beauty when she'd expected grey skies and a massive chill factor. As they pushed their overladen cases (and the special carrier bag protecting Nieve's precious wedding dress) through customs and into the arrivals hall, she could feel a wall of warmth hit her despite the air-conditioning.

'I don't see our names.' She looked around in frustration at the boards held up by drivers meeting the arrivals. 'Lorelei told me that she'd organised the limo to take us home.'

Aidan said nothing. Nieve hadn't said anything about the limo until they were on the plane, and he was a little bit annoyed with her because he knew she'd kept quiet on purpose. He would've told her that limos were far too OTT for the west of Ireland and that he didn't want to be greeted by some guy in a peaked cap. But he was one of the few who had a problem with it, it seemed, because there were plenty of people being met by drivers (although possibly not many of them driving stretch limos).

'Nieve!'

She heard her name and twirled around. Gail, dressed in a light pink suit and looking extremely elegant, was standing a few feet away, waving at her.

'You walked right by us,' said her mother as Nieve moved towards her.

'I wasn't expecting to see you.' Nieve pecked her on the cheek. 'We hired a car.'

'I know,' said Gail. 'I was talking to Lorelei about it. And I told her not to be so bloody stupid; that your dad and I would pick you up.'

'Dad's here too?' Nieve turned around again.

'You know your father, can't stand still for two minutes. He went wandering . . . ah, here he is.' Gail smiled as Stephen walked across the concourse.

'Nieve, sweetheart.' Stephen put his arms around her, hugged her and then gave Aidan a manly dig on the arm. 'And how's the groom-to-be?'

'Fine,' said Aidan.

'We're so looking forward to this,' said Gail. 'It's going to be utterly wonderful.'

'I know,' said Nieve. 'I've worked hard to make it utterly wonderful. So why have you got rid of my car?'

'Only for today,' said Stephen. 'I wanted to pick you up myself.'

'Yes, but it would've been nice for the neighbours to see us . . .'

'But sweetheart, there aren't any neighbours,' Stephen

reminded her. 'We sent you a photo of the new house. It's on land of its own.'

Stephen and Gail had moved from their Oughterard home a few years previously, much to Nieve's astonishment at the time. She'd thought that they liked the neat bungalow, which was a cut above the semi-detached house next door to the McGonigles.

'Well, I know. I didn't think it was that isolated!'

'It's not really. But the road is narrow and we're the first house and nobody would get to see the car, so it was all a bit of a waste. Besides,' added Gail, 'your dad has a new one himself that he wants to show off.'

Aidan and Nieve followed Gail and Stephen to the car park. Stephen led them to a gleaming maroon BMW 7-series.

'Nice wheels,' said Aidan admiringly.

'Good God, Dad. That's a bit flash,' remarked Nieve. 'How on earth are you managing to afford it?'

'You really haven't got the hang of the changes here, have you?' asked Stephen as he loaded the cases into the boot. 'I've done well, honey. Really well.'

Nieve stared at him and the car. Twenty-seven years ago he hadn't been doing well at all. Then he'd been made redundant and they'd had to move because of it. He had been depressed at the thought of never having a job again. And when they'd visited her in the States from time to time, he hadn't really ever given her a hint of quite how much things had improved for them. How in heaven's name had he managed to turn it all around? She knew, of course, that he'd eventually got something in a small garage outside the city. A kind of general dogsbody job, because his skills had been on the factory floor, but he had no expertise in mechanics.

'I never got any good at the car stuff,' he told her as they swung out on to the main road. 'But I was actually good at selling. They gave me a sales job in the end and the garage is now a main dealer. I'm the regional sales manager.'

Nieve blinked. She had known that her father was a sales manager, but in her mind she'd seen it as a minor job with no prospects. Clearly she'd been wrong.

'That's great, Mr Stapleton,' said Aidan.

'Yip. It is.' Stephen grinned at him. 'With things the way they are at the moment, I'm having trouble keeping the orders filled. It's all going along brilliantly. I'm earning a bloody fortune and I've no intention of retiring!'

Aidan laughed.

'But not everyone is loaded, surely,' remarked Nieve.

'Ah no,' agreed her father. 'But a lot of people – well, they're comfortable now. And being comfortable is a good thing.'

'Being stonking rich is better,' said Nieve firmly.

'Well you've certainly done well for yourself in the stonking rich stakes,' agreed Stephen. 'You'd need to have with the palaver you're putting on.'

'What d'you mean, palaver?' demanded Nieve.

'Castles, marquees, flying in guests from all over the place . . . the most expensive champagne, a dinner the night before – the night before, for heaven's sake!'

'It's a rehearsal dinner,' explained Nieve patiently. 'An informal meal for close friends and people who have travelled a long distance. My American friends will be there.'

'It's expected, Stephen,' said Gail. 'I've read up on it. It's the in thing these days.'

'Hey, listen, I've no problem with whatever she wants to do,' said Stephen easily. 'If she can afford to shell out the cash, then let her. We'll always be here to pick up the pieces.'

'What pieces?' asked Nieve.

'If it all goes wrong in that job of yours,' said Stephen,

'Get over yourself,' said Nieve. 'And you can't talk about it all going wrong in jobs, can you?'

'Being made redundant was the best thing that ever happened to me,' said Stephen. 'Obviously not at the time, of course. But if it hadn't happened I'd still probably be in that factory and earning a quarter of what I'm on now. So as far as I'm concerned, it was all a blessing in disguise.'

'All the same, it's quite a turnaround.' Nieve couldn't keep the surprise out of her voice.

Stephen laughed. 'I know, honey. I know. And did you ever think you'd see the day when your old dad would be driving a Beemer?'

Nieve sat in silence as Stephen drove along the main road, stunned at the heaviness of the traffic and at the number of new factories and office blocks that lined it. She knew now what people had been talking about when they said that Ireland had changed. She'd never quite got it before, but the gleaming glass buildings and new cars on the road were bringing it home to her. On the surface at any rate it was a different place. But she wondered how different it really could be, and comforted herself with the knowledge that despite whatever riches had come into the area, nobody – but nobody – had made the fortune she had. There was no way Gail could even think that anyone in Galway was better than her own daughter.

'Obviously I don't see many of them any more,' replied Gail in response to Nieve's question about old neighbours. 'Not regularly anyway. But I know that Helen Coyle's girl is in New Zealand now and Conor Smith is working in Johannesburg. So many people are still scattered around the globe because it's so damn expensive to relocate home. Bernie Robertson's doing well in Galway, though.'

'At what?' asked Nieve. 'As far as I recall, she was the laziest cow ever to walk the earth.'

'Makeovers,' said Gail. 'You should see her these days – quite the glamour queen.'

'Tarty, not glamorous,' remarked Nieve.

'Oh, no.' Gail shook her head. 'She's very sophisticated now. She's a qualified make-up artist and she knows lots about fashion too. Loads of people around here go to her for advice. In fact,' she added, 'she'll be doing your make-up for the wedding.'

'What?' Nieve looked at her in astonishment. 'But I thought Lorelei—'

'She has a range of people on her books,' Gail interrupted her, 'but not in Galway. And I didn't see the point in you paying for yet another person to stay over, especially when you don't even know them. Elegant Expressions is Bernie's company.'

'For crying out loud!' Nieve looked at her mother in exasperation. 'I'm paying a fortune for the best, not for friends of friends to do a bad job.'

'Bernie did the make-up for that movie they shot in Kerry

last year,' said Gail. 'If she was good enough for Nicole Kidman or whoever it was who starred in it, she's good enough for you. Anyway, it's nice to see local people doing well.'

'I've no problem with local people,' said Nieve shortly. 'I just don't want to employ them as some kind of favour to your friends.'

'Oh, and Audrey McGuiness is getting married,' added Gail, as though Nieve hadn't spoken.

'Is she?'

'To a Latvian. Lovely man. She met him in Dublin. He owns a chain of health-juice bars. They're really popular. She's done well for herself there.'

'I've done well for myself too. And I'm getting married as well.' Nieve felt that the conversation had taken a wrong turn somehow. She couldn't understand why Gail was being so positive about other people's lives when none of them could say that they were doing half as well as she was herself. But that had always been Gail's thing, she acknowledged to herself. Telling her how great everyone else was. Reminding her how hard she had to work to keep up.

She didn't have to keep up any more, though. She was way ahead of them all – ahead of Bernie and Audrey and, of course, Darcey. She wanted to ask Gail if she'd heard anything of Darcey, but she didn't quite have the nerve.

'Of course you have, sweetheart.' This time it was Stephen who spoke. 'Your mam wasn't trying to say that any of those girls are better off than you. How could they be? You're our amazing success story and everyone in Galway will be dying to know all of the details about your wedding.'

'You think?'

'Sure they will.' Gail turned and smiled at her. 'Listen, honey, none of them can hold a candle to you. You're the talk of the town, you're so successful.'

'In that case, maybe you should've let the limo pick us up. Maybe they'd have expected it.'

'There's no need to waste money,' said Stephen. 'Or to try too hard. Besides, limos are tacky. They were all the rage a few years ago, but not now. Helicopters – they were the thing for a while too. But most of us have got over that sort of stuff.'

Nieve opened her mouth to speak but closed it again. She said nothing for the rest of the journey.

Her parents' house was set in an acre of land with a view over the bay.

'It's stunning,' said Aidan as he got out of the car. 'Great views. And it's so gorgeous on a glorious day like today.'

'Every day in Palo Alto is glorious,' remarked Nieve.

Aidan laughed. 'So it's extra special when we get them here.'

Nieve made a face at him and he grinned at her. Then he kissed her affectionately on the forehead.

'Come on,' said Gail. 'You're in the dormer bedroom.'

The house was beautiful. It was warm and spacious and elegantly decorated and a far cry from the house next door to the McGonigles. Nieve felt happy for her father that it had all turned out right for him in the end. If anyone deserved good luck it was her dad. She never would forgive the management at the factory for making him redundant no matter how much of a blessing in disguise he proclaimed it to be.

'Oh, look, it could all go pear-shaped tomorrow,' said Stephen when Aidan commented that business was obviously even better than he'd said. 'It's up and down. But we're living in the here and now, and at the moment it's up and we have to enjoy it.'

He said the same later that night when they were at the newest must-be-seen-in restaurant in the city.

Afterwards, Nieve attempted to pay the bill but her father instantly stopped her. She insisted, but he somehow managed to make sure that the waiter took his credit card instead. And he told her, as they walked out into the balmy night air, that he wouldn't dream of her putting her hand into her pocket while she stayed with them. She had enough expense, he said, with her extravagant wedding.

She was touched by his concern, but this wasn't how it was supposed to be. She'd imagined herself as the one who would be paying for the swanky restaurants and flashing her exclusive charge card around the place. She was the one who was to have unpacked her cases and left her Vera Wang dress lying casually on the bed so that her mother would be stunned at the sight of it. Gail was supposed to have been rendered speechless by the Balenciaga bag that Nieve was carrying too. But she'd just looked at the dress and said that it was gorgeous and she hadn't noticed the bag at all. And why would she? Wasn't she toting the latest Chloé model herself!

'I went through the wedding list with Lorelei the other day,' said Gail later that night as they sat on the patio at home. 'What's all this about Darcey McGonigle?'

'I had to ask her,' said Nieve. 'She was my best friend.'

'*Was*,' Gail emphasised. 'I hardly think you two are friends any more.'

'I had to ask her,' repeated Nieve. 'I was asking other people who were old friends and they'd wonder why she wasn't there.'

'You could simply have said she couldn't come.'

'But I don't know who she's kept in touch with!' cried Nieve. 'If I told someone that she couldn't come and it got back to her that I'd said it though I hadn't even asked her . . .'

'Who'd care?' demanded Gail.

'I would,' retorted Nieve. 'Besides, I want her to come and see us getting married. I want her to see that Aidan and I love each other and that it wasn't my fault that he dumped her.'

Aidan shifted uncomfortably and Stephen shot him a sympathetic look.

'Don't you think it might be a bit hard on the girl?' asked Stephen gently. 'After all, you've got the man, you've got the money, you've got everything. And she's got—'

'A divorce,' said Nieve.

Aidan looked even more uncomfortable. 'Which is why,' he said, 'it might not be a good idea for her to be there.'

'Look, she was always hopeless at hanging on to men,' said Nieve. 'That's not my fault. She can't blame me for what happened.'

'Like I said before, though, she might blame me,' said Aidan.

'We're all older and wiser,' Nieve said. 'We were only kids back then. We've got sense since.'

'I hope you're right,' muttered Stephen. 'I really do.'

A few hours later, when they were lying in the double bed of the guest room together, Nieve propped herself up on one arm and looked at Aidan.

'Do you love me?' she asked.

'Of course I do.'

'More than Darcey?'

'Nieve! What a stupid, stupid question.'

'More than Darcey?' she repeated.

'I never loved Darcey,' said Aidan. 'I . . . cared about her. I was intrigued by her. But I never loved her.'

'How can you say that?'

'I was only a kid back then. I had no idea what love was all about.'

'Are you ready to marry me?' she asked.

'I've been ready to marry you for years.'

'Why didn't we do it before?' she asked.

'You didn't want to.'

'Are you sure it was me? Are you sure that it wasn't you?'

'I always wanted to marry you,' he told her seriously. 'From the moment I first set eyes on you. I knew.'

'Really?'

'Really.'

'And you won't change your mind if you see Darcey McGonigle again?'

'Are you cracked?' he demanded. 'I *left* Darcey McGonigle for you.'

'And you don't ever think it was a mistake?'

'Why would I think that?'

Nieve shook her head. 'I don't know,' she admitted. 'It's just that being here again . . . I wondered . . .'

'Stop wondering,' he said as he put his arm around her and dragged her beneath the covers. 'And start getting used to the idea of being Nieve Clarke in a few days' time.'

She giggled. 'I'm not changing my name.'

'I'm not asking you to.' His lips were on her breast. 'I know you're mine. And that's all I ever wanted.'

The following day, Nieve and Lorelei met at Rathfinan Castle to discuss the wedding plans. Stephen and Aidan had gone clay-pigeon shooting together. At first Aidan had been concerned that Nieve would want him to be at the castle with her, but he soon realised that she preferred to do all of the organising herself.

'It's not that I don't want you to be involved,' she told him over breakfast. 'It's just that it's going to be done my way anyway, so what's the point?'

He'd laughed at that and so had she. Things were always done her way. He never minded. And so he was quite happy to head off with Stephen while she borrowed Gail's car to drive to the castle to meet Lorelei.

Gail, however, had been a bit miffed at not being invited. After all, she pointed out, she'd been the one who'd had to talk to Lorelei about some of the various minor issues that had cropped up. It seemed right that she should come along. But Nieve insisted, very firmly, that this was a meeting between her and her wedding-planner and that she needed to talk to the owner of Happy Ever Afters herself. She didn't say so out loud but she knew that she would feel intimidated with Gail there and that she'd end up giving in over something ridiculous simply because she didn't know how to say no to her mother.

Gail, rather snippily, said that she was going off to have a beauty treatment anyway and that it didn't make any difference. Nieve responded that she was glad her mother had something relaxing to do. Both of them wondered why it was that they got on so much better when there was an ocean and an entire continent between them.

It was another glorious day and the sun beat down from a clear blue sky. Nieve tuned the radio in to a local music station and sang along as she hurtled towards Rathfinan. It was strange, she thought, but the blues of Ireland were bluer and the greens greener and the countryside just that bit more real than California. Beautiful though the Golden State was, and much as she loved it, there was something good about being home. Only temporarily, she reminded herself, as she spun the car around a hairpin bend, her heart beating rapidly in her throat. Ireland was nice to revisit, but these damn roads were hopeless!

She missed the turn for the castle at the first attempt and had to back up the twisting country road, terrified that something would come along and slam into her. But nothing did. The only sound around her was the gentle lowing of cattle in a nearby field and the incessant chirping of the birds in the hedgerows that lined the roads.

There was an intercom at the castle gate. She pressed the buzzer and announced herself. The gates glided gently open.

As she pulled up in front of the castle, a tall woman wearing a pale blue Chanel suit, honey-blonde hair pinned into a severe knot on the top of her head and huge Jackie O sunglasses perched on top of the knot, walked down the steps to greet her.

'How'ya,' she said breezily. 'I'm Lorelei.'

Nieve, who until now had only communicated with her by email and who'd expected a cut-glass accent to go with the Parisian chic, was startled.

'Hi,' she said in reply. 'I'm Nieve.'

'Of course you are,' said Lorelei. 'I recognise you from your picture in the emails. You're better in real life. Not,' she added hastily, 'that I'm criticising the pictures. But sometimes a person doesn't do themselves justice in one-dimensional shots. You're going to look great on the day. Your bone structure is magnificent.'

'Thanks. I think.' Nieve felt herself tense. This girl was a million miles away from the image she portrayed. She was far too familiar and relaxed. How the hell was she going to manage the kind of wedding that Nieve deserved?

'I mean it.' Lorelei grinned at her. 'And listen to me, Nieve, we're going to have the absolute best wedding in the world for you.'

'Are we?' Nieve knew that there was doubt in her voice.

'Don't you worry your pretty little head about a thing,' said Lorelei blithely. 'It's all worked out down to a tee. Come inside. Malachy has set us up in the library and I've got loads to show you. And don't look so worried.' Her voice hardened a little. 'I'm really good and I absolutely know what I'm doing.'

Nieve breathed out and followed Lorelei up the steps.

'Hallway,' Lorelei said. 'We're going to have flowers here . . . here . . . and here.' She waved her arms expansively. 'White roses. I know your preference was red, but you need something to give this place a lift because it's so dark – otherwise it'd look like a mausoleum.'

Nieve nodded.

'And there'll be a string quartet in the corner. Very tasteful music. Vivaldi mostly. It's a bit clichéd, I know, but it's absolutely the best music for this sort of thing.'

She moved rapidly through the castle.

'The access to the back will be totally planned out,' she said. 'It's actually not that far, the route we're doing it. There'll be red velvet ropes to guide people the right way.

'Here,' she continued, 'a reception room. Another quartet playing exactly the same music. The guests will be served champagne here. If we're totally unlucky and it pisses with rain they can stay here and in the adjoining room. If God is good and we have a day like today, then they can walk through here . . .' she moved forward and Nieve followed her, 'and through here . . . and *voilà*! The great outdoors.'

Nieve stood on the flagstoned area at the back of the castle where the wrought-iron tables and chairs were arranged.

'These will be dressed properly, of course,' said Lorelei. 'White silk cushions. Gorgeous. And ribbons on the back. It'll look spectacular. We'll rearrange them in the best possible way too, of course. And then there'll be a raised walkway to the marquee, which will be set up behind.' She waved at the huge tract of land in front of them. 'I know we debated whether to use the castle itself, but in the summer people want to be outside, and nice though it is, the inside of a castle is bloody gloomy. So we'll have a wooden walkway covered in a red carpet leading to the marquee. If it does rain, the carpet will be changed every hour. There'll be flowers either side of it – those white roses again, you can't beat them, miles more elegant than colours. You wanted elegant, didn't you?'

'Yes, but some colour too.' Nieve needed to exert some control over her wedding-planner. 'I mean, I specifically emailed you about colours. No yellow was what I said.'

'And I got that loud and clear,' said Lorelei. 'The floral displays on the tables in the marquee will be colours. They're gorgeous, a kind of tropical mix. Now, honey, you don't have to worry because I have a sample of everything with me so that you can see it.'

'Oh.'

'I know my brides,' said Lorelei. 'And I know brides like you who have a really exact idea of what they want. Right, let's go into the library.'

The square room, lined with books, was filled with wedding paraphernalia. Lorelei hadn't been joking when she'd said that she had a sample of everything – on the big table in the centre of the room was a variety of glasses, cutlery, crockery, napkin rings, linen, flowers, chairs and cushions, as well as the gifts for the people coming to the rehearsal dinner.

'They're lovely,' murmured Nieve as she held one of the lockets in the palm of her hand.

'Glad you like them. Right.' Lorelei began moving things around so quickly that Nieve was dazzled. 'This is how a setting is going to look.' She stepped back and Nieve saw a beautiful arrangement of white bone china with silver edging flanked by modern-design Newbridge silver cutlery, an Irish linen napkin in a silver holder, and Louise Kennedy glassware, exactly as the emailed photos had promised. A silver-framed menu card with a stylised photo of Aidan and Nieve was placed beside the setting. It looked stunning. Lorelei completed the picture by adding a Louis XV-style chair at the end of the table. 'I don't have the tropical flower display yet,' she told Nieve. 'But it's fabulous.'

'Everything else is,' agreed Nieve slowly. 'It's just how I imagined.'

Lorelei beamed at her. 'Of course it is. You were very specific.'

'I know. But I guess I'm surprised it's exactly right.'

'Honey, you're paying me a lot of money to get it exactly right.'

'So I am. In that case I don't have to worry about the marquee, do I? It's going to be OK?'

'Sure it is. We'll go outside and look back at the castle from exactly where it's going to be so that you get the general idea.'

They walked into the sunshine.

'Your dress is Vera Wang?' Lorelei looked quizzically at her.

Nieve nodded.

'You stuck to the design you sent?'

'Of course.'

'Because that little velvet ribbon detail is going to be on the place-setting names,' said Lorelei. 'I just wanted to make sure that I could give the go-ahead for them to be printed up.'

'Sounds great.'

'And you're still wearing the veil with the little tiara?'

Nieve nodded. She'd wondered whether she should dispense with the veil and just have flowers in her hair. Somehow a veil seemed an almost childish thing to wear when she was, after all, in her thirties and had lived with her future husband for the past ten years. But she'd always wanted one.

'It'll be adorable,' said Lorelei.

'The diamonds in the tiara are real.'

'Good grief.'

Nieve was pleased to see that she'd finally surprised Lorelei.

'It's my present to myself,' Nieve told her.

'Nice present.'

'Ah, it's not that big a tiara,' Nieve said quickly. 'It looks more extravagant than it really is.'

Why am I suddenly getting coy about it? she asked herself. Why am I concerned that this girl should think I'm being stupidly flashy by wearing a ridiculously expensive tiara? Why shouldn't I boast about it anyway?

'You can have the biggest tiara in the world if you like,' said Lorelei. 'This is the greatest day of your life. Go for it.'

'Exactly.' Nieve grinned at her.

'You're my biggest wedding to date,' Lorelei confided as they stood in the place the marquee was to be and looked back at the castle. 'Of course weddings have mushroomed into vast extravaganzas over the last few years, but nobody has quite matched this yet. Well, nobody who isn't some kind of celeb, anyway. I'm not into celeb weddings. This is much better. It's great for me. People will be impressed when I tell them that I did the Stapleton–Clarke!'

Nieve felt herself glow with pleasure inside.

'Have you known him long?'

'Who?' asked Nieve.

'The groom.'

'Aidan.' Nieve sighed. 'Years. We've been living together for years. That's why I want this to be great.'

'We need to talk through the guest list,' said Lorelei. 'And also plans for the rehearsal dinner the night before. Not that you're going to need a whole heap of rehearsal. The Rathfinan church is tiny – it'll be packed out by your crowd, but that'll look great. You'll just be walking a few steps up the aisle and back down again. But you need to know who's doing what. Your bridesmaids are . . .' she hesitated for a moment, 'Mischa and Courtney. They're coming from the States and staying at the castle.'

Nieve nodded. 'They'll be here two days beforehand.'

'We've organised treatments for them the night before the rehearsal at Glenkilty Spa, which is about a half a mile away,' said Lorelei. 'That way they'll be refreshed and looking good and not jet-laggy. Those bridesmaids' dresses – I love the way the colour matches your bodice ribbon – Vera Wang too?'

Nieve nodded again.

'I do so admire her.' Lorelei sighed. 'She's my absolute favourite designer. If I ever get married myself I want one of her gowns.'

'I don't blame you,' said Nieve. 'Mine is just fantastic.'

She closed her eyes and thought of her magnificent wedding dress. Tasteful, of course, Vera Wang was nothing if not tasteful. But Nieve had allowed her fantasies to take hold of her, and instead of the discreet and slinky dress she'd originally intended, she'd bought one with a wide skirt and petticoats underneath that was both girlie and stunning and that she knew looked like a million dollars on her. (As well it might, she thought, remembering the price tag.)

'I'm having such fun with this,' Lorelei told her. 'Oh, there'll be more musicians out here, of course, and what we'll do is have an outdoor dancing area too . . . We'll have anti-mozzie lanterns dotted all around this place so that it'll look very fairy grotto – I promise you it'll be the totally best day of your life.'

'Catering?' said Nieve.

'Oh yes. You saw the menu card but I was waiting to have you confirm everything before I get that printed up and tell the caterers too. We've got Ireland's absolute top people in to do it. You'll love it. They're like totally in demand everywhere and it was actually a huge coup to get them because they're usually booked up months in advance.'

'We *did* book them months in advance,' Nieve reminded her.

'Years, then.' Lorelei grinned. 'Anyway, as long as you're still OK with this, it's going to be the salmon pastrami starter – I've had that, it's absolutely fantastic; then, for mains, a choice of seared tuna with green curry sauce – to die for, that one – or the lamb cutlets or the nasi himpit with glass noodles, vegetables and a chilli sambai. Dessert to be fresh fruit followed by petit fours – we didn't make a final call on those, but I'm suggesting the banana, chocolate, apricot and kiwi tartlets. The caterers are aware that there are a number of different ethnic cultures coming, and so there are no pork products and meat will be prepared according to halal, just as you requested.' She smiled brightly at Nieve. 'We've obviously ordered crates of Moët; and according to your specifications it's a choice of Pouilly Fumé and Sauvignon Blanc for the white wine, Cabernet and Shiraz for the reds. Old and new world!'

'I can't think of a single thing to complain about,' Nieve said honestly.

'It's my job, honey,' said Lorelei. 'I knew from your emails what you wanted. Why shouldn't everything be right?'

Nieve, who'd expected to spend the day in Bridezilla mode, snapping at Lorelei that the preparations weren't good enough, blushed slightly.

'Y'see, my aim is that the bride just turns up, looks gorgeous and doesn't have to worry about a thing,' said Lorelei. 'Which is what I want to happen for you, Nieve. You're paying for the best and you deserve the best.'

'I know,' said Nieve. 'It's just . . . sometimes you don't get what you pay for.'

'You do with Happy Ever Afters,' said Lorelei. 'OK, you deserve a drink. I've got some waiting for you. And,' she grinned at Nieve, 'it's on me, so don't worry.'

'I'm not,' said Nieve as she followed Lorelei back to the castle.

The wedding-planner disappeared inside and returned with a bottle of champagne and two glasses.

'To a great wedding day!' she said as she popped the cork.

'To a great wedding day,' agreed Nieve.

They sat on the flagstoned patio area and looked over the lawns.

'Flowers,' said Nieve suddenly. 'I wanted flowers planted.'

Lorelei made a face. 'That's my one failure,' she confessed. 'We're getting around it by bringing in loads of filled planters. But the owner said that he doesn't like flowers particularly and he wouldn't let me dig up the garden area.'

'He could grass it over again, surely?' Nieve was relieved to have something to complain about at last.

'That's what I said. But he was adamant.'

Nieve thought about arguing a bit more. But the edge had been taken off her by the champagne and suddenly she realised it wasn't worth the effort. The planters would probably be gorgeous anyway.

'I guess it doesn't matter,' she allowed.

'Of course it doesn't! Honestly, Nieve, it's going to be a great day. And the dinner the night before will be great too. We've taken over the restaurant and it's by far the best in the area. It's a seafood menu with a vegetarian option. It'll be a whole heap less formal than the wedding, of course, but that's the idea.'

'I trust you,' said Nieve.

'Excellent.' Lorelei clinked her glass against her client's. 'That's exactly how it's supposed to be.'

Nieve hadn't intended to spend the afternoon guzzling champagne at Rathfinan Castle, but that was what happened all the same. And then she realised that she was absolutely unable to drive home.

'Don't worry,' said Lorelei. 'I got Archie, my partner, to drop me here. He's been over at the restaurant and running around doing bits and pieces. He'll pick us up and get you home.'

'But my car,' wailed Nieve. 'It's my mum's. She'll go mental if I leave it here.'

'Archie and I are staying in Galway overnight. I can ask him to pick you up in the morning and drop you back to collect it. No worries.'

Nieve rather thought it might be a worry. But she was feeling too buzzy from the champagne to care.

Gail was a bit miffed that her car had been left at Rathfinan, but she was mollified by the extra bottle of Moët that Nieve produced for her.

'I suppose you had to have some celebratory champers,' she acknowledged as Nieve headed unsteadily upstairs to their bedroom.

Aidan laughed at her. 'You're totally unused to alcohol in the afternoon,' he said. 'You're pie-eyed on a drop of champagne.'

'It wasn't just a drop.' Nieve's words were slurred. 'We finished the bottle. But it was fun all the same.'

'I'm glad.' There was real warmth in Aidan's words. 'It's about time you started to remember that life is fun.'

She opened one eye. 'My life is *always* fun.'

'Well, a different sort of fun then,' he amended. 'Away from graphs and charts and numbers.'

'They're fun,' she told him. Then burped slightly and giggled.

'I know. But I'm talking about the other kind,' he told her. 'I want you to remember that you let it all go today. You weren't in charge, but it turned out fine and you enjoyed yourself.'

'C'mere,' she murmured. 'I'll show you all about who's in charge and enjoying themselves.'

He laughed, picked her up and dropped her on to the bed. But she was sound asleep already.

Her head was pounding the next morning and her mouth felt like the bottom of a bird cage. She groaned as she got out of bed and stood for ten full minutes beneath the power shower in the ensuite bathroom. It was true that she really wasn't used to much alcohol any more. She remembered her early twenties when she and Darcey used to share bottles of cheap Rioja at the beachside bar without any ill effects whatsoever. Have I got sensible? she wondered as she finally stepped out of the shower. Or just boring? Or, she asked herself later, sitting in front of a bowl of the organic oats and fruit mix that she'd insisted on bringing home from the States, have I been completely suckered into thinking that my body is a temple and I shouldn't put anything even slightly addictive into it?

She groaned again and rubbed the back of her neck. The thing was, she reminded herself, she did drink local wine in Palo Alto. She drank frozen margaritas too. And beer. Just not very much and not very often. It was a healthier way to live, definitely.

'You stay here and suffer,' said Aidan kindly. 'I'll pick up your mum's car from the castle.'

'It's OK,' replied Nieve feebly. 'Archie is supposed to call me about collecting it.'

'Don't be daft. You need to recover. I'll go with your dad. That way we'll actually get to see the venue before the wedding day.'

'There's still ten days to go,' she told him. 'I did intend that you and I would go there together.'

'I know, and we will. But this time, let me.'

Nieve nodded and then wished she hadn't. Her head felt like a granite rock wobbling precariously on her shoulders.

Aidan enjoyed the drive to Rathfinan with Stephen. The two men kept up a steady conversation about Stephen's car sales prowess until they approached the castle.

'Wow,' said Stephen as they stopped outside the gates. 'Gail told me it was impressive, but I didn't realise how impressive.'

'Nieve showed me photos,' Aidan said. 'But they don't give you the whole feel of the place, do they?'

Stephen pressed the intercom and the gates duly opened. He drove slowly up the gravelled driveway before parking alongside the other half-dozen cars to the side of the impressive castle door. The two men got out of the BMW and stood staring at the building.

The door creaked open and a woman smiled at them.

'I'm Andrea Finan,' she said. 'You're very welcome. Want to look around before you take the car?'

Aidan nodded. He and Stephen walked through the same

rooms as Nieve and Lorelei had done the previous day, and the whole wedding suddenly seemed a million times more real and imminent to Aidan than it ever had before. He shivered involuntarily.

'Cold?' asked Stephen.

Aidan shook his head. 'But it's a bit gloomy in here. We'll be outside, though. Apparently there's going to be a marquee.' He moved towards the library. The samples that Lorelei had shown Nieve were still on the table. He picked up the silk cushion that was to be used on the outside chairs. He could see that it was exquisite. He could see too that the crockery and the cutlery and the glasses were all of the finest quality. Nieve had said that they'd be keeping everything afterwards, because she'd insisted on buying in everything brand new, and he'd wondered what in God's name they were going to do with nearly two hundred place settings and glasses, but she'd said that over time there'd be breakages, that the designs were timeless and that it was an investment. Just as well, he thought, that Nieve's pockets were limitless. He shuddered to think of how much the whole thing was costing her. And as he looked at the sample menus, he couldn't help feeling guilty that she was paying for it all herself.

He didn't mind the fact that she earned more money than him. He really didn't. He knew that she was a driven woman and that she measured her own success by the size of her bank balance. She always said that she measured his success differently. That his personality was different to hers. It was only now, looking at what her money was buying, that he realised how very different he was.

Why did she love him? he wondered. He knew why he

loved her. He knew why he'd fallen for her the moment he'd set eyes on her. It was her beauty, of course, and her energy and her self-belief. All those things had been very exciting to him. And, of course, she was an absolute vixen in bed. He loved that about her too. He did acknowledge to himself the down side of loving someone who really didn't ever take time out to smell the roses, but he needed her to motivate himself. When he'd been with Darcey, he'd felt content. He'd thought about changing jobs, but only to bum around Australia or New Zealand for a few years. Darcey probably would've done that quite happily. But Nieve never would. Nieve always had to have a purpose, and Aidan knew that for him it was better to be with someone with a purpose. But it suddenly struck him, standing in the Rathfinan Castle library, that Nieve was a million times more purposeful than him.

'You OK?' Stephen, who'd been looking out of the mullioned window, turned to his future son-in-law.

'Yeah, sure, fine.' Aidan shrugged. 'I was just – thinking.'

'Well just remember.' Stephen's voice suddenly hardened. 'My daughter means the world to me. The absolute world. She's bright and clever and successful and she's done it all herself. And if you do anything – anything at all – to hurt her, I'll kill you.'

Aidan raised an eyebrow.

'She's a sensitive girl,' said Stephen. 'I know she comes across a bit hard sometimes, but she's not as tough as she makes out. When I was made redundant she came up to me and said that she didn't need pocket money any more and that if I needed to borrow anything from her to let her know, because she had some in her piggy bank.' Stephen cleared his throat. 'She's my little girl and I don't want anyone letting her down.'

'I've lived with Nieve for ten years,' said Aidan calmly. 'I haven't let her down yet.'

'I know,' said Stephen. 'But living together and being married is different. And my daughter is a prize. You're lucky to have her. Remember that.'

'There are some people who'd say that she's lucky to have me.' Aidan was annoyed by Stephen's attitude.

'Listen, you're a decent enough bloke and you've made her very happy. But she's a rich woman and there has to be more to it than that.'

'If you're implying that I'm only with Nieve because she's done well . . .' Now Aidan was really angry. 'I helped her become who she is. I was there for her when times were hard.'

'But from what I gather, she was the one who got you out of the hard times.'

'I supported every decision she made. I'm part of the relationship, not some . . . some . . . accessory!'

Aidan glared at his future father-in-law, then turned and strode out of the library, across the hallway and out on to the patio area at the back of the castle. He knew that Stephen doted on his daughter, but he was almost shaking with rage at the older man's assumption that somehow by marrying Nieve, Aidan was acquiring her and her riches without really loving her. Which was untrue and unfair and just plain . . .

He turned around, suddenly sensing that he wasn't alone.

A woman was sitting at one of the wrought-iron tables, a frond of steam rising from the coffee cup in front of her. Her right hand was covering the lower part of her face so that he could only see the sky blue of her eyes above it. Her Scandinavian-blonde hair fell over her forehead and curled gently behind her neck.

He stared at her. The name left his lips without him even realising he had spoken.

'Darcey?'

She rested her left arm, still in its plaster splint, on the table and slid her hand away from her face.

'Hello, Aidan,' she said. 'Welcome home.'

# Chapter 28

He had always loved her voice.

It had enchanted him every time she spoke, whether it was in English with its soft west of Ireland cadences, or in any of her continental languages, which inevitably sounded more seductive. She'd never known just how much it had always turned him on. It had been such a sexy voice in such an unsophisticated woman that it had made him look on her as someone desirable who needed to be protected from everything around her. That was why he'd wanted to marry her. To look after her. And to stay seduced by her.

The voice was the same, but she was different. She looked quite serene sitting at the table with the coffee cup in front of her, those instantly recognisable blue eyes regarding him thoughtfully.

Her eyes never left his face as she took a sip of coffee before replacing the cup carefully on the china saucer.

He was the one who finally spoke. 'What are you doing here?' he asked.

'Having coffee.'

He wondered if she sounded faintly nervous. She didn't look nervous.

'I meant here. Why here?' His voice was fierce. 'Why at this castle? You know, don't you, that we – that I – that . . .'

'Oh for heaven's sake, Aidan, of course I know that you and Nieve are getting married here. I have an invitation, don't I?'

Not nervous, he realised. Strong. He'd never actually heard her sounding strong before.

'Is that why you're here? Casing the joint?'

She raised an eyebrow. 'Casing the joint? Why exactly?'

'I don't know,' he said. 'I just—'

'My being here has nothing to do with you,' said Darcey rapidly. 'Don't worry. You're not that important to me.'

His eyes narrowed. She'd sounded nervous then.

'But you're coming to the wedding, aren't you? You accepted the invitation.'

She shrugged.

'I don't want you to come,' he said. 'I don't think there's a good reason for it.'

'Nieve obviously does.'

'She was inviting lots of friends. She didn't want to leave you out.'

Darcey's eyes opened wide. 'That's a bit of a U-turn, isn't it?'

'Oh, come on, Darcey.' Aidan looked pleadingly at her. 'You're over all that, aren't you?'

'That would make it easy for you, wouldn't it?' she said spiritedly.

'Are you here to make trouble?' he demanded. 'I told Nieve you'd make trouble.'

'Oh, come on!' She laughed. 'I've better things to do than make trouble. I hardly think you're worth it, really.'

'Everyone says you lost it after I left.'

'You can't believe everyone,' said Darcey calmly. 'I know that this will come as a shock to you, but people get over other people dumping them.'

'That's not what . . .'

She looked at him coolly.

'Maybe I got it wrong,' he admitted. 'I heard you sort of fell apart.'

'I was upset,' she said. 'You ran off with my best friend. I was entitled to feel hurt. But I've moved on since then. And so I'm coming to the wedding to wish you and Nieve all the best and in the hopes that both of you will have the happiness you deserve.'

Why, he wondered, didn't he trust her? Her voice was calm and friendly and yet he couldn't help feeling that there was an undercurrent in everything she said.

'So – it's all OK then?'

'Totally.' She smiled at him again.

'Look, Darcey . . .' He stopped and turned towards the building. He thought he could hear Stephen Stapleton's footsteps coming towards them. Shit, he thought. If Stephen walked out here and saw him talking to Darcey McGonigle – well, God only knew what he'd think. After what Stephen had said about killing him if he didn't treat Nieve right, Aidan didn't really want his future father-in-law to see him with his ex-girlfriend, even if it was all some horrible coincidence over which he had no control.

'I've got to go inside,' he said urgently. 'It's Stephen. I have to – he can't see us together.'

'Aidan . . .'

'Really. I have to go.' His voice was anxious. 'I have to.'

He hurried back through the doorway and Darcey released the breath she'd been holding. She picked up the coffee cup, but her hands were trembling so much she had to put it down before she could even take a sip. It hadn't for a single second occurred to her that she might bump into Aidan Clarke at Rathfinan Castle. When Minette had told her that morning (Darcey's last day in Galway; she was going back to Dublin on the early train the following day) that she needed to return to the castle because she thought that she'd lost a lipstick there, Darcey had looked at her sceptically and asked if it wasn't an excuse to see Malachy Finan again.

'No,' said Minette guilelessly. 'I have definitely lost my lipstick. And it is a perfectly new and very expensive Clarins lipstick in my favourite colour. So I want to check.'

'Maman, we were all over that castle. It could be anywhere,' Darcey protested.

'I have to look.' Minette shrugged in a very Gallic fashion.

Darcey hadn't intended coming with her, but Minette had insisted. And so, as Malachy and Minette walked through the grounds, ostensibly looking for the lipstick, Darcey had sat at one of the wrought-iron tables and had a coffee.

She'd heard voices coming from within the castle but had assumed that they belonged to one or other of Malachy's brothers.

When Aidan had walked outside, she had nearly fainted from the shock. She'd felt her heart begin to race in her chest and her hand had flown to her mouth in disbelief. He was instantly recognisable. Older, of course, and a little heavier. Yet somehow more attractive than ever with his light tan, stylish haircut and casual (but expensive) jacket and jeans.

She'd been afraid she wouldn't be able to speak at all, and when the words had come out of her mouth it had seemed to her as though someone else was saying them. She'd been pleased that she hadn't appeared to sound as shocked as she felt. That she'd been cutting, even. Maybe. Her stomach turned over. He was here and he was gorgeous and he'd made her heart beat faster again. She shivered in the afternoon sunlight.

Aidan managed, with some difficulty, to persuade Stephen that it wasn't worth going outside, that they'd better get back to the house because Nieve and Gail expected them back for lunch and there'd be hell to pay if they were late. It was lucky, he thought, that Stephen was a man who loved his food and who was scared of his wife. He knew that he was talking inconsequential nonsense as they walked back to the two cars, but he felt a huge surge of relief when Stephen got into the BMW and started down the driveway. For a moment Aidan considered going back to Darcey, but he told himself not to be stupid. Stephen would wonder what had happened to him, and the last thing he wanted was the older man wondering anything at all. So Aidan got behind the wheel of the Golf and followed his future father-in-law to the main road.

But he couldn't get the image of Darcey out of his head. And as he thought about her sitting at the table with the cup of coffee in front of her, his mental picture included the fact that, surprisingly elegant though she'd first seemed, her arm had been in some sort of cast and her leg had been heavily strapped. She clearly hadn't got over being clumsy.

He had loved her, no matter what he'd told Nieve. It would have been hard not to. She'd always intrigued him with her intellectual smartness but her hopelessness with everyday life. And her way of being able to tell him that she loved him in a clatter of different languages. He'd always felt protective towards her and he'd liked that feeling.

Until the day he met Nieve. He didn't need to protect Nieve. And although he'd felt good as the protector, he felt even better being whirled along by Nieve's enthusiasm for life. Even though, he admitted to himself now, he couldn't help feeling that it was time for her to slow down. Be a bit more like Darcey had been all those years ago.

How was it, he wondered, that he'd fallen for two such completely different women? And what sort of cosmic sign was it that practically on the eve of his wedding to the woman he knew he loved, he'd met the girl he'd almost married instead?

Darcey didn't say anything to Minette about seeing Aidan. Her mother and Malachy had returned from their search of the grounds fifteen minutes after he'd left. Darcey was still trembling from her shock at seeing him but was saved from having to talk by Minette's unceasing chatter about the permanent loss of her lipstick and how silly she'd been, really, to think that there was the faintest hope of finding it.

'You must allow me to buy you dinner sometime to make up for the loss,' said Malachy.

Minette smiled at him. 'You can certainly buy me dinner, but not for any reason other than you want to,' she said.

Malachy laughed and told her that she was a breath of fresh air. He promised to call her and she nodded in agreement before telling Darcey that they should really get going.

Darcey followed her mother silently back to the car and got in beside her. Minette tooted the horn in farewell and set off for home.

'Are you all right?' she asked her daughter as they turned towards Galway. 'You're very quiet.'

'I'm fine.'

'Arm hurting you?'

'No.'

'Ankle?'

'Maman, I'm fine,' repeated Darcey impatiently.

Minette shot her a sideways look. 'You're very pale, *ma petite*,' she said.

'Not flushed with romance like you,' said Darcey.

'Oh for heaven's sake!' Minette crunched the gears and Darcey winced as the car jolted forward. 'You're not jealous because I'm having a bit of fun with Malachy, are you?'

'Of course not!' cried Darcey. 'You know that I've always encouraged you to get out and enjoy yourself since Dad was such a bastard.'

'Please don't use that sort of language about your father,' said Minette.

'Why not?' demanded Darcey. 'He is a bastard. All men are bastards.'

Minette pursed her lips and continued driving in silence.

'Is it because I made you come to the castle again?' she asked after a few minutes. 'Was it really insensitive of me because the wedding will take place there? I'm sorry, I didn't think of it like that.'

'Ah, no.' Darcey shook her head. 'Don't mind me. I'm just in a cranky mood.'

'Don't be,' Minette told her. 'Life's too short for cranky moods.'

Darcey would have agreed with her if cranky was all she felt.

Darcey had looked great, he thought. He knew that she had never considered herself to be pretty, and she wasn't really, but he'd always thought her attractive. She looked better now than she had in her twenties – in fact he'd thought that she'd looked beautiful sitting there with the sun behind her, lighting up her golden hair, her eyes still a bright, alert blue in her arresting face. He'd been surprised at the jolt that had gone through him as he acknowledged the fact that he was looking at a stunning woman.

Hell, he told himself, he'd seen hundreds of much more beautiful girls with blonde hair and blue eyes in California! He was anaesthetised as far as blonde-haired, blue-eyed women were concerned. And he was anaesthetised as far as Darcey McGonigle was concerned too. He'd dumped her because he'd fallen so hard and fast for Nieve. It was just that seeing her so unexpectedly had brought back memories he'd buried in the furthermost corners of his mind.

Memories like their first night together, when she'd spoken to him in Italian, telling him things she wanted to do with him and to him and for him, which he didn't understand but which sounded so great and so sexy and so wonderful . . . She'd said afterwards that since she was fairly inexperienced she'd just been parroting stuff she'd read in *Cosmo* and she'd never done it before either, but it sounded a million times better in Italian than English anyway. She'd beguiled him that night, made him think of sleeping with a woman as something romantic instead of something that was pure pleasure, although sleeping with her had been very pleasurable indeed. She'd appealed to a whole range of his senses and he'd never quite forgotten it.

But just because he'd fallen for her then didn't mean he was still in love with her. He wasn't. Nieve hadn't beguiled him, but she'd taken control of his heart and he wasn't about to lose it again for no good reason.

It's pre-wedding nerves, he told himself as he sat in the kitchen and listened to Gail and Nieve discuss the make-up schedule for the wedding day. This whole extravaganza is doing my head in. It's making me wish for simpler times. But I never wanted simpler times. Not when it came down to it. I wanted Nieve. And I have her.

He looked across at his fiancée. She was frowning. He wished she'd smile instead. It seemed like a long time since he'd seen her smile and really mean it.

*   *   *

It was good to be back in Dublin even though, Darcey reminded herself, if she went to the wedding, she'd be back in Galway the following week. Minette hadn't wanted her to go back at all and the twins, who'd called around the previous night to see how her injuries were progressing, told her she was crazy to embark on the train journey again.

'Take more time off!' cried Tish. 'They don't expect you to be in the office looking like an extra from *The Mummy*.'

'Have a rest,' advised Amelie. 'Crikey, I'd love to have a few weeks off from the grind and not have to bother about anything.'

'You'd go nuts,' Darcey informed her. 'As I am slowly going here. Sorry, Maman,' she added as Minette looked peevishly at her, 'but I'm used to my own space and—'

'Oh, go back to your single white female apartment,' said Minette airily. 'I don't mind.'

Darcey groaned and the twins chuckled.

'Perhaps it'll take you out of your cranky mood,' Minette said.

'Cranky? Why?' asked Amelie.

Darcey said nothing.

'Hey, you'd be at odds too if your arm was in a sling and you were hopping around the place.' Tish looked at her younger sister sympathetically. 'Sure you'll manage OK back in the big smoke?'

'I'll be fine,' said Darcey. 'Besides, I'll be getting the lighter splint next week. I need to go back for that anyway.'

She was glad to finally settle into her own living room and revel in the silence the following day. Minette had been wonderful, but Darcey was tired of being fussed over. She was looking forward to going back to work, even though she knew there'd be some fussing there too. But it would be a different sort of fussing. It wouldn't last long and then she'd be back into the swing of things. She couldn't wait. She desperately wanted to follow up on all of her Singapore contacts.

She'd called the office from Galway and had asked to speak to Neil so that she could see if any progress had been made with them (she had, after all, emailed all of her reports back to InvestorCorp on a daily basis from Singapore), but his assistant, Jenni, told her that he was away on business. She'd asked to be transferred to Anna's extension and this time had been greeted by her friend's voicemail, which said that she was out of the office for a couple of days. The two messages had made her raise her eyebrows and wonder if they were away together. If so, hardly business.

Neil and Anna. Aidan and Nieve. Darcey and . . . Rocco and Francisco and Louis-Philippe and Jose and – just possibly – Jason White. A better deal surely, when all was said and done.

She took a bottle of white wine from the fridge and opened it. Then she turned on the TV and flicked through the channels. The relocation programme, where the English family were moving to Tuscany, was being repeated. She settled down to watch it again.

# Chapter 29

She arrived particularly early at the office so that she didn't have to run the gauntlet of InvestorCorp employees oohing and ahhing over her injuries. But as she stepped into the lift on her own, she couldn't help wishing that she'd waited until someone else was there to use it too. Her slight panic was momentary, though, and as she stepped out on to the sixth floor her only feeling was of relief at being back.

She began opening the pile of letters in her in-tray (it always amazed her how much physical post she still got) and glanced through some of the trade reports that had been left on her desk. As the morning wore on and her colleagues realised that she'd returned, they dropped by to see how she was.

'You'll be a company quiz question yourself one day,' said John Kenneally. 'Which employee gave the term Singapore Sling a new meaning?'

She laughed dutifully. John was the sixth person to have used the expression since she'd come in.

'You have my total sympathy,' Laura from the support team told her. 'I broke my wrist a few years ago and it's still not right.'

In fact, thought Darcey, it was amazing how many people in the company had broken a limb at some stage in their lives, and all of them had come to her to share their stories. It was nice, she realised, to know that they cared about her, but there were only so many times she could listen to tales of woe about broken arms and legs.

When the rush of people giving her their good wishes had eased off, she was able to devote some time to checking the hundreds of emails that had collected in her inbox. One name caught her eye and she double-clicked on it immediately.

'Hi', she read. 'I rang the company and they said you'd had an accident in Singapore! I hope it wasn't after dinner with me. Call me. Jason. PS Check with your guys on the funds side for some good news.'

She smiled and dialled the investment department.

'Yeah, we got twenty-five million in from Asia Holdings,' said Walter. 'Nice going, Darce. We also got ten apiece from three of your other contacts.'

She was beaming as she typed a reply to Jason thanking him for the funds and telling him that her accident had been minor but painful and that she hoped to get back to Singapore soon.

Her phone rang again. It was Douglas Lomax.

'Are you able to drop down to my office?' he asked. She felt her heart flutter. A summons from the managing director was always nerve-racking stuff, even though she knew that she'd done well and that he had nothing to complain about. Five minutes later she was sitting in the visitors' chair opposite him.

'You should have stayed out a bit longer,' he observed. 'You look as though you were run over by a truck.'

'It's the splint and the strapping,' she told him. 'Makes it appear much worse than it is. I'm on the mend.'

'Well I wanted to tell you how pleased we were with the result of your visit. It's really impressive stuff, Darcey.'

'Thank you.'

'Have you got the next trip planned?'

'Tokyo?' She grinned at him. 'Not yet. But I'm working on it. And I'll try not to throw myself down the stairs there.'

'That was unfortunate,' he said. 'But overall you've been great. Well done.'

They talked for a further ten minutes about her plans for Tokyo and again about her success in Singapore. If she'd been able, she would have skipped along the corridor afterwards. There was something really rewarding about doing a good job. It made her feel pleased with herself and pleased with the choices she'd made in her life.

She walked past Neil Lomond's office. The door was open and it was still empty.

'He's back later this afternoon,' called Jenni, who saw her peeking inside. 'Gosh, Darcey, you're still a bit of a mess, aren't you?'

'Doesn't matter,' said Darcey. 'I feel like the twenty-five million dollars that came in from Asia Holdings!'

She didn't feel like going back to her desk yet. She was still fizzing with self-satisfaction, so she dropped in on the investment department and chatted a little more to them about the funds from Singapore, then wandered down to Anna Sweeney's office to see if her friend had returned.

But the door was closed and Anna was clearly still on leave,

With Neil? The thought nagged at her once again. She'd told Anna that she'd be happy for her to have a relationship with Neil, and of course, she was – but she was surprised at the sudden feeling of envy that grabbed her.

It wasn't envy that Anna might be dating her ex-husband. It was envy at the idea of her friend in a relationship while she wasn't. Until recently Darcey had been secretly quite proud of the fact that she didn't do real relationships and that she was the one in control of when and where she saw her male friends. Even Robert, the last Irish guy she'd dated, hadn't got close to her, either physically or emotionally. He'd lived in Donegal, which was over two hundred kilometres away, and therefore their time together was almost as fleeting as her time with some of her continental men. But in the last couple of months she'd begun to remember what it was like to feel emotionally close to someone. And even though her experiences hadn't worked out, it was a feeling she was starting to miss.

Right now, standing outside Anna's office, she suddenly wanted to be the person she'd been before. Not the uneasy, awkward Darcey who hadn't made the most of her appearance and had been hopeless with every man she'd met before Aidan Clarke. But the Darcey who'd fallen deeply in love and known what it was like to completely trust another person. She'd been unlucky that Aidan hadn't been the right person to trust, that after him she hadn't been able to trust anyone. She knew that had messed up her view of relationships. But it had saved her a lot of heartache too. It was just that for some unknown reason she was beginning to wonder whether that was really such a good thing.

She shook her head to dislodge the conflicting thoughts competing for her attention. Then she went back to her office, replied to her emails and worked without a break until two o'clock.

It was the rumble of her stomach that made her realise the time. She pushed her keyboard to one side and picked up her bag.

I'm completely over the lift thing, she realised as she limped out on to the ground floor. I didn't even think about it that time.

'Hi, Darcey, good to see you back. How're you feeling?' Sally, the receptionist, smiled at her.

'It looks worse than it is now,' replied Darcey. 'My ankle is a million times better and I'm getting a lighter splint fitted tomorrow.'

'It must have been awful, having it happen so far away.'

'The pain was awful,' agreed Darcey. 'But the treatment was great.'

'And I heard that you've got loads of new business.'

'Things worked out pretty well.' Darcey nodded.

'I think you're brilliant.' Sally's tone was confiding. 'You're my role model, actually.'

'Oh.' Darcey looked at her in surprise.

'I know I'm not qualified or anything, but I'm thinking of studying at night,' said Sally. 'Y'see, I want to move on from reception. I'd really like a job like yours.'

'Good for you,' said Darcey.

'I want people to think of me as smart,' said Sally. She

flicked her glossy brunette curls behind her ears. 'People here think I'm good at my job, but mostly they think I'm kinda good-looking.'

Darcey grinned. 'That's because you are.'

'Yes, but I'd rather they thought I was clever, like you. Anyone can make themselves look good but not everyone can land new customers and make money and use their brain.'

'If you're that determined, then I'm sure you'll do well.' Darcey was surprised but impressed by the receptionist's vehemence.

'I hope so,' said Sally.

'Well look, if there's anything I can do to help you . . . advice, whatever, just ask,' said Darcey.

'Thanks.' Sally looked pleased and Darcey smiled at her.

'I'll see you later,' she said. 'I'm just heading out to pick up a sandwich.'

'You should've ordered a delivery,' observed Sally.

'It's not far to the deli,' said Darcey. 'And I probably need a bit of fresh air.'

She walked slowly towards the revolving door, then stopped.

'Hello,' said Neil, who was on the way in. 'You're back.'

'Yes,' she said, surprised to see him. 'I came back this morning.'

'And you're OK?' His eyes flickered over her.

'Fine,' she said. 'I'm just out to get a sandwich.'

'Late lunch?' He glanced at his watch.

'Catching up,' she told him.

'Let's go.' He grinned at her. 'You need more than a

sandwich to keep your strength up. Let's go and get something to eat.'

'Oh, but I've loads of stuff still to do,' she protested. 'There are a million queries—'

'Darcey, cut loose, for God's sake,' he told her. 'Besides, I want to talk to you about the business part of your trip.'

'In that case . . .' She shrugged helplessly and followed him outside.

He turned towards the Harbourmaster restaurant and she fell into step beside him, enjoying the feeling of the sun slanting on to her face and the faint whiff of river air coming from the Liffey.

At this time of the day the restaurant was beginning to empty, and they got a table near the window, overlooking the water.

'So how've you been doing?' asked Neil after they'd ordered.

'Pretty good,' she replied. 'I went back to Galway and Maman did her best to feed me up.'

He grinned. 'I liked your mother. She had a good attitude towards food.'

Darcey smiled faintly. 'Volatile,' she amended. 'She loves cooking, of course. But the pair of us constantly bemoan our tendency to slap on the pounds.'

'I think you've lost weight since the accident.'

'You're wrong,' she said. 'I might have dropped a couple of pounds at first, but Maman feels that hot chocolate with real cream is an essential part of the healing process, so I reckon I'm heavier now than I've ever been.'

He chuckled.

Why are we talking like this? she wondered. He doesn't care about me and my weight and Maman and drinking hot chocolate! We're supposed to be having a professional conversation.

'Sorry?' She realised that he'd changed the subject.

'I asked about Asia Holdings,' he said. 'You seem to have struck gold there.'

She felt her face flush slightly as the image of Jason White came into her mind.

'Darcey?'

'Sorry,' she said again and began to talk about Asia Holdings, referring only once to its fund manager as a man who was very clued up on the technical aspects of the portfolios.

Their conversation was strictly about business all during the remainder of their lunch.

'Peter Henson sends his regards,' said Neil as he ordered coffee for both of them. 'He said he knew you'd strike it lucky in Asia.'

'When were you talking to him?'

'Yesterday. I was in New York.'

'Oh.' Not with Anna, then, she thought. Unless her friend had gone to New York with him. She didn't feel able to ask.

'So what else did you get up to in Galway?' His question was easy and relaxed.

'Not much,' she said. 'Although my mother met this guy . . .'

She broke off in confusion, aware that she'd been about to offer him some personal information, as well as realising that talking about Malachy Finan and Rathfinan Castle would inevitably lead on to her mentioning Nieve and Aidan's wedding. And of course the moment she thought of Aidan again, she felt the butterflies go crazy in her stomach.

'You OK?' he asked curiously. 'Your mother OK?'

'Sure, sure,' she said hastily. 'I . . .'

'So go on, tell me.' His eyes were open wide. 'Your mum has met someone?'

She told him about the castle. There was no point in keeping silent. And then, even though she hadn't meant to, she told him that she'd seen Aidan.

She recognised the expression in his eyes as she spoke. She'd seen it before, the very first time she'd spoken Aidan Clarke's name to him.

The memory of that night, the night she'd accused him of having an affair with Jessica Hammond, was still clear. Neil had been dismissive of Aidan as a complete shit but later, after he'd told her that he loved her; and after he'd put his arm around her and told her that they just needed to work it out a bit; and after they'd made love together in their luxurious king-sized bed, he'd asked about him again. And when she'd explained that she'd never really got over Aidan, she saw a flicker of hurt in his eyes which was immediately replaced by concern. She'd felt guilty about causing it. But she couldn't help it. Following her upending of the plate in his lap on the day she'd discovered him having lunch with Melinda McIntyre, he'd been understandably furious. Yet he'd been worried too, telling her that she had issues to resolve but that he wanted to help her to do it. She knew that he wanted to help her. But she hadn't wanted to be helped. She'd wanted to lose herself in the misery of the betrayal that she believed had ruined her life.

'I love you.' She remembered him saying the words to her. 'I want this to work. But I can't live with someone who thinks she's in love with another man.'

'Then you can't live with me,' she'd replied. 'And I can't live with you either.'

It had been excruciating. She'd known she was hurting him but she hadn't cared. Because she'd thought it was a good thing that someone else should feel what she felt.

I was horrible, she thought now as she glanced across the table. Self-centred and miserable and horrible, and I didn't deserve him.

'It was accidental,' she explained now about her encounter with Aidan. 'I was at the castle and he turned up.'

'And you spoke to him?'

She nodded. 'But only barely. He was there with Nieve's father, checking it out. I wondered why he wasn't there with her.'

Neil's eyes darkened. 'You were thinking to yourself that maybe they don't love each other after all? That because he was there on his own it's a sign that their marriage is doomed?'

'Don't be stupid.' But Darcey blushed.

'I can read you like a book,' he said.

'I did wonder,' she told him defensively. 'I mean, most couples check out the venue together.'

'Darcey, they've been together for ten years.'

'I know, I know. But . . .'

'Are you still thinking of going to the wedding?' he demanded.

'I accepted the invitation.'

'Oh, for God's sake, woman!'

'But my wrist will still be in a splint, although my ankle should be OK by then. Even so I probably won't be able to wear my decent shoes and I don't know if there's any point in going.'

'You vain bitch.'

She'd never heard him speak with such suppressed anger before.

'You want to go to this wedding and look gorgeous and somehow make him realise that he made a terrible mistake in leaving you? You want some kind of Hollywood movie moment where he jilts her at the altar to marry you instead? But you don't think it'll happen with your arm in a sling? Is that it?'

'No . . .' she protested feebly.

'I don't know why I waste my time on you,' he snapped. 'You were a selfish bitch when I married you and you're a self-centred bitch now. And I don't know what it is in me that ever thought there was something different about you. There's nothing about you that I can possibly even identify with.'

He got up and pushed his chair back from the table.

'Let me know when you're going to Tokyo,' he said. 'You can email me.'

She sat and watched him leave, stunned at his outburst. She'd never seen him so angry before in her life, even when she'd been at her worst.

How dare he? She could feel her entire body shaking with rage. How dare he say things like that about her? She wasn't self-centred and she wasn't selfish and she wasn't a bitch. Hadn't Sally called her a role model? Didn't everyone want to be like her? Wasn't she the person who'd just enhanced Neil's own career by bringing home the bacon from Singapore? The nerve of him to talk to her like that!

The waitress came over to the table.

'Would you like the bill?' she asked.

And he'd gone and left her with the damn bill too, thought Darcey as she entered her pin number on the credit-card machine. She'd been feeling guilty about seeing that look in his eyes. Now she didn't have to feel guilty at all.

But as she walked back to the office she realised that she didn't feel guilty. She felt ashamed. Because he'd seen something in her that she hadn't seen herself. And she didn't like it one little bit.

# Chapter 30

The evening of the wedding rehearsal was at the end of yet another glorious summer's day. Nieve was relieved and happy that the sun was still shining and she hoped fervently that it would continue to shine for at least another twenty-four hours. The weather forecast was good and the barometer in her parents' house was fixed at sunny, so she was in an optimistic mood when Lorelei called to the house. The wedding-planner had also brought a sample of the tropical flower arrangements for the tables, as well as a magnificent John Rocha vase which she gave to Nieve.

'A present from Happy Ever Afters,' she told her. 'You've been my best bride ever.'

'Thanks. If I am your best bride it's because you were so totally professional. Everything is perfect.'

'I like to exceed expectations.' Lorelei grinned and re-adjusted her huge sunglasses on the top of her head. 'Anyway, don't worry about anything for the rest of today. This is all casual and relaxed. The restaurant is ready for you later – I checked. No problems there. What time are your brides-maids coming?'

'In an hour or so,' said Nieve. 'Bernie will be here any minute to do my make-up. At least this way we get to iron out any problems before tomorrow.'

'She's good,' said Lorelei. 'I know you said you were a bit worried because she's a friend of a friend or whatever, but I'm adding her to my list.'

'I have total faith in you,' said Nieve. 'Which is strange, because I normally don't have total faith in anyone!'

Lorelei laughed and hugged her. 'I can't wait for tomorrow,' she confided. 'It's going to be so brilliant and utterly wonderful. And I know that tonight is going to be great fun and that all your guests are going to have the most wonderful time. As well as loving those beautiful gifts you're giving them.'

'I hope so.' Nieve hadn't yet told Lorelei that she was worrying about Darcey McGonigle's presence. She hadn't explained to the wedding-planner that her ex-friend was a possible loose cannon among the guests.

Maybe Aidan had been right about her all along. Last night he'd asked Nieve again whether they couldn't just un-issue the invitation to Darcey, something which she told him was not only impractical and impossible but unheard of.

'You were right, though,' she admitted as she snuggled up to him despite the heat. 'Asking her wasn't one of my brightest ideas.'

'You had your reasons.' Aidan sounded tense. 'But they were the wrong ones.'

Nieve realised that the whole Darcey issue was troubling Aidan much more than he was letting on. And it worried her slightly. Why was he so concerned about his ex-girlfriend being there? What could he possibly know about her that Nieve didn't?

'There is one more thing,' she said now to Lorelei. 'It's about one of the guests.'

Lorelei frowned as Nieve explained the situation to her.

'Jeez, woman,' she said, 'don't you think your wedding day is stressful enough without worrying about lunatic ex-girlfriends?'

'I know, I know.' Nieve could feel herself getting more and more panicked. 'Look, it's probably hard for you to understand this, but I asked her to prove something to her. That me and Aidan are right for each other. I wanted her to see that. But now I'm thinking that maybe Aidan is right and she's a complete space cadet who could do anything!'

'I won't let her,' said Lorelei grimly. 'I'll keep close tabs on her and I promise you that the most you might hear is a tiny squeak from her as I wrestle her to the floor.'

Nieve chuckled nervously. 'I shouldn't have asked her. It was crazy.'

'I'm glad you did something silly,' Lorelei said. 'You're far too efficient and sensible and it's nice to see that you have a warm and fuzzy side to you too.'

'Warm and fuzzy?'

'Asking your old friend, whatever the reason, is kind of warm and fuzzy.'

'No it's not,' said Nieve. 'I asked her for selfish reasons and it's coming back to haunt me.'

'It won't. She won't,' promised Lorelei. 'Now there's the doorbell. Sounds like Bernie has arrived.'

\* \* \*

The church rehearsal went off smoothly. The old building looked warm and peaceful in the late-evening sun as the reflected colours of the stained-glass windows coloured the marble floors. The only drama was the ear-splitting clatter of the motor-mower cutting the grass outside and drowning out the words of the priest. But, he assured Nieve and Aidan, there'd be no problem with motor-mowers or anything else the following day, and everyone would hear them exchange their vows.

Afterwards, as they stood in the church grounds before heading to the restaurant, Murphy and his partner Duke (not yet wearing their green suits) came up to Nieve and hugged her and told her that it was going to be the best wedding ever. And that they'd scooted past the castle in their hire car and wasn't it just fabulous? And that Ireland was everything they'd ever imagined and so, so pretty, and wasn't she crazy not to spend every summer here?

Courtney and Mischa were blown away by the beauty of the Galway countryside too and the fact that there were real sheep and cows in the fields.

'What did you think would be in the fields?' Nieve demanded.

'No idea,' said Courtney. 'But I've never seen a real live sheep before.'

Aidan sniggered at this and the American girl dug him in the ribs.

'Why should I?' she demanded, 'I live in Silicon Valley. We nurture computer chips instead.'

They were still laughing and joking by the time they got to the restaurant, where the friends who were coming to the dinner but who hadn't been needed at the church should by now have all gathered. Like the church, the restaurant was an old building that had been lovingly restored and was equally warm and welcoming, with polished oak floors and carefully set tables.

The first person Nieve saw when they arrived was Carol Jansen. She had to do a double-take to be sure it was her old schoolfriend, because Carol looked a million times more glamorous than she'd ever done in her younger days, but when she realised it was, she shrieked with pleasure and wrapped her arms around her.

'I'm so glad you came,' she said. 'I hope you have a great time.'

'It's great to see you,' said Carol. 'Rosa is here too. She's in the bar area with her husband. You wouldn't actually recognise her. She looks very . . . well, motherly.'

'And Darcey?' asked Nieve tightly. 'Did she come?'

Carol nodded. Darcey had since filled her in on the gory details of the bust-up, and Carol had sympathised with her, but seeing the expression on Nieve's face, now she felt some sympathy for her other friend too.

'Yes, she's here,' she replied. 'Poor old Darcey, she fell down a flight of stairs a couple of weeks ago and broke her wrist and wrenched her ankle. She's feeling a bit put out at having her wrist in a splint and is still hobbling around.'

'Oh.'

'She nipped out to the chemist to get some painkillers,' said Carol easily. 'She found the journey a bit jolting. I know the roads are better these days, but you know how it is, the car seems to find every pothole there is.'

'Right.' Nieve nodded. 'Well, why don't we go inside and get seated?'

She moved into the dining area of the restaurant, where the owner and his wife were waiting to greet her. She was feeling marginally more relaxed. Darcey was hurt. Darcey was on painkillers. Darcey wouldn't do anything silly. Somehow she wasn't expecting her to tonight. She was more worried about tomorrow.

Darcey was in the pub next door to the restaurant. Needing painkillers had been an excuse for escaping from Rosa's incessant chatter and from her sudden overwhelming dread at the prospect of seeing Nieve again. She hadn't wanted to be there when her former friend arrived and she'd pleaded an aching arm as an excuse to disappear for a while.

Now she was sitting in the almost deserted bar, watching Sky News on the TV in the corner but not really registering the stories of a bomb in Baghdad, the snap election called in Italy or the breaking news of a new corporate scandal in America.

Neil had been wrong when he'd asked her if she thought that Aidan would dump Nieve at the altar. In her innermost fantasies, Darcey had wondered whether on seeing her again in the restaurant he wouldn't just desert Nieve there and then. She knew that he'd been shocked by seeing her at the castle. His reaction to the possibility of Stephen seeing them together had been bizarre. He was clearly nervous about something, and it had made her wonder and wonder whether everything in the Nieve and Aidan rose garden was really all that wonderful. But the longer she sat on the bar stool with the glass of white wine in front of her, the more ridiculous she knew she was being.

Aidan had left her for Nieve. He'd made a choice and it had been the right one. He'd been with Nieve for a long time. Clearly he cared about her. He was going to marry her. Therefore he must love her. In which case she, Darcey, was the only one who was confused about her feelings. And this confusion had only started since hearing about the wedding in the first place, uprooting old memories and making past history seem important again. The past was the past. She'd moved on. Sure, she'd made mistakes along the way. But so did everyone. And there were loads of great things in her life. So she needed to get a grip, go into the dinner and somehow find the closure that she realised she really wanted after all.

She took another sip of the now warm white wine and made a face.

She hoped that Nieve really was going over the top with the celebrations and was serving some decent champagne!

Nieve saw her walk into the restaurant and felt her stomach tighten. Darcey looked great and although, Nieve decided critically, the neutral-coloured trouser suit she was wearing wasn't exactly glamorous, it was well cut and fitted her figure perfectly. She'd never seen Darcey wearing her hair in a tight chignon like that before either, but it suited her. She looked more closely at her friend and realised that she was walking with a slight limp. And as Darcey moved through the room, Nieve could see that her arm was in a splint too. She winced on Darcey's behalf as she saw her slide uncomfortably into her seat at the same table as Rosa and Carol. She watched as she picked up the small package containing her silver locket and opened it. She saw Darcey's surprised expression as she took out the locket and turned it over and over in her fingers.

She was more confident, thought Nieve critically. She'd lost that perpetually anxious look (though perhaps she was too far away to see the anxious look!). She was a different person. Nieve realised that she'd been expecting to see the old Darcey – the Darcey of Aidan's birthday night – wearing the wrong clothes and the wrong hairstyle and out of sorts with herself. The Darcey she was looking at now might have been in the wars, but she was clearly much more comfortable in herself. Nieve had always been on at Darcey to relax more, to be comfortable with who she was. She'd often felt that Darcey needed her to show her the way. It was good to see that she'd done it; it was a bit of a blow to see that she'd done it all by herself.

Nieve shot a sideways glance at Aidan and realised that he too was looking at the table where Rosa and Carol and Darcey were sitting. She swallowed hard. She wanted to know what he was thinking. But she was suddenly afraid of what it might possibly be.

'Why haven't you kept in touch with anyone?' Rosa demanded as Darcey buttered some Guinness bread. 'We've heard about you from time to time, of course. You and Nieve both – hotshots the pair of you.'

'I think Nieve has outdone me by a factor of about a zillion,' said Darcey mildly. 'I heard someone say that when whatever company she works for floated on the stock exchange the employees all became millionaires. Sadly, I'm miles away from that kind of money.'

'She does look incredibly well off,' agreed Carol. 'There's a kind of wealthy glow about her, isn't there? And this whole do must be costing her an absolute fortune. But each to their own, Rosa. Haven't you got a wonderful family?'

Darcey shot Carol a grateful look.

'And I wouldn't change them for any money.' Rosa sniffed. 'She was always into it, of course. Remember her selling those *How To Blag Your Way Through Your Exams* videos! But is she happy?'

Carol laughed. 'If she isn't happy today, I don't know when she possibly could be.'

Rosa sniffed again but conceded that Nieve Stapleton had struck lucky and that nobody could deny it.

'But why did *you* lose touch with her?' she continued to press Darcey. 'I mean, we were all friends but circumstances made us drift apart. You two were so close.'

Darcey shrugged though her heart was racing in her chest. 'Different lives.'

'It's a shame,' said Rosa. 'Friends are very important. If it wasn't for the other women in the mother and child group I'm in, I'd lose my mind completely.'

Darcey half listened as Rosa chattered on and on but she was watching Nieve and Aidan. He looked as handsome as ever in a stylish lightweight suit, his blond hair clearly newly cut and his pale shirt accentuating his California tan. Nieve was utterly stunning. Her dark hair was caught back in a jewelled clip that glittered a thousand colours in the light.

*Sheila O'Flanagan*

(Darcey was certain the stones in the clip were precious ones. She wished she could wear something like that herself but she knew she'd lose a jewelled hair ornament almost immediately!) She was wearing a deep red dress that complemented her skin tone and her dark eyes, and her fragile strappy shoes went perfectly with it. The rubies and diamonds at her throat and in her ears glittered fierily. She looked, thought Darcey enviously, a million dollars. Which evidently she was. At least.

Aidan would never leave her. She was too beautiful and too successful. And there was a spark between them. Darcey recognised it. She'd seen it the night of his birthday but it hadn't registered. But she knew that she'd felt that spark herself once before too. Only not with Aidan. It had been there between herself and Neil Lomond. It was a spark of sexual chemistry, of mutual attraction. A spark which, in the case of Aidan and Nieve, was still as bright as ever. She suddenly wished she hadn't been so daft as to let their spark put out her own.

After the dessert, Aidan got up to speak while wine waiters filled everyone's glass with champagne.

'I know that I've got to talk again tomorrow,' he told them. 'Though in that case it will be as Mr Nieve Stapleton.'

There was an amused murmur from the guests.

'But tonight on behalf of Nieve and myself I just wanted to welcome all our closest friends and those of you who've travelled to be with us and thank you for coming along. It means a lot to both of us. We want you to eat, drink and be merry – though not so much that you're too hungover tomorrow, because it promises to be a fantastic day.

470

'We'd like to say that it's great to be back in Ireland at last and I'm personally hoping that I can keep Nieve away from that great job of hers in Ennco for an extra week or two so that we can reacquaint ourselves with our country. Thanks again. This is to you, our friends!'

He raised his glass.

Rosa nudged Darcey, who was frowning as she looked at Aidan.

'It's a toast,' she hissed.

Darcey blinked and raised her own glass. She sipped the champagne, which was perfectly chilled and tasted wonderful. Nieve was, of course, serving excellent champagne.

But she was still frowning as she replaced the glass on the snow-white damask tablecloth.

'What's the matter?' asked Carol.

'I . . . I'm not sure,' she said slowly.

'You've gone into a complete daze,' muttered Rosa. 'Just like you used to do in school.'

'Yes, but that was when you were trying to figure something out,' added Carol. She looked anxiously at Darcey. 'Is there a problem?'

Darcey's brow furrowed even more and she glanced over at Nieve, who was looking at Aidan and laughing happily.

'Maybe you should go outside.' Carol was worried at the expression on Darcey's face. On the car journey to Galway Darcey had jokily commented that Aidan and Nieve hadn't known what a touchpaper they were lighting when they'd invited her to the dinner. And she'd laughed that they'd probably asked her to this evening's event so that if she was going to lose her head and behave badly it wouldn't be as

471

bad as doing something crazy at the actual wedding. Now Carol was beginning to wonder if Darcey did, in fact, have some unpleasant surprise for both of them up her sleeve.

'No . . .' Darcey was still looking up at the top table, where Aidan had just kissed Nieve on the lips.

'Hey, Darce!' Rosa was firm. 'Come back to earth.'

Darcey blinked a couple of times and looked at both her friends.

'It's what he said.' She spoke slowly. 'Aidan. About Nieve's job.'

'What about it?' asked Carol.

'The company she works for.'

'Any Co?' said Rosa.

'No,' said Darcey. 'Ennco. That's what he said.'

Carol nodded. 'And?'

'Well, when I was in the bar next door earlier—'

'What were you doing in the bar next door?' interrupted Rosa.

'I stopped off for a drink before coming back here,' admitted Darcey. 'I felt . . . I just needed to be on my own for a minute.'

Carol squeezed her arm slightly, while Rosa looked surprised.

'But that's irrelevant.' Darcey looked at her old friends, and then at Nieve and Aidan, who had stopped kissing and were laughing and joking at the far table. 'It's the company. I heard the company's name.'

'So?' Carol looked puzzled.

'It was on Sky News,' said Darcey. 'It was breaking news, some kind of corporate scandal in the States. I wasn't paying much attention but I watched out for the company name because I wondered if it was one that we did business with ourselves. It wasn't. I'd never heard of it. But it was called Ennco.'

Carol shrugged. 'Probably not the same one,' she said. 'Or maybe you got the name wrong.'

'I don't think so.' Darcey looked concerned. 'The name was flashed up on the scrolling headlines underneath. It quite clearly said Ennco. What they were showing on the TV was the company's offices being raided and the chief executive being arrested. They said that the share price had collapsed.'

The three women looked at each other and then at the top table. Nieve was sipping champagne and looking every inch the most important person in the room.

'D'you think she knows about it?' asked Rosa.

'Hardly.' Carol breathed out slowly. 'Oh my God. That can't be good news for her.'

'Maybe it won't affect her too much,' said Rosa doubtfully. 'I mean, she's an employee. So she might lose her job. But obviously they're well enough off . . .'

'It might be OK,' agreed Darcey. 'But it might not.'

'Should we say anything?' wondered Carol. 'I mean, it's the day before her wedding. Does she actually need to know?'

'And if she does, is one of us going to tell her?' asked Darcey grimly.

She was still wondering what to do when she saw Nieve walking purposefully towards her. They'd just finished coffee and people had gathered into smaller groups, while Rosa and Carol had both gone to the bathroom, leaving the seat next to Darcey empty. Nieve was making her way towards it. Darcey held her breath.

Nieve had been thinking about this meeting for years, but she'd only allowed herself to acknowledge that now. She'd been thinking of the right thing to say to get rid of the guilt that she'd been carrying around with her. Because even if she'd been cool and calculating about the way she'd nabbed Aidan Clarke, even though she'd been absolutely sure that he was the wrong person for her friend at the time, she'd known that Darcey would be devastated. She wanted to tell her that she'd done it all the wrong way. That she should have acted differently even if the outcome had been the same. She wanted to say sorry. But that wasn't something she'd ever been good at.

'You came,' she said to Darcey as she sat down beside her.

'Yes.'

'I wasn't sure you would.'

'I wasn't sure about it either.'

'You look well.'

'Under the circumstances.' Darcey held up her splinted wrist.

'Car accident?' hazarded Nieve.

'Fell downstairs,' said Darcey succinctly.

'I was thinking that you'd changed a lot . . . but if you're still falling over things, maybe not.'

'I've changed enough,' said Darcey. 'And you too. You've become really successful.'

As she said the words, and as Nieve began to talk about

her role in Ennco in reply, Darcey was thinking about the news story on the TV and the fact that her ex-friend, as compliance director (Nieve had sounded inordinately proud as she said the words), would be directly in the firing line. She wondered whether Nieve could possibly know anything about the unfolding scandal, whether she was already aware of irregularities in the company's accounts. On the one hand the idea of Nieve cutting corners wouldn't have surprised her in the slightest. On the other . . . she didn't believe that Nieve would knowingly defraud anyone. And she didn't know whether she should say anything to her or not. Well, she couldn't say anything. Not here. Not now. Not without seeming to be a complete bitch for ruining her friend's wedding. Which, she suddenly remembered, was something she'd thought about doing when she'd first received the invitation.

'But you still go into trances, I see,' said Nieve.

Darcey focused again on her friend and shrugged. What should she do? What should she say?

'If you were a bit more grounded, then maybe you would have as much as me, if not more,' said Nieve.

'Oh?'

'Face it, Darcey. You were smart. You were clever. You could've come to the States and made your fortune.'

'I rather think I would have been in the way,' said Darcey wryly. 'You'd gone with my ex-boyfriend, after all.'

'Look, I want to explain . . .'

'Please don't,' said Darcey. 'Please don't tell me that it was love at first sight and all that sort of stuff. I don't believe in it and I don't believe that people get carried away and can't help themselves and I don't believe that you couldn't have stepped back and told Aidan that no matter what you felt for each other he was with me.'

'Look, I wish . . . I wish I'd behaved differently. But once he met me he didn't want to be with you any more,' Nieve told her. 'So what would have been the point?'

Darcey nodded. 'You're right,' she said. 'There wouldn't have been any point. He was going to marry me but he changed his mind. He was entitled to make that decision.' She'd been going to leave it at that, but in the end she couldn't help herself. 'Let's hope he doesn't change it again.'

Nieve stared at her and was about to reply, but Carol, who'd just returned to the table, interrupted them to tell Nieve that she'd never looked more fabulous and that everything was marvellous and to thank her for the beautiful gift of the lockets . . . and by the time she'd said all that, Darcey had disappeared.

She leaned against the brick wall and waited for her body to stop shaking and the pain in her ankle to subside. She thought that she'd behaved as well as she could under the circumstances. She hadn't screamed or shouted or said any of the things she'd so often dreamed of saying to Nieve Stapleton. OK, so she'd got in one bitchy dig, but it hadn't degenerated any further. So all in all, she'd got out with her dignity intact.

Which was probably a reasonable result.

\*    \*    \*

'Darcey.'

She turned around at the sound of his voice and her heart began to beat faster again.

'Aidan.'

'Are you OK?' he asked.

'Why wouldn't I be?'

'You and Nieve . . .'

'We spoke.' She shrugged. 'It wasn't particularly friendly, but I didn't punch her and she didn't punch me, so you don't have anything to worry about.'

'I didn't say anything to her about meeting you at the castle. Did you?'

'Keeping things from her, are you? Afraid of her?'

'Don't be stupid.'

'Oh, Aidan, you know me. Always a bit stupid.'

'Not really,' he said.

'Over the important things.' She sighed. 'I was stupid about us and stupid about Nieve and stupid about loads of things that other people seem not to be stupid about at all. I thought you loved me and I was wrong and I let myself be blinded by that.'

'You weren't wrong,' said Aidan.

Her heart missed a beat and she stared at him.

'I never tell Nieve this, but I did love you,' he said. 'Not enough, Darcey, in the end. But I loved you. We had good times together. You mattered to me, but we were very young. It wouldn't have lasted.'

Her heartbeat returned to normal and she nodded slowly.

'I know. Nobody marries the first person they fall in love with. That's why I'm stupid. I thought we were going to.'

'Not that it matters,' said Aidan, 'but I nearly asked you.'

She was going to say that she knew, that she'd seen the ring. But she suddenly realised that saying that would probably be stupid too. But she could see it now in her memory, nestling in the box, her dreams and hopes with it. The wrong dreams. The wrong hopes.

'And now you're marrying Nieve instead,' she said eventually.

'Took us a while to get around to it,' he admitted. 'But yeah.'

'I was surprised you invited me.'

He looked at her awkwardly. 'Her idea. Not mine.'

'Thought that.' Darcey smiled suddenly. 'Showing off?'

He looked surprised. 'Probably.'

'Though maybe it was more than that,' said Darcey. 'Maybe she just wanted me to know that you and her were for real.'

Aidan looked surprised at Darcey's accurate take on Nieve's intentions.

'Why did you accept?' he asked. 'I was really surprised at that. In fact I told her not to ask you because I was afraid you might try to – to ruin the day.'

'Why would you think that?'

'I heard you hadn't dealt with the situation very well. I thought you might be holding a grudge.'

Darcey smiled at him. 'I can't hold a grudge that long,' she said. 'I came because I was curious to see both of you, and I guess . . .'

He looked at her expectantly. He was still gorgeous, she thought. He really was. Maybe even more attractive now than when she'd first known him. She was standing close to him and she could even sense the scent of the evening air on his skin. Once he'd been the love of her life. For a long time she'd continued to believe that. She'd wanted to believe it because losing the love of her life explained why she'd been so bad at relationships ever since. But no matter what she might have wanted to believe, there wasn't the spark between them that she'd seen between him and Nieve. She could sense that too. There wasn't even the spark between them that she'd had with Neil. She couldn't believe that she hadn't realised that before now. Aidan had been her first love, but that didn't mean the love of her life after all.

'What?' He was waiting for her to continue, but her attention had been caught by the sight of someone walking out of the bar next door. And suddenly the Sky News story came rushing back to her and she frowned.

'Darcey?' He knew that something was wrong.

Should she tell him? Would telling him seem like the act of revenge that he'd been anticipating? Would she actually get satisfaction out of it? Would it be better just to walk away and let them find out for themselves sometime later?

Maybe she'd got it wrong. And if she told him, he'd laugh at her, because if it wasn't Nieve's company after all, he'd feel sorry for her for being so pathetic as to want it to be. For her to be holding a grudge after all. Only she wasn't holding a grudge. And for the first time in her life, she actually wanted to be wrong.

She wished she could trust her own judgement. But then it had always been hopeless when it came to Aidan and Nieve.

'I don't want you to think that I . . .'

'Oh, for Chrissake, just tell me,' he said impatiently.

So she did. And when she'd finished speaking, she thought he was going to faint.

'What the hell's going on out here?' They both looked up as Nieve pushed open the restaurant door. Aidan and Darcey, who had been standing close to each other, sprang apart. 'Trying to persuade him, are you, that you were hard done by ten years ago? Trying to win him back?'

'Don't be silly.' Darcey shot a worried look at Aidan. 'We were talking about—'

'Oh, I can guess!' Nieve's eyes sparked with rage. 'You were telling him how I was really a horrible person and how I somehow tricked him into thinking he loved me and how he'd be so, so, so much better off with you than me – even now, you pathetic wretch, when he's going to marry me!'

'Nieve, you're getting the wrong end of the stick completely—'

'I never really figured out why we were friends.' Nieve carried on as though Darcey hadn't spoken. 'You needed me, though, didn't you? 'Cos you were lonely. You didn't have any friends until I came along. But you never accepted that. You always looked down on me. From that first day, when you told me that I wouldn't be able to read your damn French book. I was awed by you, a kid reading in another language! I thought you'd be good to know. But nobody was really good enough or smart enough for you, and don't think I didn't know that you let me get more marks than you at maths and English sometimes. That you deliberately made mistakes so that I could feel better. I knew you patronised me, but I knew too that I'd do better than you in the end. And I did. I got the man and I got the job and I know that inviting you to my wedding could be seen as rubbing your nose in it a bit, but you know what, I just don't care.'

'Nieve . . .' Darcey was stunned at what her former friend was saying.

'My mother was always on at me. "Be like Darcey. Work like Darcey. Darcey's such a clever girl." Well, who's the clever one now?'

'Nieve, honey,' said Aidan. 'There might be a bit of a problem.'

'A problem!' She hadn't meant to shriek but she couldn't help herself. 'What sort of problem? Don't tell me, don't dare tell me that this bitch has somehow persuaded you that we should turn back the clock! She was always a conniving cow.'

'How dare you!' This time Darcey was angry at her. 'Me conniving? Me? You were the conniving one, pretending to be my friend, telling me that Aidan wasn't the one for me and then running off with him instead.'

'Get over yourself,' snapped Nieve. 'They all leave you in the end. Even your husband left you, and that was hardly my fault!'

'You bitch!' Darcey raised her right arm as though to hit Nieve, but Aidan caught it. She gasped at his touch and turned to him.

'Stop it,' he said. 'What d'you think you're doing, the

pair of you! There are more important things for us to worry about right now.'

'You were going to hit me,' said Nieve in astonishment. 'I can't believe it. You were going to hit me.'

None of them had noticed that the rest of the guests had clustered near the foyer and were craning to listen to what was going on. Then Lorelei marched out and stood between Nieve and Darcey, causing Aidan to let go of Darcey's arm.

'I advised Nieve against asking you to this wedding,' Lorelei told Darcey. 'And if she's too well-mannered to ask you to leave, I'll do it for her. I have to insist that you go, and go now. Nieve doesn't need this sort of problem.'

'It's not Darcey who's the problem,' said Aidan. 'Not now.'

Nieve stared at Aidan in horror, while Lorelei's eyes darkened and she looked at the prospective groom with dismay.

'It's you?' she asked.

'Aidan.' Nieve's face was paper-white. 'Don't tell me . . . She can't have . . . changed your mind.'

'No.' Aidan turned to Nieve. 'It's nothing to do with the wedding at all. It's Ennco.'

'Ennco?' Nieve was taken aback. 'What about Ennco?'

'Mike Horgan has just been arrested,' said Aidan. 'The share price has collapsed. The story is on the news.'

'What!' It was supposed to be an exclamation but it came out as a whisper. Nieve's tone was filled with disbelief.

'I saw it on TV,' said Darcey.

'Is there a TV in the restaurant?' asked Nieve faintly.

'No. In the bar. Next door.'

'Let me see for myself.' Nieve's voice was stronger.

'It's probably all a mistake. Something you cooked up, McGonigle, to upset me.'

'No,' said Darcey. 'It isn't.' And she stood back to let Nieve walk past her and into the bar.

# Chapter 31

By now all the guests at the rehearsal dinner had realised that something was brewing and they piled out of the restaurant and into the street, following Nieve as she strode into the bar and demanded that the TV be tuned to Sky News again.

'We're watching the sports,' said a man sitting on a bar stool.

'I don't care what you're watching,' said Nieve. 'I want to watch Sky News.'

'You can't just come in here and tell us what to do,' said the barman.

Nieve looked around impatiently. There were only half a dozen people in the bar.

'A drink for everyone on me,' she said. 'And one for your-self if you'll just switch it over for a few minutes.'

The barman looked at her in surprise, but pointed the remote at the television.

It was still breaking news but this time there was a reporter at the scene. Nieve gasped as she saw the pictures. They showed the gleaming glass structure that was Ennco – a structure that looked strong and solid and made her feel that the company was strong and solid too – but then the cameraman zoomed in on Mike Horgan being hustled out of the door, down the granite steps and across the plaza to a waiting police car.

'Oh my God,' she said, as Murphy Ledwidge pushed his way through the throng of wedding guests to stand beside her.

'What the hell's going on?' he asked.

'It's Ennco,' she said. 'There's trouble.' She looked around the crowd. 'Anyone got a cell phone?'

'Here.' Darcey handed over her Motorola and Nieve rapidly tapped numbers on the keypad.

'Who's that?' she said when the phone was finally answered. 'Gene? Gene Shaw from payments? It's Nieve Stapleton, compliance director. What the hell is going on there?'

She continued to watch the TV screen while she listened to Gene speak. Her face grew whiter and her lips tighter. Aidan put his arm around her shoulders. Eventually she flipped the phone closed, her fingers clenched tightly around it.

'I have to get some air,' she said.

She walked out of the bar, followed by Aidan.

'Hey,' said the barman. 'She owes me for seven pints of Guinness.'

'Here.' Darcey undid her bag and handed over the money. 'Now leave it on Sky News. We want to see what's happening.'

The story, according to the journalists, was one of financial fraud. Mike Horgan had somehow managed to conceal a debt of around five hundred million dollars by shuffling it between Ennco and a private company that he controlled himself. If the debt had been shown on Ennco's books originally, the price at the flotation would have been significantly less. The fraud had been discovered, one reporter said, when a junior member of the compliance team, Paola Benedetti, had queried an interest payment. Now the company was under huge pressure and there was already talk of it filing for bankruptcy protection. Mike had been arrested. The authorities wanted to talk to other members of the senior management team.

'Could that include Nieve?' Carol wondered out loud. 'But she couldn't have anything to do with it. We all saw her reaction.'

'Jesus H. Christ.' Murphy Ledwidge was holding on to Duke's arm. 'That's my pension they're talking about. I have millions tied up in the company. We all do. I've got to phone home.' He stumbled out of the bar, followed by the other guests from Ennco.

Mischa, Courtney and the remainder of Nieve's American friends continued to look incredulously at the TV screen, while the Irish contingent murmured amongst themselves.

'What's going to happen to the company?' wondered Carol.

'More to the point – what about the wedding?' asked Rosa.

'What about it?' Lorelei looked at them all in consternation. 'OK, I can see that she might be losing her job and that it's not a great time to get married. But she's spending a fortune on this . . .' Her voice trailed off. 'Oh, shit. She still owes me money. She'd better be good for it.'

'I'm sure everything will be fine,' said Darcey quickly. 'Nieve's a smart cookie. She wouldn't have all her eggs in one basket.'

'No, that's true.' Lorelei looked relieved. 'And the first hundred thousand arrived OK.'

Darcey, Rosa and Carol all looked at each other. The *first* hundred thousand, thought Darcey in astonishment. How many hundred thousand was this bash costing? How much money did Nieve actually have? And how much did she stand to lose?

'It's going to be fine,' said Aidan as they sat in the limo bringing them back to Stephen and Gail's. (Nieve had insisted on the limo for the day, and this time nobody had even considered suggesting a different car. But the driver, who'd expected to be out much later, had been taken aback when he'd seen them all rush from the restaurant to the bar and was forced to abandon his own burger and chips to drive them home.)

'How do you know it's going to be fine?' demanded Nieve. 'They said bankruptcy protection, Aidan. That hardly sounds fine to me.'

'I know, I know,' he said soothingly. 'But you know how it is. There's always a big panic and then someone comes in and sorts things out, and OK, you'll have lost some money, but the company will bounce back.'

'I hope you're right.' Nieve swallowed hard. 'Aidan, if Ennco goes belly-up . . .' She stared at him with huge, frightened eyes. 'We'll lose everything. Everything. I never paid off the mortgage on the house. I didn't think it mattered. But if I don't get the share money . . . Oh, God.' She doubled over and began to gulp air in jagged breaths. 'Oh, God.'

'Don't worry,' he said. 'It won't come to that. We won't lose everything. You're just seeing the worst-case scenario right now. I bet by the time we get back to your mam's, they'll have more news. Better news.'

'Gene said that the cops just burst into the office and arrested Mike.' She sat up again. 'And that Harley is answering questions but he's not under arrest. And that they wanted to know where I was.' Tears started to fall down her cheeks. 'Aidan, they think I might be *involved* with whatever's going on.'

Aidan couldn't believe she was actually crying.

'Do you know anything about it?' he asked.

'What!' She could hardly contain her anger. 'You think I had something to do with it? That I'm some kind of *criminal*?'

'Of course not,' he said quickly. 'You're upset, you . . . you're crying – you're not thinking straight. I just wondered, was there anything you were worried about? You mentioned once something about the figures . . . I thought perhaps it was that.'

'No,' she said tiredly. 'I was on top of that. All of it.' She bit her lip. 'Harley was always on about me keeping an eye on the traders. He never said anything about keeping an eye on himself!' She wiped the back of her hand across her eyes. 'He must have known, Aidan. All the time he must have known, and he let me and the others sink more and more money into Ennco and . . .' She started to cry again.

'Sssh.' Aidan pulled her close to him. 'I promise you it'll be fine. Don't worry. Please don't worry.'

He'd never had to do this with Nieve before. Even years earlier, when Jugomax had gone under and they'd lost their jobs, she hadn't cried. She'd simply straightened her shoulders and got on with things. He kissed the top of her head as she huddled in his arms. She'd protected him before. Now she needed someone to look after her. He wouldn't let her down.

Murphy was on the phone to Karl Spain, another one of the compliance staff.

'Paola shopped him?' he said in disbelief. 'Our Paola?'

'Yeah. And everyone's wondering why nobody in compliance noticed the debt before. That's why they want to talk to Nieve.'

'Shit,' said Murphy. 'D'you think they want to arrest her too?'

'Don't know, pal. But it's mayhem here right now. The place is crawling with Federal agents and Fox newshounds. Everyone wants to know what's going on but nobody really does.'

'They're saying bankruptcy protection on the news,' said Murphy.

'I doubt they've had time to even think of that,' said Karl. 'But we're sure as hell going to need some kind of protection. Man, all my money is in this damn firm.'

'Yeah, mine too.'

'We're shot to shit,' said Karl. 'It's over for us.'

'Tell me you think it might work out,' begged Murphy.

'I could tell you,' said Karl, 'but I don't think I'd believe it.'

'What's going to happen about the wedding?' Mischa asked Courtney. 'Is it on or off?'

'How would I know?' replied her friend. 'I can't imagine she'll be in the mood for a big celebration if her whole life has just gone down the pan.'

'She must have investments outside the company,' said Mischa. 'She's not stupid.'

'Sure, but how much?'

'Will she have to sell her house?' wondered Courtney. 'It's a gorgeous place.'

Mischa looked at Courtney quizzically. 'You're not thinking of putting in an offer for it, are you? I remember you wanting to buy it before but she pipped you at the post.'

'All good things come to those who wait,' quipped Courtney.

'That's horrible,' said Mischa.

'I know.' Courtney looked slightly abashed. 'I feel so sorry for her. I really do. But it's hard not to feel a bit . . . Well, she was always so damn cocky about everything, wasn't she?'

'Hey, I know Nieve. She'll bounce back from this bigger and brighter and better than ever, so I really wouldn't try to cross her now.'

'You're right, I guess,' said Courtney. 'Still, I do like that house . . .'

Stephen and Gail were watching a DVD when Aidan and Nieve returned. They looked at the couple in surprise.

'I need to use the internet,' Nieve said to her father before he had a chance to speak. 'I need to check things out in the States.'

'What sort of things—' began Stephen, but Nieve had already walked out of the living room.

'What's going on?' demanded Gail. 'I thought you'd be out much later than this.'

'We don't have the full details yet,' said Aidan. 'But let me explain what we know.'

Darcey, Rosa and Carol were still in the bar. Rosa's husband, Roy, was with them too. He was an accountant, and he regularly punctuated the conversation with observations that the debt must have been really well hidden, because if the company that had bought out Ennco had done proper due diligence they should have found it. Darcey thought Roy was the most boring person she'd ever met in her life – even more boring than her actuarial colleagues had considered themselves to be.

'Oh shut up, Roy,' she said after the fifth or sixth time he'd said the same thing. 'The point is that they didn't find the debt and that the chief financial officer must have known about it. As far as I can tell, the problem for Nieve is that someone from her own department spotted it, which surely means that she should have spotted it, which is why the Feds might think she had something to do with it.'

'That's what I was trying to say,' protested Roy.

'So what d'you think?' asked Carol. 'Nieve – saint or sinner?'

'I wish I knew.' Darcey couldn't help remembering Nieve's

willingness to blackmail Max Christie into giving her a job, and her lack of scruples in passing off someone else's work as her own; and, indeed, her inclination to get Darcey to do translations for her and say nothing about her contribution. All of these things made her feel as though Nieve would quite happily turn a blind eye to less than ethical goings-on at Ennco. Added to that, of course, was her complete betrayal of Darcey herself in nabbing Aidan (no matter how Aidan tried to justify it by pretending that he'd fallen for her anyway). But fraudulent? Criminal? She couldn't believe that of her friend.

'She pushed the boundaries at school,' said Rosa. 'Didn't she cheat at exams?'

Darcey frowned. 'No, she didn't.'

'Oh, come on!' Rosa looked at her sceptically. 'All those times she got top marks ahead of you? She used to scratch notes on her desk with a pin.'

'No way,' said Darcey.

'Everyone knew she did,' Carol said. 'I can't believe you didn't know that, Darcey.'

'Look, I know there was a bit of competition between us, and I know that she desperately wanted to beat me all the time, but I can promise you that she didn't cheat.' Darcey's words tumbled out. 'She used to have ways of remembering things, sure. She'd make up rhymes and stuff so that she could memorise formulas or dates or anything like that. But she never cheated.'

Rosa and Carol exchanged glances.

'She was very clever,' said Darcey. 'And she was just unlucky that I had a better memory and was better at exams, because in any other year she would have been top of the class the whole time and nobody – not even you, Rosa, or you, Carol – would have stopped her.'

'So it's not true that you two fell out?' said Rosa. 'Only from what people were saying in the restaurant, and from the bit of the fracas I heard outside afterwards, you're supposed to hate each other.'

Darcey hesitated. For a moment – possibly for the first time in over ten years – she'd actually been thinking of Nieve's good qualities rather than her bad. Nieve had always been there for her. They'd spent hours in each other's houses letting off steam about the things that upset them – their parents, their teachers, other girls at school . . . spots (in Nieve's case), weight (in Darcey's), their lack of experience with boys, with clothes, with everything. Despite the fact that there'd been competition between them at school (mainly driven by Gail's pressure on her daughter), Nieve had always been supportive of Darcey's academic success. She'd always encouraged her to try harder, to do more, because, she would say, getting ahead was a good thing for women to do. And – with the obviously blatant exception of her behaviour over Aidan – she'd been great at setting Darcey up with dates too. She'd been the one to organise the trips abroad, even if Darcey had been the one to do the talking when they'd got there. Without Nieve, Darcey knew she would have been too lazy to bother. Nieve was the driving force behind almost all of her early experiences, and she couldn't now – as she had for the past ten years – forget the good things that had been part of their friendship.

'It's true that we fell out,' she said eventually. 'The thing was . . .' And she explained the entire situation regarding Aidan, expanding on what she'd already told Carol so that both her eyes and Rosa's grew rounder and rounder and even Roy looked uncomfortable. 'But that doesn't make her a criminal,' concluded Darcey. 'A bit of a cow maybe. But not a criminal.'

'And now she's got her comeuppance,' said Rosa. 'You must be feeling very satisfied about that.'

Darcey supposed she should feel satisfied. But actually, all she felt was sympathy.

Nieve had Googled every story there was about Ennco and had watched downloadable clips from the US news stations on the unfolding events at the company. But nothing could lift the sense of doom that had settled over her and none of the reports gave her any comfort that her shareholding (or indeed the shareholding of any Ennco employee) was going to be worth more than the value of a postage stamp by the time the dust had settled.

She cupped her chin in her hands and stared at the computer screen. She was ruined. Personally and professionally. There would be no seven-figure payout. No great reward for all the hard work of the past few years. Her savings were minimal, because she'd reinvested every last cent of her earnings in Ennco stock which was now worthless. Even if another company stepped in and bought them out, it would only pay a nominal sum. And there was still the possibility that she'd be arrested if she went back to the States. She was sure that she had nothing to worry about, that she'd done nothing improper during her time with the company, even though she'd sometimes allowed traders to exceed their limits for short periods of time when it was obvious that the deals would benefit Ennco. But that wasn't criminal, although it would be just as bad to be labelled incompetent. And despite the fact that the debt had clearly been well hidden, she should have discovered it. Paola had. They couldn't prosecute her for incompetence, but how the hell would she fund her defence if they decided that in some way she'd ignored the warning signals? She couldn't afford a lengthy lawsuit. She couldn't afford anything. She was broke.

She closed her eyes and started to cry again.

Lorelei rang Gail and Stephen's house and asked to speak to Nieve. Aidan, who answered, told her to speak to him instead. Lorelei wanted to know about the wedding plans for the following day. She had, she told him, caterers, musicians, waiters, florists and a whole heap of other people descending on the castle in the morning, as well as the surprise guest – the totally in demand winner of the last *Pop Idol* competition, who was arriving by helicopter – and she wanted to know if everything was going ahead according to schedule.

'Of course it is,' said Aidan, although at that moment he was wondering if he'd be able to find some Valium to help Nieve make it down the aisle. 'Call us in the morning. Nieve will be able to talk to you then.'

He replaced the phone and it rang again. It was his mother. She'd arrived at the hotel and she wanted to let him know that everything was lovely and that she and his father had spoken to each other and that they'd be coming to the church together. He'd completely forgotten about them, and of course they didn't know a thing about what had happened. There was no point in going into it now. He told her that everything was fine, he'd see them the next day, and then went down to the office to check on Nieve.

She was still in the chair in front of the computer screen but was leaning across the desk, her head buried in the crook of her right arm.

'It's not so bad,' he said in a comforting voice.

'It's a fucking disaster.' Her words were muffled. 'I'll either come out of this branded a criminal or a fool. I'm not sure which is worse.'

'Come on, honey,' he said. 'OK, it's a huge, massive setback. I'm not trying to downplay it. But we can bounce back from this.'

She lifted her head to look at him, and he could see that her eyes were red and puffy from her tears.

'Bounce back?' she said brokenly. 'Bounce back? Nobody can bounce back from losing what we've just lost. Nobody. It's my life, my career, my reputation. And millions. Our whole future!'

'Our future never depended on your millions,' said Aidan. 'And you'll come out of it with your reputation intact, you know you will. There have been cases like this in the past and there'll probably be more of them in the future. Everyone knows that there are a few bad apples, but you're not one of them. You're very good at what you do.'

'No,' she said, the tears starting to fall again. 'If I was that damn good, I would've realised what was going on. Paola found out. Paola! She's a pregnant admin clerk, for

God's sake, and she was always taking time off! I was shitty to her, kind of implied she wasn't pulling her weight. But she saw something I didn't. So stop trying to make me see an up side when there damn well isn't one.'

'OK,' he said. 'I understand that now isn't the time. But listen to me, honey, we're getting married tomorrow and nobody can take that away from us, and you need your beauty sleep tonight. So come on. Get into bed and I'll bring you up a hot drink and you'll feel a million times better in the morning.'

She stared at him. 'Are you in cloud-cuckoo land?' she asked. 'A hot drink isn't what I need. It's a few million dollars. And I won't feel better in the morning.'

Carol, Rosa and Roy had gone back to the Radisson Hotel where they were staying. Darcey had accompanied them, although she was spending the night at home with Minette. Their house was a mere ten-minute walk away from the hotel, and Darcey knew that Minette would have been offended if she'd opted to stay there instead of at home.

'So what d'you think?' asked Carol after they'd ordered a nightcap. 'Do we get glammed up for tomorrow or not?'

'Sure, she might as well get married,' said Rosa. 'She'll need him to support her, and after today she could do with a bit of fun and support!'

'Besides, women don't chicken out of their weddings,' said Roy.

'Nieve's certainly not a chicken,' agreed Carol. 'But, gosh, it'll hardly be the sort of day she wanted.'

'It's scheduled for four,' Darcey reminded them. 'I'm sure

we'll have heard before then if there's any change. We can ring the castle and check, or perhaps the wedding-planner will be in touch.'

'If it's off, she'll have a canary,' observed Carol. 'She was worried enough about the bill as it was.'

'Jeez, yes,' Rosa remembered. 'How much d'you think the whole thing was costing?'

'I bet they have insurance,' said Darcey optimistically. 'If I was planning a huge wedding there'd be insurance.'

Carol laughed. 'Why? Would you have expected something like this?'

'No, you fool.' Darcey grinned in return. 'But things have a habit of not turning out like you expect. Best to be prepared.' She flexed her wrist. The plaster splint had been replaced by the lightweight plastic one, but it was still uncomfortable.

'Our wedding was perfect,' said Rosa. 'Everything was exactly right and turned out totally in accordance with the plan.'

'Funny,' said Carol. 'Back in school and in college, I thought that getting married would be the best thing that could ever happen to me. But it wasn't.'

'It was for me,' said Rosa.

'It wasn't for me either,' said Darcey. 'But that was entirely my own fault.'

'Were you still in love with Aidan?'

Rosa asked the question in such a matter-of-fact voice that Darcey was startled.

She didn't answer straight away. For an instant she was transported back to her wedding day. She could see Neil wearing his kilt at Gretna Green, smiling at her. She could see herself smiling at him too. She'd been thinking . . . she'd been thinking then that she loved him. She really had. She hadn't been thinking of Aidan Clarke, the man she wanted to believe was the love of her life, at all.

'Not the day I got married,' she said eventually. 'But later, when Neil and I had problems, I thought I must have been.' She looked suddenly surprised. 'I think . . . I think I wanted to be able to blame someone, something else for the fact that it wasn't working out. It was easy to think that it might be that I was still in love with Aidan.'

'He's a total hunk,' Carol said. 'I'm not surprised you lost it when she pinched him.'

'She's dead lucky if only she realises it,' agreed Rosa.

'Unless he decides that she knew what was going on after all,' commented Darcey. 'Or he isn't interested in her now that she's lost everything.'

'Is he that much of a shit, d'you think?' Roy broke into the conversation. 'Guys aren't usually with women for their money.'

'That's 'cos most women don't have any,' said Rosa.

'It's different these days,' Carol pointed out. 'I'm doing quite well out of journalism. Darcey's a top-notch city girl. Nieve was loaded. We're all pretty good catches, you know.'

Rosa grinned. 'You and Darcey are both divorced. Nieve may or may not make it to the altar. Who says money buys happiness?'

Darcey and Carol looked at her bleakly. Rosa had always applied her own ruthless form of logic to everything. And she was doing it again now.

\*   \*   \*

It was after midnight by the time Darcey got home. Roy had offered to walk her to Minette's house, and when Darcey told him she'd be perfectly OK, Rosa interjected to say that she wasn't to walk through dark streets in a cast looking like some kind of victim, and that Roy would most definitely accompany her.

Darcey grumbled but agreed that Rosa had a point and promised to call them if she heard anything about the wedding. It was only later, when she was going through her bag, that she remembered that she'd given her mobile phone to Nieve so that she could call the States, and that Nieve hadn't given it back to her. Darcey conceded that returning the phone wouldn't have been Nieve's top priority at the time, but she wished she'd remembered to get it off her herself.

She took off her make-up and flopped into bed. Her wrist and her ankle were both throbbing, and she was very tired. And heaven only knew how tomorrow would turn out.

# Chapter 32

It was a fairy-tale day. Even at six in the morning the sun blazed down from a sky so blue that it actually hurt Darcey's eyes to look at it. The wild flowers and hedgerows were a patchwork of frothy colours and dappled greens, and the summer scents of freshly cut grass and rambling roses hung in the still air.

Minette, always an early riser, was having breakfast in the kitchen, the back door propped open to allow the faintest of breezes to waft through the room.

'She's got a great day for it,' she observed as Darcey greeted her, her hair tousled from a restless night's sleep.

'You'd think so.' Darcey proceeded to fill Minette in on the previous evening's events, while her mother's eyes widened in disbelief as she spoke.

'I don't want to believe that she had anything to do with whatever scam was going on,' said Minette eventually. 'But, you know, I wouldn't be in the slightest bit surprised. Nieve was always an amoral kind of girl.'

'She took short cuts,' admitted Darcey, 'and she used people. But she isn't a thief.'

Minette smiled slightly. 'No.'

'She just wanted so badly to be successful.'

'And she succeeded.'

'But to have it snatched away like that . . .' Darcey sighed. 'I can understand how she feels. It's not like I ever wanted that level of success for myself, but, well, I've done OK, and I know that if it all went horribly wrong at InvestorCorp, I'd be devastated.'

'Would you cancel your wedding as a result?' asked Minette.

'Ah, hell, there's probably no chance of that ever happening.' Darcey grinned at her. 'Need to have someone else fool enough to ask me first.'

Minette laughed. 'I guess so. What now?'

'Who knows?' said Darcey. 'We'll just have to wait and see.'

She'd only just finished her shot of espresso when the phone rang.

Minette answered it and then handed the receiver to Darcey, her eyes darker than ever.

'It's for you,' she said. 'Aidan Clarke.'

Darcey took a deep breath and took the receiver from her mother.

'Hello,' she said.

'Hi, Darcey.' Aidan sounded wretched. 'I wasn't sure if this was still your number.'

'Sure it is,' she said as calmly as she could. 'What can I do for you? How's Nieve?'

'That's the thing,' said Aidan. 'I don't know. She's left me. I thought you might be able to help.'

\*   \*   \*

Darcey made an arrangement to meet Aidan at the castle in an hour's time. She was able to drive Minette's car now, even though it made her ankle ache, and she pulled up outside the huge granite building with ten minutes to spare. But Aidan was already there, standing at the top of the steps, Malachy Finan beside him.

'Your mother's not with you?' Malachy asked as she clambered out.

Darcey shook her head. 'She felt sure she'd be in the way. She sends her regards.'

'Come through to the back of the castle,' said Malachy. 'I'll organise some coffee for you both.'

He led them through the now familiar passageways and out to the flagstoned patio. Darcey shaded her eyes with her hand against the glare of the sun on the enormous white marquee that had been set up on the lawn.

She turned to Aidan. 'Any news?'

He looked utterly dejected. His face was pale beneath its California glow, and there were dark circles under his eyes. He shook his head.

'No. Just the note. Nothing else.'

He'd told her about it on the phone, and now he handed it to her. He'd finally fallen asleep sometimes in the early hours of the morning, and when he'd woken a couple of hours later, Nieve had disappeared, leaving the note on the pillow beside him. It said, quite simply, that she needed to be on her own and that she understood it was over between them. She wished him well in finding somebody else: Darcey McGonigle, she suggested, who was probably still in love with him, and who would have been a better bet all along, would be only too willing to step into the breach.

Darcey swallowed hard as she read Nieve's words.

'Why is she thinking this?' she asked him. 'This is crazy.'

'I suppose . . .' Aidan spoke slowly, 'I suppose you're not the only one who felt that the situation between the three of us didn't end very satisfactorily. I know she and I kinda ran off into the sunset together, but she always felt a bit guilty about it. And I think she sometimes wondered if I wouldn't do the same to her some day.'

'Oh, come on! I can't believe she ever said that.'

'Not – well, you know Nieve. Every so often she'd wonder out loud how you were doing and ask me if I thought I'd made the right decision by leaving you, and I guess deep down she felt bad about it.'

'Is that why you didn't get married before now?' asked Darcey.

He shrugged. 'Not really. She wanted the money and stuff before we did it, and sometimes I thought it was because she needed to prove to me that I had made the right choice . . .'

'Y'know, Aidan, I don't like that one little bit.' Darcey snorted. 'It's as if the two of us were like something on a shelf waiting for you to choose us. It wasn't just your choice, you know. We had something to do with it ourselves.'

He laughed. 'That's what I remember best about you. And loved about you. You used to argue with me.'

'Not enough, obviously,' she told him. 'Look, what do you want me to do? Why have you come to me at all? Surely there are other people who can help? Friends, family?'

'You were her best friend,' said Aidan. 'And she still thinks of you more than anyone else. So I thought that maybe you'd know where she's most likely to have gone.'

Darcey shook her head slowly. 'There was nowhere special,' she said. 'All our good places were abroad. France and Spain. Italy, maybe, though that was my favourite, not hers.'

'I don't know what to do.' His voice was desolate. 'She's got it all wrong. Got me all wrong.'

'Maybe she hasn't got me all wrong, though.' Darcey sat down on one of the wrought-iron chairs with the note still in her hand.

Aidan sat opposite her and looked at her warily. 'How?'

'I never got over you properly,' Darcey told him. 'I suppose she could see that. That's why she said what she said in the note.'

'You seem to have got over me pretty well,' he said. 'You look a million dollars and you were pretty cool with me before.'

She smiled faintly. 'Yeah, well. What's a girl to do? Anyway, I guess we should be focusing on finding Nieve, not worrying about us.'

'I don't worry about us,' said Aidan. 'But I'm sorry how it turned out.'

'Me too,' said Darcey. 'I suppose . . .' She looked at him uncomfortably. She needed to say it. 'I just need to settle one issue. You were going to ask me to marry you. You'd bought a ring.'

He looked surprised. 'How did you know that?'

'I looked in your jacket pocket the night of your birthday.'

He stared at her.

'I know I shouldn't have,' she said. 'But I did. And that's why I was so devastated.'

'Oh, Darcey!'

'And I think the reason I was so angry with both of you was that it seemed particularly shallow to dump me when you'd been about to ask me to marry you, and she – well, the thing is, Aidan, we're two very different people. I simply couldn't understand how you could be about to marry me and then run off with her instead.'

'You're different people, but in some ways you're very alike,' said Aidan, and Darcey looked at him in astonishment. 'Oh, look, you're both bright and smart and . . . and interesting people who know your own minds. I like that in a woman. I really do. I need to be bossed around a bit. You know me, I'm a bit lazy really. You're smart and sassy but not bossy. She had it all.'

Darcey nodded slowly.

'And that's why she's the right person for me. She's good for me and I'm good for her and I want to be with her for ever, and I really can't believe she's done this.'

Darcey looked at the marquee again. She noted that the patio chairs had all been swathed in off-white silk, while hundreds of planters overflowing with a blaze of tumbling flowers filled the gardens, and she thought that it was probably the most romantic setting in the world for a wedding.

Malachy appeared and left them some coffee. Darcey watched Aidan as he poured the dark brew into one of the white cups. She could see that his hand was shaking and she felt very sorry for him.

'Are you all right?' he asked her.

She nodded slowly. 'Yes. Yes, I am.'

'I know I hurt you. Maybe I shouldn't have called you. You just seemed the right person somehow.'

'Oh, look, everyone gets hurt.' She smiled at him. 'I'm way, way over that.'

And suddenly she realised that she was. Because she knew that she'd been feeling hurt for the wrong reasons. Sure, it had been horrible to lose her almost-fiancé to her best friend. But the hurt that she'd carried around with her and that still sometimes crept up on her was the hurt of embarrassment and betrayal, not the hurt of losing the one person in the world who meant the most to her. She'd got over that. But she hadn't been able to get over the feeling of shame that being dumped had given her. And as she looked at Aidan sitting there, the sun glinting off his fair hair and the pain of Nieve's disappearance in his eyes, what she also realised was that she'd actually got over him a long, long time ago. What she hadn't got over, but what she was gloriously and wondrously over now, was feeling sorry for herself.

And now she felt it was important that Aidan and Nieve should get back together. They'd been together for ten years. Ten years! How could she possibly have thought they would last that long if they didn't love each other? She'd been more of a fool than she'd realised.

'We need to find her,' she said firmly. 'She's trying to get through this on her own because she feels like a failure. She always hated failure.'

'Who are you telling?' Aidan looked disconsolate. 'I wish I could talk to her. She was in such a state last night that she wouldn't listen to anything, but today might be different.'

'I can call her.' The thought hit Darcey quite suddenly. 'She has my mobile phone. I'll call it. She might answer.'

'My stupid cell doesn't work here,' said Aidan.

'I'm sure we can use the castle phone,' said Darcey.

She got up and led the way inside. There was a phone on one of the occasional tables. She picked up the receiver and dialled. Her own voicemail cut in and told her to leave a message. She grimaced, shook her head at Aidan and hung up.

Nieve heard the insistent ring of the Motorola but didn't at first realise where it was coming from. She opened her bag and fished out the phone, which had by now stopped ringing. It took her a minute or two to remember that this was Darcey's phone. She turned it over and over in her hand.

The call was probably for Darcey. From Rosa or Carol probably. Wondering what was going to happen about the wedding. She supposed they'd all be wondering that. And then they'd realise that it wasn't going to happen. The wedding of the year, the glittering social event on which she'd spared no expense to make them all envious of her, wasn't taking place. Instead of lording it over people at Rathfinan Castle as she'd planned, she was sitting here in a bed and breakfast somewhere in Galway county, on her own.

She started to shake. She wished she hadn't run away. It wasn't like her to run away. But she'd been so horrified and upset and so sure that people would think the worst of her regardless . . . They always thought the worst of her, she knew that. They'd thought it over the Darcey McGonigle affair (Gail had told her that the talk of the neighbours had been that Nieve had done the dirty on her friend, but that she was putting them right – some chance!); Max Christie hadn't given her a chance after the Jugomax collapse, and she was sure that he blamed her for it in some way . . . There'd be people at this wedding who were supposed to be her friends but who would now be thinking that she was as corrupt as Mike or Harley. The thing was, running away would make them think that even more. She should go back. She wanted to go back. She wanted Aidan. But she couldn't go back to Rathfinan Castle, where everything would be set up for what was supposed to have been the best day of her life. It was too hard. Way too hard, even for her.

Darcey and Aidan were still sitting at the wrought-iron table when Lorelei arrived. She was wearing another one of her Chanel-style suits, but this time her huge sunglasses were shielding her eyes.

'Ah,' she said when she saw Aidan. 'The groom. At least one half of the happy couple is here. Where's Nieve? There's a lot to do today.'

'Um, we don't know where Nieve is,' said Darcey.

Hidden by her sunglasses, Lorelei's eyes narrowed.

'The other woman,' she said sharply. 'And what exactly are you doing here?'

'Helping me track Nieve down,' said Aidan.

'She's disappeared,' said Darcey. 'She left Aidan a note.'

'Oh, bloody hell.' Lorelei pushed her sunglasses back on top of her head. 'She can't do this to me. She can't.'

'She was very upset by the news last night,' Aidan told her. 'What did you expect?'

'That she'd be as professional as me,' snapped Lorelei. 'This is the biggest wedding I've ever done. It's important to me. It isn't all about the romance, you know.'

Darcey laughed sardonically. 'It's a *wedding*,' she told Lorelei. 'Surely it *is* all about the romance. But I don't think Nieve is feeling very romantic today.'

'Not with you sidling in and trying to grab her future husband, I guess.'

Darcey looked at Lorelei angrily and felt Aidan's hand on her arm, restraining her.

'Darcey's helping me,' he said. 'I want to find Nieve. I want this wedding to go ahead.'

'So do I,' said Lorelei. 'But I can't see it happening when you're having a cosy tête-à-tête with your former lover.'

'Put an effing sock in it!' cried Darcey. 'I'm not here to ensnare Aidan. I'm not here to wreck anything. I'm here to try to sort things out if I can.'

'Yeah, well you're not having much success and you don't look like you're trying very hard.' Lorelei pinched the bridge of her nose. 'I asked her to get a damn mobile phone here so that I could keep in touch, but she told me that it was fine to ring her house. I've just spent half an hour talking to a very hysterical mother of the bride. I want to make sure that there *is* a bride for the mother to be hysterical over!'

'We'll find her,' said Darcey. 'We'll find her and we'll sort it. You just get on with whatever it is you're supposed to be doing.'

'I'm supposed to be with her while she gets her hair done!' snapped Lorelei. 'That's a schedule that's gone haywire already!'

'It doesn't matter about her hair,' said Aidan. 'Or her make-up.'

Darcey smiled at him. He smiled back at her.

'Oh for crying out loud!' Lorelei stared at them. 'Don't tell me there isn't anything going on between you two. Don't tell me that half of the problem isn't to do with you. If it was only a question of the business problem, Nieve would be here. But she's not here, because she knows that it's more than that. I'm going to talk to Malachy. We have some major problems going on here. Major.' And she stalked back inside the castle.

'I'm sorry.' Darcey watched as Lorelei barged angrily through the doors. 'I seem to be causing you more trouble.'

'No you're not. And I'm glad you're here,' said Aidan.

'Maybe I shouldn't be,' said Darcey. 'Maybe everyone will think—'

'I don't care what they think,' said Aidan. 'I'm glad you and I have talked. To be honest, you've always been a bit of an unspoken thorn in the side of my relationship with Nieve.'

'Why?'

'I told you. She felt bad about it. And so did I.'

'If you felt that bad, all you had to do was apologise years ago,' said Darcey.

'I tried.'

'I guess I wasn't in the mood to listen,' admitted Darcey. 'Anyway, it doesn't matter any more. Right now, we have to find her.'

'D'you think she's tried to get out of the country? Gone somewhere else? All of her stuff – her credit cards, her passport, her money – everything's missing.'

Darcey shook her head. 'I honestly have no idea,' she told him. 'I'm sorry, you've come to me for help and I'm really not sure what I can do . . .' She sighed. 'I guess I'm not as dynamic and efficient as I pretend to myself either.'

'Are you?' he asked. 'Dynamic and efficient? What do you do these days?'

'Work in finance,' she said.

'What about the farm in Tuscany?' he asked.

Darcey blinked.

'You told me about it loads of times,' he said.

'Well, sure,' she said. 'Maybe one day that's what I'll do. But I've changed. I like my job. I'm good at it.'

'I've changed too,' he said. 'I like my life. I love Nieve. And she'd never want a farm in Tuscany.'

'I know that. What she wants is to be married to you,' said Darcey. 'We just have to remind her of that.'

'You got married, didn't you?' he asked curiously. 'We heard about that.'

'Yes, but it didn't work out.'

'Any reason in particular?'

She shook her head. 'Probably because we weren't right for each other.'

He was looking at her and she knew he was wondering if she was telling him the truth.

'I wasn't mature enough to get married,' she added. 'I regret that. But I've had a great life, Aidan. I travel a lot, earn loads of money, and have a lot of really close male friends.'

'You were coming to the wedding alone.'

'Yeah, well. Rocco's in Italy at the moment, so . . .' She shrugged.

'Italy? You've got an Italian boyfriend?'

She grinned. 'Sure I have. What did you expect?'

He sighed. 'I told Nieve that she shouldn't invite you to the wedding because you might flip. That you might still hate us. That you might have some kind of revenge thing going on. I thought – God, this sounds so flipping self-important – that you might still have some feelings for me.'

'Oh, come on,' she said. 'It was years ago. I'm *so* over you.'

But way more importantly, she told herself, I'm so over me!


Darcey left Aidan and Lorelei at the castle. She told him that it was his job to prove to the wedding-planner that the hitch in their plans had nothing to do with her but was entirely down to the fact that Ennco's managing director was languishing in a prison cell somewhere in California (or, more likely, she added, had been bailed out to contemplate life in whatever fancy pad he lived in), and to the fact that Nieve had plummeted from being a mega-rich hotshot to a stony-broke hotshot in the space of a few hours.

'I'm not sure I should go with the "broke" motif too much,' Aidan had said. 'I get the feeling that Lorelei is quietly freaking out about the money side of things.'

'She can't be owed very much, surely?' Darcey looked concerned. 'She was muttering about having been paid hundreds of thousands yesterday.'

'The money is the least of my problems,' said Aidan. 'I'm sure that I can deal with her when she calms down. It seems to me that she's more worried about the bad publicity of one of her weddings not actually happening than anything else.'

'Good luck with that,' said Darcey. 'Nieve sure picked a barracuda wedding-planner.'

'That's Nieve. Look, if I hear anything, I'll call you.'

'Sure,' she said. 'Let me know as soon as you locate her.'

She went back to Minette's house and joined her mother, who was sunbathing in the back garden. She updated her on events and then rang Rosa and Carol to tell them how things stood too.

'If she doesn't show and everything is definitely off, d'you want to join us for dinner tonight?' asked Carol. 'We'll book a table at the hotel.'

'OK,' agreed Darcey. 'But hopefully she'll turn up.'

By four o'clock, the time at which the wedding should have taken place, there was still no news of Nieve. Aidan had spoken to Lorelei and she had made what she called an executive decision aimed at containing events. She had contacted all the guests, telling them that there would be a buffet meal provided at the castle and they were welcome to attend. Most of them did, on the basis that if there was anything new going to happen, the castle was the place to be. Besides, they all knew that Nieve had organised the most wonderful food and they wanted to eat it. As well as gossip.

Aidan kept ringing Darcey's mobile, but it continued to divert to her voicemail. Gail and Stephen had phoned hotels and bed and breakfasts around the county in the hope of finding her, but with no success.

'I can't believe this has happened.' Gail stood in Nieve's

bedroom looking at the beautiful Vera Wang wedding dress on its hanger. Aidan stayed leaning against the door jamb. 'Why couldn't she just come back and go through with it? It's not as though she's done anything wrong. Now all this hard work and expense is totally wasted.'

'I know,' said Aidan.

'She could be anywhere now . . . I wish she'd call me.'

Aidan didn't want to say to Gail that she was probably the last person Nieve would call. Nieve would think that she'd let her mother down by not giving her the glamorous occasion she'd wanted. He thought, though, that Nieve might have been wrong about that. Gail Stapleton was upset not because of the cancelled wedding, but because she was worried about her daughter.

'Why oh why didn't you wake up when she got out of bed?' demanded Gail. 'You're supposed to be her fiancé, for heaven's sake. You should have known how distressed she was.'

'I did know,' said Aidan. 'I knew because I know exactly how she felt when she heard the news. Devastated. And I'll tell you why she was so damn devastated. It's because she thought she'd let everyone down. You especially.'

'What d'you mean, me especially?'

'You always went on and on at her about being the best. Well, because of that, she became the best. The trouble was, she couldn't cope with anything less.'

'It's not my fault!' Gail raised her voice. 'I only wanted her to achieve her potential. That's all.'

Stephen came bounding up the stairs.

'There's no need for us all to get in a state,' he said. 'It's not the end of the world. The most important thing is to find her and to let her know that we love her.'

'I know,' said Aidan miserably. 'I know.'

The right thing to have done, Nieve thought, was to have gone back. To have got into her wedding dress and held her head up high and gone through with it all. That was what a real winner would have done. Instead she'd run away. She'd never run away from anything in her life before. But now she was sitting in the living room of the unlisted B&B, watching the TV, because she didn't have the heart to do anything else. She'd turned from a winner into a loser. In the normal course of events she'd never have stayed in a place like this, but she didn't have a choice. She'd asked for something for two nights and had been shown to an unexpectedly pretty room with a white-tiled bathroom. She'd paid cash (worrying that somehow she'd be traced through her credit card, and then thinking that she'd watched too many Hollywood movies and that nobody in Galway would be tracing people through credit cards, for heaven's sake!) and had dumped on the bed the small overnight case she'd packed with toiletries, clean knickers and a few T-shirts.

The owner of the house, a surprisingly young and cheery woman who introduced herself as Mary Mackle, had asked if she'd like a map of the area, but Nieve had said no, that she was really tired and just wanted to rest. And so she'd lain down on the extremely comfortable bed and, much to her surprise, fallen asleep.

In the afternoon she'd sat in the back garden, her legs

stretched out under the blazing sun, and stared across the lawn to the sheep in the fields beyond. She wondered whether Lorelei had got sheep for Rathfinan Castle. She wondered what people were doing, whether they'd gone to the castle anyway, whether Aidan had organised drinks for them (which was what she would have done in the circumstances), whether they were talking about her.

Well of course they were talking about her! What else was there to talk about? She'd wanted them to talk about her, hadn't she? Only not like this. Not as someone who'd been part of a failure. Only as someone who'd been a success. But they'd be doing that age-old Irish thing of nodding wisely about her misfortune, murmuring that she'd got a bit above herself, and sure, wasn't it only inevitable that something like this would happen?

She wondered about Aidan himself. How was he coping with the mess she'd left behind? She felt terrible about it and she knew she should call him, but she just couldn't. He'd try to be upbeat and she didn't want to be upbeat. He'd probably say something about it being a sign that they needed to downsize, but she didn't want to downsize. He'd be looking for the bright side for her, but there was no bright side. Not this time. She was ruined, and it was all very well for people to say that as long as you had your health and your family everything would be OK, but she'd never felt that way. She wanted the money too. She felt adrift without it.

God, she thought, she was a shallow, selfish cow. Just like people thought. Like Darcey thought. Surely it couldn't be that her friend had been right all along?

At half past four two children – a boy and a girl, both, Nieve estimated, around the ages of five or six – ran joyfully into the garden and stopped when they saw her. They muttered to each other for a moment and then the boy came over to her and said that his name was Davey and was she staying at the house. And the girl said that she was his sister, Eimear, and that she wanted to be a fighter pilot when she grew up. Then Davey shoved Eimear and she pinched him and the two of them were rolling around in the grass when Nieve told them to stop it this instant. She used the voice she'd used when she'd been an au pair to Guy and Selina. It still worked. Davey and Eimear stopped instantly, and looked at her expectantly.

'Where's your mam?' she asked.

'Talking round the front,' said Davey.

'If you don't behave, I'm going to have to tell her,' said Nieve.

'We'll be good,' said Eimear. 'S'long as he doesn't do stupid things.'

And they suddenly started playing together, quite amicably, in the large sand-pit at the back of the garden.

This is what Aidan wants, thought Nieve. Two kids slugging it out and me keeping an eye on them. This is what he thinks is a good life here in Ireland. Maybe by not turning up today I'm actually doing him a favour. Because, in the end, he'll always want this, and I . . . She looked at the two children and swallowed hard. She didn't know what she wanted any more.

She heard Mary walking around the side of the house and looked up as the younger woman waved and said hello.

'Would you like anything to eat?' asked Mary.

'No, I'm OK,' Nieve replied.

'A cup of tea?'

'No thanks.'

'It's no trouble. And it's on the house.' Mary beamed at her. 'I'm making some for myself. And I've got some soda bread in case you fancy a piece.'

'Thanks anyway, but I'm fine just sitting here.'

'Whatever you like,' said Mary. 'Don't forget that the sun is very strong today. I hope you're wearing some sunscreen.'

Nieve wasn't, but she wasn't worrying too much about the sun. She lived in California, for heaven's sake. She knew all about sun. But after a couple of minutes she went inside and stayed there, the curtains half drawn against the light, watching daytime TV.

The Mackles didn't have satellite and so she couldn't tune in to Sky or CNN or Bloomberg TV and see if there was any more information on Ennco. But at six o'clock she turned on RTÉ to see if the national channel was covering the story. Typical RTÉ, she thought, after it had gone through a range of news items but nothing about Ennco. International business just didn't register on its radar at all. And then she gasped in horror as a picture flashed up of Rathfinan church and the camera zoomed in on a reporter.

'There has been local fallout from the story in the US this week that businessman Mike Horgan of Ennco, the US financial firm, has been arrested and charged with wire fraud. A senior employee of the firm, Nieve Stapleton, from the Galway region, was due to get married here in Rathfinan this afternoon. But following yesterday's arrest of Mr Horgan, Miss Stapleton left a celebratory dinner and has not been seen since. Friends and family of the bride-to-be are very concerned at her disappearance. Following the scheduled ceremony in the small church behind me, Miss Stapleton and her fiancé, Aidan Clarke, also from the Galway region, were due to celebrate their marriage with an extravagant reception at Rathfinan Castle.'

The camera cut to a shot of the castle, looking perfect in the summer sunshine. It zoomed in on the red carpet leading up to the marquee, bordered by pots and pots of white roses. Nieve could see people in the marquee. So Aidan had gone ahead with some kind of reception after all. She smiled forlornly.

The reporter walked towards the marquee, microphone in hand.

'I'm here with Darcey McGonigle, a local woman and a friend of the bride,' he said. 'Miss McGonigle, where do you think Miss Stapleton is now? And what have you to say in response to the stories that she has disappeared with a significant amount of the company's money?'

Nieve gasped in horror. Were they trying to pin it on her? They couldn't do that! She hadn't known anything about it. And now Darcey . . . Omigod, Darcey could ruin her reputation in a second now just by not denying it!

'I don't know where she is.' Darcey looked straight into the camera, her blue eyes frank and honest. 'None of her friends do, but we're all naturally very concerned. We know that she had nothing to do with this at all. We're confident that her name will be totally cleared.'

Nieve continued to stare at the TV even as the news coverage moved on to something else. And then she became aware that Mary Mackle was standing in the room behind her.

By seven that evening, everyone had left the castle and Aidan, who'd continued to ring hotels in his search for Nieve, was feeling utterly defeated.

'I'm getting really worried now,' he said anxiously. 'She's a sensible person, but she's so upset and – well, what if she does something stupid?'

'She won't,' said Darcey comfortingly. 'Look, why don't you join me at the Radisson? I'm meeting Carol, Rosa and Roy there.'

'I'm heading to the airport now,' said Aidan. 'To see if she's trying to get a flight out. There's an evening one, and she might be on it.'

'It's a mess,' said Darcey.

'I know. But it's not Nieve's mess. She's a victim too.'

'I guess she is,' said Darcey. 'I guess that's a new feeling for her.'

Later, as she sat with Rosa, Carol and Roy, she thought about Nieve as a victim. She couldn't help feeling extremely sorry for her friend. She tried to analyse exactly how sorry she felt, wondering if, as Rosa had suggested previously, she wasn't taking a bit of satisfaction from the fact that it had all gone so horribly wrong for Nieve, but in the end she didn't really think so. And the main reason for that was because she'd spent so much time talking to Aidan.

Despite the fact that everyone else was in shock about the Ennco situation and the loss of money for everyone involved, Aidan was far more concerned by the disappearance of his fiancée than the disappearance of her fortune. Darcey was actually stunned that he was able to take the loss of so much money with such apparent equanimity (although she'd always known that money wasn't his thing). Nevertheless, it was one matter to say that you didn't care that much about it, another entirely to see so much money disappear from under your nose.

It was that that made Darcey see how much he loved Nieve. And always would.

Nieve was still sitting in Mary Mackle's living room, but this time with a laptop computer in front of her. Mary had offered to let her check out some internet news sites to see if she could find out any more information about Ennco. She'd listened sympathetically as Nieve had explained what had happened and cursed Mike Horgan and everyone around him. Nieve had been touched by the younger woman's immediate acceptance of her explanation.

'But sure why would I think you were some kind of criminal?' asked Mary. 'If you were, you'd be staying somewhere bigger and flashier than this.'

'I'd probably be keeping a low profile,' said Nieve, 'which would make Bayside Meadows the perfect hideaway.'

'Ah, get away with yourself!' Mary grinned at her. 'I can tell anyhow. You're not a bad person.'

At Mary's words, Nieve felt the now familiar, but generally unaccustomed, prickle of tears in her eyes.

'You know, you should be answering that phone,' said Mary as the mobile rang yet again. 'Your poor fiancé is probably doing his nut.'

'Probably,' agreed Nieve as she clicked on a *Sun Herald* piece about Ennco. 'But this isn't my phone and all those calls are probably for the girl who owns it.'

'In that case you should get back and give it to her,' said Mary, 'because someone sure wants to speak to her.'

'I'll switch it off in a minute.' Nieve frowned as she scanned the online article. 'They've arrested Harley Black too. I knew it! I knew the two of them had to be involved. It wasn't possible for Mike to be in it all on his own. That bastard Black! He tried to imply that any problems with the company would be entirely due to my staff. Shithead! Oh, sorry.' She looked apologetically at Davey and Eimear, who were watching her accusingly.

'She has to put money in the swear box,' said Davey. 'A euro.'

Nieve picked up her bag and opened her purse. 'I've only a fiver left,' she said. 'What about I put the whole lot in and then I'll have some words to spare.'

Davey looked at his mother in puzzlement and Mary laughed.

'Ah, with all that's happened, maybe you can have a few for free,' she said. 'If it was me, I'd be cursing and swearing too.'

Aidan arrived at the Radisson around nine o'clock that evening. Darcey, Rosa, Roy and Carol were sitting in the bar area chatting. Darcey stood up and waved as she spotted him.

'Any news?' she asked when he joined them.

He shook his head helplessly. 'I don't know why she's doing this to me. She knows I must be worrying about her.'

'She always was a bit of a selfish cow,' said Rosa, and then winced as Carol dug her in the ribs. 'Ow! Sorry, but she was.'

'She sees things from her own perspective,' agreed Aidan. 'But that doesn't mean she's selfish.'

'I think it's bloody selfish to run off and leave you to deal with the mess,' observed Roy.

'Look, if all you guys are going to do is trash her, then I'll leave.' Aidan looked around at them angrily.

'We're not trashing her.' Darcey put her hand on his arm. 'Really we're not. We've just known her a long time and we know what she's like.'

'No you don't.' Aidan was still angry. 'You don't know how hard she's worked over the past few years. You don't know how she already brought us back from financial ruin to having a great home in a great part of town. She fought for everything we have and I owe her everything, and I won't listen to you talking about her as though you guys know more about her than I do. She's close enough to being my wife and I won't have you diss her like that.'

They all exchanged penitent looks.

'I'm sorry,' said Darcey eventually. 'You're right. We haven't seen her in a long time and we're basing our reactions on how she was, not how she is now.'

'Dammit.' Aidan rubbed his eyes with the tips of his fingers. 'I know that she can come across as a bit self-centred, but that's the way our life is. I wanted her to stand back from it a bit. I wanted to come home, start a family, and she kind of agreed, but deep down, I know she didn't think she was ready. Maybe she would have changed her mind anyway. Maybe this gave her the perfect excuse.'

'I hardly think that's likely,' said Rosa sympathetically. 'If she'd wanted to call off the wedding, she would have done it differently. You're not thinking straight, Aidan.'

'Give me your phone,' said Darcey. 'I'll try the mobile again. You never know, this time she might pick up.'

'I should have been dancing by now.' Nieve looked at her watch as Mary sat beside her. 'We had a load of string quartets and stuff for earlier, then there was to be a big band playing jazz and Glenn Miller numbers, and that girl who won *Pop Idol*. Plus a DJ for later.'

'Crikey,' said Mary. 'Sounds fun.'

'It would have been great.' This time she gazed out of the window at the still bright garden. 'It was a perfect day for it.'

'It's not the end of the world,' said Mary. 'You can do it again.'

There was a touch of hysteria in Nieve's laugh. 'I don't think so,' she said. 'I couldn't afford to do it again.'

'You don't need the hoopla,' Mary pointed out. 'Getting married is something between two people. The rest is just padding.'

Suddenly Nieve started to cry. Slow tears at first, and then convulsive sobs that racked her body. Mary put her arm around the other girl's shoulder and hugged her tightly.

Then the phone rang again.

'This is a waste of time.' Darcey listened to the phone ring. 'It's just going to divert to my mailbox again. Of course she could just have it switched off and so she doesn't even know it's . . . Oh . . . oh, hello. Nieve?'

'No, my name is Mary Mackle. Nieve is staying with me. Who's this?'

'Darcey McGonigle,' replied Darcey. 'Nieve is . . . my friend. That's my phone you're holding, she took it by mistake. Is she there?'

'Hold on.'

There was a slight flurry and a murmur of voices while Darcey looked expectantly at the group of people around her.

'Hello.'

'Nieve!' Darcey's voice was filled with relief. 'Where are you? Are you OK? Aidan's here. He's worried sick.'

'I'm fine,' said Nieve. 'I'm in a B&B about thirty miles from town. I hitched here this morning.'

'Nieve!'

'Ah, come on, no big deal. We did it through Europe, remember?'

'Yes.'

'So it's cool. I'm fine. I just needed some space.'

Aidan was hopping up and down, pointing at the phone and then his ear, making it plain that he wanted to talk to her. Darcey frowned at him and shook her head slightly.

'You scared the life out of us. Especially Aidan.'

'Is he there? With you?'

Darcey spoke carefully. 'We're all here. Rosa and Carol and Aidan and me. We're worried about you.'

'Tell him I'm sorry.'

'Tell him yourself.'

'I've given him a way out.' Nieve spoke quickly. 'I've left him, Darcey. It's for the best.'

'No, it's not.'

'He'd be tainted by association with me. It doesn't matter whether I had anything to do with the Ennco mess or not. Mud sticks. He's better off without me.'

'He doesn't think that way.'

Nieve laughed raggedly. 'I told him he could have you. It's what you've always wanted.'

Darcey gulped. 'But not what *he* always wanted,' she said. 'And Nieve, not what I want at all. Not what I've wanted for years.'

'Really?' Nieve sounded doubtful.

'It's been a long time,' said Darcey. 'We're all different people now.'

There was a silence at the other end of the phone.

'Does he hate me?' Nieve asked eventually.

'No,' said Darcey slowly. 'No, he doesn't.'

'He should. I've totally ruined our lives. I let this terrible thing happen. It wasn't my fault, I had nothing to do with what went on, but I should have guessed. You probably think that I did guess, because you probably think that after everything that went on in Christie Corp and how I got the job and how I got on . . . well, I don't blame you if you think I knew about this. But I didn't.'

'I do believe you.'

'Why?' asked Nieve. 'You know what I'm like.'

'Sure I do,' said Darcey. 'You're not a fraudster, though.'

'Thanks.' Nieve's voice was wobbly. 'Thanks for saying it on TV too. It means a lot to me that you think that.'

'It doesn't really matter what I think,' said Darcey. 'In the end it's what you know and what Aidan knows that really counts.'

She flapped her hand at him as he continued to mouth at her that he wanted to speak to Nieve.

'I'm sorry,' said Nieve again.

'Oh, it's OK,' Darcey told her. 'We're sorry that we didn't have the great day that we'd been looking forward to, but what the hell, we had a few drinks and toasted you anyway.'

'I didn't mean sorry about the wedding, you dope. I'm sorry about . . . about Aidan.'

Darcey was silent.

'Darce . . . are you there?'

'Yes,' she said slowly.

'I honestly didn't mean things to turn out the way they did. Darcey, I know I behaved really badly, but the truth in the end was that I fell in love with him.'

'Love happens,' said Darcey, 'even when you don't expect it.'

'I do love him,' said Nieve. 'I know you might not believe that, but I do.'

'Better tell him, so.'

'Jeez, Darce . . . I dunno. I ran away from our wedding! That was totally selfish. He must hate me.'

'Nieve, don't be so damn silly,' Darcey said firmly. 'He loves you too. Now talk to him and sort things out.' She thrust the phone at Aidan and walked away from him and into the foyer of the hotel.

# Chapter 33

'So what happened next?' Anna Sweeney looked at Darcey in anticipation. It was noon and they were sitting in the Italian coffee bar, two wide cups of frothy cappuccino and two Danish pastries in front of them.

'I actually went into the loo and cried for a bit while he talked to her,' admitted Darcey. 'When I came out, he'd gone to get her.'

Actually, she hadn't exactly come out. Rosa and Carol had both come in and banged at the cubicle door, telling her that Aidan had headed off to the B&B and asking if she was OK. She hadn't been sure whether she was OK or not. Her conversation with Nieve had set off a chain of thoughts in her head and, sitting in the cubicle, staring at the door, she was thinking that she had wasted the last ten years of her life. Not in the sense that she hadn't got on with things and worked hard and got a good job and been the sort of person that she never believed she could be – nobody could truly notch that up as a waste – but that she'd spent so many years feeling hard done by simply because a guy she loved had fallen in love with someone else. She hadn't let herself move on from it and she'd let it mess up her own life when it really didn't have to. It seemed to her now that she'd wasted an awful lot of her emotions on the wrong thing. And as for the things that truly mattered, well, she hadn't given them half enough of her emotional energy at all.

'Did she come home with him?' asked Anna.

Darcey nodded. 'Apparently it was a love fest. He cried. She cried. They swore undying love for each other.'

'You've got to admit that it's very romantic.'

'It probably would've been more romantic if she'd talked to him sooner and they could've got married like they planned,' said Darcey.

'So did they in the end?'

'No. She wanted to go home and deal with all the Ennco shit first. She said that she didn't want to marry him without a clean bill of corporate health. She had to find out whether there were any charges against her and all that sort of stuff first, although obviously if there are charges – and we don't know that yet – she'll be fighting them. Of course it doesn't matter to Aidan, he wants to marry her anyway, but it matters to Nieve.'

Darcey had met her friend the evening after the wedding should have taken place. Nieve had called at Minette's house with her mobile phone. Darcey had answered the door because Minette was out shopping and had been startled to see Nieve standing there.

She was a different Nieve, devoid of the make-up she usually always wore during the day, her long dark hair pulled loosely back from her face. She looked more like the pre-Max Christie Nieve, but although she was simply wearing jeans and a T-shirt, and although her look was casual, Darcey couldn't help thinking that she was still stunning and probably always had been, only she'd never really noticed it before.

She'd invited her in.

'It hasn't changed,' Nieve said, looking around her. 'Well it has, of course. New colour on the walls and new furniture, but . . . it still feels the same.'

'Not all of us moved on the same way as you.'

'Darcey, please don't get at me.'

'I won't. I'm not. Would you like some tea?'

Nieve shook her head. 'No thanks. My mother keeps offering me cups and I feel like gallons of the stuff is sloshing around inside.'

Darcey grinned.

'Anyway, I'm just here to give you back your phone and say thanks for . . . well, I guess for looking after Aidan and not actually persuading him to run away with you.'

'I didn't want him to. And he wouldn't have,' said Darcey. 'He's bonkers about you. You're lucky.'

'I know.' Nieve shrugged. 'Of course I don't exactly feel lucky right now, what with everything that's going on, but I do know that I'm lucky to have him. He was fantastic last night . . .'

'He's really proud of you,' Darcey told her. 'He admires all that go-getting thing that you do.'

'Oh well.' This time Nieve sighed. 'I'm not sure how much get-go is left in me, to be honest. There's only so many times you can climb a mountain.'

'I bet you can give it one more go.'

'Perhaps,' said Nieve. 'But hell, Darcey – I've lost so much damn money this time . . .' She swallowed hard. 'For a while there I was really living my dream. I had everything I ever wanted. Now it's come crashing down around me and I'm finding it really, really hard to pick myself up.'

'Was the dream always about money?' asked Darcey.

'Pretty much,' admitted Nieve. 'It just seemed to matter to me. I guess because it's a really easy way of proving you've achieved something. And, Darce, I was making millions from the Ennco deal. Millions! Me, Nieve Stapleton, whose family once had to move to a smaller house because my dad lost his job, had millions in the bank. I got such a buzz out of it. It made me feel so good. That's why I went loopy with the whole wedding thing. To show off.'

'If I had that kind of money, I'd probably show off as well,' admitted Darcey. 'What's happened about your wedding stuff? That planner of yours was going mental. When she realised you'd disappeared, I thought she was going to blow a gasket. I think she was ready to haul you up the aisle no matter what, just so's her wedding would go ahead!'

'I feel really sorry for her,' confessed Nieve. 'She worked so hard to make everything perfect and I was the one who messed it up. Plus I owed her the balance of the money because I hadn't paid everything up front just in case there were problems. Anyway, she's sorted out now.' Nieve cleared her throat. 'Dad . . . Dad paid her. He said he'd been saving for my wedding since the day I was born. He quite liked the idea of giving me money. I'm hoping to sell my stupid diamond tiara on eBay or something and get enough for it to pay him back.'

'And at the end of it all, have you come to that great conclusion about money not buying happiness?' asked Darcey.

Nieve laughed. A genuine laugh. 'It mightn't buy happiness, but it can buy a lot of things that help. All the same . . .' She looked confidingly at Darcey. 'There is one thing that maybe proves I'm not a complete hard-hearted money-bitch.'

'What?'

'I wanted Aidan to sign a pre-nup.'

Darcey looked enquiringly at Nieve.

'I went to my lawyer and he put me in touch with someone. I got it all drawn up.'

'And?'

'And in the end I couldn't ask him.'

Darcey smiled. 'So, a softie after all, then.'

'Despite myself. And he's been so damn great since, that every time I think about it I break out in a cold sweat. You won't tell him, will you?'

'Of course not,' said Darcey. 'Anyway, now that you're back and sorted, there's no need for me to talk to him about anything. He's your fiancé. I don't matter.'

'I was afraid that after I scarpered he and you might realise that you were meant to be together after all.'

'You know, Nieve, he made it perfectly clear to me that that would never happen,' said Darcey.

'Do you still . . .'

Darcey shook her head. 'I'm glad I met him again,' she said. 'It's showed me how little any of it matters any more.'

Nieve still looked doubtful.

'So what now?' asked Darcey quickly.

'We're heading back to the States tomorrow,' Nieve told her. 'There's loads of things to sort out. I need to talk to the investigators about Mike's scam. It wasn't my responsibility or something I necessarily should have known about, but the fact that someone on my staff spotted it and I didn't is a worry.' She winced. 'You would've spotted it, Darce. I know you would.'

'Maybe not.'

'Oh, come on.' Nieve sighed. 'You look at numbers and it's like they're a completed jigsaw for you. You'd have seen it just the way Paola did, and you'd have been the whistle-blower, and you'd have come out on top like you always do.'

'Come out on top?' Darcey looked at her sceptically. 'Nieve, I never did. You were always that person.'

'Give me a break,' said Nieve. 'In school, at college – even if I beat you I always knew that you could've done better. And the times that you did beat me, you were so far ahead. You were great when I was with Max Christie and you did all that translation stuff for me, and I never really thanked you properly.'

'You bought me jewellery,' Darcey reminded her.

'And I pinched your boyfriend.'

Darcey said nothing for a moment, then she exhaled slowly.

'Yes, you did. And I know you're still a bit suspicious about how I feel, but in the end it was for the best,' she said eventually. 'I've been thinking about it a lot lately. Hard not to, of course. Nieve, I was crazy in love with Aidan. But he was my first love. Crikey – how many people marry their first love? Hardly anyone. I just had these daft ideas that because it was so great and wonderful with him then it should be great and wonderful for ever, and life isn't like that.'

'Darcey – he would've married you.'

'I know. And . . . and . . . it would've been a mistake.'

Nieve looked at her searchingly.

'You really think so?'

'Yes,' said Darcey. 'I really do.'

This time Nieve's look was less doubtful.

'Truly,' added Darcey.

'Thank you,' said Nieve. 'Thank you for everything.'

'You *will* come out on top in the end,' said Darcey confidently. 'You always do.'

Nieve looked worried. 'Maybe this time I won't.'

'I wouldn't bet against it. And you always have Aidan.'

Nieve nodded. 'That's the thing. The dream might have come tumbling down, but he was there for me. And that's probably the bit you were talking about when you asked me about money buying happiness. It didn't buy Aidan. And he's the most important part of my life.'

Anna spooned froth out of her cup. 'So are you guys friends again?'

'Ah, come on!' Darcey made a face at her. 'The cow still pinched my boyfriend.'

'But, after everything . . .'

Now Darcey laughed. 'I meant it when I said she probably was right to pinch him. We would've broken up eventually anyway.'

'You really think so?'

'I don't really know.' Darcey's tone was serious. 'Maybe we would've been the best thing since sliced bread. Maybe it would've been spectacular. But it's all maybe, isn't it? I have to stop thinking about the maybes, and how things might have been, or how I thought they should have been. I have to accept things the way they are. And the truth is, Anna, he's besotted with her. So whether she pinched him or not doesn't matter. They're right for each other. I was only fooling myself to think any differently.'

Back at her desk that afternoon, Darcey busied herself with her emails. There was one from Rocco, telling her that the new business development manager for Italy was a nice enough person but not half as nice as her, and wondering whether she was planning a trip to Milan again in the near future. A new restaurant had opened within walking distance of her usual hotel and it was superb. He wanted to show it to her.

She smiled to herself. A trip to Milan would be nice. Seeing Rocco again would be nice too. But her feelings towards him, towards all her continental men, had changed. Yes, they'd been great to know. Yes, they'd been exactly what she needed. The trouble was that she didn't know if they were what she needed any more. In the last couple of months the focus of her life seemed to have shifted, and the things that had seemed important to her before had lost their hold on her.

'Busy?'

His voice startled her and she looked up from the computer screen. She hadn't spoken to him since the day he'd left her to pay the bill in the Harbourmaster. She'd been so angry then, she realised, but suddenly she didn't want to be angry with him any more.

'Hi.'

'Can you spare me a few minutes of your time?'

'Sure.'

'It's about your travel plans.'

'What about them?' Hell, she thought, maybe he doesn't trust me to go to Tokyo after the Singapore débâcle. Maybe he wants to go himself.

'There's been a bit of a change.'

She felt her stomach sink.

'Oh?' she said calmly.

'Well, the US crowd have just employed an ex-fund manager from Japan. He has brilliant contacts there already and we're thinking that maybe you doing Japan is reinventing the wheel a bit—'

'Oh for heaven's sake!' she interrupted him, her concern about her future making her tone more abrupt than she intended. 'What are you guys like! Choose a strategy and stick with it.'

'I understand that this hasn't been the best way to deal with it. That's why we want you to come to Edinburgh and discuss things.'

'Again?'

'Yes. If you wouldn't mind.'

'When?'

'Next week?'

She called up her desktop diary. 'I guess so. Whatever day suits. Just let me know.'

'Probably early in the week. I'll email you when I get confirmation.'

She nodded.

'You OK?' he asked.

She nodded again and smiled awkwardly at him. 'Um . . . there was just one other thing . . .'

'What?' He looked at her warily.

'When we went to lunch, at the Harbourmaster . . . we talked about Aidan and Nieve and their wedding and you called me self-centred and selfish—'

'Actually,' he interrupted her, 'I'm sorry about that. I was way out of line.'

'No,' she said. 'You weren't. And I wanted to say that you were right. I *was* being self-centred, and maybe I have been for a long time. And so I'm sorry about that.'

'Oh.'

'So can we put that incident behind us and get our working relationship back on an even keel, because there's so much to do and so many opportunities out there, and I don't want to be uncomfortable with you.'

'Of course.' He was looking at her as though he'd never seen her in his life before.

'Great,' she said. 'Well, I look forward to hearing the day for the Edinburgh trip.'

He stood in front of her, not leaving.

'Did you go to the wedding?' he asked finally.

'Sorry?'

'The wedding. Did you go?'

'Didn't Anna tell you?'

He shook his head. 'I haven't seen her the last couple of days.'

Darcey frowned slightly.

'Well?' he asked.

'There wasn't a wedding.'

He looked at her in astonishment.

Darcey explained about the Ennco situation and Nieve's difficulties. 'But hopefully it'll all work out,' she said.

'And you're all right with this?'

'Of course,' she said.

'You're sure?'

'Very.'

'Well, what d'you know,' he said as he turned away from her desk. 'I think pigs are flying around the room.'

When she got home that evening, she threw open the windows of her apartment and let the air circulate. She stood in the centre of her neat living room and wondered whether it would be an idea to do a bit of home decorating. She actually liked the current style, but she hadn't changed it since she'd moved in. And although taupes and creams were very restful, she wondered if it wasn't time to jazz things up a little with a few splashes of colour. Purple, she thought. Like my Singapore shoes.

She went into the bedroom and took them out of the wardrobe. She slid her feet gingerly into them. The swelling of her foot and ankle was now almost nonexistent, and they fitted her perfectly. Maybe there'll be another event I can wear them to in the future, she thought. Or maybe I'll find myself a new boyfriend and wear them on a hot date with him. Only this time maybe I'll find someone I can share the spark with, instead of looking for someone who doesn't really matter to me at all.

She walked out of the bedroom and back into the living room feeling particularly restless. She knew that it was in part because her life had been turned so upside down by the accident in Singapore and then the excitement of Nieve's non-wedding that she was finding settling back into her old routine more difficult than she'd expected. She'd been looking forward to the Tokyo trip as a way of feeling the buzz again, but now she was pretty certain that they'd give Japan to the ex-fund manager. She thought she could do a good job, but if the other guy was a Japanese market specialist, then he had her beaten hands down. And Neil Lomond would want the best person on the job. An experienced fund manager versus a vain and selfish bitch would win every time.

Maybe he wasn't thinking of her like that now. Maybe he could see that she was changing.

When he'd first come to Dublin, she'd been perfectly happy for him to think of her as the flaky blonde who'd given him so much personal grief; but since Singapore she'd thought that they'd become, if not friends (which was asking a bit much), at least somewhat closer. She didn't want him to dislike her or to think badly of her. And it would be worrying if, because he didn't like her, he took Japan away from her. If that happened, then what future did she have with InvestorCorp? She'd quite suddenly managed to move on from everything to do with Aidan

Clarke. Maybe now she had to move on from everything to do with Neil Lomond too. Maybe she had to move on, full stop.

InvestorCorp was a much bigger organisation than Global Finance had ever been, and decisions were going to be made at board level that would affect her life in ways that maybe she didn't want any more. She'd enjoyed the Singapore trip, but she wasn't sure that travelling halfway around the world was really what it was all about for her. The truth was, no matter what kicks she got out of it, she preferred Europe.

An olive farm in Tuscany, she told herself as she sat on the edge of her bed. Maybe that's still my dream after all.

# Chapter 34

The sun was shining in Palo Alto when Nieve and Aidan arrived home. Nieve stood at the kerb, her hands thrust deep into the pockets of her loose white trousers, while Aidan paid the cab-driver. As the car pulled away, Sienna Mendez waved at her from the garden of the house opposite. Nieve swallowed hard and waved back. Sienna, who hardly ever spoke to her in the normal course of events, trotted across the street.

'How you doin'?' she asked. 'I saw all that stuff on the news. You guys OK?'

That was the great thing about America, thought Nieve. No bullshit. Just cut directly to the chase.

'I don't know,' she answered her neighbour. 'Obviously it's all been a bit traumatic, and of course we were away, so I don't have a good handle on what's going on. But I'm heading into the office tomorrow to find out.'

'Hey, I'm sure it'll all work out for you,' said Sienna.

'Thanks,' said Nieve. 'Have you heard anything about it yourself?'

Sienna shook her head. 'The news stations are totally

dissing Mike Horgan. There've been quite a few of your colleagues doing interviews and stuff, and the investors sounding off, of course. But what can you do?'

'Heaven knows,' said Nieve. 'Anyway, Sienna, we'd better get inside and unpack.'

'How was the wedding?' Sienna glanced at the garment-holder containing the Vera Wang dress. 'This cast a cloud over it?'

Nieve glanced at Aidan. 'No,' she said firmly. 'Not at all.'

She put the dress over her arm and tugged her Diane von Furstenberg case towards the house.

'Why didn't you tell her?' asked Aidan as he opened the front door.

'Why should I?' she responded. 'Besides, I feel married.'

Aidan laughed. 'What about your clean bill of financial health?' he asked.

'Once things are sorted out, once I know that there are no charges to face and that everything is fine . . . then we'll get married. But I don't want anyone to know what happened.'

'They will eventually,' he said. 'All of our American friends will tell them.'

'Yeah, well, I'll worry about that later.'

'I would have gone through with it, you know,' he told her.

'Yes, I do know. But that's not how I wanted it to be,' she said. As he went to speak, she covered his lips with her fore-finger. 'And I don't mean that I wanted the whole grand event thing to happen. I want to know that we're OK with every-thing when we get married. I want it to mean something.'

'Wouldn't it have meant something anyway?' he asked.

'Of course,' she answered. 'But that wasn't the point. I couldn't just pretend everything was all right when it wasn't. I can do bravado, but not that much. We'll do it soon. I promise.'

'Nieve?'

'What?'

'It doesn't have to be perfect,' he told her. 'You don't have to have your so-called clean bill of financial health. We don't need a wedding-planner. Getting married is a very simple thing between two people who love each other.'

She stared at him. And suddenly found her eyes filling with tears.

'Hey, hey,' he said. 'I'm sorry. I didn't mean . . .'

'Don't be sorry.' Her voice was choked. 'Don't be sorry for being the kind of person who knows what's important in life. Don't be sorry for being the kind of guy who's sticking with me despite the fact that I so totally lost it in Ireland! I'm so damn lucky to have you, Aidan Clarke. And I don't think I ever appreciated you properly before.'

'Of course you did,' he said.

'No, I didn't. I thought I was the great one in the relationship, making the money, doing all this stuff. But you're there for me. Always.'

'I know.'

'I love you,' she said.

'I'll always love you,' he told her as he scooped her into his arms and carried her into the house.

\* \* \*

There were forensic accountants in Ennco as well as Federal investigators. All the desks were covered with files and papers and nobody was allowed to log on to their computers without permission. According to Paola Benedetti, the company had filed for bankruptcy protection, but Decker Benson, a rival brokerage firm, had now made an offer for it and it seemed as though a takeover was going to happen. The offer was nominal and meant nothing in real-money terms to the share-holders, but it offered a certain amount of security to the employees.

'You did some job, Paola,' said Nieve as she waited to talk to one of the investigators.

'It was a fluke,' said Paola. 'I shouldn't even have been looking at that report. I hit print for the wrong one and it just caught my eye.'

'Better to be lucky than smart,' said Nieve wryly.

Paola shrugged.

'Hold on,' said Nieve apologetically. 'That's unfair. You were both lucky *and* smart. Once you saw it, you knew there was something wrong, and you dealt with it.'

'Thanks,' said Paola.

'I guess they'll keep you on in the new firm,' Nieve said. 'Probably open a crèche specially for you and everything.'

Paola grimaced. 'I'm sure they'll keep you too.'

'I don't know whether that's good or bad,' said Nieve. 'I really don't.'

Five hours later, after an extensive grilling by the people who were checking out the company, she wasn't sure whether she ever wanted to be involved in a financial business again. The investigators had focused in on the fact that it had been

Paola, an administrative clerk on her staff, who discovered the error, and continued to press Nieve for the reasons why she'd missed it herself. Nieve wondered how many times she'd have to say that that particular report wasn't her responsibility, that Harley Black was the man in charge, that Paola shouldn't even have been looking at it, before they'd actually believe her.

Afterwards she and Murphy Ledwidge sat in her office and contemplated the future.

'I just hate having the money snatched from under my nose,' Murphy complained. 'When I didn't have it I had a focus in trying to earn it. But when it was there, so close . . .'

'I know how you feel.' Nieve had made tea for both of them from her special pack that she kept for emergencies. 'Although actually I've got around to thinking that the whole thing was a dream. That there never was any money.'

'For us there wasn't,' said Murphy sourly. 'Did you know that there have been death threats made against Mike?'

'No!' She looked at him aghast.

'Oh yes,' he said. 'And given half the chance . . .' He shrugged. 'Well, maybe not. But he deserves to have something really bad happen to him.'

'I agree with you there.'

'When I listen to all these business people talking about how he built up the company, and how great he was and everything . . .' Murphy made a face. 'He got rich thanks to us and he would've continued doing it. He didn't need to scam the company as well.'

'At what point, I wonder, would people have found out about his secret accounts?'

'Oh, eventually, I'm sure,' said Murphy. 'Thing is, if they hadn't, he probably would've paid them all back eventually and no one would ever have known.'

Nieve sighed. 'I was thinking that myself. And thinking that in some way maybe it's my fault, because I was always on Paola's case about putting in extra time to make up for the days she had to rush off to look after her kid or go to an ob-gyn appointment . . . Perhaps if I hadn't made her feel so bad about that, then she wouldn't have been looking at the accounts . . .' She trailed off. 'Well, I suppose it had to come out, we could hardly have stayed working for a company that was being defrauded, but I wish it hadn't happened when it did.'

'There's never a good time for something like this,' said Murphy.

'Still, I can't help feeling that there's a message in all this for me. There's a rumour going round that they want to make Paola head of compliance!'

Murphy laughed. 'Which makes me wonder if the new guys will be any better than the old.'

'I wonder if we'll ever work in this town again.' Nieve placed her empty cup on the filing cabinet and looked gloomily at her colleague.

Murphy laughed. 'Don't be so pessimistic. Of course we will. I bet we'll have offers in the next few days.'

'I hope so,' said Nieve. 'But to tell you the truth, Murph, I just don't know if I have the energy to start over again.'

Murphy told her that of course she had, that she was one of the most dynamic people he knew and that she was great at what she did.

But Nieve couldn't help wondering if that was true any more.

By the end of the week she was completely wrung out by the investigation. She was confident now that she'd be cleared of wrongdoing, and had been told by Decker Benson, the new owners, that there was a probable role for her in the compliance department when they'd completed the takeover. She'd thought that the news would both cheer her up and fire her up, but the truth was, as she told Aidan that evening, she wasn't sure that she wanted it.

'It's crazy,' she said as they sat on the swing-chair on the porch. 'I need the money. We need the money. But there's a part of me that just doesn't want to bother any more.'

'Hon, we need money, but not necessarily all that much,' he told her. 'You seem to forget whenever you think about our finances that I have a well-paying job myself. And that my salary can cover our mortgage payments.'

'They're repossessing my Acura,' she said glumly.

'So?'

'I need a car.'

'There's always the Prius.' He grinned at her. Then his expression became more serious. 'We could go back to Ireland,' he said.

She drew her knees up beneath her chin and looked at him thoughtfully.

'I know it's an option,' she told him. 'Though like I said before, everything about Ireland is expensive these days. It was fine when I could've swanned in and bought whatever

I wanted, but the way things are now, we couldn't even afford a one-bed apartment in the city!'

'But you'd be at home,' he told her. 'Perhaps that would be better for us.'

'If you truly want to go back to Ireland, I will,' she said slowly. 'I'm happy to do whatever you want. But to be completely honest with you, Aidan, this really is home to me now. I felt like a stranger in Ireland. I don't want to go back. I love it here. I want – I want us to bring up our family here. Eventually.'

'A family?'

'Not just yet,' she said hastily. 'I'm not quite ready. But I suppose I'm thinking that having a good job is all very well, but having people you love is better. And I reckon that we'd have some very smart kids.'

He laughed. 'You bet.'

'Well then,' she said. 'Let's go and get some practice at making them.'

'You read my mind,' he told her as he followed her up the stairs.

Even though she was tired, and even though their love-making had left her feeling lazily languorous, she still couldn't sleep. She hadn't slept properly since the day the news about Ennco had broken and she wondered if she'd ever sleep properly again. She pushed back the comforter and Aidan moved slightly.

'OK?' he mumbled.

'Absolutely,' she reassured him. 'I can't sleep. But don't get up. I'm fine.'

He grunted and buried his head in the pillow.

She tiptoed into her home office and switched on the computer.

She couldn't access the Ennco files any more. That might not be a bad thing, she told herself, as she looked at the company's home page, which had already been redesigned by Decker Benson. I probably spent too much time looking at the damn files. Pity they were the wrong ones.

However, she had her own records. The investigators hadn't asked her about her personal files yet, which had surprised her. She felt that they should have. Not that it mattered. For once in her life she was truly blameless.

But she'd stored memos and emails and a whole heap of other information on her computer. She needed to let them know about it. She would. After she'd saved everything first.

She burned all of her files on to DVD. Then she sent a few emails and logged off the computer. This time, when she went to bed, she fell asleep straight away.

# Chapter 35

They made an arrangement to meet at the boarding gate, but Darcey actually saw Neil in the café, where she was having her usual espresso. She wasn't sure whether to signal to him, but then he looked across the tables and saw her. He waved and made his way to the seat beside her.

'Good morning,' he said.

'Hi,' she said.

She drank her coffee in a single gulp and replaced the tiny cup on its white saucer.

'I'm sure that's not good for your stomach,' he said mildly.

'My stomach can take care of itself,' she assured him. 'And I totally need the hit at this hour of the morning.'

'I see you've got rid of the splint.'

'The other day,' she said.

'How's the wrist?'

'Fine, thanks.'

He might not be thinking of her as a bitch any more, she thought, but something had changed. There was an edginess between them that she couldn't quite fathom. She glanced at her watch.

'Plenty of time,' said Neil.

'I know.' But she got up anyway, suddenly wanting to be on her own. 'I have to use the bathroom. I'll see you at the gate.'

She bought a newspaper on the way, so that by the time he joined her she was engrossed in the business stories. He glanced at the headline over one that said 'Decker buys Ennco' and cleared his throat. She looked at him questioningly.

'Yes?'

'I was wondering how things were with them. Have you heard anything?'

'I got an email from Nieve,' she told him. 'She thinks she's in the clear but she's not certain. It's still a bit up in the air. Apparently there might be a job for her in the new outfit, but she doesn't think she'll take it.' She smiled shortly. 'It seems like she's had it with high finance for the time being.'

'Leaving you as the business executive and her as the also-ran,' said Neil.

Darcey looked at him in surprise. 'I don't think like that,' she said.

'Don't you?'

'Of course not!'

'Aren't you just a teeny bit pleased that she's got her comeuppance at last?' he asked. 'The girl who ruined your life has been ruined herself. Doesn't that make you happy?'

She said nothing.

'You said it to me once. You wanted her to know what it was like to have everything she'd ever wanted snatched away from her.'

'That depends,' said Darcey slowly, 'on knowing what you really want. And recognising when it's been snatched away.'

She wished that she could read the expression that crossed his eyes as she spoke, but she'd always been hopeless at that.

'We'd better go,' she said into the sudden silence between them.

He nodded, and they made their way to the gate.

They didn't talk much during the flight, or on the drive to the business park either. Darcey was convinced that there was a definite tension between them, and she suddenly began to worry that Neil didn't want to talk to her because he was part of the board that was going to get rid of her. Fire her. Move her sideways. Something. They'd brought in a Japanese guy. Maybe they were bringing in other new people. Maybe he didn't want his ex-wife working in the office. Maybe he couldn't handle it. He was more important to the organisation than she was. And so, as they drew closer and closer to the company's head office, she could feel the butterflies in her stomach fluttering around ever more anxiously and she wiped the palms of her hands along the skirt of her suit.

'Darcey. Good to see you.' Gordon Campbell smiled broadly at her as she walked into the boardroom. The other board members, already standing around drinking coffee, acknowledged her arrival too.

'Coffee, tea?' asked Gordon.

'Thanks,' she said. 'Black coffee, no sugar would be lovely.'

He poured her a cup and then motioned for her to sit down. She slid into a seat near the centre of the table. The other board members followed suit.

'So, Darcey,' said Gordon. 'A good result from your trip. And I believe we've had follow-up funds since then.'

'Yes.' She nodded. 'Media Holdings sent us twenty million yesterday.'

She'd been delighted with that. Media Holdings had been the first company she'd seen, when she was still nervous and unsure of what she was doing. She hadn't really expected anything from them.

'So the only ones who haven't stepped up to the plate yet are . . .'

'Orchard Investments,' she supplied. 'But I spoke to Tricia Lim, one of the managers there, yesterday, and I'm fairly confident we'll get some business after month end.'

'And have you recovered from your fall?' asked Michael Banks.

She nodded. 'It all looked worse than it actually was. But thank you very much for your concern. I really appreciated Neil coming out to check on me.'

'It hasn't put you off going abroad for us again, has it?' asked Alec Burton, another director.

What a stupid question, she thought. Honestly, sometimes board members could be very patronising.

'Of course not.'

'Well, Darcey,' said Gordon, changing the tone and direction of the conversation. 'We wanted to talk to you about that. And what you could be doing in the future.'

She was worried again now. He sounded too serious for her liking. Too much like he was going to impart bad news. But that wouldn't be fair. She'd done a good job. Everyone was agreed on that. Her mind skimmed over all of the hard work that she'd put in, from before the takeover, when she was business development manager for Global Finance, to now, when she'd had to adapt to being an InvestorCorp employee. She worried that somehow, despite the money that had come in from Singapore, they thought there was someone better for the job. She'd always worried that there was someone better for the job, always been afraid of being found out. It was only now, sitting among them, that she believed that there was nothing to find out. That she was good at what she did. Despite herself.

'. . . and so . . .'

She tuned in again, having missed most of what Gordon had said because she was so anxious about his conclusion.

'. . . we think that the right move for us to make is to offer you the position.'

She blinked. What position? She hadn't heard him properly. But she couldn't ask; she'd appear a right fool if she asked.

'What do you think?'

They looked at her expectantly. She swallowed.

'It's a big change,' said Neil, who'd been watching her. 'Director of new business.'

But, she thought, that was his job. That was what he did. She frowned.

'I'm happy myself with replacing Douglas at InvestorCorp in Dublin,' said Neil. 'But it seems to me that you're a perfect replacement for me.'

She'd missed all that entirely!

'I – um – didn't catch what was happening with Douglas,' she said.

'He's moving back to Edinburgh,' said Gordon.

'We think Neil will be an excellent replacement,' added Michael. 'And just as sure that you'll be an excellent replacement for him.'

'So?' Gordon Campbell's voice was still expectant.

'Um, I'm really . . . very honoured,' she said. 'A bit taken aback, to be honest.'

'Why?' asked Michael. 'You deserve it.'

I deserve it, she thought. I deserve to be . . . Omigod, I'm going to be a director! Director of new business. It's a big, big job and they've offered it to me. It was never about being fired – why did I think that? It was about being good at my job. Even though I never think . . . Well, I know I'm good at my job, but still . . . a director. Me!

She began to laugh and stopped quickly. She thought she sounded slightly hysterical. 'Would I be based . . .'

'Here,' said Gordon.

She nodded.

That would be a good thing. Sure, she'd have to move away from Dublin and her lovely apartment and all her friends, but maybe that would do her good. She'd been feeling restless; this was a chance to get rid of that feeling. Her personal life had changed too – seeing Nieve and Aidan again and dealing with all the stuff that she'd never dealt with properly before had lifted the self-imposed burden she'd carried around with her for so long. It was time for change, and this was the best possible change.

'Can I take it you're accepting?' asked Gordon Campbell.

It still seemed totally unreal to her. She couldn't help thinking that she didn't deserve it, that she'd fallen into this job and this life and she hadn't wanted it as badly as Nieve but she still had it. (OK, she told herself, you can get a grip now. It's not like InvestorCorp will make you the multi-millionaire that Nieve so nearly became.) But still! She was an important person. She was director of new business. She was a success! She tried hard not to let the excitement fizzing inside of her show on her face. She wanted to appear as though being promoted was a perfectly normal thing for her. As though she was accepting nothing more than her due.

'Of course,' she said. 'I'm just so – delighted. I didn't know what to say.'

'Excellent.' Neil got up from the table and went into the anteroom. He returned carrying a bucket with a couple of bottles of champagne on ice. 'Congratulations, Darcey,' he said as he gently eased the cork from the first bottle. 'Here's to the new InvestorCorp director of new business.'

'Thanks.' She realised that her hands were shaking. 'Thanks, everyone. I'm . . . I wish I knew more words. I'm . . . well . . . delighted.'

A few hours later, flushed by three glasses of champagne and still buzzing with the surprise of it all, she boarded the return flight to Dublin with Neil. They'd hardly spoken on the return journey to the airport or while they'd waited to board the plane (she'd been still in a daze), but as she flopped into her seat she looked at him and asked him why he hadn't told her.

'I really thought you'd guess,' he said as she fastened her seat belt. 'It seemed so obvious.'

'Why?' She was struggling with the tension of the belt. The person who'd sat in the seat before her had been about five times her size. But the champagne had made her woozy and she couldn't get to grips with it.

'Oh for heaven's sake let me do it.' Neil pulled it tighter for her.

'Thanks.'

'Everyone knew that Douglas wanted to come back to Edinburgh,' he said as he sat back in his seat. 'Unless I totally cocked up, I was a good bet for his job. And everyone was saying how well you'd done I was sure you'd have copped that we'd offer you a directorship.'

'Why?' she asked. 'Why would I think that? Sure, I can get the job done, but I'm not really a director sort of person. I'm just . . . an ordinary bod really.'

He laughed. 'You're totally a director sort of person,' he said. 'Sometimes you're so much so you even scare me.'

'I doubt that.' She smiled faintly,

'Oh, Darcey, you always had the ability to scare me.' His smile was equally faint.

She didn't know what to say, so she said nothing. Then the plane pushed off from the stand, trundled to the runway and climbed steadily into the sky.

They were over the Irish Sea when the captain switched on the seat-belt signs and told the crew to take their seats too as there was a bit of weather ahead that they couldn't avoid and it might get a bit bumpy.

Darcey glanced at Neil, who was immersed in another newspaper, and then pulled her own seat belt a little bit more securely around her. The plane jolted sharply and she caught her breath.

'You OK?' Neil folded the paper and put it in the seat pocket in front of him as they shuddered through a patch of dark cloud.

She nodded and glanced across the aisle. A priest in the window seat opposite blessed himself as the plane lurched sideways and the woman behind them let out an involuntary shriek.

'I hate this,' Neil remarked tightly. 'I know that it's OK really, but it's the fact that I have no control over what's happening that bothers me.'

'*Que sera sera*,' Darcey said.

'Very philosophical.' He tightened his grip on the seat rest.

'No other way to be.' She shrugged. 'It's like being trapped in the lift. It'll be all right or it won't. Worrying about it won't make any difference.' She gasped as they seemed to plummet earthwards before levelling out again.

'It'd be a blow to InvestorCorp to lose the ex-director of new business and the new one in the same day.' Neil tried to keep his voice light, and Darcey suddenly laughed.

'Maybe it's a plot by one of our rivals,' she said.

The plane pitched and Neil inhaled sharply. 'It's at times like this that people tell each other their innermost secrets.'

'Ah, there's plenty of time left for that yet,' she joked. 'When they start shouting "Brace, brace" you can tell me that we were never divorced or something like that.'

He glanced at her and she saw a sudden unreadable expression in his eyes.

'We *are* divorced,' she said urgently. 'I mean – that's not one of your secrets, is it? I saw the papers. They weren't faked.'

'Of course we're divorced.' His tone was vaguely irritable. 'What a stupid thing to say.'

'It was the only dark secret I could think of,' she said wryly. 'Have you any?'

He shook his head.

'There you go then,' she said. 'Though surely it's a bit tragic that we don't have one dark secret between us.'

The plane shuddered again and both of them winced.

'Well, look, I don't have a secret, but I do want to apologise,' said Neil.

'For what?'

'Calling you vain and selfish.'

'You apologised already.'

'Yes, but I still feel badly about it. You're not vain and you're not selfish and I shouldn't have said you were.'

'Neil, I may not be vain – what's the point when you're not drop-dead gorgeous! But I am selfish. I'm terribly selfish, only I didn't realise it. I thought that I was deep and thoughtful and all that sort of stuff. But actually I was just obsessed with myself. Thinking that I'd been dealt a rotten hand because my friend was a bit mean and the bloke I was in love with didn't love me back! I mean, how pathetic can a person be!'

'It was a bit more complicated than that,' said Neil.

'Not when you come down to it,' she said. 'Sure, there were loads of things that I wasn't great at dealing with. But you know what, I met you, you were great to me, and instead of acting like an adult, I decided to wreck our lives too. I married you because I could, not because I should. I was totally wrong to do that, and if anyone should be apologising, it's me for being – just like you said – totally selfish. And actually you were partially right on the vanity thing too. I wasn't thinking of going to the wedding and pinching Aidan from under Nieve's nose, but I did want to look great and make him think that I was far more gorgeous than her. So vain is probably reasonable under the circumstances.'

'Wow.' He grinned at her. 'That's quite a statement.'

'I know.'

'But you're being a bit hard on yourself.'

'I don't think so.'

'It wasn't all bad,' said Neil. 'Being married to you.'

She smiled. 'Thanks. But when it goes wrong, you tend to focus on the bad bits and forget the good.'

He nodded. 'Like our Christmas in Scotland.'

It had snowed. She'd been ecstatic because it had been so wonderfully and unexpectedly traditional. On Christmas night they'd gone for a walk in the extensive grounds of the hotel where they'd been staying. They'd crunched their way beneath the silver light of an almost full moon through the snow and towards the small patch of woodland at the edge of the grounds, leaving their tracks behind them – the large prints of his boots beside the smaller ones of hers.

They'd sat on a felled pine tree and sung 'White Christmas' together, and then, when she'd complained about the cold, he'd taken her in his arms and slid his hand under her tartan miniskirt while she'd giggled that her bum would freeze and he'd told her that he had ways and means of keeping her warm . . .

She blushed furiously as she remembered and hoped that he wasn't remembering too. She tried to keep her face impassive. Apologising to each other was one thing. Being nice to each other was something else. But she didn't want to remember making love to him. He was her boss, for heaven's sake! And he was going out with her best friend. As she thought about Anna, she was jolted even more firmly back to the present. I've moved on, she reminded herself. And so, very clearly, has Neil. There's no room in our present for what happened in the past.

Another violent shudder ran through the plane and she swallowed hard as it seemed to plunge downwards before levelling out again.

'Are they going to get married, d'you think?' Neil's voice broke into her thoughts.

'Huh?'

'Nieve and Aidan. Will they definitely do it?

'I think so. I expect so.' Darcey shrugged. 'I don't care about it any more. Honestly.'

He nodded. 'Sorry. I'm just talking because it's distracting me from the fact that we're being shaken around like a can of peas here.'

'OK then,' she said. 'Just in case it all goes horribly wrong, and so you don't die wondering, I talked to Aidan and I talked to Nieve and . . . well, I don't think I'll ever be her best friend again, but I don't hate her any more.'

'And him?'

'I don't hate him either.'

'Do you still love him?'

The question hung between them.

'I loved the idea of him,' she said finally. 'I loved the idea that I'd met the man of my dreams and we were getting married and if I'd been with him my life would have been perfect. I used him as an excuse for everything that ever went wrong for me. But he's a different person now. I am too. So of course I don't love him.'

The worst shudder yet racked the plane and she gasped. Even though she never minded flying in bad weather conditions, she'd never experienced anything like this before. And she supposed that it wasn't out of the question that perhaps the captain might make a basic error and somehow their perfectly normal commuter flight back to Dublin could end up being a lead story on the evening news.

Unconsciously, she grasped the armrest herself and felt Neil's warm, dry fingers beneath her own.

'Sorry,' she said.

'It's OK. It's nice to have the comfort.'

And then, just as suddenly as they'd been plunged into the turbulence, the jolting eased and the plane began flying evenly again.

'Apologies for all that,' said the captain cheerfully over the intercom. 'Couldn't avoid it. But the weather in Dublin is fine.'

Darcey slid her hand back into her lap and loosened her seat belt, though still keeping it fastened.

Neil let go of the armrest and flexed his fingers.

'Nervy stuff, though,' he said.

'Ah, the champagne helped,' she told him. 'Dulled any potential terror.'

The seat-belt sign came on again and both of them looked at it warily, but this time it was because they were making their final approach to Dublin airport.

'How about we go for something to eat?' he suggested after they'd disembarked from the plane. 'To celebrate.'

'We already celebrated,' she pointed out. 'Lunch with the board and fizzy drink.'

'No, you dope. Celebrate the fact that we didn't end up as wreckage on the runway.'

She laughed. 'That was never going to happen.'

'Whatever.' He looked at her questioningly and she shrugged.

'Why not? Where have you got in mind?'

They went to Roly's in Ballsbridge, where Darcey only just stopped Neil from ordering more champagne.

'A glass of wine is enough for me,' she said. 'I can't hold my drink these days.'

So he ordered a crisp Sauvignon Blanc to go with the Caesar salad she'd requested and a Pinot Noir for himself to accompany his beef.

'I don't know why I'm so hungry,' he remarked as the waitress offered them bread and he helped himself to a selection. 'We ate well at lunchtime. I think it's being saved from certain death in the skies.'

'Fool.' She grinned at him and declined the bread.

'You're very healthy these days,' he remarked. 'Very little

alcohol, a sensible diet – you didn't eat much at lunch, I noticed.'

'Oh, well, I try to be a bit more balanced about everything in my life now,' she told him. 'Everything in moderation.'

'Must make things a bit dull sometimes.'

'Not really. Manageable, I'd say.'

He nodded.

'So, come on, since we've escaped certain death and since we've got over you calling me a vain stuck-up cow or whatever, tell me what you've been up to over the last ten years,' she asked after she'd taken an appreciative sip of the chilled wine. 'You know all about me. What about you?'

He started to talk, mainly about his career and his stints overseas and his eventual promotion to the job that she was going to take over. His accent grew softer as he spoke, warm and gentle, as it had been at the Christmas party when she'd danced with him and thought he was lovely. She remembered how she'd felt when he'd put his arms around her. Comforted by him. Suddenly secure. And how she had, for an instant, forgotten all about Aidan Clarke and Nieve Stapleton and how things should have been.

Why didn't I love him? she wondered. He cared enough about me. I cared enough about him. He made me feel happy. So why didn't I love him?

She felt a sudden, sickening lurch in her stomach, just as she had when the plane had hit the turbulence.

She *had* loved him, of course she had. She'd loved him when he'd asked her to marry him and she'd loved him when they'd gone to Gretna Green. She'd loved him when they'd messed around with Häagen-Dazs and when they'd made love in that damn freezing-cold forest in Scotland. But she'd decided that she hadn't really loved him when things had become a little more difficult, when he'd been busy with work and had gone to meetings and left her behind, because she'd been paranoid that he'd find someone else just like Aidan had. And so she'd concluded that she had never really loved him at all. That she'd married him because she might as well marry someone. And then he'd stopped loving her and she'd told herself that she was glad she hadn't really loved him either.

But she'd been lying to herself. She didn't love him now. But she'd loved him then. She really had.

'Darcey? Are you all right?'

She nodded, although she looked away from him so that he couldn't see the confusion in her eyes.

'And then there was Megan,' he said bluntly.

'Megan?'

'The girl I nearly married,' he reminded her.

'Oh, God, yes. Megan.'

'Lovely girl. From Glasgow, though.' His eyes twinkled.

'Och well.' She smiled back at him. 'Ye cannae have everything.'

She'd said that to him before. In a restaurant too. Somewhere in London. Shortly after they'd been married. He'd said that the only thing that she was missing to make her his perfect dream woman was a multimillionaire very elderly father. It had been a fun-filled night. She remembered it perfectly now. Not the name of the restaurant but its location, near the King's Road. A chi-chi kind of place that she liked but that he found a bit too girlie. But she'd told him that she was a girl and so just for once girlie was good. And he'd said that he had to agree with her there, that she was in fact the perfect girl. And then he'd mentioned the father and she'd made that 'cannae have everything' remark. They'd laughed about it and she'd complained that her dad had been nothing more than a jilting bastard. She'd been going to add something along the lines of 'like all men' because she'd been thinking of Aidan Clarke, but right then she'd looked into Neil's eyes and decided that he'd never leave her. Never jilt her. And that was when she became afraid that someone else might try to take him away from her.

She closed her eyes to blot out the memory.

'Sure you're OK?' he asked. 'Wrist hurting you?'

She realised that she had closed her right hand around her left arm and was squeezing it tightly. She opened her eyes again.

'I'm absolutely fine,' she said, although it seemed to her as though the words were being spoken by someone else. 'A bit tired maybe.'

'Do you want to leave?' he asked.

Actually she did. But she shook her head and said no, she was OK again, and asked him how he felt about taking over in Dublin and whether it was what he'd wanted all along.

'I didn't have a career plan to end up in Dublin,' he said. 'But it's a good office and the people are nice and so I reckon it'll be good for me.'

'It's funny that you're staying in Dublin and I'm going to Edinburgh,' she said.

'Yeah, well, that's how these things work out in corporate-land,' he told her. 'Maybe in a few years I'll have had too much and so will you and one day we'll meet at that olive farm in Tuscany.'

'I think I've given up on the farm,' she said. 'My dream is different these days.'

'Sure.' He nodded. 'Power suits and power lunches and giving it socks in the boardroom.'

'I still think it's so not me,' she confessed. 'But if other people . . .'

'Other people think it's definitely you,' he assured her.

'Was I your choice for the job?' She looked at him curiously.

He nodded. 'I can't believe that those cretins in Global Finance hadn't promoted you long ago,' he said. 'Your hit rate of business is phenomenal. When we looked at the figures in Edinburgh, we were astounded.'

'It's so weird.' She giggled, knowing that it was the alcohol making her feel a bit silly, and abruptly tried to stop. 'How things turn out.'

'You're going to be great,' said Neil. 'And . . . well, I'm really proud of you.'

'Thanks.' She wanted to reach out and touch him. She didn't know why she wanted to, but she did. She wanted to hold his hand in hers and to twine her fingers around his. She wondered if he still had the callus on the side of his left hand that, he'd said, he'd got from doing karate badly when he was younger. Andy McNab action hero, she thought.

His phone beeped with a text message and he looked at it.

'Anna,' he told her as he punched a reply. 'Wondering how you'd taken the news.'

'Anna knew already?'

'Of course. She's the director of HR in Dublin after all. I've told her I'll ring her later.'

But why would he ring her later? To talk business? Or not? Darcey was conscious of a burning sensation in her stomach as she thought of Neil and Anna talking about her later. Neil saying that it was OK, she'd accepted the Edinburgh job and she'd soon be happily working somewhere else. And Anna being relieved that Darcey would be out of the way, because no matter how strong their friendship, there was a definite awkwardness about her dating Darcey's exhusband.

This can't be happening to me, Darcey thought, as she pushed her food around her plate and took careful sips of her wine. It can't be that the feeling I'm suddenly having is . . . jealousy of Anna. And of the fact that she and Neil are an item. And that, even though he's here with me and we're having dinner and we've spent the whole day together, he's just my boss after all.

He's not my boss, she reminded herself. He's my equal. I'm a director too. And I'll feel differently in the morning.

# Chapter 36

Darcey wasn't sure how many people would turn up at the Excise Bar for drinks on the Friday night of her last week in Dublin. She'd issued a general invitation and had asked the bar staff to cordon off an area for Investor-Corp employees, but she was worried that there'd only be a few people there and that her reserved space would have an empty look about it. However, by eight o'clock the place was heaving and she realised that three-quarters of the staff had come along to wish her well.

'Of course they came.' Anna looked at her as though she needed her head examined. 'Why wouldn't they?'

'There's a football match on tonight,' Darcey said. 'And you know what the company's like when it comes to footie.'

'Yeah, but they want to celebrate with you more,' Anna told her.

Darcey grinned. 'Well, I guess I'm in the mood for celebrating.'

'Are you looking forward to Edinburgh?' asked Anna.

'Of course I am,' replied Darcey. 'I'm nervous, but that's

natural. To be honest, I'm terrified. But I've got to try.'

'Attagirl.'

'My first meeting is with that guy they brought in to go to Tokyo,' said Darcey with amusement. 'Which should be interesting, I guess.'

'He's probably terrified of you,' said Anna. 'The big gun from Dublin to be in charge.'

'You think?'

'Totally.'

Darcey laughed. 'I don't believe you, but thanks.'

'Hey, Darcey!' Walter came up and patted her on the back. 'Well done, I hope you're mega-successful in Edinburgh. I know you will be.'

'Thanks,' she said.

She spent a lot of the night saying thank you to all of the people who wished her well in the future. She was touched that they truly seemed to think that she deserved her promotion, and pleased that even people whom she'd locked horns with in the past were telling her that she'd be a great director. Sally from reception confided that she'd applied for a position in the client services department and was scheduled for an interview on Monday.

'Be positive,' Darcey told her. 'I'm sure you'll do really well. And don't forget you can always call me if you need advice.' Sally nodded and said that she would, and that she hoped to be a director herself one day. Darcey smiled and said that she hoped so too.

'It's great that you got the job,' John Kenneally told her later as they were chatting together. 'But who am I going to get to replace you on the quiz team?'

She chuckled. 'Neil Lomond?'

'Feck off,' said John amiably. 'But maybe . . .' His eyes roamed over the crowd. 'He might be a good sub.'

She followed John's gaze and saw Neil pushing his way through a knot of people.

'Hi,' he said. 'Sorry I'm late. Had a few things to do in the office.'

'No problem,' she told him. 'Good to see you. Can I get you a drink?'

'It's OK,' he told her. 'I met Gareth on the way in. He's ordering a pint for me.' Neil grinned. 'I think people are on the "buying a drink for the boss" track.'

'They're just friendly,' she told him sternly. 'Nobody here cares that you're the boss.'

'Probably not,' he agreed cheerfully as Gareth, one of the accounts staff, came over and joined them, handing him the drink. 'Cheers.'

The evening went by in a blur. Darcey drank champagne (she wondered whether she was getting a taste for it: maybe it was a director thing!) and enjoyed the buzz of good-humoured conversation around her. She overheard two of the junior members of staff wondering if you had to be really clever to get on in the company, and she interrupted them and told them that you didn't, you just had to want to succeed. And afterwards she wondered why it was that she had decided that she wanted to succeed when it had never seemed important to her before.

By the time the bar was finally closing, the only people left were herself, Anna, Neil and half a dozen younger staff members who planned to go clubbing. Both Neil and Anna said that they had no intention of clubbing, and Darcey also declined the invitation.

'Too old,' she told them. 'I can't hack that sort of thing any more. I'm going home to bed.'

'D'you want us to come with you?' asked Neil.

'To bed?' she laughed.

'In the taxi. Make sure you get home OK.'

She shook her head. 'I'll be fine. You can make sure I get into one if you like, but I'll be grand by myself.'

So they walked her to the rank outside the Financial Services Centre and waited until a cab showed up.

'It's not like it's some terrible goodbye,' said Anna as Darcey opened the door. 'I'm sure you'll be back and forward a lot, and of course I'll email you all the Dublin gossip.'

'Sure,' said Darcey easily. 'I'll give you a shout on Monday anyway and let you know how it's going.' She hugged her friend tightly. 'Thanks for everything, Anna.'

'Good luck,' said Anna. 'You deserve it.'

'Yes,' said Neil. 'You do. I'm sure we'll be keeping in touch too. You'll probably be sending me all sorts of impossible targets for Dublin to beat.'

'You betcha,' she said.

He hugged her too. The scent of him was still familiar. As was his hug. She swallowed hard as she hugged him back and then got into the cab.

The storm hit at about two in the morning. She'd spent ages sitting in front of the mirror in her bedroom, slowly taking off her make-up and moisturising her face, not entirely sure why it felt different to be doing this tonight. And then she decided to make herself hot chocolate. Not instant, as she normally did, but with some of the real chocolate Minette always sent her home with whenever she visited Galway. She didn't, of course, have the cream that should go with it, but she still took her time over making it, stirring the chocolate slowly over the heat, savouring its rich, addictive aroma.

Minette, Tish and Amelie were positive about her relocation to Edinburgh. They all agreed that her promotion was a fantastic achievement and a wonderful opportunity for the future, and Minette pointed out that since she could just as easily get direct flights to Galway from Scotland as from Dublin, it didn't make a huge amount of difference where she lived. And she said that it was probably a good thing for Darcey to get out of the country again for a while. It wasn't like her to be so settled!

Darcey had teased her that she wanted her out of the way so that she could continue to flirt outrageously with Malachy Finan without wondering if her youngest daughter would drop in unexpectedly, and Minette had replied that any flirting she did would be in the castle and well out of sight of her daughters. Then Darcey had asked a little more seriously if there really was something going on with Malachy.

'Nothing to worry yourself about,' Minette replied airily. 'But I'm enjoying myself.'

Well, thought Darcey now as she sipped her hot chocolate and watched sheet lightning rip the skies while rolling thunder followed it like bowling balls along an alley, if Minette was to have fun, it was good that she was doing it with someone who owned his own castle! And she wondered if Minette felt that she'd ended up with the better half of the deal since Martin's departure. Darcey's father was, she knew, still struggling to repair his relationship with Clem, and it wasn't easy.

She sighed. It was so easy to have a plan of how things should be, but life sometimes got in the way. Things hadn't worked out as expected for her parents. Or for Anna. Or Nieve. Or Aidan. Or even for Neil. None of them had got what they'd originally anticipated. But the question was whether this was a bad thing or not. She only wished she knew.

Her mobile rang and startled her. She put her half-finished mug of hot chocolate on the kitchen counter and answered it.

'Hi, Darce.' It was Nieve. 'Hope I didn't wake you.'

'Surprisingly, no,' replied Darcey after she'd got over her astonishment at hearing Nieve's voice. 'But it's the early hours of the morning, you know. Is something wrong?' She suddenly thought that perhaps it had all gone pear-shaped for Nieve after all. That they'd found a good reason to indict her on the same charges as Mike and Harley. That she'd been involved even unwittingly in the scam. Her stomach contracted.

'No,' said Nieve. 'Everything's right. Totally, totally right. And I had to ring you to tell you.'

'Oh?'

'Aidan and I got married today.'

'Nieve!'

'I got the all-clear from the Feds eventually,' Nieve explained. 'So we talked about it. We were thinking of maybe having a small ceremony here and having a few friends over, and then I suddenly thought that it was becoming a big deal all over again and I didn't want that any more, and so we just got a licence and did it and now we're married.'

'Congratulations.' Darcey realised that she was truly pleased for Nieve. For both of them, really. Bloody hell, she thought, why did I spend so much time and energy hating her? What was the damn point of that?

'It's freaky,' said her friend. 'I keep saying Mrs Nieve Clarke over and over like I'm a kid or something. I didn't realise how much it would mean to me.'

'I'm glad you're happy,' said Darcey. 'And I'm really glad about the Feds.'

'Jeez, so am I.' Nieve's tone was heartfelt. 'I'm telling you, Darce, it's been a lot of stress. But it's all worked out for me. That's the other bit of what I wanted to tell you.'

'Have the new owners offered you a job?'

'In the end – no,' said Nieve. 'They've given one to Paola all right. Y'know, you'd get on with her, Darce. She's determined in the same way as you. Pregnant, actually, but determined.'

'I'm not sure what connection we have there,' said Darcey drily. 'I'm certainly not pregnant!'

'No, I just mean that she sort of reminds me of you. All quiet but not really. You know?'

'Maybe.'

'Anyhow, she's got the job, but me – I'm changing career!'

'How?' asked Darcey.

'You'll love this,' said Nieve. 'You really will.'

'I'd better.'

'I'm writing a book.'

'What?'

'Yeah. I am. I have a contract and everything.'

'What sort of contract? What sort of book?'

'All about Ennco,' said Nieve happily. 'One night I was looking through my files and I realised that I had loads of background information and stuff, and I emailed my attorney, who knew a guy who knew a guy . . . Anyway, bottom line is that he put me in touch with an agent and there's a real interest in the inside story and I know that I can do this. I was always good at putting stuff together, even if I wasn't so good at developing it in the first place. So I'm writing the story of yet another American corporate scandal and the money is – well, it's not what I was going to make, but it's not bad at all. So things are looking up.'

'You're amazing,' said Darcey. 'You really do always land on your feet.'

'I have to do a whole lot of twisting as I fall to get that way,' said Nieve wryly.

Darcey laughed.

'But, you know, they're talking about making a TV drama of it and everything.' Nieve sounded cheerful again. 'So the whole thing is that I'm in the middle of it and I feel . . . better about things. I'll be able to pay Dad back some of the money he had to shell out for Lorelei, which is good too.'

'You know, I wouldn't rush to pay back your dad,' said Darcey slowly.

'Huh?'

'Nieve, I think he liked being able to help you out. I think it made him feel good.'

Nieve was silent for a moment. 'Perhaps you're right,' she said. 'I never thought about it like that.' She chuckled. 'Good grief – a human insight from Darcey McGonigle!'

'Sod off.' But Darcey's tone was light.

'D'you want to talk to Aidan?' asked Nieve.

Darcey hesitated.

'Go on,' said her friend. 'You might as well.'

Darcey heard the phone being handed over and then Aidan's voice came on the line saying hi. She congratulated him on the marriage too and he thanked her again for being around in Galway, and she said that some day they'd probably all meet up somewhere, maybe at the film premiere or something, and he laughed and said that Nieve was a dynamo about the book and that everything was just going to be totally peachy.

'I hope everything works out great for you,' said Darcey sincerely.

'And we hope it works out for you too,' said Aidan. She nearly told him about her promotion but she didn't want to appear as though she was trying to trump Nieve's news. So she simply said goodbye to her friend again and then closed her phone.

They were finally married. Any stray ideas that they might not, that it would all go wrong, that Nieve might still be arrested, were over and done with.

And Nieve had turned disaster into triumph just as she always did. Just as she always would do, thought Darcey, because that was the sort of person she was.

And me? she wondered. Am I the complete opposite? Is that my problem? That I always want to turn triumph into disaster instead? She thought, for an instant, of her ill-fated marriage and squeezed her eyes closed. She'd managed to stop regretting Aidan; she couldn't now start regretting Neil instead. She had to get on with her life. And she was. She was moving to Edinburgh.

Her hot chocolate had gone cold. She rinsed the mug in the sink and wandered over to the patio door again. It had stopped raining, but the thunder was still crashing around in the sky. She slid the door open and peered out into the city. She loved thunderstorms. She loved the light and the noise and the sheer exuberance of it all. She loved the way people talked about them afterwards – always surprised by the power of nature to put on such a show.

That's the thing, she said to herself. It's like all our plans. Nature can muck them up for us if that's what she wants to do.

A flurry of wind surged through the open door and blew papers from her table and shelves. She swore softly under her breath as she closed the door again. It was all very well, she thought, communing with nature and having all sorts of existential thoughts at gone two in the morning, but she really needed to keep her wits about her.

She got down on her hands and knees and picked up all the various bills and flyers she'd dumped on the table over the past few weeks. And then her hand closed on a small piece of cardboard and she realised that it was the scratch card that Nerys had bought her for her birthday months earlier. She'd never bothered to scratch it because she was so sure she wouldn't win.

'Maybe it'll be different tonight,' she said out loud.

Perhaps because of the fact that she was changing jobs and changing her life and changing everything, the fates would also allow her to win something for the first time ever.

She took a coin from her bag and held it over the card. Realistically, she told herself, things didn't change that much. You might want them to, but they didn't. She was still the person who didn't make birthday wishes or win on scratch cards, because that wasn't how her life turned out. She got things when she worked hard. She didn't get things just because she wished for them.

The latest roll of thunder was the loudest yet and it made the windows shake. Oh hell, she thought as she brought the coin down on the card, there's no point in not doing it. Maybe I'll get three stars and go into the prize draw.

She didn't win three stars. She won a hundred euros. She thought she might spend it on buying some coloured T-shirts to brighten up her wardrobe.

# Chapter 37

It was hot in Milan. She hadn't intended to come back at all, but there had been the sudden opportunity to pitch for the business of a very successful retired rock star who'd made his home on the shores of Lake Como and whose financial advisers had asked to meet with Investor-Corp. Robin Barrymore, who had taken responsibility for the European client base, was on a week's paternity leave, and although he'd phoned the office and told her that he was perfectly prepared to meet the rock star's finance people whenever they wanted, Darcey had told him not to be so silly, that she'd go herself. It was only after she'd put the phone down that she realised that in all likelihood Robin hadn't thought of himself as being silly to want to give up part of his paternity leave. In her experience men didn't usually think that way. And the sudden thought struck her that perhaps he was a fan of the rock star!

The meeting wasn't (unfortunately, she thought) in the star's palatial home near the lake, but took place in the modern air-conditioned offices of his financial advisers, who grilled her comprehensively about the InvestorCorp products and whose questions were much more searching than she normally had to deal with.

'He was stung before,' said Antonio Mantovani when she pointed this out. 'We want to be sure that everything is exactly as you say. Our client doesn't really want to have to work any more at this time of his career.'

Nice idea, Darcey thought, as she went through the information yet again for them. Though it's kind of hard to imagine a seventies hellraiser wanting to spend the rest of his life quietly contemplating the Italian lakes.

She didn't feel at all positive throughout the meeting, and so she was surprised when Antonio and his colleague asked her to come to dinner with them that evening. They chose a really nice restaurant, not far from the one she normally went to with Rocco, and she spent an enjoyable night chatting to them and agreeing with them that there wasn't a more beautiful place in the world and that the ageing rock star was lucky to live there and that he was right to want to spend his time admiring the view instead of touring with his band.

And because the next day was Friday, she decided not to rush back to the chillier air of Edinburgh but to treat herself to a weekend in what actually was one of her favourite cities in the whole world. The treat was all the sweeter because the next morning the financial advisers called her to say that the rock star had agreed to go ahead with his investment. She thanked them profusely, closed her phone and punched the air in delight.

She decided to go for a short stroll around the town, then did some shopping in the fashionable stores and sighed in envy at how gorgeous and stylish both the men and the women looked, despite the fact that the sun was splitting the rocks and that it was far too hot to be walking around the city at all.

After lunch she thought about calling Rocco to see if he wanted to meet that evening. But she kept putting it off, knowing that seeing Rocco would be a backward step and not wanting to look backwards any more.

As she strolled along a shaded side street, her attention was caught by an estate agent's window and she stopped instead to look at the photos of new, old and utterly ruined villas for sale in the surrounding district. Quite out of the blue, she decided to go and look at some properties near the lake.

An hour later she was standing in a field in front of a practically derelict building, the heat of the sun scorching her shoulders and dried stalks of grass scraping at her bare legs. It wasn't exactly the mansion that the rock star owned, she admitted to herself, suddenly realising that seeing the photos of his pink stuccoed house was what had made her feel itchy about looking at property (even if she was in Lombardy and not Tuscany). The house she was looking at was a complete wreck, with weeds growing out of the roof and shutters at half-mast across the windows.

'There is some restoration work to be done,' said the estate agent with a mastery of understatement. 'But it is a beautiful property. And from the top you can see the lake.'

Well, thought Darcey, it had a lot of potential. But she wasn't sure that she was the person to unlock it. After all, she did have a whopping mortgage on her Irish apartment already. (She hadn't decided what to do about the apartment yet. She'd been thinking about renting it out, but she hated the idea of someone else living in her space. The company was temporarily paying for her current apartment in Edinburgh, but dealing with more permanent living arrangements was something she kept pushing out of her mind.) Borrowing more money to buy an Italian ruin surely wasn't the sensible way to go about things. But, she mused, as she walked around the sandstone walls, it's a lovely, lovely house and it does have lots and lots of potential. Pity the scratch card was only for a hundred euros instead of a hundred thousand!

She knew the estate agent was watching her. Probably thinks I'm a nut, like that family who wanted to own their own olive farm, she thought. The ones who had struggled to make it work in the sleepy little town off the beaten track and who'd nearly had nervous breakdowns in the process. But it *had* worked for them, she remembered. By the end of the programme they'd all been eating stone-baked bread dipped in their own olive oil, and had insisted that their dream had come true.

Maybe my dream come true isn't actually owning a crumbling ruin, but becoming managing director of Investor-Corp, she told herself as she smoothed down her skirt and walked back to the estate agent. Maybe my problem all along has been not understanding what my dream really is.

She allowed the agent to talk about various other properties all the way back to the city, and ended up giving her her email address and phone number so that she could be kept up to date with Fontana Properties' latest offers. In order that the agent's hopes weren't raised too high, Darcey insisted that she was only barely thinking about the possibility of buying a property and that it would be ages before she was even close to making up her mind; but the estate agent simply smiled and told her that everyone wanted to live in Italy, and that her life would be a million times better under the Italian sun, and that of course when she saw the right property she would know.

Darcey smiled and nodded and eventually made her escape back to her hotel, slightly irritated at herself for being so silly as to organise a property search for something she truly wasn't about to buy, but still feeling that she'd enjoyed the afternoon much more than she'd expected.

When she got to her room, she showered, then wrapped herself in a heavy towelling robe and sat at the window. It overlooked the back of an apartment block, which meant that she could actually see people sitting on their own balconies in the slightly cooler evening air. She enjoyed watching them talking and laughing and eating and living their lives outdoors. When the aroma of food wafting through the open window started to make her feel hungry, she grabbed the room service menu and looked through it. But then she decided that there was something a bit forlorn about sitting in her room on her own when so many people were out and about and enjoying life. So she got dressed – though only in a pair of jeans and a vibrant pink T-shirt (from the coloured selection she'd bought with her scratch-card money). She didn't dry her hair, still damp from her shower earlier, because she couldn't be bothered to spend ages on it tonight. She didn't care if she looked unkempt just for one evening.

The dining room, which was on the second floor and opened on to a small terrace overlooking the courtyard at the back of the hotel, was half full. A waiter showed Darcey to a small table tucked near the terrace and brought her a menu. She ordered spaghetti carbonara and a half-bottle of Frascati, and then opened the Italian gossip magazine she'd bought in the city earlier.

She read and ate at the same time, savouring the perfect combination of spaghetti and sauce and the refreshing qualities of the cold white wine. She wasn't thinking about it but she knew, deep down, that she was feeling content and relaxed and happy.

'Hi.'

She'd just popped a forkful of spaghetti into her mouth and she swallowed it in one gulp.

'What's wrong?' She looked up anxiously. 'Why are you here?'

'Nothing's wrong,' said Neil Lomond. 'Mind if I join you?'

She shook her head and laid her fork beside the pasta dish.

'I'm sorry if I'm disturbing you,' he said.

'Of course you're not disturbing me.' She closed the magazine and put it to one side. 'Is there a problem? Have you been trying to contact me? I'm sorry, I switched my phone off.'

'No problem at all,' he assured her. 'And I'd switch my phone off in such a gorgeous place too.'

She looked at him enquiringly.

'Don't let me stop you eating,' he said. 'Go ahead.'

'I was nearly finished.'

'Sorry.' He didn't look very contrite. Instead he grinned at her. 'You're the only person I know who could eat spaghetti elegantly.'

She laughed slightly. 'Not really. That's why I always order it with a pale sauce.'

'At least you manage to get it on the fork and keep it there,' he said. 'I was watching you before I said hello. It's impressive. Really.'

'Um, thanks. Look, I don't want to be rude or anything, but . . . is there a reason you're here?' As she spoke she smoothed her hair, uncomfortably aware that it was probably sticking up in errant clumps around her head.

He pulled out a chair and sat opposite her. She poured him a glass of wine from her half-bottle.

'How are you liking Edinburgh?' he asked casually.

'It's working out well,' she told him. 'There's a good bunch of people there and I get on with them, and I'm devising our strategy for next year. This trip . . .' She smiled slightly. 'This was an unexpected bonus. It's not in my game plan to be traipsing around the world. But it was nice to come here again.'

'Your favourite place,' he said.

She shrugged. 'My favourite city for sure.' Then she smiled slightly. 'I looked at some houses today. Well, drove past some houses and looked at a total ruin which the estate agent told me had potential.'

He raised an eyebrow. 'Thinking of chucking it all in after all?'

She shook her head. 'I don't think I'm quite ready to chuck it all in yet. At least . . . my life isn't like that right now. Some day, yes. I suppose I could leave InvestorCorp and sell my apartment and move to Italy and get a job here. But that's just changing location, not my life. When I'm ready to change my life, then I'll do it.'

'Is that the only way you'd change your life?'

'Unless I win the lotto.' She grinned. 'You never know. I netted a hundred euros on a scratch card a while ago.'

'You always told me that you were the world's unluckiest person when it came to things like that.'

'I am,' she said wryly. 'That's why I wondered if it was an omen. But I don't think so. I don't really believe in omens.'

'If you did chuck it all in, what would you do here?' he asked.

She shrugged. 'That's the thing. More of the same, I guess. I need to earn a living. I'm not like Nieve, who can turn her hand to bloody anything to make money.'

He looked at her quizzically, and she told him about Nieve's phone call on the night of her going-away do.

'So apparently she's penning the blockbuster reveal-all story of corporate greed,' said Darcey. 'Which is kind of ironic, I guess, but very typical Nieve.'

'And are you really and truly OK about them getting married?' he asked.

'I guess it took me a long time to be OK with anything to do with them, but yes, I am. Totally.'

'How did you know?' he asked.

She stared at him.

'This is a really, really weird conversation, Neil,' she said. 'I haven't spoken to you for weeks. Now you're in my hotel in Milan asking me about a man I thought I was in love with. I don't know how you even knew I was in Milan in the first place. Or why you're here interrupting my dinner. So please don't get mad at me, but what the hell is going on?'

'Humour me,' he said. 'Tell me how you know you're OK about Nieve and Aidan.'

She sighed. 'I just know. I think about him and I don't get this stabbing pain in my heart like I used to. I think about her and I'm not filled with rage. When I think of them together I don't want to rip her face off or throw my arms around him and sob. I am, I suppose, a little bit sad that I messed up my life by not being able to do this before now, but I'm glad that it's happened. I don't love him. I probably haven't loved him for years, only I couldn't admit that to myself. So, in fact, I'm over him.' She smiled. 'Actually, I've never said that out loud before and it's rather liberating. I'm over him.' She raised her voice for the last three words and then laughed. 'Yup. Definitely. I'm over him.'

'But I'm not over you.'

She was suddenly very still.

'Sorry?' she said.

'You heard me,' said Neil.

'I know I heard you, but I . . . I'm not sure I heard you properly.'

'Of course you heard me properly.'

'OK. You said that you weren't over me. Which is just a little bit weird and freaky.'

'I know,' he said. 'But it's true. I'm not over you, Darcey. When I think of you I still get a stabbing pain in my heart and sometimes I'm still filled with rage too. There's nobody whose face I want to rip off, but I understand the sentiment.'

'Neil!'

'Strange, huh?'

'But – but you nearly got engaged to someone else. You're dating Anna. You forgot about the Marmite.'

He looked at her in astonishment. 'I what?'

'At the quiz,' she said. 'The French word for cooking pot. You forgot it.'

'No I didn't,' he said.

'You lost the quiz because of it. I thought because of what . . . what it had meant to us that you'd remember. But you'd forgotten.'

'Häagen-Dazs,' he said quietly. 'Afterwards.'

She swallowed hard. 'I asked you and you said you didn't know what I was talking about.'

'I was hardly going to say anything else.'

'Why?'

'And let you know?' he demanded. 'That I did remember? That I still cared?'

She stared at him wordlessly and ran her fingers through her hair. She felt its soft curls and instinctively tried to pat it flat. He watched her.

'Your hair is fine,' he said. 'I like it like that.'

'Neil, this is too crazy. You're freaking me out here.'

'I know. I'm sorry. It's just that lately I've been feeling freaked out myself.'

'Why?'

'Meeting you again,' he said. 'Seeing you. Talking to you. Finding out how brilliant you were at what you do. Realising that you'd more or less worked things out. Wishing you'd done it when we were together. Missing you.'

'Neil, it's been eight years!'

'It doesn't seem like it.'

'No,' she said softly. 'It doesn't.'

'It's been driving me mad,' he said. 'And one way or the other I just felt that I had to talk to you about it. Sort it all out. Whatever sorting it out actually means for me.'

'What about Anna?' She said it abruptly. 'She's my friend and you've messed with her and I *told* you not to mess with her. And if – just if – you and I became . . . if we . . . I'd be like Nieve. I'd have pinched her boyfriend.'

'Anna's the one who made me come here,' said Neil. 'She says that I'm not facing up to how I feel. And I told her a million times that I was and that she should butt out and that I knew exactly how I felt about everything, but she wouldn't listen and she made me come.'

'But I thought you and she . . . I thought she . . .'

'Early on, Darcey, early on I thought that she and I might have something going. But equally early on she realised that it was impossible. She knew that because she knew that I totally wasn't over you. That actually I was still crazily in love with you. And as much as I tried to tell her that I wasn't and that I was looking for someone new, she spent most of her time pointing me back in your direction.'

'But she asked me how I felt! She said she wanted to have a relationship with you!'

'And then she found out that I haven't been able to hang on to a woman ever since we split up. She's one of the cleverest, most intuitive women I've ever met, and maybe under different circumstances she and I might have worked, but there was no chance, Darcey, and she knew that well before I did and so she was having none of it.'

Darcey stared at him in silence. 'She never said anything to me.'

'She thought you weren't facing up to things either. But she reckoned that if she said anything to you, you'd take the stubborn approach and not want to talk.'

'Poor Anna,' said Darcey after a moment or two. 'She so wanted someone.'

'Um, yes. She said you might come out with that sort of guff. She said that someone isn't important. The right someone is.'

'Maybe,' said Darcey. 'But sometimes you think you've found the right someone and you're wrong. And you regret the fact that you didn't realise it sooner.' She gazed unseeingly out at the terrace.

Neil watched her without speaking.

'I'm sorry if I'm embarrassing you,' he said eventually. 'She told me to come and she told me I might make a fool of myself but that I had to do it. And I have. And I'm sorry, because we have a professional relationship and if I've got it wrong now then I've screwed that up.'

'Our professional relationship is fine,' she said.

'When you behaved the way you did at ProSure, I was utterly humiliated,' said Neil. 'I was glad when you left me and glad to divorce you and very, very glad that the whole sorry episode was behind me. And I told myself that I'd had a lucky escape. Which, in some ways, maybe I had. But then afterwards I told myself that perhaps I should have fought for you. Made you realise why you'd married me in the first place. That Aidan shouldn't mean anything to you. But I let you go because I thought it was for the best, and I think I've regretted it ever since.'

'Please stop,' she said quietly. 'Please stop making it seem as if you should be blamed for something.'

'I know I shouldn't be blamed for anything, but I still feel that I should have done something different.'

'Oh, Neil. I feel like that all the time.' She smiled faintly. 'There isn't one aspect of my whole life that I don't think I should've done differently. And most of all what I wish I'd done differently was to treat you better. Not to have hurt you or humiliated you or done anything to make you feel the same way I did. I know I'd been hurt and humiliated myself but that didn't mean I had to inflict it on you. Yet I did and I am so, so sorry for that. I really am. I behaved in a dreadful way and I justified it by telling myself that I'd been badly treated. That wasn't any justification at all. I'm going to allow myself a little bit of leeway and say that I hadn't coped very well and that I wasn't really myself at the time. The bottom line is the same, though. I married you for the wrong reason and I didn't think enough about your feelings and I was a horrible person. And I'm sorry.'

'You don't have to say sorry to me,' he told her.

'Oh, I do,' she said. 'I have to take responsibility for what I did and how I did it, and you know, I didn't really manage to do that at all until that whole wedding débâcle thing, which made me realise that I was in danger of blowing away my whole life on a mistake!'

'You've changed,' he said. 'I never realised anyone could change so much. You went through your worst time and came out the other end and you're fine. It's a great story. It's just that I wish it had been different too.'

'Why haven't you got over me?' she asked.

'I don't know,' he said. 'Maybe it's the way I remember you looking every morning when you woke up. Your hair sticking up all over your head like it is now and your eyes unfocused. Sort of vulnerable and yet tough at the same time. The way that you remember all sorts of useless information that one day actually ends up being useful! The way you laugh. The way you cry. The way—'

'Stop!' She pushed her hands through her mussed-up hair. 'God, Neil, stop saying stuff which makes me seem like a great person when I was the biggest crock that ever walked the earth and when you were kind of right to call me vain and selfish and all those things because I totally was. Don't tell me that you're not over me, because there's nothing to be over.'

'Bit of a blow then,' he said shakily as he looked intently at her. 'I'm here to declare undying love to my ex-wife, and she's not really interested.'

'You don't love me, Neil,' she said. 'It's like me and Aidan. You think you love me. But you don't. It's just that you're . . . you're used to the feeling.'

'I can see how that might be true,' he agreed. 'But the thing is that I was glad when we got divorced. Utterly delighted, in fact. I didn't think about you for a whole year.

And then I met Megan. She was a great girl, a wonderful woman, and any bloke would've been happy to marry her. And I thought I was that guy. Until one day I woke up and realised that I wasn't. That I couldn't marry her because she wasn't you.'

'Neil, listen to me – you're not in love with me. It's not real. And for the first time in her life I think Anna Sweeney has got it completely wrong. You shouldn't have come here and you should go back to Dublin and marry her, because she's a million times better for you than I'd ever be.'

'But she's not you,' said Neil.

'That's a good thing!' cried Darcey.

'OK.' He smiled in resignation. 'I gave it my best shot. I'm really sorry to have messed up your evening.'

'I . . . you didn't.'

'Cold spaghetti carbonara. I'd call that pretty messed up.'

'Well, yes. True.' She looked at the pasta congealing in the dish.

'Are we OK for the office?' he asked briskly. 'Not that it matters too much, with you in Scotland and me in Ireland, but on those occasions when we have to talk to each other, are you sure our professional lives are OK?'

'Of course.'

'Excellent.' His smile nearly reached his eyes. 'Good.'

'Well, um, goodbye.' Her smile was crooked. 'Thanks for, um, dropping by and for everything you've done for me and all that. And I'm sure I'll see you around again.'

'Yeah. Sure.'

They looked awkwardly at each other for a moment and then she stood up and kissed him on each cheek.

'*Ciao*,' she said.

'*Ciao*.' He smiled again. 'By the way, I like the colour of your T-shirt.' Then he turned around and walked away.

As soon as he'd left the dining room, she sat down abruptly on her chair. Her body was shaking. She couldn't believe what had just happened, what he'd said. She couldn't believe that he'd felt the way he did and that he still felt the way he did and that he'd laid it all out on the line for her like that. She couldn't believe that Anna had told him to come to her because Anna herself believed in how he felt. It was all too weird and too emotional and not the sort of stuff she wanted to know about any more. It was like birthday wishes and scratch cards coming up trumps, and dreaming about living in another country. These things didn't happen to her. These things weren't part of her life.

And then she remembered that she'd seen a lovely house in Italy. That the scratch card had come up trumps after all. And that he liked the colour of the T-shirt she'd bought with the money.

She got up from the table and hurried out of the dining room. She clattered down the two flights of stairs and into the cool marble foyer of the hotel. Neil was standing near a square pillar, almost but not quite leaning against it. His back was to her and he was staring out of the open hotel door to the street beyond.

'Neil!'

He turned around and looked at her quizzically.

'Tell me again,' she said.

'Tell you what?'

'How you feel.'

'I can't go through it all again,' he said. 'I said it once. I—'

'In one sentence,' she asked. 'Just once. Once more. Summarise it for me.'

'I love you,' he said simply.

She swallowed hard and opened her mouth, but no words came out. He moved towards her and put his hands on her shoulders.

'I love you,' he said again.

She bit her lip and he smiled.

'I love you.'

This time she smiled too. '*E ti amo.*'

He looked directly into her eyes. 'It's your turn to say it again.'

'*Ti amo. Je t'aime. Te quiero.* I love you.'

Then she kissed him.

Everyone in the foyer of the Milan hotel looked at them and smiled in understanding, because they were in Italy, and Italy is the perfect place to be in love. And Darcey, as she kissed Neil once again, knew for certain that this time they would get it absolutely right.

# SHEILA O'FLANAGAN

# Yours, Faithfully

Iona Brannock wants everything *now*. She's always been that way – didn't she marry a gorgeous man on a beach after just a few months of good times and great sex? Four years later, she's got a fabulous job, a stunning house and, best of all, a blissfully happy relationship. When she *finally* gets pregnant, life will be complete . . .

Sally Harper has loved her husband for almost twenty years. They've built a home, raised a daughter and are still passionate about each other. Blessed with a fantastic family, Sally couldn't want for anything more – least of all, another baby . . .

Two different women. Two perfect husbands. But being in the wrong place at the wrong time means Iona and Sally's lives are about to collide with an almighty bang. And, shockingly, they've got a lot more in common than they realised . . .

Praise for Sheila O'Flanagan's bestsellers:

'Engaging characters and flowing dialogue . . . an eventful, compelling and ultimately satisfying journey' *Irish Independent*

'Sheila O'Flanagan is one of the blinding talents on the female fiction scene' Scottish *Daily Record*

'A must-read' *Woman's Own*

978 0 7553 0760 9

headline
**review**

# SHEILA O'FLANAGAN

# Connections

'A journey of intrigue and romance' *Irish Examiner*

Welcome to the Caribbean resort of White Sands, where the sparkling turquoise sea laps against the glittering shore, lush green palms sway gently in the breeze, and everyone has a story to tell.

Jennifer is here to marry the man of her dreams, but could an unexpected wedding guest turn her perfect day into a nightmare? Sahndhi, disillusioned winner of Pop Princess, has come to escape the media glare. Or so she thinks. Grainne and Aidan celebrate their twenty-fifth wedding anniversary, while secretly wondering if it's all a sham. Divorced dad Rudy arrives for a rare holiday with his beloved little boy – though his ex-wife may not see it in the same light. And thriller-writer Corinne observes all from the sidelines, as she battles with writer's block and self-doubt. Is the inspiration she needs closer than she thinks?

Join these and many other holidaymakers for a journey of intrigue and romance, as intertwining tales unfold from beach to bedroom to bar. Together they create a delightful collection of stories, the ideal escape to pure paradise . . .

Praise for Sheila O'Flanagan's bestsellers:

'The perfect book to bring on a flight' *Evening Herald*

'Vastly entertaining' *Ireland on Sunday*

'The Sheila O'Flanagan guarantee is a pretty powerful one' *Irish Independent*

978 0 7553 2345 6

headline
review

Now you can buy any of these other bestselling books by **Sheila O'Flanagan** from your bookshop or *direct from her publisher*.

FREE P&P AND UK DELIVERY
(Overseas and Ireland £3.50 per book)

| | |
|---|---|
| Suddenly Single | £6.99 |
| Far From Over | £6.99 |
| My Favourite Goodbye | £6.99 |
| Isobel's Wedding | £6.99 |
| Caroline's Sister | £6.99 |
| Too Good To Be True | £6.99 |
| Destinations | £6.99 |
| Dreaming of a Stranger | £6.99 |
| Anyone but Him | £6.99 |
| How Will I Know? | £6.99 |
| Connections | £6.99 |
| Yours, Faithfully | £6.99 |

TO ORDER SIMPLY CALL THIS NUMBER

**01235 400 414**

or visit our website: www.headline.co.uk

Prices and availability subject to change without notice.